Seafled

Seabound Chronicles: Book Three

Jordan Rivet

Staunton Street Press
HONG KONG

Cover Design by James at GoOnWrite.com
Book Layout & Design ©2013 - BookDesignTemplates.com
Author Photo by Shannon Young

Seafled / Jordan Rivet

First Edition: November 2015

This one's for Seb.

Table of Contents

And now the STORM-BLAST came, and he
Was tyrannous and strong.

−SAMUEL TAYLOR COLERIDGE

1. Preparations

ESTHER CARRIED HER STEEL toolbox through the *Lucinda*'s main corridor. She wiped away the sweat trailing down her face, realizing too late that her palms were covered in grease. She had just finished checking the generator system for the tenth time. The power output still surprised her, even though she'd built and installed dozens of the contraptions over the past few months. The *Lucinda*'s had been one of the first, and she had to make sure nothing could go wrong on this voyage.

She climbed the ladder to the deck, where the crew was busy with preparations, and headed toward the pilothouse. Luke and Cody, who had once worked on the Metal Harvesters ship *Terra Firma*, had spread all the *Lucinda*'s weapons out in the sunlight to take inventory. A small pile of stage guns sat to one side, remnants of the *Lucinda*'s escape from the *Galaxy Flotilla*.

Esther set her toolbox by the pilothouse door and opened it to find David Elliot Hawthorne sitting on the floor with a sketchpad across his knees. Charts littered the ground around him. He glanced up at her and smiled.

"You look like you just crawled out of an oil drum," he said.

"Who says I didn't?" She nudged the toe of his boot with her foot and sat cross-legged beside him.

"How's the work going?" David asked.

"The biofuel system is all set for the trip. I made some changes based on suggestions from that engineer on the *Sebastian*. How about you?"

"Almost finished with the route." David showed her the map of the western coast of North America on his sketchpad. Intricate doodles filled the corners of the paper.

"So Baja is still our best bet?"

"Yes. There'll be too many mountains in our way if we go through California. It's already September, and it's still pretty cold there."

"Sounds nice, actually," Esther said, wiping her forehead again.

David grinned, touching her cheek with his thumb. "You have a smudge on your face the size of a footprint."

Esther caught his hand between hers and pulled it down to rest on her knee, entwining her fingers with his.

"You shouldn't make fun of me, or I might accidentally do something to sabotage your precious ship."

"You wouldn't dare. You know I love the *Lucinda* more than anything."

"Anything?"

"Yes, ma'am," David said solemnly. He leaned in to kiss her gently. Then he slid his arm around her back, pulling her closer. He brushed a finger across the long, thin scar on her cheek, and his hand came away smudged.

Esther was about to slip her hands under the edge of his sweater when something pelted her in the face.

"Oy! Aren't you guys supposed to be working?" Zoe had appeared in the doorway to the pilothouse. She carried a handful of prawn crackers, and she threw another one at the couple as Esther pulled away from David.

"I'm done for the day," Esther said.

"Uh-huh. Sure you are."

Zoe joined them on the floor, stretching her long legs out in front of her. Her blond hair was covered by a bright-red scarf, a gift from Luke, who had been trying desperately to get Zoe to go out with him ever since he left the Harvesters to join the *Catalina*. The harder he tried, the more she acted like she didn't care, but Esther had noticed that Zoe always used, wore, or ate Luke's gifts, even if she pretended not to be impressed by them.

"So what's up?" Esther asked.

"Neal wants to talk to you," Zoe said, popping a prawn cracker in her mouth. "I needed some fresh air, so I volunteered to come over."

"Why didn't he just radio us?"

"*Lucinda*'s gear is all disconnected. We're tweaking a few of her instruments over on the *Catalina* to get ready for the trip."

Zoe had taken over the radio and satellite duties for the *Lucinda*. She would be the chief communications officer on their voyage.

"I should head over anyway," Esther said. "I need to see if any more help requests have come in."

"They're keeping you busy," David said.

"It's crazy how many people are using my system. It's only been what? Two months?"

Ever since Esther had sent the algae oil separator design out to the satellite network, she had been inundated with requests for help. Crews all over the New Pacific wanted her advice as they adapted her plans to suit their own vessels. Esther's system was being used on everything from warships to fishing trawlers to gigantic cargo vessels. There had even been a memorable few weeks when she had spent nearly every waking hour on the satellite phone with the head machinist of an aircraft carrier thousands of miles away. It still amazed Esther that the satellite connections were now good enough for them to talk like that.

She felt proud of her work, and she enjoyed walking people through the issues that came up as they built their own versions of her system. It was even better when they reported back on what a difference the system had made in the daily lives of their people, now free from their dependence on crude oil. In fact, it made such a big difference that a difficult decision had been weighing on her.

David was preparing to take the *Lucinda* on an expedition to land. Neal had been communicating with a farming community in Kansas City, survivors of the eruption of the Yellowstone volcano nearly seventeen years ago. The community had managed to produce a harvest for several years now. They hadn't ventured very far toward the West Coast, however. The *Lucinda* would sail to the coast, and then the crew would make an overland trek to Kansas City. David hoped to gain an accurate picture of the conditions on land along the way. He wanted to find out if they could all move back to land one day soon. If life was now better there than at sea, he would find a place for them.

But Esther was thinking about not going with him.

She hadn't told him she might stay behind. In fact, she hadn't told anyone except her father, who had been helping her think it through over the past few weeks. Ships came to her from all over the New Pacific asking for help, and she couldn't justify leaving all that behind for an expedition that could take months. She was needed at sea right now.

"Come in, Esther, do you copy?" Zoe threw another prawn cracker at her.

"Huh?"

"I said are you packed?"

"For?"

"The grand land expedition? That journey we've been planning for months? Leaving in three days?"

"Oh, um, I don't have that much stuff," Esther said.

Zoe rolled her eyes. "You mean as long as you have your tool belt, you're set, right?"

"Something like that. I'm gonna go see what Neal wants. Are you guys coming back over for dinner?"

"It's cod night," David said. "I never miss cod night."

Esther squeezed his hand and stood, brushing off her trousers. "Why don't you bring your route map over? My dad would like to see it."

"Sure. See you later."

David returned to his sketchpad, and Esther hesitated for a moment. Everything had been good between her and David over the past few months. Very good in fact. He'd helped her save the *Catalina*, and then she'd saved his life. Things had been pretty clear after that: they were a couple. She hated the idea of being away from him for months, but she finally felt like she was doing something important and useful as she helped other mechanics build her system. The system was already installed in the *Lucinda*, and maintaining it was the easy part. She didn't see what she could contribute to the expedition that someone else couldn't handle just as well.

Esther and Zoe left the pilothouse and crossed the *Lucinda*'s promenade, heading for the gangway connecting to the lower door of the *Catalina*. The *Lucinda* was less than a third as long as the *Catalina* and not nearly as tall, but she was fast and agile. She'd already proved useful when Esther and Zoe went to rescue David and needed to be picked up. That was when Luke and Cody had joined the crew, risking their lives to get Zoe out of the Harvesters' clutches. The *Lucinda* was the perfect ship for the mission to land.

Zoe hummed as she sauntered along beside Esther, pointedly not making eye contact with Luke when they passed. He stood up from the ammunitions pile, grinning, a semiautomatic rifle resting in his arms. Esther waved at him, but Zoe studied a bulbous cloud formation.

"Don't you think it's time to cut him some slack?" Esther asked when they reached the gangway. "Tell him how you feel about him?"

"That's rich coming from you, Esther," Zoe said. "You're the queen of pretending your feelings don't exist."

"I'm turning a new gear."

"I just can't stand the whole seal pup act. He's trying way too hard."

"You'd be happier if you're honest with him about it," Esther said. "I should know."

"When the time's right," Zoe said lightly. "Speaking of being honest with people, when are you going to tell me your big secret?"

"What secret?"

"Whatever has kept you so preoccupied lately," Zoe said. "Tell me. You're pregnant, aren't you?"

"What? No, of course not."

"Are you sure? You two have been doing a lot of—"

"It's not that."

"Then what?"

They made their way through the ship toward the bridge and the broadcast tower. The *Catalina* bustled with activity as everyone wrapped up their work for the day or prepared to trade shifts. A group of children darted through the corridor, one little boy chasing the others with a slimy piece of kelp. Esther waited until she and Zoe stood at the bottom of the ladder to Neal's Tower before she answered.

"I'm not sure I should go."

Zoe's eyebrows threatened to climb into her headscarf. "Say again?"

Esther frowned and picked at the white paint flaking off the ladder. "This expedition to land is important," she said, "but my role in it isn't. What can I add to the crew that a dozen others couldn't? I should keep helping the other ships with their bio-fuel systems. No one can do that as well as I can. I'd be leaving people high and dry here."

"They can call you on the *Lucinda* every bit as easily as on the *Catalina*."

"But not on land. The spotty communications there are why we have to make this trip in the first place."

"I just assumed that because David—"

"That's the problem," Esther said. "He has to go with the *Lucinda*. He wants it more than anything. I wouldn't ask him to stay behind with me, obviously, but I can't justify going with him."

"I can see why you don't fancy talking about it," Zoe said slowly. "Esther, I thought *you* wanted to see land. It's not like you were only going because of David."

"I do want to, but the timing is wrong. It would be selfish to go off on an adventure when people need me here. Judith might be right after all about doing what's best for the community. I'll go in a later expedition, or if we end up moving back. But right now . . ."

"Esther, you know I love ya, but I can't believe you'd miss this."

"That's not making me feel any better."

"All right, no guilt tripping," Zoe said, "but I don't think this'll go down well with the elegant Mr. Hawthorne."

Esther sighed and began to climb the ladder. Of course it wouldn't. That's why she didn't want to talk to him until she had made her decision. Still, she thought it might be the right thing to do. It had been reckless of her to run off to save David from the Calderon Group. She couldn't keep taking senseless risks when she was doing something so valuable here. David was important to *her*, but this time he wasn't being kidnapped by pirates.

Red sunlight filled Neal's Tower when Esther and Zoe pulled themselves up through the hatch. The sun was sinking through the clouds, washing the sea with scarlet and gold. A large chart taped to one of the windows glowed pink in the sunset.

Neal sat with his feet up on the computer console and a pen in his mouth, headphones hanging around his neck. He leaned backwards in his swivel chair when they entered.

"Hey Es, Zee."

"What's up, Neal? You called?"

"You got three more help requests today. We've been busy with the *Lucinda*'s stuff, so I didn't get a chance to let you know." He waved at a jumble of instruments spread out on the floor. "You should keep a handheld on you."

"I'd never get anything done then. Who were the requests from?"

"Two new ones, and then another message from that Harvester—you know, the one who's been calling almost every day?"

"Ugh, yeah. The guy really doesn't know what he's doing. It'd probably be faster if we just sailed over there and I did the installation for him." Plenty of people who worked on the sea did jobs they weren't suited for out of necessity, but Esther almost wished that particular ship hadn't figured out how to use the satellite network.

"I'm starting to feel like your secretary," Neal said. "You get more calls than I do."

"Oh come on, you love talking to all these people."

Neal managed one of the main communications hubs on the new satellite network. Zoe worked with him now, but most of the ship's news still came through Neal. Only Marianna, his former love on the *Galaxy Flotilla*, had better connections. She had been the first to regain contact with a handful of people broadcasting from land. Now she oversaw the primary communications hub from the *Galaxy*, despite the reservations of the *Galaxy* captains.

Neal nodded sagely. "True. True. Speaking of which, check out that map." He gestured toward the large diagram taped to the window. It was a hand-drawn approximation of most of the western hemisphere. Neal had placed a dozen markers seemingly at random on the map. There was something strange about the placement of the markers, but Esther couldn't put a finger on it.

"What am I looking at?"

"Those are the locations of the land-based communities that have tapped into the satellite network," Neal said.

"There are so many!"

Esther realized why the map looked odd to her. She was used to maps of the sea, but all those markers were places on land. For sixteen and a half years they'd only been in contact with other ships that had escaped the eruption of Yellowstone and had chosen to stay at sea to avoid the famine and unrest on land. Now, everything was changing.

"Some of the settlements are just a handful of people holed up in the wilderness," Neal said. "That pin in Alaska represents only one guy. He was some sort of mountain man before, and he had a lot of supplies stored away. He said it's freakishly cold there. I'm surprised he hasn't tried to leave by now." Neal swiveled back and forth in his chair as he talked. He had been in high spirits lately. It was nice to have him back to normal after his mournful infatuation with Marianna had ended.

"How much do you know about these communities?"

"Not much. The connections still aren't great, and some folks only check in every once in a while. Two of those marks are just guesses, because the people on the other end are paranoid about revealing their actual locations."

"One woman I talked to," Zoe added, "thought we wanted to eat her children. She told me to 'freeze off' and never call her again. Makes you wonder what other kinds of people have contacted her." Zoe shifted aside the spare headset and took a seat at the next console.

"It's crazy," Neal said. "For the first time in years we're reaching people really far away, and they don't want to talk."

Esther studied the map. The mark for Kansas City was the largest. As far as they knew, it was now the main settlement for survivors. There had been no word yet of any survivors in a large portion of the West. The volcano must have wiped out everyone and everything within hundreds of miles. The ash and famine would have done the rest.

"There's not much near the coasts," Esther said, scanning the jagged borders of the continents. The *Lucinda* would need to find a safe harbor before the expedition inland.

"Yeah, like we've suspected for a while, it hasn't been safe there, because of the storm surges. The group that's closest to the sea—at least the closest of the ones that have managed to reach the satellites—

is way down in Mexico, on a lake. There." Neal pointed to a dot on the map.

Esther leaned closer and read the label in Neal's scratchy handwriting. "Lake Aguamilpa?"

"They're about two hundred miles from the coast up the Santiago River. I gather they're mostly English speakers, and they traveled down from the US after the volcano."

"They're bonkers, though," Zoe said. "There's only one guy who will talk to us, and they've got this weird religious cult thing going."

"Yeah?"

"Our contact there told us about it when we asked him about the List."

"What list?"

"Oh right, that's our new project. It was my idea," Zoe said. "Show her, Neal."

"Sure thing. This is still a work in progress, so we're not ready to announce it to everyone yet." Neal fired up the computer in his console. A rudimentary window loaded slowly, filling the screen with names and locations. Esther recognized most of them as people who lived on the *Catalina*.

"It's a survivors database!" Zoe said proudly. "See, we only sent out the request for names a few days ago, and it'll take some time to compile all the responses, but anyone who can access the satellite network will be able to read it. We're working on getting a record of everyone who's still alive out there so that family members can find each other."

"This is amazing," Esther said. "Do you have a space for missing people, too?" She thought about her sister, Naomi, and her mother, Nina. They had been lost in the destruction of San Diego when she and her father, Simon, had escaped on the *Catalina*. There was no way they had survived the avalanche of volcanic ash, but she couldn't help looking for their names as the List scrolled past.

Neal grimaced and shifted in his seat. "There would be too many to count," he said. "We're optimistic about the number of survivors we've been able to reach now that the comms are better, but really there are far more people who didn't make it through the famines. We don't have the capacity to list all of them. We figured it'd be more practical to start with the names of the people we know are still alive."

"Makes sense."

"So we got in touch with all the ships and all the land-based communities," Zoe said, "and asked them for their rosters. The results are trickling in."

"When are you going to announce it?"

"After we have ten or twelve groups. People will have to come up here to look at the names, and it would be good to have more of them before then. Plus we'll add in a search function so the database will be easier to use."

"This is great."

"Yup. Anyway," Neal said, "do you want me to connect you with the ships that had questions, or do you want to deal with it tomorrow?"

"Let's get it wrapped up before dinner," Esther said.

"Sure. You still have a lot to do before the trip?" Neal asked as he turned back to the computer.

Esther glanced at Zoe, who raised an eyebrow.

"There's always a lot to do," Esther said. She thought about asking Neal for advice, but she was afraid of what he would tell her. He knew better than anyone how much people needed her help. She hoisted herself onto an unused console next to Neal's computer. "Okay, who do I need to call first?"

2. Cod Night

ESTHER, ZOE, AND NEAL walked down to the Atlantis Dining Hall together. It was a large space, somewhat the worse for wear after their sixteen and a half years at sea. Many of the windows had broken and were now patched with salvaged fiberglass from a dozen wrecks. The people of the *Catalina* filled the tables with their usual babble.

Cally, Esther's engine room apprentice, had been born on the ship the day they fled the disaster. Now she sat beside a solemn ten-year-old girl named Thera, trying to get her to laugh. Cally's boyfriend, Dax, hovered behind her chair, pulling faces for the little girl. Thera's parents, Byron and Sylvia, who had come to the *Catalina* from the *Galaxy Flotilla* earlier in the year, sat on the other side of the table with Cally's mother.

Over the last few months the divisions between the original Catalinans and the former Galaxians had diminished, and there were more newcomers now too. In addition to Luke and Cody from the Harvesters, the *Catalina* had picked up a few residents at the *Amsterdam* and from the other ships they had encountered with their newfound mobility. Esther's invention and subsequent regular contact with other ships had opened the floodgates, ending the policy of isolation that had ruled the *Catalina* for over a decade. Some of their number had moved on too, including Adele from the *Galaxy*, who had joined the Calderon Group, but it didn't feel like an irreversible decision anymore. The barriers that had kept the floating communities apart became more permeable every day. It was a source of regular frustration for Judith, but she wasn't the only person in charge anymore.

Esther, Zoe, and Neal helped themselves at the buffet and then went over to what had become their usual table next to the boarded-up windows. They'd removed a panel to reveal a bit of the sky outside and even a handful of stars. Luke and Cody were already there when they arrived, but there was no sign of David.

"How's the food?" Zoe asked, plopping down beside Luke.

"The cod gets better every day," Luke said. His curly hair had grown out in the past few months, and he kept sweeping it back out of his eyes.

"Did you guys hear about Dirk and Judith?" Cody said, leaning forward eagerly. He had round shoulders and dark hair, and his face was still babyish. "Reggie just told me."

"What about 'em? Did she finally snap and drive a stake through his head?" Luke asked.

"You stab a vampire through the heart, not head," Zoe said, "and I'm pretty sure it would be the other way around."

Cody shook his head. "Gracie Cordova overheard them talking," he said, "and she's been spreading it around. They were arguing over council business as usual, and Judith said something about Dirk's sea-blasted incompetence. Then Dirk goes, 'You didn't think I was so incompetent last night when you were screaming my name.'"

"No!" Zoe said. She looked like her coffee ration had come early.

"I totally saw it coming," Luke said immediately. "Those too have way too much friction. And Judith ain't bad looking for a mature lady."

"Judith isn't even that old," Neal said. "She's under forty."

"I don't buy it," Esther said. "This is Gracie Cordova we're talking about. You can't trust anything she says."

"I can't believe you're defending Herr Judith," Zoe said. "Don't you still hate each other?"

"I don't hate Judith." Esther took a bite of her cod and looked around the dining hall. Judith was nowhere to be seen. Neither was Dirk, the oilman from the *Galaxy* who had challenged Judith's reign, nor most of the other council members for that matter. Esther felt like she was slowly coming to understand Judith. She had a single-minded devotion to doing what was best for the community. That was a model Esther was starting to think she should follow. "I do hate Gracie Cordova, though, and I won't participate in her games." Gracie was the conniving eldest daughter of Rosa, the matriarch of the Cordova clan and one of Judith's longtime supporters.

"I thought Gracie was on Judith's side. Why would she spread rumors about her?" Cody said. "*Reggie* believed it."

"Has to be some other play," Zoe said. "Maybe Gracie's trying to take down Dirk, or maybe she wants to undermine both of them for some reason." Most people on the ship liked Dirk. He was gruff but less abrasive than Judith, and he wanted to make changes to the *Catalina*. He had urged them to officially end Judith's long-established isolation policy and to stay in closer contact with other ships. Dirk and Judith were rarely separated these days, primarily so they could prevent each other from scheming behind each other's backs.

"It's not worth getting into it, trust me," Esther said. "I don't think it's true."

"You're no fun, Esther," Zoe said. "Anyway, if Dirk and Judith are secret lovers, my chips are on that making their fights worse. People don't start getting along just because they're sleeping together. Look at Toni and Anita."

Cody choked on his water. Luke slapped him on the back, while Zoe grinned slyly.

"What, you didn't know?" she said.

Esther laughed and stood up. David had just entered the dining hall. He shook hands with a few of the newer Catalinans as he made his way toward the buffet, greeting them by name. Esther went over to join him in the fish line, and he dropped a kiss on her forehead.

"How's your baby?" she asked.

"Almost ready to go. Got the charts here to show your dad." He gestured to the rolled-up paper under his arm. He'd used the reverse side for another sketch of the *Lucinda*. He was quite good at drawing, as far as Esther could tell. She'd heard the *Catalina*'s resident artist, Bernadette, praising his work before. She'd even talked about getting David to help her redo the murals on the dining hall walls. Slowly but surely David was becoming integrated in *Catalina* life.

"My dad's not here yet. You should check out Neal's map up in the Tower. He's got the locations of everyone with a satellite link."

"I was up there this morning. Has he told you about the List, by the way?"

"Just now, yeah."

"That's going to be an important record. We should encourage any survivors we come across to transmit their names as soon as possible." David smiled as he piled his plate high with a double helping of cod. Now that they didn't have to worry as much about conserving energy, they could take the speedboat further out and had even rigged up a vastly superior trawling apparatus. They had more than enough food these days. Her system had already improved their lives exponentially. It was yet another thing reminding Esther that she needed to help all of the ships get her technology set up too.

"Hey, can I talk to you for a sec?" she said, pulling David aside as he finished filling his plate.

He smiled at her expectantly. She hesitated. He acted much happier these days than he had on the *Galaxy Flotilla*. His life here was so different from the luxurious one he led as the captains' spokesman, but he loved his new purpose as the captain of the *Lucinda*. Even the way he stood was different, looser somehow than the rigid posture of a man who was constantly on guard against saying the wrong thing. As soon as he recovered his health after being kidnapped by the Calderon Group, he had thrived.

"Look, David," Esther said, "I've been thinking that maybe I shouldn't go with you—on the expedition."

David blinked. "We're leaving in three days."

"I know, but I still have a lot of requests for help coming in, and the other ships need me. I'm not sure it's the right time."

"And you're bringing this up now?"

"I've been thinking about it for a while."

"Have you," David said flatly.

"By the time you get back, my work should have let up a little."

David frowned and blew out a long breath between his teeth. He didn't say anything more. Esther had expected him to try to talk her into coming along. He always had something persuasive to say.

"David?"

She'd wanted to make it clear she hadn't decided for sure to stay behind yet and that it would be temporary. It was not like she was trying to break up with him. But he stared at the plate in his hands, seemingly struggling to maintain his usual cool.

"It would just be this trip," Esther said. "Next time you head out somewhere, I'll come with you. I promise."

Unexpected emotion rioted across David's face like storm waves across a deck. He looked up sharply.

"And what if I don't come back?"

"But the plan—"

"The plan was for you to come with me," he said. "We've been working on it for *months*, Esther. You can't just change your mind at the last minute without discussing it with me first."

"I haven't decided anything yet," Esther said.

David stiffened, his back ramrod straight. "How gracious of you."

"What do you—?"

"Maybe I *will* stay on land. I don't know, Esther. We'd better sit down." He turned and walked away from her across the dining hall, the plate of cod still in his hand.

Esther stared after him. Something in his tone stopped her from responding. She knew she had left it late, but she thought she had explained she was trying to do the responsible thing for once. She had thought David would understand, but he seemed . . . hurt.

She followed him to the table to rejoin their friends. David didn't look at her when she sat down. She tried to catch his eye, but he leaned further over his plate and stabbed at the flaky white fish with his fork.

Zoe, Neal, Luke, and Cody were talking animatedly and didn't notice any tension between Esther and David. They had moved on from speculating about Dirk and Judith, and Neal was telling them about the Lake Aguamilpa people and their strange practices.

"They live on a lake, right?" Neal said. "And they have to do these offerings. Every time they get a particularly good catch of fish, they give something back to the water, a bit of food or produce they would otherwise use, something the remaining fish can eat. The lake is like a god they need to appease. They've developed a whole religious system around it."

Esther barely listened. She picked at her meal, stealing glances at David. He kept his gaze determinedly on his food. He hadn't given her a chance to explain.

"Why the lake?" Cody asked. "I mean, why not worship the dirt or the trees or something? Or, like, God?"

"I don't think they worship it exactly," Neal said. "It's more like a healthy respect bordering on reverence. They worship God too, and the lake is tied to that somehow. Not sure I have the full story yet. I'll see if I can get their comm guy to tell me more."

"Well, I respect the salt out of the sea, but I'm not making offerings to it," Zoe said. "I'll keep all the food I can." She poked Luke's hand with the bent prongs of her fork. "Speaking of which, any chance you guys can get something besides cod next time you go out? I'd kill for a nice big garlic shrimp right about now."

"One garlic shrimp, hold the garlic, coming right up," Luke said. "I still can't believe you grew garlic on the *Galaxy*."

"You wouldn't believe a lot of the things we did on the *Galaxy*," Zoe said, "but at least with the Harvesters you got to see the world a bit."

"Just different parts of the sea. It all looks the same."

"I can't wait for the expedition," Cody said. "We'll get to see real grass and trees again. Trees!"

"As long as you don't get kidnapped and eaten by any crazy lake people," said Zoe.

"Aren't you excited, Esther?" Cody asked, nudging her with his elbow.

"Huh?"

"For the expedition?"

David stood up so fast he would have knocked his chair over if it hadn't been bolted to the floor.

"I've got some work to wrap up," he said. "Want to finish my cod, Luke?" He left the dining hall without waiting for a response. The door swung shut behind him.

"Dude, what's up with him?" Luke said, already digging into the mostly full plate.

"I'll venture a guess that he's not going to work," Zoe said. She picked up the rolled-up charts David had left on his chair.

"Are you guys fighting, Esther?" Neal asked.

"I guess the fish is out of the net anyway." Esther sighed and pushed her own plate away. "I'm thinking about skipping the expedition because I have so many people asking for help with their generators still."

Cody frowned. "I'd hate for you to miss it."

"I know. I'm still not sure what to do."

"So that's why David's acting like someone stole his favorite sweater," Luke said through a mouthful of fish.

"I just told him I *might* not go. He . . . he seems pretty upset about it. Wouldn't even talk to me." There must be something she was missing, something to warrant such a strong reaction. Everything had been great between them just a few hours ago.

"It's not like Hawthorne to *not* wanna talk, is it?" said Zoe.

"What did you say to him exactly?" Neal asked, looking at her thoughtfully.

"I just said I'd been thinking maybe I shouldn't go this time because of all the ships that still need my help with their generators. He got all steel-faced and stalked over here and, well, you saw. I *did* tell him I hadn't decided for sure, but he's still pissed." Esther looked around the table at her friends. "Do you guys understand why he's mad?"

"I haven't always seen eye to eye with the guy," Neal said, "but this is kind of sudden. He probably wanted you to talk it over with him before making a decision."

"I haven't decided," Esther said.

"You sure about that?"

Esther hesitated. "Well, that's what I told him, and he went off pouting." *Had* she decided? People really needed her here, and there were no guarantees they could stay in contact throughout the entire trip. It would take months even if everything went according to plan.

"You're supposed to leave in less than three days," Neal said. "You can't dump stuff like this on him at the last minute. I should know." Neal took a forkful of David's cod from the abandoned plate.

"Also, Esther," Luke said, "don't take this the wrong way, but maybe what you thought was 'talking it over' sounded to David like 'telling him your decision.'"

"I don't have to ask his permission," Esther grumbled. She looked down at her plate, beginning to lose her appetite. So what if she had decided? She was trying to do the right thing. He should see that.

"The guy used to be the king of diplomacy on the *Galaxy*," Zoe said. "Things have changed a lot, but he probably would have appreciated a little more conversation about something that affects him. And a tiny bit more notice."

"Yeah, that's what being in a relationship is about," Luke said. "Talking things through and doing what's best for you as a team while respecting the needs of each individual. Communication is key."

Everyone stared at Luke. Zoe's mouth dropped open slightly.

"What?" Luke said, shoveling up another bite of cod. "It's what my mom always says."

"Maybe," Esther said slowly. Had David really meant what he'd said about staying on land for good? She hoped not. Even if she had duties here, she was not willing to be done with David Hawthorne. They would work it out.

Esther knocked on the door to David's cabin on the *Lucinda*. It was late, but she didn't want to let the night pass without talking to him. She had his roll of charts tucked under her arm. The passageway was dark and very cold. She knocked louder, shivering as she waited for a response.

Finally, she called, "Are you in there, David? It's me."

There was no answer, but Esther thought she heard movement inside the cabin. Pacing. He was there after all.

"Answer me!" She banged harder on the door. "I'm salting sorry. I didn't know it would bother you this much. Can we talk it over?"

Esther hoped her friends were right and this was just a misunderstanding. If skipping the voyage meant losing David, she would reconsider. At the same time it infuriated her that he would allow it to get to that point. He was being unreasonable. She raised her hand to knock again. David opened the door.

Involuntarily, Esther took a step back at the sight of David's disheveled appearance. His hair stood on end, and his face was dark as a thunderhead. He put one hand on the doorframe, preventing her from coming in.

"What would you like to talk over, Esther?" he said. His voice sounded like a stranger's. A very polite stranger's.

"I'll come with you on the trip," she blurted out, shoving the roll of charts against his chest.

For a long moment David simply stared at her. His expression didn't change at all.

"Don't jerk me around like this, Esther," he said. "You can't save my life one minute, be with me the next, send me off to sea because you're busy, and then come knocking on my door."

"David—"

"I've tried, Esther." Some of the composure slipped from David's face. "I've tried a lot harder with you than with any other woman because I know what I want."

"I—"

"But you don't know how to be in a relationship with someone, you don't know how to communicate, and you don't know what you want."

"I want to be with you," she snapped. "The world is just crazy right now. I have work to do. I thought the timing—"

"Maybe it is the timing," David said. Pain flashed across his face, and the roll of charts crinkled in his palm. "Maybe you're just too young for me, Esther. Do your work. Stay with the *Catalina*. I don't care."

He turned back to the cabin and jerked the door shut behind him.

Esther stepped back against the cold bulkhead, fuming. *Too young for him? We'll see about that!*

She glared at the door, angry tears forming in her eyes. He'd be back. He'd realize he was being petulant, and *she* was the one with the maturity to put the needs of everyone else first. And the maturity to come work things out. *I'll just give him time to come to his senses.*

The door remained closed.

He *would* be back. He had overreacted. He would realize it in a minute. She'd be the one to graciously accept his apology. *Too young for him indeed!*

Still the door didn't move.

After a few minutes Esther rubbed her eyes angrily and turned to stomp toward the hatch. If he wanted to be like that, then *fine.* He could come to her.

She made it halfway up the corridor before she whirled around, marched back to David's door, and banged on it with her fist.

"You don't get to be like this, David Hawthorne!" she shouted. "We've been through too much together. Rust, I'm not going to grovel if you're going to act like a child. I came back here to admit I was wrong for not talking it over until the last minute. If you want to be angry, then fine! But you don't get to slam the salting door in my face. Now open up!"

Esther pulled her wrench from her belt and was about to begin prying at the lock when the door swung open again. She froze, with the wrench poised at waist level. Blood rushed to her cheeks.

David looked down at the tool in her hand, then back at her sheepish expression.

"You should see your face, Esther," he said.

"Don't slam doors on me when I'm trying to talk to you. It's not fair."

"Well, don't abandon me," David said, a crack appearing in his smooth voice.

"Temporarily! You're the one who threatened to stay on land for good."

"You started it."

"I started it? Seriously? Aren't you supposed to be the skilled orator here?"

David gaped at her, his composure wavering. Then he threw up his hands, stepped forward, and covered her mouth with his. The momentum carried them all the way out into the corridor. He kissed her more earnestly than he ever had before. Her wrench clattered to the floor as she wrapped her arms around his neck. His fingers were in her hair, his lips pressing hers. All thought swam straight out of her head.

As suddenly as the kiss had begun, David released her. He set Esther back on her feet and stepped away, adjusting the glasses that had fallen sideways on his face.

"I meant what I said about not wanting to be jerked around," David said, completely serious. "You make me crazy, Esther. Let's both cool down, give it some thought, and talk in the morning."

Esther waited for him to continue, still catching her breath. But he just walked backward until he was in the doorway of his cabin again. Then he saluted, and with slow, exaggerated movements he closed the door.

Esther had spent most nights in David's cabin on the *Lucinda* over the past few months, but now she crossed back to the *Catalina* and climbed up the service stairwell to the Mermaid Lounge, on the ninth deck, where Zoe, Anita, and Toni had lived ever since they arrived from the *Galaxy*. Her father's girlfriend, Penelope Newton, had moved into the cabin Esther used to share with him, so she couldn't go back there. She had been getting used to the idea of her father's newfound happiness with Penelope. She had moved to the lounge to give them space without being asked, but it still grated. Esther and her father had been a duo for the past sixteen years, and she wasn't quite ready to welcome Penelope into their family.

Most of the space in the Mermaid Lounge was taken up with tables, chairs, and a long bar in front of the sea-facing windows. Bright portraits of mermaids and a handful of carved sconces decorated the booths against the walls. Cots that had once been in the ship's spa (long since dedicated to storage) were spread out in one corner.

Esther hadn't slept up here in weeks. The way she felt with David made her not want to be anywhere else. She loved spending time with him in the *Lucinda*'s pilothouse or in his cabin when they weren't working. She had thought she could handle being away from him for a few months while he made the expedition he had been dreaming of for so long. Now she felt a void like a drop-off on the seafloor.

No, she didn't just love spending time with him. She loved him. Every fiber and joint of her loved him. She wouldn't let him go over something this stupid, and she didn't think he'd let her go either.

"So did you sort things out?" Zoe asked when Esther sat down on the cot in between hers and Toni's. Her straw-blond hair hung loose around her face, and she knotted and twisted the red headscarf in her hands.

Toni lay stretched out on her stomach, reading a book that was on the verge of disintegrating. She had been making her way steadily through the *Catalina*'s meager collection since arriving from the *Galaxy*. She didn't look up.

"I'm not sure," Esther said.

"Did you at least talk?" Zoe prompted.

"Sort of." Esther pulled her thin blanket up to her chin and peered over the tattered edge. "I yelled at him, and then he kissed me, and then I left."

"You guys are crazy," Zoe said.

Toni snorted and turned a page in her book.

"We care about each other, though."

"You have a weird way of showing it."

"I think we're okay," Esther said. Hopefully they'd be able to talk things over more reasonably after a solid night's rest. They did care about each other. David would never lose his cool if he didn't. They'd figure out a way for them both to be happy, even if they had to be apart for a little while. They *had* been through too much together.

Zoe frowned at her for a minute, looking conflicted. Then she sighed and stood, letting the red scarf drop onto her cot.

"This is silly. I'm going to find Luke," she said, and strode toward the exit.

Esther laughed, startled.

"It's about time!" Toni called.

Zoe turned when she got to the door. "And you?"

"I'll fix things with David in the morning."

"Atta girl."

3. News

B UT THE NEXT MORNING everything changed. Esther awoke to Neal shaking her shoulder insistently. She pushed him away and sat up.

"What, Neal?" She rubbed her eyes, adjusting to the early-morning light streaming into the Mermaid Lounge.

"Esther, I've been looking everywhere for you. Are you awake?" Neal knelt beside Esther's cot. His clothes were rumpled, and he had dark circles under his eyes. Toni stirred in the next bed but she didn't wake up.

"Not really. What time is it?"

"Just after five."

"Are we sinking?"

"No, Esther, I need you to see something. Get up."

"Okay, okay, I'm up. Where?" As her brain kicked into gear, her thoughts immediately jumped to the worst things: something had happened to her father, to David, to Cally.

"In the Tower. On the computer."

"You woke me up at five to show me something on the computer?" Esther grumbled. "Salt, Neal, really?"

"Trust me, Esther, you'll want to see this."

Within minutes they were jogging through the corridors of the *Catalina*. Esther trailed her fingers along the bulkhead, still feeling groggy. She had no idea what could have caused Neal to rouse her this early.

"Look, Esther, you should take this with a grain of salt, okay?" Neal said as they neared the broadcast tower. "I don't know anything for sure, and I'm only going off the name, so promise you won't freak out."

"Freak out about what?"

"It's your sister. I think she might be alive."

The corridors of the *Catalina* vanished. Esther had the sensation of fog closing in or maybe a wave crashing over her head. Something obliterated all her senses.

"What the rusted *hell* are you talking about?" She had stopped walking. Truths she had known for over sixteen years tumbled around in her head.

Esther's sister was dead.

Esther's sister had been at a dentist appointment in San Diego when the ash cloud descended.

Esther's sister had been eight years old.

Esther's sister had been with her mother.

"Esther," Neal said, "please stay calm. It's a slim chance, but I knew you'd want to know right away." He tugged on her arm, and she followed him numbly.

Neal kept talking as they climbed the ladder to the tower. Esther had to stop him and make him start his explanation over again. She tried to focus.

"We told you about the List, right?" Neal said. "The database of survivors? Well, I got a batch of names in late last night. I've been putting them into the system, and one of them caught my eye. The name was Naomi Harris. Now Harris is a common name, so that's why you can't do anything rash."

Esther felt queasy, like she'd been hit with an unexpected bout of seasickness.

"It's very common, Neal."

"But let me finish. We've been asking people to provide places of origin and birth dates for the database to make it easier to tell people apart. This particular Naomi Harris is from San Diego, which is why she caught my eye. And she's about two years older than you."

Esther swallowed hard. "What's the full birth date?"

"That's what I brought you up here to see." Neal's voice seemed to fade in and out, like he was on the radio. "I thought you should check before everyone else gets up. If it's not her, I want to prepare your dad before he starts looking through the List and comes across that name."

"Thank you, Neal," Esther said. She looked over at the computer terminal. She felt like she had just seen a fin jutting out of the water and didn't know yet whether it was a dolphin or a shark. It could be something good, or it could be incredibly painful. At least she could spare her father that.

"Show me the date."

Without speaking, Neal sat down at his computer. He tapped a key, and the screen lit up. His finger trembling slightly, he pointed at one line.

The words seemed to shift and blur before Esther's eyes, but she read, "Naomi Harris. Origin: San Diego, California, USA. Location: Lake Aguamilpa, Mexico." And there, next to a date about two years before Esther's own birth year, was July 27.

Esther's legs folded under her, and she sat straight down on the floor.

"Is it her?" Neal asked.

Esther nodded.

Alive.

Naomi was alive.

It couldn't be real. There had to be a mistake.

Her sister was alive.

"Wow. Man, Es, I thought there was a chance, but this is crazy," Neal said.

Esther shook her head, unable to answer. Neal sat beside her on the floor and put a hand on her shoulder.

"There's more, Esther. Please don't freak out, but you need to know."

"My mom?" Esther whispered. Her hands found the flat planes of the floor. Pressed downward.

"Her name's not on the List. I'm sorry. No, it's something else."

Esther closed her eyes for a moment, gathering herself. "What is it?"

"Naomi Harris is in Lake Aguamilpa. Remember that's where they have this strict religious thing going on? Well, the guy I usually talk to didn't want to give me their roster. No one else there is even allowed to communicate with the outside world, and he said they couldn't expose themselves like that. I'd sorta given up on them. Then late last night I got a transmission with a text-only message containing all these names. He didn't say anything, just sent them over with the Lake Aguamilpa location clearly listed. He may have been going against orders by sending their roster, so I don't know if we'll be able to talk to Naomi."

"You have to make him put her on the phone."

"There's only so much I can do from here," Neal said.

Esther stood, her next course of action crystal clear.

"We'll just have to go get her."

Esther arrived at her father's door fifteen minutes later, still trying to process what she had just found out. The wild combination of joy and shock was like being outside in a storm while lightning cracked gorgeous, deadly patterns across the sky.

Esther knocked several times before she got an answer. Her hands shook, and she hooked them in her belt to steady them as she waited for Simon to respond. He finally called out that he was coming, and a few muffled words indicated that he'd woken Penelope.

The door opened. Simon wore a "Catalina: Your Island at Sea" T-shirt. His curly salt-and-pepper hair stuck to his forehead, and he had a red crease in his cheek. Esther remembered how he'd looked during their first days on the *Catalina*: sad and tense and determined all at once. When the people on the *Catalina* learned San Diego had been completely covered in ash, he had explained to six-year-old Esther that it would have been impossible for Naomi and her mother to survive. He'd told her about the cloying, suffocating effects of ash if it got inside your lungs. He'd held her close and told her she would never see her mother and sister again.

"What's wrong, Esther?" Simon said quietly. He looked back at the darkened cabin and stepped into the corridor with her. "Is everything okay?"

"Dad, there's a chance . . . We think Naomi is alive."

"Naomi?"

"There's this List . . . Neal has been collecting names . . . She's in Mexico . . ."

Simon watched her, confusion furrowing his brow. Esther realized she probably wasn't making sense.

She breathed. Started again.

"Neal and Zoe are making a database of survivors. They're collecting names from everyone on the satellite network. Naomi Harris is one of them."

"Harris is a common name, button."

"I know. But Neal has birthdays and where people are from. It's July 27, Dad, Naomi's birthday. She just turned twenty-five. And the List says she's from San Diego."

"How is that possible? The ash . . ."

"I have no idea. But do you think it could really be her?"

"No one could have survived in San Diego," Simon said, his voice unbearably sad. "The ash was too thick and it spread too quickly."

He had said as much many times before. He'd said they had to accept it. At first she'd been hurt that he didn't hold out hope for her mother and sister, but she understood later that he'd been looking out for her. Following his example, Esther had accepted the truth of their deaths years ago. She had moved on. But now she heard the familiar words in a different light. What if her father hadn't moved on at all? Had he believed there was a slim chance they could have survived? Had he been protecting her all this time?

"There had to have been some exceptions," Esther said, her brain whizzing through the possibilities she hadn't been able to entertain before. "What if they started driving straight from our house instead of going to the dentist?"

"I don't think there would have been enough time. Is . . . is your mother—?"

"She's not on the List, no," Esther said quickly.

Simon nodded. Exhaled.

"Naomi was only eight years old," he said. "I don't see how she could have escaped on her own."

"But the birthday, Dad. Do you think there was another Naomi Harris from San Diego born on the very same day?"

"It's possible. Unlikely maybe, but possible. Can you talk to her on the satellite phone?"

"Neal's trying to find out. That's the other problem. She's with this crazy group where they're not allowed to have contact with anyone. We need to go and get her."

"But if it's not her—"

"Do you want to take that risk?" Esther said. "We'll see what Neal can find out, but I think we should go look for her in the *Lucinda* if there's any chance at all that it's her."

Simon put both hands on her shoulders. "Esther, I don't want you to get your hopes up. The likelihood—"

"I know. You're right. It seems impossible, but we have to try, don't we?"

"Yes, we do. I'd like to talk to Neal, find out what else he knows about this group she's with. Just let me get my shoes." Simon released Esther's shoulders and turned back toward his cabin. He hesitated. "Are you sure your mother wasn't on the list?"

A picture of Esther's mother rose before her: dark hair, a strong nose, bracelets that slid along her wrists. Nina laughed, danced with Simon in the kitchen, kissed Esther's cheeks in a soft cloud that smelled like apple blossoms. The image was bright and warm, like her dreams of land.

"She wasn't," Esther said. "I'm sorry."

Simon's shoulders drooped, as if he had just picked up a heavy load after setting it down for a moment. He went back inside his cabin to retrieve his shoes.

4. The Meeting

ESTHER CROSSED THE GANGWAY to the *Lucinda* as the sun climbed upward. She felt unmoored, almost delirious. She jogged to the passageway outside David's cabin and hammered on the door.

"Wake up, David. We need to talk."

He opened the door and let her in immediately. He wore his trousers but no shirt. A shiny, round scar marred his shoulder, no bigger than Esther's thumbnail.

"You didn't sleep out here, did you?" He sat back on his bunk, rubbing his eyes and reaching for his glasses. "I didn't want you to do that just because we were fighting. I was wrong to act like—"

"That doesn't matter now. Listen, my sister is alive!" Esther paced back and forth in the small cabin. She needed to do something. "She's in that weird town in Mexico. We have to find her."

"Slow down a minute," David said. "Who? What town?"

Esther quickly explained about finding a Naomi Harris with the same birthday as her sister on the list of survivors from Lake Aguamilpa. "We need to go get her in the *Lucinda*. We're heading through Mexico anyway. Lake Aguamilpa is a lot further south, but it's on a big river. *Lucinda* might be able to sail all the way from the coast. We should leave tonight and—"

"Hold on, Esther," David said. He was frowning. "*Lucinda* isn't your ship. You can't make a route change like that."

"What?"

"We have a mission, and it involves the entire crew. We can't go running off after a rumor until we discuss it with them."

"Are you serious? My sister is alive, David. I can't wait."

"I appreciate that you feel like you have to do something right this instant, but you have to think of other people sometimes."

"I am. I'm thinking of my sister." So much for choosing to do what was best for the greater good. When it came down to it, Esther's family was more important to her than the whole world. The other ships would have to do without her for a while.

"Esther, we can't just do whatever you want because you happen to have a forceful personality and a good purpose," David said.

Esther stopped pacing and stood stock still in the middle of the cabin. "I can't believe you're not on my side."

"This isn't about sides," David said. "Hopefully we will go after Naomi in the *Lucinda*. I know what this means to you, but I will not change the plan out of the blue without discussing it with the crew."

"I thought you—"

"That's my final decision."

"Is this because you're mad at me?!"

"This isn't about you and me anymore, Esther. And I wasn't mad because you were thinking about staying behind. I was mad because you just made your decision at the last minute and without talking it over with me. I thought we had a partnership. You can't act like you're the only one who gets to decide things for both of us. In this case the decision affects every member of the *Lucinda*'s crew, and they deserve to have a say."

"What do you mean 'had' a partnership?"

David sighed and rubbed his hands over his face. "Let's talk about it with the crew, okay? If we're going to change our route, we'll need to do it soon."

"Okay, fine," Esther said. "I'll call everyone to the Mermaid Lounge. See you at 0800?"

"Aye." David began pulling on his boots.

Esther hesitated, not sure whether she should kiss him before heading out the door. She rested her hand lightly on the smooth skin of his shoulder. Her fingers brushed over his scar. He took her hand for a moment but didn't look up. She turned toward the door.

"I had a family too, Esther," David said quietly, still bent over his boots. "I understand how you feel."

She looked back at him, but he didn't meet her eyes. She pulled the cabin door closed behind her.

Esther darted through the *Lucinda*'s corridors, banging on doors to rouse the crew for the meeting. Luke and Zoe emerged from one bunk together, Luke grinning foolishly. Zoe winked at Esther, about to say something until she saw Esther's face.

"How can we help?" she said, reaching for her pocketknife.

"Get the team for the expedition over to the Mermaid Lounge. It's important."

She hurried back across the gangway to round up the last of the crew on the *Catalina*. Toni, Anita, and Zoe were in the lounge by the time Esther returned to the ninth deck. Toni's lanky frame was sprawled over a lounge chair. Anita sat beside her, folding and unfolding her pale hands. Luke brought Cody, who he'd roused from his own bunk on the *Lucinda*. Other members of the *Lucinda*'s crew took seats alongside them, many still rubbing their eyes and staring blearily around the room. Oilmen. Former Galaxians. A few longtime Catalinans.

Neal arrived with Dax, his friend Raymond from the *Galaxy*, and Esther's father. Simon looked pale. He'd wrapped his green scarf haphazardly around his neck, and the end trailed along almost to the floor. He sat at a table between Esther and Neal, his face solemn.

"Did you talk to the Aguamilpa people?" Esther asked.

"Sort of," Neal said. "It was weird." He glanced at Simon.

"What do you mean?"

"Well, I got in touch with my usual guy," Neal said. "He's the only person there I've ever talked to. I brought up the List and the Aguamilpa roster, and he sounded confused. It was like he didn't know what I was talking about. Then he said he had to go and hung up real quickly."

"He didn't remember your conversation about the List?" Esther felt a surge in her stomach, like the ship had tipped sideways. What if it wasn't true after all? "Are you sure you had the right location?"

"If I didn't know better," Neal said, "I'd think he was surprised I had their roster at all. He acted like I must be mistaken."

"We think he may have gone against the instructions of a supervisor to provide it to us," Simon said. "He could be pretending not to know what Neal was talking about to avoid getting in trouble."

"Doesn't bode well for our chances to speak to Naomi," Neal said.

Esther frowned. She didn't understand what kind of supervisor or leader would insist on keeping the identities of their people a secret. They couldn't get access to the List without sharing their own names. And who wouldn't want to know if their families had survived?

"All the more reason to get there as soon as possible," she said.

"I agree," Neal said.

Esther grabbed his hand and squeezed it gratefully. Neal, at least, was on her side. He came from a small family, and his mother had died of pneumonia aboard the *Catalina*. But he knew, as Esther did, that any whisper of surviving family members could not be ignored.

Esther tapped her hands impatiently along the wood tabletop, counting the remaining crew as they made their way in, some with breakfast clutched in their hands. The youngest Newton boy, Ike, a tow-headed young man of twenty, was the latest addition to the crew. He waved at Simon and Esther as he entered the lounge, but Simon didn't notice. He was too busy picking apart the worn threads of his scarf, brow furrowed in thought. For her part, Esther had resisted spending any time with the Newtons since her father started dating their mother. She had no interest in forming a new family, and she was about to get her real sibling back anyway.

At precisely 0800 David entered. He was dressed immaculately, his hair neatly combed. He strode to the bar by the sea-facing window and took charge before Esther could say a word.

"Good morning, everyone. Thank you for gathering here on such short notice. We have been planning our voyage to land for a while now. As you know, our primary objective is to assess the conditions on the coast of northern Mexico and southern California and possibly discover a secure harbor. At that point, if all is well we plan to make an inland journey, exploring as far as we can. If conditions on land are acceptable, we may go as far as the settlement in Kansas City, assessing any areas along the way that may have potential as a home for us in the future. That is the plan we've agreed to as a group, and the *Lucinda* is stocked with this purpose in mind."

David looked around the lounge. He met Esther's eyes, his expression cloaked.

"One member of our crew," he continued, "has proposed a route change. The new course would take us farther south, to the mouth of the Santiago River in Mexico. Before she explains the reason for this change, I want to make it clear to you that the *Lucinda* may not be able to take this detour and still make it all the way to Kansas before winter sets in. We've all been working for this, and we need to understand the consequences before any decisions are made. I may be in command of the *Lucinda*, but it's important that we all agree before embarking on this voyage. Esther?"

Esther stared at David for a moment before going up to join him by the bar. What was he trying to do? Did he want to talk people out of the trip?

"I'll make this quick, guys," she said. "I found out that my sister is alive. I want to go get her in the *Lucinda*. I don't care about being all diplomatic about this. If you found out someone in your family was still alive, you'd want to go after her too."

"Where?" Zoe gasped. "And how?"

"She's on the List."

"She's at Lake Aguamilpa in Mexico," Neal put in.

"The crazy ones?"

"Yeah, and they won't let their people talk to anyone, except for one communications guy," Esther said. "We need to go there."

"Hold on a minute," Luke said. "How are we going to get to this lake?"

"The Santiago River flows all the way there from the coast," Esther said.

"Is it passable in the *Lucinda*, though?" asked one of the oilmen. Jackson was a big-shouldered, amiable man in his late thirties. He was turning a dented water bottle around and around in his hands as he listened to the discussion.

"I don't know."

"That," David said, "is exactly why this needs to be a group decision. It is entirely possible we will sail up this river and find that we're either stuck or unable to proceed. At that point we'd need to continue on foot or turn back. Even if we manage to sail *Lucinda* all the way to the lake, we would be engaging a reclusive and potentially hostile community about which we know almost nothing."

"But it's Esther's sister," Dax said.

"I know," David said. "But we all need to understand the risks. Some of us could be killed if we embark on this mission."

"That's always been on the cards, hasn't it?" Luke said. "If it was my mom and we were talking about storming the *Amsterdam* to help her, I reckon I'd be asking you all to do the same. I'm in."

"Obviously, I'm in too," Zoe said. "I can take a little danger, even though the Aguamilpa people are whaleshit crazy."

"Thank you," Esther said. Why couldn't David have agreed with as little hesitation?

"We want to explore land anyway, so I get why you think we can change our route, but what about *our* families?" Toni said. She sat up in her chair. "We all lost people on land. My family lived in Florida. What if they're still alive? Can we take the *Lucinda* all the way through the Panama Canal?"

"Maybe we can," Esther said. "I'm not asking you to do anything I wouldn't turn around and do for you. Right now it's my sister that we found."

"So we'll go to Florida next then," said Toni, "followed by Michigan to find Anita's family, and then maybe New York City to see if anyone survived there?"

"I don't know . . ." Esther said.

"It's gotta be all or nothing, Esther." Toni stood and addressed the group. "I don't think we should change our plan. It's a real long shot that we could even find the lake. Seriously, isn't it kind of a stretch that this is really Esther's sister?"

A few people in the crew nodded, including Dax's friend Raymond. Jackson leaned over to speak to another of the oilmen in a low voice.

"She has the same birthday," Esther said.

"Great," Toni said, putting her hands on her narrow hips. "Let's all put our lives at risk to fetch someone who has the same birthday as Esther's dead sister. That's fair."

"You don't have to come," Esther snapped.

"Oh really? I don't have to come, when I've been working to plan this voyage just as much as the rest of you? Now I don't have a say because I'm not sleeping with Hawthorne?"

Esther started forward, but David put a hand on her shoulder, silencing her.

"You do have a say," David said. "That's the point of this meeting. I haven't made any decisions about our voyage beyond bringing this possible route change to you for your consideration. Let's keep the discussion from degenerating into juvenile personal attacks, if you don't mind."

"This *is* personal," Toni said. "You're making it personal by trying to change the plan to benefit your own family."

"I don't have a choice," Esther said.

"Well, I do," Toni said. "I didn't escape the *Galaxy* to be subjected to someone else's whims. I'm out." She turned on her heel and strode to the door. Anita started up from her chair, fluttering between standing and sitting for a moment, then remained where she was.

David cleared his throat. "Would anyone else like to offer something constructive to this discussion?"

"Look, I'm not saying we shouldn't do this," Jackson said, "but Toni has a point. Are you sure it's really your sister?"

Esther swallowed. She barely knew Jackson and some of the others. But she was going to ask them to do this for her anyway. She had no choice.

"No, I'm not," she said. "I wish I knew for certain, but it could turn out to be a stranger. What I do know is that there's hope. Not only are there people alive on land that we can communicate with, but some of them have to be connected to us. The whole point of our mission on the *Lucinda* is to find out whether it'll be possible to go back to the land. This is just a detour. Even if this isn't really my sister, there's hope on land for the first time in years. Haven't we had enough of living without hope?"

"Hawthorne, what do you think we should do?" Anita asked quietly.

"I think we should go," David said without hesitation. "But we all have to understand the risks. As the captain of the *Lucinda*, I will not force anyone, but I'm with Esther on this one."

He met Esther's eyes, the morning light catching in the cracks in his glasses. A hot flash ignited in her chest, like fuel in a combustion engine. He was with her.

"Esther hasn't steered us wrong yet," Zoe said. "Let's do it."

"I agree," Dax said.

"It's still land," Jackson said, lifting his wide shoulders, "and we're ready to go anyway. I'm okay with a detour."

More voices rose in agreement. Esther tapped her foot impatiently, but David waited until the entire crew had given their consent to the route change. Raymond looked like he wanted to protest, but he buckled under David's gaze and nodded. Once everyone had agreed, David relaxed visibly.

"Okay, that settles it," David said. "We'll need a replacement for Toni, though. Do you know of anyone who wants a spot on the boat?"

Simon stood then. He stepped forward and extended his hand to David.

"Count me in."

5. Judith

WORD OF WHAT HAD happened traveled quickly amongst the Catalinans as the crew scrambled to adjust their plans. Rumors spread through the ship like ink in water. By the following afternoon a long line of people snaked away from the entrance to Neal's Tower. They all wanted to see the List to find out if their families were alive too. The people waited anxiously, bouncing on their toes, peering toward the ladder, asking questions raw with hope.

Neal tried to warn everyone that the List wasn't complete yet and it would be better for them to wait until he had more names, but no one listened. They refused to waste a minute while there was a chance they could find their lost loved ones. Neal relented and called them up a few at a time to scroll through the List. Each of them must now be half expecting the impossible to happen to them too.

Esther spotted Penelope Newton in the line as she headed for Neal's Tower. Penelope looped her arms through the arms of two of her sons, Isaiah and Ike, and prayed out loud, repeating her husband Jeb's name many times in quick succession. Jeb had been lost in the destruction of San Diego, and Penelope had found solace with Esther's father. Esther wondered what would happen between Simon and Penelope if Jeb had lived after all. She couldn't let herself follow that line of thought. It only led to her mother.

Esther bypassed the line, and no one tried to stop her. Eyes laced with envy followed as she scrambled up the ladder. Inside the Tower, the entire Cordova clan crowded around the computer console. The adults jostled each other for a better view of the little screen, while the children ran around the small space, pushing buttons and giggling to each other. Neal hovered nearby, tufts of his mousy hair sticking out at odd angles.

"I keep telling you," he said as Esther entered, "there will be more names later. Please, can you wait?"

"Stand back, young man," said old Mrs. Cordova. She had control of the keyboard and was clicking down the List one name at a time. "I have twenty-one cousins who were still alive right before the disaster. And my two brothers were living in Mexico.

You have a roster from Mexico right here, and I will not wait."

Neal threw up his hands and turned away, spotting Esther by the trapdoor. He skirted around Gracie and Maria Cordova and pulled a spare headset out of the hands of one of Gracie's children.

"Hey Esther," he said. "How's things?"

"We're set to leave at first light if the weather holds. Any news here?"

"I've barely had time to check." Neal gestured helplessly toward the large family filling his workspace.

"Have there been any others?"

"Not yet. A few near misses. I keep reminding everyone that lots of people have the same name, but they keep wanting to tear off after anyone whose name is vaguely similar to that of someone they know."

Esther let out a sigh of relief and immediately felt guilty for it. She wanted to set out immediately, and she worried about the inevitable delay if anyone else found a family member's name on the List. She knew it was selfish, but she didn't want to worry about anyone but Naomi.

"Have you been able to get anything out of your comm guy in Aguamilpa?"

"Unfortunately, no," Neal said. "There's only the one. He's chatty when he's around, but sometimes he steps out for a cigarette break and doesn't come back for days. I haven't been able to reach him since that weird conversation about the List. I'm not sure you guys should set out until we get a bit more intel."

"We can't afford to wait," Esther said, "and you'll definitely be able to reach us while we're still at sea. Winter will set in while we're traveling overland if we delay." She glanced out the window. The late-afternoon sun sparkled across the gently rolling sea. The *Lucinda* bobbed beside them, her decks crawling with tiny figures. They were almost ready.

"I'll keep trying," Neal said. "I should warn you that the comm guy has always been cagey about odd things, though. He's happy to talk about the village in general but gives away almost nothing about himself. He won't even tell me his name."

"He gave you their roster, though. Why wouldn't he talk to you now? Is he being watched?"

"It's possible." Neal swept up one of the children who had decided to jump on the cot where he slept. "Oof. That's enough playing for you. Go ask your grandma for a snack." He set the girl down and turned back to Esther. "The roster *did* come through in the middle of the night. Hope he didn't get in trouble for it if he really was going against orders."

"Hmm." Esther didn't like this. She had hoped to actually speak to Naomi before they set out. It could still be the wrong person. "Next time you talk to your guy, maybe you shouldn't tell him we're coming. And don't mention Naomi. We don't know who else might be listening." She didn't want Naomi to end up in trouble, especially if the comm guy had to sneak around to give them information. Who knew what the leaders there would say if someone started asking after the Aguamilpa residents by name?

"Maybe he could help," Neal said uncertainly, "or send Naomi to meet you at the coast or something."

"We'll figure it out along the way. Find out everything you can from the guy without making him—or whoever is listening—suspicious." Esther forced down her anxiety. There was no time for second thoughts. If the leaders of the lake community were going to cause problems, there was nothing they could do about it right now.

"Sure thing, Esther," Neal said. "It's too bad you can't trade your separator technology for information." He looked over at the crowd around the computer. The children had started taking apart his mobile of cutouts from ancient sports magazines. He sighed and didn't bother trying to stop them. "It'd be less dangerous than going in guns blazing like Luke and Cody want to do."

"That ship has sailed," Esther said. Just a few months ago she had given their very best bargaining chip to the entire world in order to stop the fighting between the Harvesters and the Calderon Group. For the first time she regretted it. "Maybe they'll need help with their generator at least. The last thing we want is to start a fight."

There was a commotion outside. An angry voice shouted something about cutting in line and how long they'd been waiting. Seconds later Manny's head popped through the trapdoor. He looked harassed.

"Judith is looking for you, Esther," he said, a bit out of breath. "Why aren't you answering your radio?"

"Been a little busy." Esther still hadn't actually used the handheld. She had too much to worry about without people calling her at all hours.

"She wants you now."

"Okay, I'm coming." Esther glanced over at Gracie Cordova, who was making a show of inspecting a piece of radio equipment nearby. She lowered her voice. "I don't trust those Aguamilpa people, Neal. Be careful what you tell them."

"They won't know you're coming," Neal said.

"Thanks."

Esther followed Manny out of the Tower and made her way through the restless crowd outside. She tried not to make eye contact with anyone. The jealousy and hope on every face was too painful to witness.

"Your father is there already," Manny said as they circled around toward the main bridge entrance. He scratched at the scar above his eye. "Judith is telling me to keep Dirk occupied."

"Thanks, Manny," Esther said.

She pushed open the door to the bridge, which stretched across the front of the ship. The huge panel of windows revealed a broad view of the late-afternoon sky. Computer consoles and control panels marched across the wide, quiet room. Ren, the reclusive navigation officer who normally worked here, was nowhere to be seen.

Judith and Esther's father stood in the center of the bridge, where two windows met. Their relationship had improved recently, but Esther was still surprised to see them meeting alone. They didn't turn when Esther came in. Judith had both arms wrapped around her thin frame. Her presence usually seemed to take up so much space, but now she looked small against the panorama of the endless sea behind her.

"I'm in a precarious position thanks to Dirk," Judith was saying. "He's becoming too popular with the crew, especially with Reggie on his side. He'll put the *Catalina* at risk, Simon. We've had our differences, but I can't lose you as an ally now."

"This is my daughter," Simon said quietly. The sunlight made his gray hairs shine like silver. "She needs me."

"I need you," Judith said, her voice breaking.

Esther stopped abruptly. Judith was on the verge of tears. That was something she had never expected to see. She waited by the furthest computer console, feeling awkward about interrupting.

"I won't be gone long," Simon said.

"Don't leave us," Judith said. "You're the heart and soul of this vessel."

"You've been so brave and so strong, Judy. You are the heart of the *Catalina*, not me. You'll be okay."

Simon reached out to Judith and hugged her. Esther's mouth dropped open. Her father had been a mentor to Judith long ago, but it had been years since the two had worked together without tension and resentment boiling beneath the surface. Esther herself had been angry for a long time about Judith's role in usurping Simon's leadership.

Now, as Simon squeezed Judith's shoulders reassuringly, Esther remembered their early days on the *Catalina*. Judith had been twenty-two when the disaster struck. She'd helped Simon eagerly, coordinating the survival efforts and keeping the peace among the passengers. She had been businesslike and even bossy. But Esther remembered an evening when Judith held her tight as a storm raged outside. Simon had watched over them both while Esther drifted in and out of sleep, curled up with her arms wrapped around Judith's waist, utterly certain that Judith would take care of her. Esther hadn't thought about that in years.

She cleared her throat loudly, pretending she had just entered.

"What's up, Judith?" she called. "Manny said you wanted to see me."

"Glad you're here, Esther," Judith said, stepping away from Simon and pulling her ponytail tight. "You need to tell your father not to go on this voyage."

"Are you crazy?" Esther's voice sounded harsh in light of the exchange she'd just witnessed, but she didn't want to let on that she had seen Judith display such vulnerability.

"Or persuade him. Whatever." Judith stood with her hands on her bony hips, resuming her usual authoritarian posture. "He's not as young as he used to be. You should convince him to stay behind for his own safety as well as the good of the *Catalina*."

"My dad can do what he wants," Esther said.

"Thank you," Simon said dryly. "Judith, we'll come back, but right now we have to do this."

Judith gave a sharp nod and turned back to the window. "Fine. Fine. We're done here. You may return to your duties."

"Shall we give Judith a minute, Esther?" Simon said.

"Uh, okay, but was there anything else you needed? Manny said—"

"No, I'm sure you have a lot to do," Judith said, still not looking at them. Her thin shoulders quaked almost imperceptibly. "I'll see you at dinner."

Esther and Simon left the bridge without speaking. They walked together toward the plaza. After a few minutes Esther broke the silence.

"I've never seen Judith like that."

"This is hard for her . . . us finding Naomi," Simon said.

"Because it makes her think of her own family?" Esther recalled the awkwardness as she passed the people waiting for a chance to look for their own loved ones' names. The raw, heartbreaking envy. "She wishes it was her sister instead of mine?"

"In a manner of speaking," Simon said. "I think Judith wishes *she* was your sister, Esther."

"Huh?"

"Judith has become part of our family in her own way. I think it's hard to see us leaving her behind for the sake of our real family."

"Did she say that?"

"No, but I've known Judith for a long time. She's been through a lot, more than you might realize. We haven't always seen eye to eye, but she's like a daughter to me. She doesn't want to let on that she feels that way too."

Esther didn't answer. Did Judith really think of Simon and Esther as her family? After everything they'd been through, she was surprised to realize that she understood. She might even miss Judith too.

And speaking of people she considered family, Cally was waiting for them in the plaza.

"You have to let me come with you, Esther!" she shouted, running over to meet them at the bottom of the grand staircase. She skidded to a stop, her red hair flying.

"Sorry, Cally, it's too dangerous."

"I'm about to turn seventeen next spring," Cally said. "I'm basically an adult."

"Not until you're eighteen, like Dax," Esther said.

"What if my mom says I can go?"

"She won't, and if she did I still wouldn't allow it."

"What if Hawthorne says I can go?"

Esther smiled. "Same thing. I won't allow it."

"I *never* get to go on any of the adventures," Cally said, pushing out her lower lip. She had developed a scattering of freckles on her nose, evidence of increasingly sunny days.

"You need to be around to fix things in the engine room." Esther reached up to put a hand on her young assistant's shoulder. Cally was now a full head taller than her. "You did a great job of taking care of the *Catalina* last time I was gone."

"But I want to help find your sister!"

"We'll bring Naomi back here," Simon said. "Then you can give her the full tour. Can you figure out somewhere for her to stay when we get back? We're running out of cabin space."

"I guess so," Cally grumbled.

"We'll be counting on you to make her feel welcome," Simon said.

"*Okaaay.*" Cally sighed dramatically. "What's Naomi like anyway?"

Esther and Simon exchanged glances.

"It's been a long time since we last saw her," Simon said carefully. "She's a lot older now."

"What was she like as a kid then?"

"She loved to read," Esther said. She chose her words slowly, picking her way through memories long since rusted over. "She always had her nose in a book, and she didn't like it when I made too much noise or bothered her while she was reading. She was a lot more girly than I was. She even wore dresses to school sometimes." Naomi had been warm too, Esther remembered. Kind. Esther could always go to her big sister when she had trouble with kids at school or needed help with her homework. For some reason it was hard to put that into words without her voice catching in her throat.

"Did she like school?" Cally asked. "I wish I could go to a real school."

"Yes," Simon said, smiling. "She was what we used to call a teacher's pet. She always knew the answers and got good grades. She hated getting in trouble, even for little things."

Esther wondered what her sister had made of this new world. And she'd been on land the whole time. It had to have been hard.

As if he'd read her thoughts, Simon said, "We don't know what she's had to go through. It must have been difficult no matter how she escaped from San Diego. She might be different than we remember."

"If it's her," Esther said.

Simon hesitated. "Yes, of course. We shouldn't get our hopes up too high." He gave a half smile and turned to walk back up the stairs. "I'm going to collect Penelope for dinner. I'll see you both later." He limped away, eyebrows drawn together.

"What happens if Naomi doesn't want to come back to the *Catalina*?" Cally asked as she and Esther watched him go. "She lives on land! It must be magnificent, better than living on this rusty old ship anyway." She swept her arms wide, indicating the three levels of the plaza. The old chandelier hanging above them tinkled softly. People milled around, going about their work or leaning against the rails of the upper levels, chatting. It was a familiar scene, the only world Esther had known for a long time.

"It's more important to be with family," Esther said. "I'm sure she'll see it the same way."

"What if she wants you to stay with her on land instead?" Cally said, panic darting across her face.

"I—"

"What if you never come back?!"

"We'll be back, Cally. Don't worry," Esther said, even though she wasn't sure if it was true. The *Catalina* was her home, but she was beginning to realize that its days were numbered. Their life here couldn't last forever. The purpose of the *Lucinda*'s voyage was to see if living on land was now better than living at sea. One day it would be time to go back for good.

"Maybe we'll find a place for all of us to live, and you can come meet us," Esther said. She brushed a frizzy curl out of Cally's eyes. "Hey, what do you say we head to the dining hall to get our dinner early, just you and me?"

"Oh, um, I promised to help my mom with something, and then I have to find Dax to . . ." Cally shifted from foot to foot. "I'll see you later, Esther!" She spun and darted for the opposite side of the plaza, her long limbs swinging. Esther watched her go, shaking her head. She was going to miss Cally very much.

6. Farewell

THE CATALINANS THREW A leaving party for the *Lucinda*'s crew after dinner that night. They gathered in the plaza, filling the space with chatter and warmth. Everyone received a single piece of candy or a slice of sweet dried fruit from a supply they'd acquired at the *Amsterdam*. The plaza crackled with the crinkling of plastic and foil wrappers, which were duly collected for reuse by a group of children. The brief bursts of sweetness conjured expressions of nostalgia and longing on the faces of the assembly. The sea outside was calm, and they could almost forget they were still drifting in the middle of the ocean.

There was no official agenda for the party. Those staying behind eagerly surrounded the departing crew to wish them well. They put in their last-minute requests for the type of home they wanted the *Lucinda*'s crew to find: mountain, valley, forest, farm. They called up the long-forgotten features of land, waxing lyrical about the plants, the rocks, the sounds and smells.

Esther answered questions about her sister for as long as she could take it, and then she retreated to the second level of the plaza. She found a table by the balcony railing and settled in to watch the activity. She spotted her father and Penelope deep in conversation beside an old gallery. They were not fighting. That much was clear. As Esther watched, Penelope put a hand on Simon's cheek and said something, the soft purr of her words lost in the chatter. He took her hand and held it. There was something sweet and sad about the way they looked at each other, no hint of resentment or hurt. Esther remembered what her father had once said about how he understood Penelope and what she was trying to do for her family. Maybe Penelope understood Simon too. She would know when it was time to let him go, at least for a little while.

Reggie and his band had set up their instruments at the center of the plaza beneath the darkened skylight. Under Reggie's direction, the Catalinans pushed the chairs and café tables to the edges of the space. The band had been working on more upbeat music, expanding their folksy repertoire with the help of a newly acquired saxophone, and Bernadette and Anita had offered to teach a few dance moves to go with the new music. They stood in the middle together, an old woman and a young one, and worked through all the steps they knew in common. Their laughter and enthusiasm was infectious, and soon more people were joining them.

As the music swelled, Bernadette pulled big, burly Dirk out to the dance floor, and he twirled her around, her long white hair swinging loose. Anita meticulously walked each of her partners through the steps, smiling shyly. Zoe danced wildly with everybody except for Luke, who hung around the edges of the dance floor and watched her with a silly grin on his face. Simon and Penelope disappeared before long. Cally sang with the band for the first set, but she too snuck away before the end of the evening to be with Dax before his departure on the *Lucinda*.

David climbed the staircase to join Esther at her side table overlooking the dancers. He had been busy fielding questions from the Catalinans about the route, the List, and their plans. He dropped into the chair across from her and reached for her hands with a tired smile. They hadn't had much time to talk since the decision to go after Naomi. Esther thought they were okay again, but she hadn't had a chance to really thank him for siding with her.

She was opening her mouth to speak when Byron came over to their table.

"Hi, folks, sorry to interrupt." Byron smiled at Esther, his handlebar mustache twitching, and shook David's hand. "Had an idea. Might prove useful in light of the route change."

"Let's hear it," David said.

"I got to thinking about the river," Byron said. "Sailing inland could save you some time in the long run, even though you're starting further south than planned." Byron glanced at Esther. "What do you think about bringing another one of the smaller boats with you on the *Lucinda* in case you need to continue through shallower water?"

"We're pretty tight on space," David said. They'd been arranging and rearranging the supplies for their journey like a puzzle. They had packaged up individual sets of provisions in salvaged backpacks and suitcases for the overland part of their trip. Each one contained tightly packed cubes of dried fish and seaweed, jugs of freshwater, which would need to be refilled along the way, and charcoal filters. Realistically, they wouldn't get far if they couldn't find uncontaminated water. They had no idea what effects from the volcano might linger in the streams and wells of the continent.

"We have the inflatable life rafts already," David said, "but to make room on the *Lucinda* for another boat big enough to carry all twenty-eight of us would mean—"

"Not for everyone," Byron said. "Just a small team to press on if the mission fails." He looked at Esther again. "*Some people* might have a reason to keep going up the river even if the *Lucinda*'s gotta turn back. That way you won't be left without any of your life rafts."

David was silent for a moment. "You're right," he said after a while. "Which boat do you have in mind?"

"A little speedboat we picked up from the last cargo giant Esther helped out. They gave her to us as thanks for our assistance. Carries four comfortably enough. She's durable too, and light."

"I see where you're going with this," David said. "What would we have to move to bring her along?"

"Just stick 'er on deck and tie 'er down good. She'll add a bit of weight, but with the algae fuel system working as it is, I think *Lucinda* can take it."

"Okay. Let's get to work then." David started to stand, but Byron waved him back into his seat.

"Naw, you enjoy your final evening. I'll round up some of the off-duty fishing boys to take care of it. They don't have to be sharp in the morning."

"Thanks, Byron. You're a good man."

Byron touched his cap with a weathered hand.

"Wait," Esther said as he turned to go. "Could this boat make it up the whole river? For example, if the *Lucinda* dropped me off at the mouth and then continued straight up the coast, could I sail it all the way to the lake?" She didn't look at David.

"Yes, she ought to be able to handle it," Byron said without hesitation. "You could make the whole river journey by yourself if you chose."

"Understood," Esther said. "Thank you, Byron."

His mustache twitched again, and he headed for the lower decks. Esther knew what Byron was trying to do. He was giving her an out, a way to let the mission proceed as planned without dragging everyone with her. Continuing on in that little boat would mean leaving David and everyone on the *Lucinda* behind. She wouldn't be able to get back to the *Catalina*. But she could get to Naomi, and if she needed to she could do it alone.

"Esther," David said quietly. She met his eyes and was relieved to see that he didn't look hurt. Only a little sad. He reached for her hands again. His grip was firm and warm. "Promise me you'll talk to me before doing anything rash. I know there are things you might have to do. I understand that. But no surprises, okay?"

"Okay. I promise," Esther said, her heart thrumming painfully in her chest. "And thank you. For everything."

David brought her hands up to his mouth and left a soft kiss on each palm.

The evening had begun to wind down. Bernadette collapsed into a chair, fanning herself and chuckling. Many of the older Catalinans had gone to bed. Zoe finally took Luke's hand and dragged him to the dance floor. A few other couples swayed in corners, the fancy steps of the dance forgotten.

Reggie began a new song then, his raspy smoker's voice caressing the words. It was one of the originals Cally and Anita had written together.

Starlight find a way for me
Find me in the swaying sea
Give me shelter, help me see
Starlight find a place for me

Roll roll roll
Sea of slumber sway with me
Toll toll toll
Bell of thunder play for me
Soul soul soul
Pretty lover help me be
Whole whole whole
Give me cover
Stay with me

Twilight hover over me
Cover me in dying light
Ocean, lover, give me sight
Twilight hide me in the night

A full moon filled the skylight above them, lighting the plaza with a soft radiance. David's white-blond hair seemed to glow, and shadows from the thick frames of his glasses lined his face.

"Let's not talk about plans anymore," he said, standing and pulling Esther to her feet. "Dance with me."

"I don't know how," Esther said.

"Yes, you do."

David took Esther's right hand in his and placed her left hand on his shoulder. He curled an arm around her waist and pulled her close. She rested her head on his chest, her ear level with the scar underneath the soft wool of his sweater. She sometimes forgot how tall he was. David moved in slow, rocking steps, and she followed. There was a kind of rhythm to the gentle dance. The music drifted up to them, quieter now, as they relaxed into each other.

Daylight break into the storm
Draw me close into your arms
Moon and stars give stolen glow
Daylight save me when you show

Roll roll roll
Sea of slumber sway with me
Toll toll toll
Bell of thunder play for me
Soul soul soul
Pretty lover help me be
Whole whole whole
Give me cover

Stay with me

"Do you remember the tango we saw on the *Galaxy Mist?*" David murmured.

Esther smiled into his shoulder. "We don't look like that."

"No, but this is nice. We should dance more often."

"Yes."

Wind and rain and death will fight
Lover hold me in the light
Pretty lover stay with me
Make me whole and set me free

Storms may rage and
Ships may break
But your love keeps me
Wide awake
Pretty lover make me whole
Give me shelter from the storm

David held her closer, and Esther let some of the tension run out of her body. Her family would be okay. They could do this. Together.

Reggie stopped singing, and instrumental music floated around the plaza, a formless, soft jazz. It felt quiet and solemn, like the sea.

"What was your family like?" Esther asked after a while. "You don't talk about them much."

David traced the calluses on Esther's right palm, swaying to the music.

"They loved dinner parties," he said. "They were always inviting over my father's business associates and their partners. Many of my father's friends didn't have kids, but he liked me to be around when we entertained at home. My mother always made me wear a tie, even if there were other kids coming over. I got made fun of for that."

Esther tried to imagine David as a young boy. She pictured him in miniature, with the same straight posture and clean haircut.

"You know I didn't have any siblings," David said, "but I had cousins. My mother was always competing with her brother and sisters. They'd compare whose kids were the brightest or most accomplished or had the best manners."

"Did that make you feel bad?" Esther asked.

"Just the opposite," David said. "I got the best grades. I was the best at talking to adults. All those dinner parties paid off, but I got to be pretty arrogant pretty quickly. My cousins hated me."

"I probably would have hated you too," Esther said.

David laughed and kissed her forehead. "Yes, probably. I was fourteen when the disaster hit. Most fourteen-year-old boys are awkward. I was just a little jerk. My parents went on vacation to Europe and flew me off to Seattle to go on a cruise with my relatives. I think my mother wanted to show me off to my aunts. All I talked about for the first few days was the debate tournament I had won in New York before spring break. My cousins were about ready to beat me up. That's when we boarded the *Galaxy Mist*."

"Seattle would have had some of the worst ash fall," Esther said. "You're lucky you left when you did."

"Yes, we were three days at sea when the news came through. I'd spent most of those seventy-two hours throwing up, though."

"Really?"

"Really. I was violently seasick. It was humiliating. There I was, thinking I'd solidify my status as the best of the cousins, and I could barely leave my cabin without needing to lean over the railing."

"But the *Mist* was really big . . ."

"I know. I didn't think the motion of a big ship like that would affect me so much, but it was an absolute nightmare. After the *Galaxy* ships formed the Flotilla, we never returned to land, so I was seasick for the better part of two years."

"Seriously?"

"By the time I finally got my sea legs, I was a much humbler person."

"Not that much humbler," Esther said.

"No, not that much," David agreed. For some reason that made Esther want to hold him tighter.

"What happened to your cousins?"

"They moved to a different *Galaxy* ship years ago. They wouldn't have wanted to come to the *Catalina*. They resented my status and my friendship with Boris."

David tensed as he said the name. Esther knew better than to ask for more details about what had happened between David and his *Galaxy* captain friend. It was still a sore subject after all these months.

"What about your parents?" she asked instead.

"They may have been in Europe still when the Great Storm hit New York," David said. "Maybe I'll find them on the List one day."

"I hope so." Esther hesitated, then asked the question that had been weighing on her. "Do you think they're in Kansas City? Is that why you were hesitant to take this detour for Naomi?"

David didn't answer. They danced in slow circles, bathed in moonlight. The low hum of the music floated over the balcony. David's heart beat through his sweater, quicker than before.

Finally, he said, "It's possible, but with the storms, famines, and violence people have dealt with on land, it's too much to hope that anyone made it." He drew back and looked down at Esther. "The truth is I can't hope for something like that. It's too painful."

Esther hugged him fiercely and didn't let go even when the music faded away below. There had to be hope. Otherwise, what was all this for? She would show him. They would find hope together. On land.

7. Land Bound

THE MORNING SUN DAWNED bright and raw, throwing the *Lucinda*'s preparations into sharp focus. Esther checked the biofuel system and engines and took inventory of her toolbox for the tenth time. Dax darted back and forth, carrying the remaining food supplies to the galley. Neal hovered around the *Lucinda*'s new and improved comm system, quizzing Zoe on its features until she kicked him out of the pilothouse. At least one shouting match broke out—over bunk allotments—but for the most part the final arrangements went smoothly. Simon boarded the ship serenely with a small satchel of belongings, looking like a tourist embarking on a leisure cruise.

Before heading to their stations, the crew gathered on the foredeck to mark the beginning of the voyage. Nervous energy spread amongst them. They numbered twenty-eight—the *Lucinda*'s full capacity—and included David, Esther, Simon, Zoe, Luke, Cody, Anita, and Dax. They had considered reducing the number of crew members to make room for more supplies for their overland trek, but they'd need to leave some people on board to guard the *Lucinda* if they found a harbor.

When the full crew had assembled on deck, David stepped up to the bow. He stood tall, framed by the clear blue sky, and thanked everyone for their commitment to the voyage. He looked impressive, Esther thought, with the sea behind him and his white-blond hair glowing in the sun. More importantly, he looked ready.

"We don't know what we'll find on land," he said, "but I'm proud to have such a fine crew aboard the *Lucinda*. I will do everything I can to keep you safe no matter what dangers we face. May we have good weather and calm seas, and may we find a safe harbor once again."

Zoe whooped, and a smattering of applause rippled through the crowd. People filled the balconies and railings of the *Catalina* above them, and they cheered too. Some waved shirts and bits of cloth like flags.

Judith came forward on the lower deck of the *Catalina* where the gangway stretched across to the *Lucinda*, a loudspeaker in her hand. Dirk, Neal, Mrs. Cordova, and the other council members stood around her, forming a farewell committee. Judith addressed the crew through her loudspeaker.

"Be careful out there," she said. "Send updates whenever possible. And don't do anything stupid." Then she turned on her heel and strode back into the *Catalina* without further ceremony. At least Judith was still Judith.

Eager to get moving, the crew said their goodbyes quickly, shook hands, grabbed brief hugs. It wasn't until they were pulling up the gangway and shoving off that Esther realized she hadn't spoken to Cally since the night before. She searched the faces peering over the *Catalina*'s rails above them for her young friend. She caught sight of a flash of red hair on the lido deck, but it was gone before she could wave. Esther fought off a pang of sadness, but it was just as well. She didn't want to see Cally's disappointment as they left her behind.

They pulled away from the *Catalina* slowly, and the faces on her decks disappeared one by one. The *Lucinda*'s wake lapped against the *Catalina*'s battered sides, which were no longer white but a crackled grayish, like the scales of a giant black jack. She creaked and groaned with every roll of the sea. The *Catalina* was getting old. Her hull still held, but it had been patched and repaired dozens of times.

It was bittersweet, this voyage. The *Catalina* was the only world Esther had known for years. The vast, seething sea was never still, never forgiving, but the *Catalina* endured. She had kept them safe.

Yet Esther had dreamed of this departure for nearly seventeen years. They were finally on their way to seek a new life. They would get answers about what had happened when they left the land behind and maybe find a final harbor after all this time.

As the *Catalina* shrank behind them, the *Lucinda* sailed swift and true, still the fastest ship Esther had ever encountered. The voyage to the shores of Mexico from their current position should take five or six days, barring adverse weather, and they would cover over three thousand nautical miles. Esther hadn't sailed that far in a straight line since the *Catalina* first fled the ash from the eruption. But the *Lucinda* was the perfect vessel for the job.

She was a *Cyclone*-class patrol ship, 179 feet long and 331 tons, built by the old US Navy. She had a maximum speed of 35 knots, though they didn't need to sail quite that fast now. Her strong prow cut through the waves beneath Esther's feet, the breeze sweeping across her face. The pilothouse stood out over the main deckhouse, its windows like wide fish eyes. The lookout tower and guns rose above the pilothouse, sharp against the sky. They didn't fly a flag, though. Countries no longer existed as far as Esther knew, but she wished they had fashioned one for this trip, something to mark their allegiance to the *Catalina* and to the sea.

The crew got to work, settling into their routines as they coaxed the ship through her first hours at sea. The crew was divided into eight-hour watches of nine or ten people each. Many of the *Lucinda*'s systems were automated, and now that the new fuel system had been installed she operated quite efficiently. A healthy bustle filled the decks, everyone moving with a spring in their step. They couldn't help looking forward across the rolling sea. Toward the land.

Esther went belowdecks to monitor the engines for most of the morning, watching for problems or inefficiencies. The engine room hummed with a familiar music. As she knelt beside her biofuel machine to check for leaks, she thought about her childhood on land.

She had only been six years old when the disaster struck, too young to have had many real experiences on land. She remembered images and feelings more than actual details. She remembered riding her bicycle around their cul-de-sac and accidentally pitching off into a patch of gravel. She could still feel the sting of the scrapes on her knee but had no memory of anything that happened afterwards. She remembered sneaking into Naomi's bedroom at night to play tricks on her, like dripping water from an ice cube onto her face from behind the bed. She felt the sharp cold of the ice on her fingers and heard Naomi's shriek of surprise but couldn't recall the appearance of the room itself.

What would it be like to see Naomi again? Would she even recognize her? She wasn't even sure what she'd say to her. Well, except for one thing. The first burning question she would ask Naomi was what had happened to their mother.

Esther's memories of her mother were different, more dreamlike. As a child at sea she had imagined that her mother escaped the ash cloud and disappeared into the jungles of Brazil to live amongst the trees and flowers and snakes. Despite her father's insistence that this was impossible, Esther had held on to the idea. One day her mother would find them. She would swim across the sea and emerge like a goddess with seaweed in her hair and dolphins following in her wake. Esther had imagined it so many times that the image was sharper than many of her real memories. But now she would know the truth of what had really happened on the terrifying day when the world changed. The prospect sent shivers along her spine.

Esther shook away the feeling, reached for the wrench in her belt, and tightened a bolt needlessly. She wrapped her fingers around the metal until it warmed in her grip. For now all she could do was focus on the ship and the journey.

The *Lucinda* sailed onward. By the second shift change, some of the crew's nervous energy had dissipated. The novelty of the voyage began to wear off as they settled into the monotony of their work. They had many days at sea ahead of them.

Esther went up to the mess after her shift, where Luke and Cody had started a card game. To Esther's surprise her father was with them. She found the three of them caught up in a heated argument.

"That's how they played it in my day," Simon said as Esther crossed the narrow room to join them.

Tables and benches packed the mess hall, and a doorway at one end led to the galley. Like most of the lower cabins, it had no portholes, so it was a close, dank space. Stacks of cards littered one of the tables. Simon tried to pull a small pile of washers and twists of fish jerky toward his side of the table.

"No way!" Luke said, waving a bent playing card at him. "Aces are ones! You can't just make them the highest-value card, you old whale."

"Old whale, am I?" Simon chuckled. "Which one of us is actually old enough to have played casino games in real casinos? Aces are high, son."

"That makes no sense. There's only one fin on it!"

"That's a spade."

"Whatever. You can't make up your own rules." Cards fluttered off the table as Luke crossed his arms.

"You could do something to settle it," Cody suggested. "I've got some dice here somewhere." He searched through the many pockets sewn onto his green jacket.

"No dice," Luke said. "Arm wrestling."

"You're on," Simon said.

Esther rolled her eyes and went to join Dax, who stood in the doorway to the galley watching the spectacle, his sleeves rolled up above his elbows.

"How's it going, Dax?" Esther leaned against the bulkhead beside him. The usual fishy odor came from the galley. Dax was the official cook for this voyage. He had asked to be called Silver after the famed pirate cook from *Treasure Island* until the guys threatened to nickname him Long John instead. He had quickly abandoned the idea.

"They're going for best out of three," Dax said. "Your dad won the first game, and now Luke's trying to redeem himself. Guess he decided to play to his strengths."

Esther laughed. "Serves them right if they both pull a muscle."

The two men strained over the steel tabletop. Luke began pushing her father's arm closer to the table. Simon grabbed the edge with his other hand, sending more playing cards flying. Finally, the younger man prevailed, driving the back of Simon's arm down all the way. Luke whooped, but he was sweating profusely.

Simon shook Luke's hand while Cody thumped him on the back.

"Nice one," Simon said. "Aces are still high, though."

"He's tough for an old guy," Dax said.

"Don't let him hear you say that. What do you think of the *Lucinda*'s galley?" Esther asked. The men had picked up the cards scattered across the floor, and they began dealing out another game.

"It's not bad. A little cramped." Dax glanced back at the small kitchen space behind him.

"Mind if I check on the equipment?" Esther said. "I want to make sure all the power links are okay under the hood."

"Oh! Um, now?" Dax tugged on his hair, pulling at it, though he no longer wore it spiked quite so high.

"My shift just ended, but since I'm here anyway . . ."

"Right, um, well, I need to get started on dinner, so maybe this isn't the best time," Dax said.

"Actually, that's perfect. You really need to be running the equipment for me to test it. Once you get the stove fired up—"

"Can we do it tomorrow?" Dax interrupted. "It's pretty disorganized in there right now. You just finished your shift, and I'm sure you probably want to spend time with your dad for a bit."

"I have my gauge right here." Esther indicated her tool belt. "Besides, he's busy."

"No, you hang out. I'll let you know when I'm cooking tomorrow." Dax gave Esther a nudge toward the card game and disappeared into the galley, closing the door behind him. She shrugged. He was up to something, but knowing Dax it was probably just a special meal plan he didn't want anyone to know about yet.

Esther sat down beside her father at the bench and leaned her elbows on the tabletop.

"Hey, Esther. You seen Zoe?" Luke asked.

"She's on duty," Esther said. "How was your first shift?"

"Hasn't started," he said. "I'm in the third rotation."

"Shouldn't you be sleeping instead of playing cards?"

"I would be, but your dad came in and challenged me. Can't have that."

"You talk a big game, son," Simon said. "Guess you can do that if you make up your own rules."

"Rules are fluid, old man," Luke said, grinning as he checked out his hand. "You in, Esther?"

"Why not?" She took a few damp playing cards from the stack and studied them. Some of the cards were so faded she could barely read them.

"How're things down in the engine room so far?" Cody asked.

"Pretty smooth," Esther said. "We're making good time."

"What do you think it'll be like when we get there?" Cody scrubbed at the stubble on his upper lip. He had decided to grow a mustache for the voyage, and it was slow going.

"I barely remember anything about before," Luke said.

"Same here," Esther said. "Dad?"

Simon narrowed his eyes at his cards. "I remember it too well. This'll be easier on you kids, I think."

"Well, what was it like?" Cody asked. "I was only four when everything went down." Cody had been traveling with his parents on a freighter. It was originally meant to be a low-budget adventure for their family. They ended up surviving on the canned contents of the shipping containers for many years before drifting within range of the *Amsterdam Coalition*, where Cody had eventually joined the Metal Harvesters with Luke.

Simon tapped his cards on the tabletop, thinking for a moment.

"It was stable," he said. "Solid. We didn't think about it like that, though. We complained a lot on land. Someone was always ranting against politicians or the state of the culture or their neighbors. We were a little worried about the changing climate, but many treated it like a problem for the next generation. Now we're at the mercy of the environment, and we're ultimately focused on survival. Back then, at least in North America, survival was basically a given."

"We do all right now, though," Cody said. "I wouldn't say I worry about starving or getting killed most of the time anymore."

"That's hard-won," Simon said. "We've really had to struggle to make this life at sea work. And the vast majority of our time and effort is still spent gathering food. It's hard to comprehend now, but back on land we didn't even know where most of our food came from."

"Farms, right?"

Simon laughed and took a card from the stack on the table. "Yes, but those farms were often hundreds of miles away, and we didn't think about them much. You all know how to fish. You can all identify every edible type of seaweed and shellfish. You take it for granted. I kept a garden at our home in San Diego, so I knew a bit more about how things grow than the average person, even though I only managed to produce a few vegetables and herbs each year. And hunting! Some people did it for food, but it was more of a sport than a means of sustenance."

"You think people have gone back to hunting and growing things for themselves after the volcano?" Cody asked.

"They'll have had to. I expect they scavenged for canned food at first, and then eventually got together to grow things again, starting from scratch."

"Neal told me they already have big farms in Kansas City," Esther said. She wondered if she'd ever see that settlement now. She took another card, then pulled a washer from her pocket to drop onto the betting pile.

"That was an agricultural region before too," Simon said. "We drove through there once, though I don't know if you were old enough to remember, Esther."

"I vaguely recall a really long drive when I was four or five. It was very flat."

Simon chuckled. "That about sums it up."

"Did you ever go to Mexico, where we're headed?" Luke asked.

"Only once. I went to Cabo San Lucas with my wife shortly after we moved to San Diego from the East Coast." Simon tossed a chocolate-covered squid onto the pile and folded his hands over his cards. "It was hot and dry and packed with tourists. Brightly colored umbrellas covered the beach as far as you could see. People would weave among the tourists selling handicrafts and cold beverages. I bought my wife a bracelet on that beach that she wore nearly every day afterwards." Simon smiled at Esther. "It was the carved wooden one. Do you remember it?"

Again, Esther wished her memories were sharper. It had been so long ago. "I remember some of her bracelets. Did the pattern have swirls in it, like breaking waves?"

"That's the one."

An image came to her then. Esther sat on her mother's lap and traced her fingers around the wooden swirls, the smell of apple blossom perfume surrounding her. She saw her mother's soft-brown eyes, her strong nose. But she couldn't summon the sound of her voice or anything that she'd said. The image faded.

As the *Lucinda*'s movement hummed through the soles of her boots, Esther fought down the hope that her mother had survived. Her name hadn't been on the roster. Naomi had managed to survive over the past sixteen and a half years, but Esther couldn't allow herself to expect that her mother had too.

"Man, I wouldn't mind sitting on a hot, dry beach," Luke said, bringing Esther's attention back to the table. He fiddled with the pile of items in the center. "I've had enough of the cold."

"That was farther north than we're going," Simon said. "I don't know much about the Santiago River region, but I imagine it used to be pretty hot there."

"And the lake?"

"It was a fishing destination, I think. One of my colleagues used to go every year. I expect that's why this group settled there. If the fish survived, it would have been a way to sustain themselves until they could start growing food."

"What do you think the people will be like?" Cody asked.

"I don't know." Simon frowned. "We've been able to start afresh to an extent. Because we've been at sea, it's been like living on a different planet. A clean break. We don't have to walk the streets of derelict cities or face constant reminders of all the people who died. It must have been difficult for them."

"Standing on solid ground again will be nice, though," Luke said. "There's another thing I barely remember."

"Yes, I'm looking forward to that." Simon took a peek at his cards and smiled broadly. "I think you're in trouble, son."

"Well, I fold," Esther said. "I'm not going to win a single nut or gear against you guys. We should go back to dice." She tossed down her cards and headed for the exit. She turned back for a moment when she reached the door. Her father was laughing at something Luke had said, a warm, full sound. It was strange to think that their family could be together soon. Together, and standing on solid ground.

8. The Crew

AFTER DINNER THAT NIGHT Esther found herself at the captain's cabin door once again. Officially, she had her own bunk now. After Toni's comment about them, Esther and David had agreed it would be best to maintain a more decorous relationship during the voyage. She didn't think it would hurt to debrief with him about how the journey was going so far, though. They could be discreet.

David paced across the compact cabin, full of energy, and raved about how well the *Lucinda* had handled the first day.

"She's so sharp!" he said. "Given everything this ship has been through, it's amazing how smooth she handles."

"You've done a lot of work on her," Esther said. She sat cross-legged on his bunk and pulled his threadbare blanket over her knees.

"So have you. Have I told you how brilliant your system is lately, Esther?"

"I don't mind hearing it again."

David grinned and sat beside her, nudging her to make room.

"We can go anywhere if she continues to sail this well," he said.

"What happened to settling on land?"

"Maybe sea travel will still make the most sense for a while. After Aguamilpa we could head down to Panama, or even Tierra del Fuego! I'd hate to say good-bye to the *Lucinda* so soon."

"I like the sound of that," Esther said.

"We'll make it work, Esther." David stretched out on the bunk, put his arm around her waist, and tugged her down beside him. "We always do. We're a good team . . . and if the crew gets along well . . . have to see how the next few days go . . ." He trailed off.

"Um, David?" Esther tapped his shoulder. "You were saying?" He had fallen asleep.

Esther removed David's cracked glasses and curled up beside him, just to enjoy being wrapped up in the warmth of his blankets and his body for a moment. She'd return to her own bunk in a minute. They had to be decorous after all.

David's breathing slowed, his chest rising and falling beneath her arm. His heartbeat was loud and steady in her ear.

She closed her eyes, listening to David's breath, his heart, the slow, steady rhythm of his body. She couldn't bring herself to leave to return to her own bunk. She thought of the extra speedboat, sitting atop the rear portside deck. If she had to separate from the group and go after her sister alone, she wanted to make the most of every second they had together right now.

She had often heard older folks talk about the things they wished they had done before it was too late, before the old world ended. They regretted missed time with their loved ones, the moments just appreciating what they had before it was gone forever. Esther's seabound life was about to change, and she didn't want to waste this time with the most precious thing she had. Esther drifted to sleep, holding on to David like it was the end of the world.

In the early hours of the morning, Esther tiptoed back toward her aft cabin with her boots in hand. As she passed the entrance to the head off the main corridor, someone rushed out of the door, also with boots in hand, and slammed into her.

Esther stumbled back, stunned. A shock of a red hair. A familiar squeal.

It was Cally.

Esther caught her arm before she could dart through the door to the mess.

"What the hell are you doing here?"

"Uh . . . Hi, Esther. Surprise!" Cally wore a thick pair of woolen socks and a sheepish smile.

"How did you get here?" For a second Esther wondered if she'd dreamed their departure, but she was definitely in the corridor of the *Lucinda* on the way to the coast. And so was Cally.

"I hid in the galley," Cally said. "I didn't want to miss another adventure."

"Did Dax help you? I'm going to kill him!"

"He doesn't think it's fair I didn't get to go either. He's only a little bit older than me. You can't treat me like a kid forever."

"I can if you act like a kid," Esther said. "We are turning this ship around right now."

"What's the commotion out here?"

The crew had begun to come out of their cabins at the sound of raised voices in the corridor, many rubbing their eyes. It immediately felt crowded in the narrow passageway.

"Keep it down out there," someone yelled from a nearby cabin.

"Do you know how early it is?"

Cody emerged wearing only boxer shorts, his dark hair tousled. He yelped and turned bright pink when he saw Cally, then darted back into his cabin.

"Oh, you're in big trouble, Cally," Zoe said, grinning as she leaned jauntily against the bulkhead. "Nicely played."

Dax tumbled into the corridor, skidding to a halt when he saw the crowd with Cally in their midst. His face went scarlet, and he tried to edge away.

"Hold it, Dax," Esther said. "You're off the ship too. You should know better than this."

Dax dropped his head and shuffled forward to join them.

"You can't turn around," Cally exclaimed. "What about Naomi?"

"Rust," Esther swore. Cally was right. It would waste so much time to go back now. They would never be able to get to Naomi and have any hope of completing their trek if they kept sailing back and forth. "It's the captain's decision." She grabbed Cally's arm and tugged her toward the fore. When had she gotten so tall?

"Don't be mad, Esther. You'd do it too," Cally said, walking beside her without resistance. Dax followed them up the corridor.

"I'll be mad if I damn well please," Esther said, though she couldn't work up too much real anger against Cally. She understood why Cally wanted to come along. But now she had one more person to worry about if things went badly.

Esther marched the two young people to David's door so he could pass judgment on them, but the cabin was empty. David must have already gone up to the pilothouse to relieve Luke at the helm. They continued up the ladder at the forward end of the corridor. The crew followed eagerly.

"Don't you people have work to do?" Esther snapped.

"I'm not on until next shift and—" Ike Newton said, but he fell silent when Esther gave him a dirty look. He slunk back toward his bunk.

They passed Luke on his way down to bed from the night shift. He didn't even notice Cally as he shuffled sleepily to his cabin.

When they reached the pilothouse, David was flipping through the charts. He tossed them onto the dash and listened, expressionless, as Cally and Dax explained that she had been hiding in the galley since the night before their departure.

"It was super-cramped," Cally said, smiling weakly. "I learned my lesson."

David was not amused.

"She's only one person," Dax said, "and she doesn't eat that much. You'll barely notice her."

"So you think you know best, do you?" Esther said. She was well aware that she herself was guilty of stunts like this, but she really was trying to be more responsible.

"This is insubordination," David said. "Dax, you directly disobeyed orders and disrupted the mission of this crew."

"But—"

"Do not interrupt me. We carefully planned our supplies for a specific number of people. Having

Cally on board throws us off. This is your responsibility, Dax, as a member of the crew."

"We can make it up to you," Dax said. "And she doesn't eat very much." He tugged at his hair, his face as pink as a conch shell. "Please don't kick us off the ship."

David sighed. "You and Cally have officially volunteered yourselves for all the least pleasant jobs on this ship for the duration of the voyage. Starting with cleaning the head, then the bilges. Get to it as soon as the breakfast shift is up. Got it?"

"Yes, sir," Dax said.

"Sure thing!" Cally chirped. "I knew we'd get caught eventually. I'm ready to work!"

"And you will maintain a professional attitude about it," David said.

"Aye aye, Captain!"

David tried to scowl, but Esther detected a hint of a smile. It was impossible to stay mad at Cally for long. She should know.

"Oh, and Dax," David said, "there's something you can do for me today. It's extra work, and I hadn't wanted to trouble you too much, but I've changed my mind about that."

"What is it?" Dax hesitated. "Sir?"

"I want you to arrange a special dinner for the whole crew tonight. Nothing too fancy, but I want everyone to get better acquainted with each other. It would be nice to have a little something extra to eat while we're at it."

"I can handle that," Dax said eagerly. "I have an idea I was hoping to try out on this voyage."

"Good. All right. Get out of here, you two."

"Yes, sir!" Dax and Cally waltzed from the pilot-house, not looking nearly contrite enough.

When they were gone, Esther grinned ruefully. "At least it wasn't Gracie."

David snorted.

"I'm going to do rounds, make sure we're not in for more surprises," Esther said.

"Good idea," David said. "Check on morale while you're at it."

"Will do. What's up with this dinner tonight, by the way?"

"The *Galaxy* captains held regular dinners on the *Crown* to reward their favorites. They were important for keeping the most powerful people in line, but I think we can expand on the idea to help the crew bond. We're mostly dining in shifts, but I'd like us to have a meal all together every once in a while. We should also work on identifying the leaders amongst the crew."

Esther stood on her toes to kiss his cheek. "I'll leave the politicking to you. I'm sure Dax would help you with extra-special dinners every night if you wanted, though."

David laughed and turned back to his charts. "Oh, he'd better after this."

When Esther left the pilothouse, the sun was rising. It was shaping up to be another beautiful morning. The crisp, clean air filled her with energy, as did the speed of the ship beneath her feet.

Esther made her way along the starboard promenade to the stern, where the spare boat was tied down beside the *Lucinda*'s main rafts. It was a simple thing, with a sturdy outboard motor and a watertight compartment for supplies. It could prove useful if they ended up encountering surprises more unpleasant than a stowaway. Or if she needed to set out on her own to keep the Lucindans out of danger.

Jackson, the oil tanker man from the *Galaxy*, was checking the lashings on the boat, and he nodded to her as she passed. A handful of other crew chatted in a circle nearby, former Galaxians who had left the *Flotilla* along with Zoe, Anita, and the others to start a new life. Esther said a brief hello and headed for the portside promenade. She had leapt across this promenade with a group of oil tanker men the day they hijacked the *Lucinda* from the *Galaxy*. Now she climbed back down into the bowels of the ship and inspected the hold, the engine room, and the main corridor.

The ship was compact, with no wasted space, so it didn't take long to check that everything was in order. She peeked into a few cabins where off-duty crew were resting or talking. Ike Newton was playing cards with Raymond on one of the bunks, and he waved at Esther when she strode past his door.

Luke was sound asleep in his cabin. Zoe sat on the floor beside his bunk, sharpening her pocket-knife. She had the same shift as Esther today, so she wasn't on duty yet. She gestured toward Luke and put a finger to her lips, then stood and joined Esther in the corridor.

"Murdered Cally yet?"

"No, but I want to talk to you about that." Esther drew her friend further away from the cabin door to avoid disturbing the sleepers.

"*I'm* not even mad," Zoe said. "I'd say mildly chuffed about covers it."

"Can you promise me you'll look after her?" Esther said. "No matter what happens?"

"I always look after her," Zoe said. "Seriously. You, me, and Anita will keep her in line."

"I mean if anything happens to me, or if I have to separate from you guys at some point."

"Separate? What's gotten into you?" Zoe twisted her pocketknife between her fingers. It flashed in the cold, artificial light of the corridor.

"Nothing. It's just . . . I couldn't stand it if anything happened to her or my dad or David. Or you and the guys of course. I just want to make sure she'll be okay."

"She will. Esther"—Zoe put her hands on her shoulder—"we are all going to be fine. You can't protect everyone all the time. Trust us to look after each other, okay?"

Esther hooked her fingers in her tool belt. She wanted to protect all her friends, all the people she loved. But her first priority had to be Naomi. If she was going to find her, she might need to let go of the others, at least for a little while.

"Okay. You're right."

"I'm always right," Zoe said. "Now let's grab some breakfast. I could eat a giant squid."

9. Evening

THE WHOLE CREW COULDN'T fit in the mess at once, so they gathered on the foredeck for dinner that evening. David instructed them to make sure their stations were in order, and then he cut the engine, allowing the ship to drift for a few hours so everyone could eat together.

Despite such short notice and limited supplies, Dax's efforts were impressive. He had fixed seaweed pasta—one of their staples—and mixed it with a colorful assortment of sea urchins, iridescent fish scales, and prawns still in their shells. The colors alone were enough to make the meal appealing. He had also added a squid-ink sauce and a side of delicately prepared—and strategically saved—canned vegetables.

The crew filed eagerly through the galley to fill their bowls and then climbed through the hatch to eat on deck in the fading light. David took on a hint of his old spokesman's persona. He made the rounds, stopping to shake hands and talk with each crew member individually. He carried himself differently now that they were under way. He was the captain, and he had to establish his authority at sea.

Esther let him get on with it and looked around for her father. Simon had been on duty in the lookout tower for most of the day, so she hadn't had much chance to talk with him. As she scanned the deck, a woman with a round face and black hair named Sarita came over to stand beside her.

"Good way to kick off the night shift," Sarita said, holding up her bowl of pasta.

"Sure is," Esther said. "Hey, weren't you a cook on the *Galaxy*?"

"Guilty." Sarita had been one of the defectors, a small band of people who had been dissatisfied with the inequalities on the *Galaxy*. The hijacking of the *Lucinda* had been their chance to break away.

"You didn't want the galley job on the *Lucinda*?" Esther asked.

"I'm damn tired of scaling fish," Sarita said. "Happy to let someone else handle it for a while."

"We're happy too." Jackson came up beside her with a bowl in hand. "I remember your seaweed pasta too well."

"Oh, go eat a blowfish," Sarita snapped.

Jackson chuckled.

"You two gonna fight?" A third former Galaxian joined them. Wade had been an oilman like Jackson. Both big men in their late thirties, the two could have been related. Wade jerked his head in a casual nod to Esther. "This is some party."

Sarita rolled her eyes. "Doesn't take much to count as a party these days, does it?"

"Guess not," Wade said. "I'm saving up my energy for when we get to land. I'm gonna get damn festive. I'll run around in the dirt. Maybe go camping. What're the chances I can find myself a truck?"

"Better than they are at sea," Esther said. David passed them, heading for the hatch to go below. He noticed Esther talking to the former Galaxians and gave her the slightest nod. She turned to the trio. "So, how are your quarters?"

"Wade snores," Jackson muttered.

"You got the lower bunk," Wade said, chewing on a hunk of seaweed. "I won't hear no rustin' complaints from you."

"It's better than the tanker," Jackson said. He picked a bright-purple sea urchin out of his bowl with his fingers. When he popped it in his mouth, Esther noticed he was missing a few teeth.

"True. True."

"I'll sleep like a baby no matter what," Sarita said. "*Lucinda* runs easy, but I'm beat."

"You wanna bunk with Wade then?" Jackson asked. "If it won't bother you—"

"I'm good actually," Sarita said quickly.

"We have a long voyage ahead of us," Esther said. "Guess it's best for everyone to get comfortable."

"We've been on a near-seventeen-year voyage," Jackson said. "We can handle five more days."

"Ain't that the truth," Wade said.

Esther spotted her father sitting with his back against the starboard railing. She left the group of Galaxians, and they put their heads together to talk more quietly as she walked away. She was sure they'd get to know each other much better as the journey progressed.

Esther joined her father and sat cross-legged beside him on the deck, balancing her bowl on her knee.

"I heard about our little stowaway."

"Can't believe she actually did it," Esther said, shaking her head ruefully.

"I can," Simon said. His legs were stretched out in front of him, and he set his empty bowl aside to massage his bad knee. "Don't be mad at Cally, Esther. What's done is done."

"I'm not mad," Esther said. "I just don't want her to get hurt."

Simon smiled. "Maybe now you'll understand what I went through when you went off with the Harvesters a few months back."

"Yeah. I am sorry about that." Esther took a large bite of her pasta. She felt a crunch and spit out a piece of boiled prawn shell. "I would have been go-ing crazy."

David returned from belowdecks then with a tall bottle in his hand.

"Everyone," he called. "I've been saving this for a special occasion. Got enough for a sip or two each. I want to propose a toast to the crew. Thanks for all your hard work so far. May we continue to have smooth sailing."

"Hear, hear!" Luke shouted.

David twisted open the bottle and handed it to Luke first. He took a swallow and passed it to Zoe. The bottle made the rounds, and each crew member took a swig. Sarita handed it off to Ike Newton, who brought it over to Esther and her father. He plopped down on the deck beside them. Ike had a pale, earnest face, and Esther had always considered him the nicest of his brothers.

"I've never tasted alcohol before," he said. "My mom says it's from the devil."

"I won't tell if you don't," Simon said.

Ike grinned nervously, then tipped the bottle back and took a swig. He nearly spit out the drink but managed to choke it down, eyes watering. He handed the bottle off to Esther with a grimace.

Esther looked at the label. It was cola. Her father winked at her. Ike was still making faces and shaking his head. She took a sip of the warm, flat beverage and passed it on.

The evening was cool. The ship rocked gently. The sun hadn't set, so Cody got out his dice to get a game going while they still had a bit of light. Cally darted around the deck collecting empty bowls and introducing herself to the few crew members she didn't already know. Luke jogged over to Esther, her father, and Ike.

"Simon," he said, "me, Jackson, and Wade are gonna race around the deck. You in?"

"Sorry, son. My knee can't handle it."

"What happened to you anyway?" Luke said. "Old age?"

"Careful," Simon said dryly.

"Yeah, you've had a limp for ages," Ike said. "But I don't think I've ever heard the story."

"It was about six years after we moved onto the *Catalina*. Esther was twelve years old at the time, so you would have been around ten—is that right?"

"Yes, sir," Ike said.

"It happened the day we almost blew up the *Catalina*."

"Blew it up?" Luke said. "Sounds like a story." He waved Zoe over and shouted for Cody to pause his dice game. Jackson and Wade drifted over too. Soon a little knot of people had formed around Simon.

"I was heading up the leadership council on the *Catalina* at the time," Simon began. "In those days there was still plenty of salvage floating on the sea. One day we happened upon an abandoned navy ship. I don't know what happened to its crew, but it was listing badly and most of its munitions were gone. We couldn't use the ship itself, so we stripped it for materials. While we were at it, we found two crates of explosives in the hold."

"That never ends well," Jackson said.

"Tell me about it." Simon shifted around to ease his knee. A few more crew members had joined the little crowd. "The plan was to lift the explosives up to the deck using our lifeboat winch. It's not really my area, but the fishing crew was out, and Reggie needed an extra pair of hands. We had some retired navy men on the *Catalina* who oversaw the operation, but they were a bit too old to help with the manual labor. Well, I probably wasn't the right choice either. One minute I'm on the other ship attaching the crate to the winch. Next thing I know, the ship sinks right out from underneath me. I jumped up to grab the crate and ended up swinging from the thing. As I tried to get a better grip, my movement made the crate swing harder. Of course, the rest of the crew had the good sense to jump into the water when the navy vessel sank. I realized pretty quickly that I was going to swing this box full of explosives right into our hull."

"Shit," Luke said.

"Yeah. I had no choice but to scramble onto the crate and get my legs between it and the *Catalina*. One collision at the wrong angle and we could have sparked the explosives and blown a hole in our home. I was agile enough at the time that I managed to clamber onto the crate and get my legs between it and the ship. Took the full impact on my right leg, but it kept the thing away from the *Catalina*. After a few kicks against the hull, I managed to slow the crate enough that Reggie could get control and pull it aboard. By that time my leg was pretty banged up, not to mention the rope-burned hands and pulled shoulder."

"Ouch," Ike said.

"Rope burn's the worst," Wade growled.

"Have to disagree," Simon said. "The shattered knee was pretty terrible—and permanent. On land I'd have gotten surgery and probably been right as rain, but at sea . . ." Simon gestured to his leg. He'd lived with the limp for a decade. "I was stuck in the clinic for over two months. Judith took care of things around the ship for me while I was incapacitated."

"And she used that time to get people on her team," Esther muttered.

"That was convenient for her, yes," Simon said. "She laid the groundwork for her big coup then."

"And I bet you never even used the explosives," Cody said.

Simon chuckled. "Not until earlier this year when we encountered the *Orchid*."

"That was creepy," Ike said. "That's the biggest ship I've ever seen sink. It was like watching the *Catalina* go down."

Esther glanced at him. She had felt the same way as the *Orchid* sank beneath the surface. It had been a strange sort of chill, almost like a premonition.

"Wait a minute, the *Orchid*?" Jackson said, rubbing a hammy hand against his chin. "She a big cruise ship?"

"Yes," Simon said. "You knew her?"

"I'll say," Jackson said. "The *Orchid* was the talk of the *Galaxy* for months. She was our quarantine ship."

"What?" Esther looked around for David. He stood at the back of the group, listening intently to the discussion. She had never mentioned the *Orchid* to him, the ship they sank so it couldn't spread disease to them. That encounter had taken place just days before they met. She should have made the connection.

"There was an outbreak of some virus on the *Galaxy*," Sarita explained. "It was vicious. Killed ninety percent of the people who got it."

"They say the *Orchid* brought it in the first place," Wade said.

"You buy that?" Jackson said. "That was a captain's lie I'll wager."

"Why don't we ask him?" Wade said roughly. "Mr. Captain's Lies himself."

The group parted as everyone turned to David, united in their accusing glares. This probably wasn't the kind of bonding he'd had in mind for the crew. Esther had thought the Galaxians were long past their suspicions of David. He had proven himself to be on their side more than once.

"Actually," David said smoothly, "the *Orchid* did bring the disease. Did you ever hear of anyone getting it before they arrived?"

"I guess not," Wade mumbled.

"It was a sad situation, but we had to cut her loose or risk infecting everyone on the *Galaxy*. The disease was far too contagious. I'm glad you sank her."

"Judith insisted," Simon said. "I'd have tried to help the people on board. But sometimes being a leader means making tough choices and understanding when things are out of your hands." He met Esther's eyes. "We all do the best we can."

An awkward silence fell on the crew. The Galaxians still looked at David suspiciously. Ike's brow was furrowed. Luke seemed to be at a loss for words. Zoe fidgeted with her pocketknife.

That's when Cally barreled into their midst. "Come to port quick! You guys have to see this!"

The awkwardness snapped like a broken anchor line as everyone followed Cally, drawn by her excitement. She dashed back to the opposite side of the ship. Esther offered her father a hand to help him to his feet, and they followed. The crew gathered around Cally, lining up on either side of her to lean over the railing.

"What is it?"

"What are we looking for?"

"Shh!" Cally said. "You have to watch."

They stared out at the rippling water. The setting sun cast a muted glow across the sea.

"I don't see anything," Cody said.

Cally slapped him on the shoulder to get him to be quiet.

The whole crew waited, holding their breath as one. Then the water rippled about a hundred yards from the *Lucinda*. It spun like a whirlpool, swirling around and making the sunlight dance across its peaks like fire.

"Are those fish?"

The churn intensified. Silvery creatures began to leap from the boiling water frantically, as if they hoped to take flight and escape the sea.

"I know what this is . . ." Simon began.

Then a massive shape erupted out of the water. A huge mouth closed around the leaping fish. Esther gasped. An instant later a dozen more mouths rose out of the sea, capturing the fish in one huge gulp after another. Their domed shapes glided up, sharp against the sky, before sinking down together. Whales. They had come upon a pod of whales.

"Those are humpbacks," Sarita said, her voice hushed and reverent.

"I've never seen them this far south," Wade said.

The whales circled around, swimming just beneath the surface and blowing massive spouts of water into the sky. Their bodies glistened in the dying sunlight.

"They're the biggest ones I've ever seen," Cally said. "Aren't they beautiful?"

Esther didn't answer. She didn't have to. The crew watched, entranced, as the pod swam near the surface for a few minutes, holding them captive. The creatures' backs were the glistening silvery black of iron. The biggest whale came nearer to the *Lucinda* and rolled sideways, revealing its pale underside to the watching crew. Its large black eye surveyed them, uncurious and unafraid. Then it flipped downward and dove. Water slid over its hump and down its magnificent length. At the last moment its huge tail rose upward into the sky, waved at them, and sank into the sea.

The other whales followed, arching down into the depths, their tail fins flipping upward in a final farewell. Then as quickly as they had appeared, the whales were gone.

No one moved on the deck of the *Lucinda*. They waited respectfully as the churning waters calmed, smoothing out to a gentle roll.

The sun had reached the horizon. A cool wind began to blow. The crew drew a little closer together, borrowing each other's warmth, as they waited for the last threads of daylight to sink into the sea.

10. Old Friends

O N THE THIRD DAY of the expedition, Zoe's voice crackled through the intercom while Esther was on duty in the engine room. "There's a ship on the satellite phone asking for you, Esther."

"I'm on my way."

Esther had continued fielding questions about her generator system throughout the voyage, as expected. Another ship must have heard about her. She jogged up to the pilothouse, where Zoe manned the communications. David winked at her from the helm.

Esther picked up the microphone attached to the satellite call system. "Esther Harris here."

"This is Captain Boris of the *Galaxy Flotilla*. How is our young mechanic these days?"

"Salt, it's Boris," Esther said, putting a hand over the mic. David stiffened. "Where did this call come from, Zoe?"

"They were broadcasting a request for contact with the *Lucinda*. When we identified ourselves, they asked if you were aboard," Zoe said. "Sorry, I thought it would be another tech question."

Esther cleared her throat. "Hello, Boris. It's been a while."

"I understand you're still sailing my stolen ship," Boris said. Esther didn't answer. "How are you enjoying the little beauty?"

"What do you want?"

"You, as a matter of fact. I was rather annoyed when you stole my very favorite ship, not to mention my friend David Hawthorne."

"You killed Paris," Esther said. The image of her friend dropping over the side of the destroyer HMS *Hampton* sprung to Esther's mind. She saw the swing of a lifeboat against the ship's iron side as Paris fell into it headfirst. Her heart had crumpled at the certainty that he couldn't have survived. And Paris had done nothing but help them.

"You stole my ship," Boris said. "Now, as it happens you also recently provided us with an invaluable tool. You may remember escaping from my destroyer with a bit too much ease. The destroyer was operating on inferior fuel under inferior command. Recently, however, we've installed a rather ingenious algae biofuel system."

Shit. Esther should have known it was only a matter of time before her design made it into Boris's hands. She didn't know he held such a grudge, though.

"The destroyer runs quite well now," Boris said, his voice dripping with contempt. "It would give me great pleasure to blow you out of the water, but I do want my ship back."

"We're not with the *Catalina*," Esther said quickly. "If you hurt her, it won't get you any closer to your ship."

"And where, pray tell, are you now?"

"On our way to California," Esther blurted out. She had to keep the destroyer as far from the *Catalina* and *Lucinda* as possible. "You'll have to look for us there if you want your ship back."

"You expect me to believe you?"

"Ask anyone. We've been planning this voyage for ages—to Los Angeles. Come and get us."

Esther put the microphone back on the console and turned it off.

"That's not going to work," David said.

"As long as they know we're not with the *Catalina*, it doesn't matter." Esther's heart raced. She should have known Boris wasn't finished with them. "Zoe, can you get in touch with Neal and tell him they need to move again? They can't tell people their location until we get back to protect them. The

Catalina is vulnerable without the *Lucinda* and her weapons."

"On it."

"What do you think, David? Is Boris bluffing?" Esther asked.

"You can't trust anything he says." David frowned and looked out at the horizon. "The real question is whether he has enough contacts on the satellite network to find out where we really are. Zoe?"

"Only if Marianna helps him," Zoe said. "I can't see her doing that." Marianna had been Paris's wife.

"Good, but I think he has something else up his sleeve," David said. "He didn't accomplish anything with that phone call except to warn us to be on our guard. Boris doesn't make that kind of mistake."

"Could he do something with the system while we were on the line?" Esther asked. "Rig it to track our movements somehow?"

"Hmm. You might be onto something," David said.

"I'll look into it," Zoe said. "Neal should know whether that's possible. We may want to stay off the phone for a while."

"I shouldn't have answered," Esther said.

"Can't help it now."

Something else bothered Esther about the exchange. She turned to David. "Why didn't Boris ask to talk to you?"

"No idea." David took off his glasses and wiped them clean on his sweater. "Maybe he doesn't know I'm still with you and the *Lucinda*."

Esther didn't like this one bit. The *Galaxy Flotilla* had seemed so far away for so long. But now that Esther's generator design was out there for anyone to use, any ship could travel without worrying about fuel expenditures. Including their enemies.

"We'll be within sight of land in three days," Esther said. "We should be okay then."

"But won't we be trapped as soon as we start up the river?" Zoe asked. "Like crabs in a pot?"

"I'm not so sure about that," David said. "*Lucinda* may be able to sail all the way to the lake, but I doubt the *Galaxy*'s destroyer can do it. She's got a pretty deep draft."

Esther nodded, drumming her fingers on the dash.

"And what if Boris goes after the *Catalina*?" Zoe asked.

"Let's get some of our satellite friends to keep tabs on him," David said. "If need be, I'll let him know I'm with you too. That ought to make us an even more attractive target."

"Boris wants me, though," Esther said. "It's personal. Maybe he won't waste time with the *Catalina*."

"Nothing would make it more personal for him than going after your home," David said. "Maybe we should have Marianna tell him your father is with us, try to make him think the *Catalina* doesn't matter quite as much to you."

"That's a start at least," Esther said. She thought of the ship they had left behind, the place that had been her home for almost seventeen years. The *Catalina* stood little chance against the destroyer. Their escape from the *Galaxy* had been too easy. She had been foolish to think this was over. "Zoe, can you find out where the destroyer is now through the network?"

"I'll do my best."

"Okay. I better go finish my shift," Esther said. "Keep me posted."

Esther returned to the bowels of the *Lucinda*, trying to ignore the worry roaring through her stomach like fire in a fuel cell. As her father said, she couldn't focus on things that were out of her hands.

She headed back to the engine room, thinking about Captain Boris, his raven-black hair and sneering smile. He had been friends with David once. If anything, he had more cause for a personal vendetta against David than against her. So why hadn't Boris asked about David? It might be time for her to find out what had happened between them after all.

The voyage continued without any more messages from the *Galaxy*. They were still far away, and hopefully the *Lucinda* was getting further out of Boris's reach every day. Zoe screened all calls, only patching people through with tech questions if they'd had prior communication. She didn't tell anyone where they were really heading.

The crew spent their spare time carrying out their duties and playing cards in the mess or dice on the deck. In the evenings they'd tell stories and speculate about what it would be like when they reached land. It grew warmer as they sailed south. They didn't hear from Boris again, and they drew nearer to the coast by the hour.

Esther got a chance to talk to Neal on the satellite phone one evening while Luke was on duty at the helm. Neal told her he hadn't been able to catch the communications man at Lake Aguamilpa at his station since the morning after he sent out the roster. This was the longest Neal had ever gone without talking to the man. There was no way to find out whether he had gotten in trouble for sending the roster in the middle of the night. Esther wished she could speak directly to Naomi and make sure the voyage was going to be worth it. What if she didn't want to leave with them in the end? What if it wasn't even her? What if they had left the *Catalina* vulnerable for nothing?

"I spoke to Marianna, though," Neal said, his voice surprisingly sharp through the satellite link.

"And?"

"It's less awkward to talk now. We don't have the same chemistry that we used to, but I think we can be fr— "

"What'd she say about Boris?!"

"Oh right. She says he doesn't trust her anymore, so he had someone else fix up his satellite phone system in the destroyer. HMS *Hampton*, right? She didn't know anything about his plan to come after you until the *Hampton* set out the same day he contacted you. She's scrambling rumors through all our contacts about your plans, though. Boris ought to hear from multiple sources that you and the *Lucinda* aren't with the *Catalina*, and that you're heading for the Los Angeles area. We're also keeping our coordinates a secret."

"Good," Esther said. "Do Judith and Dirk know what's going on?"

"Yup. They're cooperating. Judith's kinda smug about going back to the isolation thing, actually."

"Do you think I should send the *Lucinda* back to you guys for protection? We're almost to the coast, and I can set out on my own there."

Luke glanced over at Esther from the helm, eyebrow raised.

"The sea is a big place," Neal said. "We're hiding right in the middle of the ocean. Hopefully you'll have plenty of time to sort things out in Mexico before Boris is finished searching the California coast. Stick with the plan. We can look out for ourselves."

"Okay. Thanks for being my ears, Neal."

"No worries. Oh, one more thing. Boris is using your system in the *Hampton*, but Marianna says the *Galaxy* captains haven't allowed any of the other ships to install it. They are dead set on staying at sea and keeping the *Flotilla* together."

"Unbelievable," Esther said. "The people won't stand for that forever. The ships will rust, and time's going to run out for them."

"I agree. Anyway, got another call coming in. Be careful out there, Es. And come back soon."

"You got it. Over and out." Esther set down the microphone.

"Going somewhere?" Luke said.

"Only if I have to."

Luke nodded, his brow furrowing.

"David knows it might come to that, if that's what you're worried about," Esther said. She and David had talked about it again the night before. They were getting good at talking. Esther was surprised how much it eased her worries to confide in him. He understood that they might have to part ways, at least for a little while.

"I noticed the last-minute addition of that cute little speedboat in the stern," Luke said. "Figured it wasn't just for fishing."

"Yeah. If we get to the river mouth and find it's impassable for the *Lucinda*, I'll head upriver in that to find my sister. The rest of you can continue as planned."

"You got a crew picked out?" Luke asked.

Esther hesitated. "My dad, obviously. We can do it on our own, but there's space for four."

"Well, if you want to take Zoe, I'm coming too," Luke said. "It's too late for her to get rid of me now that she's admitted how dashingly handsome she finds me."

"I figured as much," Esther said. She *had* been thinking of Zoe, of course, and Luke was dependable, but that would leave no room for Naomi if she decided to come back with them. David would stay with the *Lucinda* and the mission. It would be for the best. Esther hooked her fingers in her belt, forcing away the sadness that came with the thought.

"Don't worry so much, Esther," Luke said suddenly. "We're going to reach the coast, and the river mouth will be open. All the folks you care about will be fine and dandy. You and David will spend the rest of your lives having dumb fights and being in love, and Zoe and me will get married and have seven strapping young sons. Everything that could go wrong in the world already has, so there's no reason to worry about things that might not happen at all."

Esther smiled. "You're a perceptive guy sometimes, you know that, Luke?"

"Shh, don't tell anyone." Luke grinned and swept his curly hair away from his eyes. "Now go grab some shut-eye. Big day tomorrow."

11. Storms

AS THEY APPROACHED THE coast, the weather turned sour. The blue skies of their early voyage fled, replaced by iron clouds and sheets of rain. The sea tossed angrily. Howling winds heralded a gathering storm.

Esther went to the pilothouse to discuss their course with David, Luke, and Zoe. The swells were growing large and dangerous.

"We can't search for a harbor in this," Luke said as the *Lucinda* pitched over the crest of another tall wave.

"We're so close," Esther said. "If we get to the river before the storm, we can take refuge in the mouth."

"It's not going to work," David said. "We need to pull back. We can't risk getting thrown onto the shore."

"We don't even know exactly where the river is," Luke said.

Storm clouds roiled in the sky. It was an all-too-familiar sight. Esther was frustrated at the delay. She wanted to get to Naomi. She had created an entire picture in her head of Naomi's life on land, more blurry and perilous than Esther's life had been. Naomi still looked like an eight-year-old girl in her mind. Esther had become increasingly nervous for her sister the longer it had been since Neal last talked to the comm guy at the lake. It felt like she was going to disappear, to vanish from the face of the earth as Esther thought she had years ago.

The *Lucinda* rolled sideways in another wave.

"Can you see the shore?" Zoe asked. She had a map in one hand and a pair of binoculars in the other. "The coastline is pretty steep on this old map. We should be able to see the cliffs by now."

"If the cliffs are still there," David said.

"Man, it's getting dark out there," Luke said.

"Got anything on radar yet?"

"Nothing."

"All right, cut the engines," David said. "We need to wait until this clears."

Esther gripped his arm. "But if we can just get to the mouth of the river—"

"I said cut the engines, Esther. We wait until we're clear."

The horizon was a smudge of gray and black. The rain swept away any identifying features. Esther leaned toward the windscreen, trying to make out some sign of land. Wind hissed through the bullet holes in the thick glass.

"We should be able to see it," Zoe said again.

Lightning cracked across the sky, illuminating the tossing sea in front of them.

"Wait, are those breakers?"

The shoreline suddenly appeared before them. There were no cliffs. It was a flat, wasted expanse of gravel and rock, as if the entire coastline had been washed away. The land was so low they almost hadn't seen it at all. Lightning cracked again, revealing just how close they were to running aground.

"Pull back!" Esther shouted.

David was one step ahead of her. He sprung into motion, putting full power into the forward thrusters.

"Come on, come on!" Sweat poured down David's forehead. He gripped the controls like a lifeline.

The *Lucinda* teetered before the shore, lurching atop the swells. The land before them was a threatening, unassailable mass. They could smack against sand or rock any minute. But then a retreating wave sucked them farther away from the beach. David's knuckles whitened against the wheel. The next wave tossed them forward. Again, Esther was sure their hull would strike the shallow seafloor. Then the waves sucked them out again.

"We have to get away from here until we find the river mouth," David said.

"We're supposed to be a mile out still," Zoe said. "I don't get it."

"Doesn't matter right now. Alert the crew."

They battled against the swells and the looming shore. The *Lucinda* caught in a seemingly endless cycle of waves, pulling the ship closer to the land, breaking against the treacherous coastline, and pushing it back again.

The tossing of the sea was violent, raucous. A storm far out to sea was made of deep rolls and colossal waves. They could ride it out as long as they stayed upright. But this storm was a jagged, jarring affair. Each wave smacked against the land, uneven and angry. The breakers were rough and unpredictable, and the tow of water was nearly as dangerous as the crashing of the waves. Any second they could be dashed against unseen rocks. The wind raged and howled, tearing around them like a sea demon.

They fought their way back out to sea. The storm still raged further from the shore, but it was safer than this.

Hours passed. No one slept. Those who weren't on duty held on to their bunks to keep from pitching against each other. Esther tried to rest for a while but soon found herself back in the pilothouse, standing watch as David fought the sea. Her father was supposed to be on lookout duty, but that would mean tethering himself to the crow's nest and risking being struck by lightning. Esther had made sure he was taking shelter belowdecks. When she left him, he was doing what he could to keep people calm as the storm raged.

The waves became so erratic that the crew began to get sick. David had to leave the pilothouse more than once to vomit over the side, his face as pale as his hair. Esther had never seen him seasick before, but this storm would get to anyone. Luke took the helm whenever David had to leave, but he too was barely holding on.

In the early hours of the morning the weather began to calm. They had gotten far enough away from the coast to escape the dangers of the rocky bottom and nearly invisible shore. As far as they could tell, they hadn't hit anything.

The seas were still unsettled, throwing deep, rolling waves beneath the hull of the *Lucinda*. But the winds had calmed, and light began to peek out over a long gray bar on the horizon. Land.

"We've got a problem," Zoe said as the light strained through the ravaged clouds. She and Esther were back in the pilothouse with David. Luke had gone to rest for a while. "Our maps are wrong."

"What?"

"Either the shore has changed more than we thought or we're in the wrong place. I can't make sense of anything here."

David took the charts from Zoe. "Could be either one," he said. "If the weather has been like this a lot over the years, the coast must have taken a beating. We could be in exactly the right place, but the shape of the land has changed."

"Well, we're looking for a big-ass river," Zoe said, "and it's not here."

"So what do we do?" Esther said.

Zoe threw up her hands. "Sail along the coast until we find the mouth?"

"Which direction?"

"Hell if I know," Zoe said.

Esther groaned. "Salt."

"You can say that again."

Esther felt a sea-deep weariness from the night's watch, but as the sun crept further up, the sight of the land transfixed her. The coast beyond the bow was flat and indistinct. With the sun in her eyes it was hard to make out the details, like it was just another mirage.

"It's very flat, isn't it?"

"We were supposed to have arrived near the hills surrounding the river mouth," David said. "Flat isn't good."

Esther took Zoe's binoculars from the dash.

"I can't see any trees," she said. "Aren't we supposed to be in a jungle region?"

"I think it's safe to say we're not near the river," David said. "According to our charts, there's a flatter region far south of the river's mouth. We could be there, but that would mean we've overshot our mark drastically. I thought our navs were better than that. If we're actually north of the river, it means the coastal topography has changed a lot. That's kind of in line with what we heard back in the early days, that the seas had gotten so bad they were destroying anything on the coasts. And the river itself could have been rerouted."

Esther blew out a breath. "You think we should sail south?"

"I do," David said, "but it's a gamble either way."

"Let's do it," Esther said. "I'll gamble. Anyway, our destroyer friend may turn up further north."

"South it is," Zoe said. "I hope you're right."

As they sailed they eased closer to the coast again, watching for any signs of the river—or of life. By the time the sun climbed halfway up in the sky, everyone who wasn't on duty had gathered on deck. They were tired after their night in the storm, but no one could resist the pull of land.

Cally and Dax, their fingers reddened from scrubbing the salt off the decks, stood together at the railing. Cody hovered nearby, studying the shore. Simon climbed up to the crow's nest. His scarf flew in the wind, green against a gray sky.

Esther joined the others on the deck, and they watched the coast together. They drew closer. The land that appeared flat as glass from far away was actually quite rocky and strewn with debris. Decayed ships littered the beaches hundreds of feet inland. Twisted pieces of metal stuck out of the sand like whale bones. Driftwood and seaweed mingled near the waterline, alongside huge knots of rubber and plastic.

There were things on the beach that hadn't come from the sea: cars and tires, a refrigerator, a collection of school desks, even what Esther recognized as a streetlight. It reminded her of childhood games of Red Light, Green Light with Naomi and their neighbors in the cul-de-sac.

Beyond the tangled detritus, scraggly trees and bushes began to emerge. The vegetation was untouched, and it was slowly pushing back against the advance of the sea. There were no signs of any new settlements, however, only the wreckage of the old world coughed up across the shore.

The crew fell silent. Esther had expected to see something besides total destruction. Neal's communications on the satellite network had given her hope. She had imagined people rebuilding on land, humanity reemerging after near extinction. Irrationally, she had thought they might even find a town or two by the beach. But as she stared at the blasted shore, she remembered just how close to annihilation they had come.

When the sun was directly overhead, they reached the mouth of a river. The banks were wide and shallow, as if the river had flooded repeatedly over the years. The water had retreated somewhat, leaving vast mudflats scattered with seaweed. Esther was surprised to see so much seaweed simply lying there. The people should be collecting it for food. It would rot if they left it. Maybe any people living near the river didn't eat seaweed. Or there were no people at all.

They had no way of knowing whether this was the correct river or if they'd sailed in the right direction. They could only hope. They sailed into the open mouth. The *Lucinda* lurched as they crossed the invisible line between the sea and the river. They had arrived.

The river narrowed quickly, the muddy delta funneling them inland. They stuck to the center, unsure how shallow it would be closer to the banks. Bare mudflats surrounded them. Further ahead trees and bushes crept closer to the waterline.

Behind them the sea suddenly had boundaries. They were sailing away from the wide-open expanse that had been their home. Esther felt a brief flash of claustrophobia at the sight of the shores closing in on them, but she pushed it aside.

"Wait a second," Cally said as the river narrowed in front of them. "Is that a ship?"

They came upon the spectral shape of a massive cargo vessel lying on its side. The carcass must have been nearly eight hundred feet long, and it blocked the river where the banks began to draw closer together. It was like someone had placed a giant floodgate directly across the river, leaving only a narrow gap on one side. Water swirled around the bow, white and rough. It was hard to tell with the shallow bank, but the gap seemed dangerously small.

"We'll have to see how deep it is around that opening," Esther said as they drew closer. "I'm not sure we can get through." They were still several hundred feet away, but Esther thought they would just make it.

Then Simon shouted something from the lookout tower. Cally tugged on Esther's sleeve.

"Uh . . . I think we have a problem."

Another ship had emerged out of nowhere behind the *Lucinda*. It floated at the rear, cutting off their access to the sea. With the cargo ship on one side and the newcomer on the other, they were trapped.

12. The River Guards

THE STRANGER SHIP WAS perhaps eighty feet long—smaller than the *Lucinda*—and it had been painted in a multitude of bright colors: yellow, red, purple. It had crept in behind them as the *Lucinda* approached the wreck blocking the river. It was some sort of fishing vessel, with a tall profile and multicolored flags flying from every corner. People swarmed across its decks, clad in a bright mishmash of colors. They were armed.

"Let's get below," Esther said. "We don't know what they'll do."

"I don't want to miss—"

"Off the deck, Cally."

Esther waited to make sure her young charge went below. She studied the other ship. It gave no discernible signal, making no move to attack. The people aboard watched the *Lucinda*, guns raised and steady. Belatedly, Esther felt a wave of shock. Survivors. They had found survivors.

The river mouth was still very wide here. If they waited for the right moment, the *Lucinda* might be able to get around the other ship and make a run for the sea, but they'd have to leave the river behind.

Esther hurried back up to the pilothouse.

"What've we got?"

"They're speaking Spanish," Zoe said. She pulled the radio headset half off her ear. "I'm trying to tell them I don't understand, but they keep talking at me. Wish we had Neal."

"Can you call him on the satellite phone to translate?"

"Working on it."

"They're definitely armed," Esther said. "I got a good look from the deck."

"They don't sound friendly," Zoe said. Her hands flew across her communications console. "Ringing Neal now."

"What do you think, David? Can we squeeze through?"

He had brought the *Lucinda* in a slow turn so they could get a better view of the stranger ship. The wrecked cargo ship and the narrow opening to the river waited at their backs.

"We can't take any chances," David said. "The river's too narrow here." He turned on the ship's intercom. "All hands to weapons stations. We're on high alert. Hold your fire unless provoked. Let's move, people." David kept his attention on the other ship, which was only a few hundred yards away now.

"We can't get into a fight," Esther said. "That's not why we're here."

"They don't know that."

"Neal!" Zoe waved at Esther and David to be quiet. She spoke into the satellite phone. "Hey, Neal. No time to explain. I need you to translate some of what these guys are saying to me on the radio." She held the mic for the satellite phone up to the speaker for the radio. A tinny tirade came from the speakers. The people on the radio were speaking fast, and Zoe was right: they did not sound friendly.

"What do you think, Neal?" Zoe said, pulling the mic away from the speaker for a moment. "Yeah, uh-huh, that's what we gathered. Give me a second. I'll patch you through."

Zoe tapped some buttons on her console. "They're telling us to go away and never come back. Neal's gonna try talking to them."

"Think they'll attack?"

"Hopefully Neal will clear things up before it comes to that."

Zoe kept the speakers close together, allowing Neal to communicate with the strangers from his perch far away on the *Catalina*.

Esther and David watched the other ship. It made no move to fire. The *Lucinda*'s crew would have reached their stations by now. Anyone who was off duty would be belowdecks. Esther wished her father were below instead of exposed up in the crow's nest. He didn't need to be involved in this fight, if a fight it would be.

The console buzzed with another call from Neal.

"*Lucinda*. Yeah. Okay. Understood." Zoe put down the mic. "We got a problem. They want everyone out on deck with weapons laid down before they'll negotiate anything."

"Not a chance," David said. "We can't expose ourselves like that."

Zoe talked to Neal, and then he relayed the message on the radio. They waited. The other ship was getting closer to them. More men came out on deck, leveling their weapons toward the *Lucinda*. It drew nearer still.

"If it comes to it, *Lucinda* can take that ship," David said quietly. "Look at it. It's built for fishing, not fighting."

"We don't need a fight," Esther said. "You guys should make a break for the sea, and I'll see if I can slip through to the river in the speedboat without them noticing."

The other ship was edging in, trying to force them back against the wreck.

David shook his head. "I don't want a fight either, but I'm not going to let these guys intimidate us." He reached for the intercom again. "This is the captain. Fire a single warning shot."

Esther held her breath.

A blast split the morning air. The shot landed in the river beside the trawler, sending a spray of water onto the deck. The trawler veered off abruptly. The men crouched low, weapons still pointed toward the *Lucinda*. They had stopped advancing.

"Wait!" Zoe said. "They're changing their tune." She listened to what was being said through the headset, still relaying the communication between Neal on the satellite call and the Spanish speakers on the radio.

Esther realized she was gripping David's arm and released it.

"Okay, Neal says they'll talk," Zoe said. "They're asking us not to fire. He says they're scared. They haven't seen another ship in ages. We need to bring one of them up here to get Neal's translations for the negotiation. They're working out the details."

The trawler made a wide circle and pulled around closer than ever to the *Lucinda*. The brightly colored paint went all the way around the hull and covered most of the tall cockpit. The strangers watched the *Lucinda* warily from their positions crouched on the deck.

"Wish one of us spoke Spanish," Esther said. "Neal should have come with us."

"I took French in school," David said. He was still tense and kept one hand on the intercom button. He'd order another strike without hesitation.

Neal called Zoe back again and filled them in on the plan. They would do an exchange. While two people from the trawler came aboard *Lucinda*, they had to send two of their crew across to the other ship.

"Send Simon," David said immediately.

"What?" Esther whirled around to stare at him.

"He's the oldest of us, and he has a calming presence," David said. "Since we can't communicate with them, we need to send someone who will keep his head."

"No. I'll go," Esther said.

"Esther, do not argue with me on this."

Esther folded her arms, scowling at David.

"I don't want him to—"

"This isn't a discussion. Send Simon and Cody. If that ship is afraid of us now, we need to show it we're in control but not overly threatening. They're the best ones for the job."

David met her eyes, and the set in his jaw told her he wouldn't change his mind.

Esther stalked out of the pilothouse to fetch her father. She hated sending him into further danger. She waved him down from the crow's nest and sent Anita up to replace him, keeping an eye on the guns on the stranger ship. They found Cody in the inner corridor with Cally, Dax, and Raymond.

"We're negotiating with that other ship," Esther explained. "They're guarding the river and want to talk. We're supposed to send two people over there while we meet with some of their people here. Hawthorne wants you to go, Dad, because you'll keep your head, and he wants Cody to go with you."

"Why me?" Cody asked, looking surprised.

"No idea. Look, you don't have to do this," Esther said to her father.

"Nonsense," said Simon. "I'm very curious about that ship. I'll be fine, Esther. Let's go, son."

"Yes, sir," Cody said. "Don't worry, Esther. I'll keep him safe."

"You be safe too!" Cally said suddenly. Cody's baby face blushed a furious red, and he followed Simon and Esther up the ladder.

Back on deck, Wade and Sarita waited for them on the promenade, guns at the ready. Wade flexed his biceps and nodded when Esther, Simon, and Cody arrived at the railing. Sarita's teeth were clenched, her finger hovering near the trigger of her semiautomatic. Sweat trailed from beneath her blunt bangs.

The *Lucinda* and the trawler drifted closer together. The men on the other ship all had black hair and sun-darkened faces. They kept their guns raised too, watching the *Lucinda* with blank expressions.

When they were within reach, the sailors on the trawler extended a long plank of wood from their deck. *Lucinda*'s deck was taller, so the men would have to scramble across the two-foot-wide plank on hands and knees, exposing themselves to the other ship.

No one moved as Simon and Cody approached the plank, the mood tense among both crews. Two men from the other ship stepped forward too. They handed their guns to their compatriots—and waited.

The two crews stared at each other. The ships creaked, and water rushed between their hulls.

Still no one moved.

Suddenly, Simon waved.

"¡*Buenos dias!*" he said. "Nice weather we're having."

One of the men on the other ship laughed.

"¡*Buenos dias!*"

Simon grabbed the railing and stepped carefully onto the plank. He balanced on the wobbling board, wavering on his bad knee for a moment, then stood up straight, extending his arms like the wings of a bird. As lightly as if he were walking on the deck, he crossed the plank to the other ship. Someone reached out a hand to help him down, and as soon as he landed on the deck he gave an exaggerated bow. A few men on the other ship laughed.

The tension eased perceptibly. Simon shook hands with the men waiting on the other side before gesturing toward the plank. The first man didn't try to imitate Simon's tightrope walk, instead clambering on hands and knees over to the *Lucinda*.

Esther followed her father's lead and shook the man's hand as he alighted. He didn't smile, but his handshake was warm and firm. He was a few inches taller than Esther, with wide brown eyes and a bushy black mustache. His face was wrinkled, and he looked older than most of his shipmates.

"Good morning," he said. "I am Emilio. I speak little English."

"I'm Esther. Welcome to the *Lucinda*."

Emilio nodded and eyed Wade and Sarita and their weapons. His gaze was sharp and intelligent.

Cody made his way across to the trawler with less grace than Simon. At the last moment he stumbled, and one foot slipped off the plank. The men on the other ship reached out to pull him aboard. Cody's face looked a little green, but he was okay. The other men slapped him on the back. Emilio's companion then scrambled across to the *Lucinda*, and the trade was complete.

"He is Jorge," Emilio said of his companion. "He speak no English."

Jorge was taller and thinner than Emilio. He wore an orange bandana, pulled low above thick eyebrows. When Esther extended her hand, he took it briefly, barely making contact before dropping it again.

"Come with me," Esther said. "Our friend on the radio speaks Spanish."

"Good, good," Emilio said.

Esther led the two men back toward the pilot-house. The crew gathered around, wary of the newcomers as they crossed the deck. She glanced back at the trawler. Simon and Cody were still on deck, Simon communicating in gestures and broken words with the people on board. Even with just a word or two of Spanish, he seemed to put the strangers at ease.

David met them at the door to the pilothouse. He shook hands with Emilio and Jorge and greeted them with a few simple words in Spanish. Esther got the impression he had asked Neal to teach him the phrases in the few minutes she had been out of the pilothouse. David seemed to grow taller as the strangers entered. He stood close to the shorter men so that they had to look up at him looming over them. He looked like someone in command, like someone people listened to.

Zoe handed over her headset, and Emilio began speaking in rapid Spanish to Neal on the other end of the line. He threw in English words occasionally. Esther hoped Neal's language skills were advanced enough for this.

Jorge surveyed the pilothouse, his arms crossed over his polyester jacket. He carried no weapon, but Esther got the impression that he wouldn't need one to do some damage. She met his hard eyes.

The pace of Emilio's conversation picked up. Finally, he laughed and handed the radio back over to Zoe. She listened for a moment while Emilio spoke to Jorge in a low voice.

David caught Esther's eye and adjusted his broken glasses. "We're okay," he mouthed.

"Here's the deal," Zoe said as she finished listening to Neal. "These guys don't like the Lake Aguamilpa people, and they thought at first we were with them. They're locals who survived the disaster, and they're just trying to get on with their lives. The Aguamilpa folks have been creating trouble for them upriver. Neal told them we're not Lake People, and we're just looking for someone. As long as we leave them alone, they're willing to guide us upriver in exchange for weapons they can use to defend themselves."

"Does Neal trust them?" David asked.

"Enough. He thinks we should do it."

"What do you think, Esther?" David said.

Esther studied Emilio. She wasn't particularly good at reading people, but his face seemed guileless. Compared to the Harvesters and the men from the Calderon Group, he was practically friendly.

"I think we should go for it," she said. "They can give us information about the Lake People. I want to know more about the trouble they caused."

"I won't hand over any weapons, though," David said. "Let me talk to Neal about alternative payments. Esther, would you let the guys out there know that we're coming to an agreement. I don't want to leave your dad hanging."

Esther left David to haggle and returned to the deck. On her way past the main hatch she spotted Cally and Dax ducking out of sight as soon as she appeared.

The scene by the railing had hardly changed since she left. Wade and Sarita waited by the plank, guns held low. On the other ship Cody shuffled awkwardly from foot to foot, but Simon leaned against the railing, seemingly at ease.

"Hey Dad," Esther called, "things are going well in there. I think we'll be working with these guys to get the rest of the way up the river."

"¡Muy bien!" Simon said, and the people around him laughed.

The men hadn't put away their guns. They seemed to have plenty, and Esther couldn't help but wonder whether they were really helping just so they could get weapons. But they relaxed a bit. The Lucindans had found their first friendly land-dwelling survivors after all.

13. River Town

ESTHER SCANNED THE SHORES on either side of them while she waited for David and the strangers to emerge from the pilothouse. Low hills were visible now, some topped with new green life. Esther still hadn't seen any people on land. The skies had begun to clear, though. The light flooding the land had a different quality than what they were used to at sea. Even the clouds looked more golden and muted than the ominous shapes they knew well.

Simon had moved to the bow of the trawler, invisible from where Esther stood. She felt nervous about him being on the other ship, but he had seemed comfortable enough with the strangers. She returned to the rail and studied the space between the cargo ship and the shallow bank. The gap leading into the river really didn't look big enough for them. The *Lucinda* wouldn't fit through it. They had to figure out some way to clear it or she'd be using that speedboat after all.

The trawler had drifted a bit. The path to the sea was clear now. The *Lucinda* could make a run for it, but they held steady. David must be working something out. The crew waited anxiously for further instructions.

Finally, David and Emilio emerged from the pilothouse and joined Esther on deck.

"There you are!" David said. He was smiling.

"How'd it go?" Esther asked.

"Swimmingly."

"I don't think we can clear the gap," Esther said, gesturing toward the sunken cargo ship.

"Not until the tide comes in," David said. "We'll have to wait it out."

"The tide?" Of course! Things like tides mattered on the coast.

"Yep. Emilio thinks it should be high enough in about four hours."

Esther nodded. "So we're stuck here until then?"

"Not stuck," David said. "Their trawler has a shallow enough draft to fit through now, so we're taking a group in to see the local settlement. We'll have to wait for the water to rise enough for *Lucinda* to squeeze past. Plus we need to give our new friends their payment."

Emilio grinned and looped his arm through Esther's.

"Oh?" she said.

"Your tech," David said. "Their village isn't on the satellite network yet. You'll give them your biofuel generator plans in exchange for safe passage through the mouth and a guide to help us sail up the river."

"I see." Esther extracted herself from Emilio's grip. He gave her a friendly smile. He seemed to think he'd gotten a pretty good deal.

"Yes, and on our way out Zoe will set them up with a satellite link. I convinced our friend here that we might need our guns when we reach the lake." David looked rather pleased with himself.

"All good news," Esther said. "Can my dad come back now?"

"He's going with us in the landing party, since he's already made such a good impression. Luke will take the command here, and Zoe will stay on comms. You and I will go to the shore with your dad, Cody, and Dax."

"Whatever you say, Captain Hawthorne," Esther said.

David grinned. "Lead the way, Emilio."

They fetched Dax and prepared to cross over to the trawler. Jorge would stay behind on the *Lucinda*. Wade and Sarita stationed themselves on either side of him, while the others headed for the other ship. David reminded them to be polite to their guest. Sarita snorted in response.

Esther was the last to step across the gangplank to the trawler. The river rushed beneath her as she stomped across the narrow board. She jumped off before she had a chance to get scared, her boots thudding on the deck.

"Welcome to *Santa Julia*," Emilio said.

Sailors crowded the ship, dressed in the same bright colors they had painted their vessel. David was busy shaking hands all around the crew. Dax and Cody stood nervously near the railing. Strangely, Dax seemed to be eyeing Cody with as much suspicion as the strangers.

As the trawler's loud, coughing engines started up again, Simon joined them. He introduced "*mi hija*, Esther" to his new friends.

"You okay?" she asked him.

"This is fascinating," her father said. "Many of these people lived in this region before the disaster. They've held on against all odds and dealt with famine and floods for nearly seventeen years."

"How many are there?"

"We'll find out soon enough, but I think their settlement is fairly small."

"You're making friends quickly," Esther said.

"I wish I could take notes on all this," Simon said, smiling and nodding at the strangers. "They've been on land all this time! They can't have had it easy."

The trawler slowed as it approached the narrow gap between the mudflats and the shipwreck. As they neared the half-sunken cargo ship, the men and women around them held on to the railing or squatted low to keep their balance. Esther and the others followed their lead.

The water roughened as the trawler drifted dangerously close to the capsized ship. Graffiti marred the smooth planes of its hull. It was mostly names, but there were bright paintings and symbols as well, many overlapping each other.

"*Los muertos*," a voice said suddenly. Esther jumped. Emilio had come up beside her. He gestured toward the names on the hull. "*Los muertos.* The dead."

"I understand," Esther said. "I'm sorry."

The *Santa Julia* shuddered in the white water around the sunken hull. Esther clutched the rail. Then the trawler slipped through the gap without a scrape. They were on the other side of the barrier, leaving the *Lucinda* bobbing in the delta. They had truly left the sea behind them.

The climate on the opposite side of the cargo ship seemed to change almost immediately. As they cruised slowly up the river, it grew muggy. The banks on either side spread wide and muddy, like at the mouth of the river, but eventually they gave way to jungle-green hills.

Up ahead the river split into two branches, a wider one to the left and a narrower one to the right of a small island. The island looked like a man's head shaved bald on the sides, with bright-green sprigs rising from the center. They pulled into the narrower branch of the river, to the right of the island. As they passed it, revealing more of the bank on the opposite side, Emilio beckoned all the Lucindans to the bow.

"Old town," he said, pointing.

Another mudflat spread before them on the far right bank. It had been partially hidden by the island until now. About halfway between the water and the jungle a group of structures emerged from the mud. Most were no more than shells: walls and partial roofs growing out of great dark piles of mud. Debris stacked like barriers suggested attempts had been made to protect the buildings from the floodwaters. A bus sat in front of one building, half-submerged in mud. It too bore names and pictures in lurid paint.

"New town is there," Emilio said, gesturing to the jungle. "We go now."

The trawler passed the swamped village and drew near to a long, thin dock. It was a rudimentary structure, floating loosely from a large concrete block so it could adapt to changes in the water level. As they got closer they saw that the concrete anchor was the wall of a sturdy building now sitting mostly beneath the waterline.

They climbed down a ladder from the *Santa Julia* onto the dock, which bobbed under their feet, pulling at the concrete anchor block. Emilio and some of his crew joined them. With Emilio leading the way, Esther and her friends crossed the dock.

When they reached the end, Esther reached for her father's hand. He grasped hers without a word, and together they took their first steps onto the land. Esther's boots sunk into the mud, leaving distinct footprints in the earth.

When everyone had reached the shore, the trawler coughed and sputtered, then sped away, heading back in the direction of the *Lucinda*. It disappeared around the island, leaving them stuck on land without a ship in sight. Gentle waves lapped at the shore. The water tore at the sand on the river beach with each pulse. The sound of the sea was softer here, like a shell pressed to the ear.

A small boy emerged from the shadows behind the anchor block. He wore a faded baseball cap, and mud stained the bottoms of his too-big jeans. He shouted a question at Emilio, who answered in a rapid stream of Spanish. The boy put both thumbs up and let out a shrill whistle. Half a dozen children popped out from various nooks and crannies around the anchor building and the drowned village. They darted off into the jungle together, chattering animatedly.

Emilio beckoned Esther and the others down a hard-packed path leading away from the concrete anchor building. They walked across the damp sand. There was debris here too, but it had all been pushed to the side to clear a path from the dock to the jungle. Soon the driftwood, plastic, and seaweed gave way to scrubby plants, and finally trees.

Esther had never seen anything like these trees. Even during her childhood, the trees had been tame, relegated to planters by the sidewalks or one corner of their little backyard. These trees grew in every direction, some sloping drunkenly almost to the sand, others standing in tight, impenetrable packs.

The air thickened as the trees closed in around them. It was damp and cool, and the moisture sank into Esther's skin. The path narrowed, forcing them to spread out into a double-file line. Emilio and David led the way. Esther walked with Dax behind Simon and one of the *Santa Julia*'s crew, a woman with her thick hair cut short above the collar of a bright-green jacket.

Birds sang in the trees. A buzzing sound suggested insects too. It was surreal. And the smells! Earth and moss and something sweet, perhaps some sort of tropical flower. Esther felt like she was wading through a strange dream.

She turned to Dax. "How are you doing with all this?"

"Fine. Fine." He tugged at his hair.

"Nervous?" she asked.

"Yeah."

"Same."

"Can't believe I'm worried about this after every-thing we've been through."

"Everything we've been through so far has in-volved a ship or two," Esther said. "This is new terri-tory."

"I mean, I've really put myself out there for her, you know?" Dax said.

"Huh?" Esther glanced over at Dax and stumbled on a root beneath her feet. He didn't notice. He was staring in front of them without really focusing on anything.

"I get that things change sometimes," he said, "but I thought we'd be different."

"We?"

Dax sighed. "We have something special, you know? And he's not that great."

"Emilio?"

"What?" Dax looked at her then. "No, of course not."

"What are you talking about?" Esther asked.

"What are *you* talking about?"

"Emilio and his crew," Esther said. "The locals guarding the river? The jungle?"

"I was talking about Cally and Cody," Dax said.

"What about them?"

"He loves her," Dax said miserably.

Esther nearly tripped over another root. "Cody loves Cally?"

"I think so," Dax said.

"You guys are still a couple, though, right?"

"Yeah, but I'm not sure she still wants to be. The way she looks at him . . ."

Esther glanced back at Cody. He walked near the end of the group, beside a skinny man with a thick beard. He stared wide-eyed at the jungle around them. He still looked very young to her.

"Are you sure you're not imagining things?" Esther said.

"Ever since I smuggled her aboard, she's spent almost as much time with him as she's spent with me," Dax said.

"Doing what?"

"He just comes around to talk when we're working. He even helped scrub the decks the other day."

"Have you talked to Cally about it?" Esther asked.

"No." Dax turned to her hopefully. "Do you think you could ask her about it, Esther?"

"You've gotta be able to talk to her yourself."

"Yes, but you're her friend," Dax said. "Maybe you could find out what she's thinking."

"I couldn't exactly report back to you."

"I know." Dax frowned. "I'm wondering if I should have stayed on the *Galaxy* after all, you know?"

"I don't know what to tell you, Dax." Esther looked at the strangers in front and behind them. The trees looming beside them. "Things are changing quickly for everyone. Maybe you'll end up being in the right place because you left the *Galaxy* even if things don't work out with Cally. I mean, look at Neal. He's happy and busy again, even though at first it seemed like he'd never get over Marianna."

"I guess so."

Esther nudged him with her elbow. "Let's worry about this some other time. We're on land! Isn't it amazing?"

Dax released his hair and grinned. "I guess so."

"Don't worry about Cally," Esther said. Behind them the skinny bearded man had begun chatting to Cody in Spanish. He looked increasingly nervous, sweat beading on his round forehead. "You'll work things out if you're meant to."

"Thanks, Esther."

They walked for almost fifteen minutes. They were getting awfully far away from the shore. Esther began to feel slightly claustrophobic as the trees closed in around them. There was no space!

Her nervousness increased as the minutes passed. Their guides showed no signs of stopping. They were surrounded on all sides by trees or strangers. What if they needed to escape from these men? If they ran into the jungle, they might never find their way out again.

Esther hooked her fingers in her tool belt. She would not give in to panic. These people were helping them. And they might have important information about the lake.

Finally, they heard people calling greetings up ahead. The trees parted, and they stepped into a wide clearing. Or more precisely they stepped *up* to a clearing. The settlement was on a low hilltop that had been shorn of vegetation. Sunlight bathed a few clusters of houses constructed of concrete and debris. A hard-packed path encircled the hilltop. A woman driving a motorbike along it pulled up suddenly when she saw the strangers. She watched the group carefully, poised for flight.

Emilio led the way as they climbed a flagstone path toward the village. Narrow streets wound between the buildings. People dressed in bright clothing, like the crew of the *Santa Julia*, began to congregate as they noticed the arrival of the Lucindans. The group of children led by the little boy had expanded. The children gathered around the newcomers, pointing and giggling.

"There are so many young ones," Simon said to Emilio. "Many children."

"Yes," Emilio said. "We need children."

A little girl broke through the crowd, tugging a tiny boy by the hand.

"¡Abuelo!" she called, and wrapped her arms around Emilio's leg, dragging the little boy with her. The boy grabbed Emilio's trousers to keep from falling down.

"*Mi hija*'s boy and girl," he said, and swept the little boy up into his arms.

The boy giggled and turned to stare at the newcomers. He laughed and pointed at David, transfixed by his white-blond hair. David smiled, took the little boy's hand, and shook it solemnly.

"Here!" Emilio said. "You hold. He is Carlos." He put the little boy in David's arms.

Surprised, David and the little boy regarded each other, green eyes meeting round brown ones.

"Hi there, Carlos," David said.

Little Carlos reached up and grabbed David's hair with his fist.

Emilio roared with laughter. "We eat now."

The group followed Emilio toward one of the larger structures at the center of the village, an open-air pavilion with a large stove inside it. A few people were already sitting at the long picnic tables that filled the space. Emilio ushered Esther and her friends to the tables and told them to wait.

Everything was brightly painted, from the tables to the support posts for the pavilion to a mural covering the outer wall of the nearest building. It depicted the village on the hilltop, with the river spread out beneath it. It was full of people with cartoonish heads and smiling faces.

Esther sat down beside David, who was still holding little Carlos. David had managed to extract his hair from the boy's fist and was now making strange babbling sounds. Carlos giggled and tried to grab David's glasses.

"Wanna hold him, Esther?" David said.

"Uh, no, I don't think so . . ."

"What's the matter? Are you afraid of babies?"

"No! I mean, not really. Didn't you tell me you don't like kids?"

"I said I don't want to bring kids into this world, not that I don't like them when they're already here," David said. "Isn't that right, buddy?" he cooed in that strange babbling voice.

Esther stared at David as he got the little boy to smile and laugh. Listening to his baby talk was almost as strange as being on land. She remembered a moment months ago on the *Catalina* when she had spotted David sitting with a group of children in the plaza and teaching them a ball game. It had been hard to reconcile the image with that of the imperious spokesman she had first met standing on the deck of a *Galaxy* yacht. But she had learned a lot about David since then.

Esther felt a tap on her shoulder. She turned around to see the little girl, Carlos's sister, standing there, her face right at Esther's eye level. She started chattering in quick, birdlike syllables.

"I . . . I don't understand," Esther said.

The girl chattered on as if she had understood Esther's every word. Esther looked around for an adult who might belong to the girl, but everyone seemed preoccupied with fixing up big plates of food for the guests.

"Looks like you've made yourself a friend," David said. "What's her name?"

Esther shrugged.

"You're hopeless, Esther." David leaned around her and waved to the little girl. He put a wide palm on his chest. "David," he said. Then he pointed to the little boy. "Carlos." A hand on the top of Esther's head. "Esther." He pointed at the girl.

She giggled and twisted her fingers in the folds of her bright-yellow dress. "Amalia!" she said, then repeated Esther and David's names. "¡Y Carlos! Mi hermano."

"It's nice to meet you, Amalia," David said cordially, and the little girl giggled again.

"How are you so good with kids?" Esther said.

"I'm good at everything." David grinned and leaned in to kiss Esther on the cheek, making Amalia giggle even harder.

Soon Emilio and the others from the settlement were setting overflowing plates in front of their guests. Some sort of grilled animal, a bit of rice, a large pile of green and yellow vegetables, and a wide, flat bread filled the plates. Esther watched the others pile everything onto the bread and roll it up to eat. She did the same.

The flavors were strange and surprisingly spicy. Esther's eyes watered, and her tongue tingled and burned. It was so different from the bland fish she had been eating for years.

Someone set a dented metal bottle filled with water in front of her. It looked just as clean as the water they put through the desal system. She sipped cautiously. It had a distinct earthy flavor.

Emilio and Simon had joined Esther and David for the meal. Emilio was the only person in the village who spoke any English, and he and Simon made liberal use of gestures and facial expressions as they talked. Simon asked Emilio to explain what had happened with the Lake Aguamilpa people.

"We are friends first," Emilio said. "They come for many years. We go to lake sometimes for *los pescados*—for the fish—but later they say no. The Big Man says no. They kill us."

"So you fought them?" David said. He met Esther's eyes briefly. "A war?"

"Not war," Emilio said. "Only fighting. Now we are here, river only, and they are there, lake only. Not *amigos*."

"But they gave you fish before?" Simon asked. He mimed an exchange. "You traded?"

Emilio nodded his understanding.

Simon gave his shoulders an exaggerated shrug. "What changed? Why not friends now?"

Emilio rattled off an explanation, but Simon wasn't able to decipher it.

"I'm sorry . . . something about death . . . church . . . I don't understand."

Emilio sighed. "They kill us, and they kill them."

"Wait, who else do they kill?" Esther asked. A dull fear grew in her stomach like nausea.

"Them," Emilio said. "The lake men kill the lake men. The Big Man says."

Esther and her father exchanged glances. Civil war? Had there been fighting amongst the Lake People themselves? It seemed that at some point the lake men had decided they no longer wanted to trade with Emilio's people. But what had they done to each other? Esther wondered if this "big man" was the one who hadn't wanted his communications guy to share their roster with Neal. If he didn't like trading with the locals, he probably wouldn't want to cooperate with strangers from the sea either.

"I think I understand," Simon said. "We don't want to fight. Will they talk to us? Before they shoot?"

"I speak little English," Emilio said. "You speak lot English. They talk to you maybe."

"Hmm. So they seem to be sticking to their own tribe, in a manner of speaking," Simon said.

"Just because we speak the same language doesn't mean they'll be happy to see us, though," David said. "We'll have to be very careful."

"Or you don't go to lake," Emilio said. "Better maybe."

"We have to go," Esther said.

"You want what with them?" he asked.

"*Mi hija*," Simon said quietly.

Emilio nodded, eyes solemn, and passed Simon another piece of the flat bread.

"*Sí*," Emilio said. "They talk to you."

Esther hoped he was right, but this didn't sound promising. Emilio's people were peaceful, even friendly. As soon as they knew the Lucindans wouldn't hurt them, they had provided food, help, and hospitality. Emilio had even offered them a guide to help navigate the river. It sounded like they had gotten along with the Aguamilpa settlers at first. But then they had fought with the men of the lake. It had to be more than a communication problem. Whatever had happened, there must be something wrong with Naomi's group and their "big man."

Esther spotted Cody and Dax further along the table. They sat side by side, not making eye contact. She hoped they'd sort out whatever was going on between them and Cally soon. They had to be a team when they reached the lake. They might run into more resistance than they had expected if they tried to take Naomi away.

Dax stuffed the last bite of his meal into his mouth, stood, and approached the women serving the food. He asked them questions, mostly using sign language. After a few minutes one of the women pulled some vegetables out of a sack by the table and started showing Dax how to chop them up, laughing at his clumsy attempts. One of the others from the *Santa Julia* brought an extra helping of food over to where Cody was sitting. She sat beside him and chattered in Spanish while he stammered and stared.

The band of children darted down the aisle between the brightly colored tables. David had given

Carlos back into Amalia's care while they ate, but the pair returned as soon as they finished their own meals. They stared at Esther, David, and Simon with wide eyes as they finished their food.

Emilio led the way to another open pavilion after lunch, and his grandchildren followed. David kept turning around and pulling faces, making them giggle and shriek. After a few minutes Amalia pulled a pretty blue stone out of her pocket and handed it to him shyly. David bowed low over her hand as he accepted the gift, making the little girl smile even wider. Esther shook her head. She didn't know how he did it.

They arrived at the second pavilion, and Esther felt more at home instantly. Machines and spare parts filled the shady space beneath it. A couple of mechanics, one man and one woman, were at work on a motorbike when they walked up. A handful of other motorbikes and one rusty car awaited their attention. The two mechanics straightened when Esther and the others approached. Emilio spoke to them in Spanish, gesturing to Esther as he did.

"Looks like it's time for you to build a biofuel system, Esther," David said.

"You got it."

"We'll go take a look around if you don't mind," Simon said.

"Sure thing. Don't forget to take notes."

The mechanics showed Esther their toolboxes, and she got to work right away, digging through the piles of gear until she found everything she needed to construct a quick prototype of her generator. Emilio took Simon, David, and the others off to explore the rest of the village while Esther worked.

The mechanics watched her closely, and one scribbled notes on rough green paper. Esther peeked at the sheet, where he was drawing and labeling each step with an impressive level of detail. This guy knew what he was doing.

Through rudimentary sign language she got the mechanics to help with the machine so they would be able to assemble more on their own. She had to improvise a bit using the parts they had in their workshop. The most important thing would be the algae to create the biofuel, but there should be plenty of it growing in the river.

Esther and the mechanics worked until the sun began to sink and Emilio and the others returned. David had acquired a few more admirers: children who laughed and danced around his knees to get his attention. Someone had given Simon a scarf woven from red and orange wool, and Dax had a huge sack in his arms overflowing with vegetables. Cody made no effort to help him carry it.

Esther made a few notations on the mechanics' drawing so they could finish assembling the machine. Then she shook hands with the pair and wished them good luck. The tide would be high enough now that the *Lucinda* could sail past the sunken cargo giant and make her way onto the river. It was time to move.

14. Rio Santiago

THEY MADE THEIR WAY back through the jungle, boarded the *Santa Julia*, and sailed toward the mouth of the river. The water level had risen. It ate further into the shore, lapping at the edges of the derelict town. They sailed until the telltale glint of the *Lucinda*'s hull appeared in the fading light. She waited for them beyond the little island making a fork in the river.

As they got closer, they could see Cally waving enthusiastically from the deck. Dax and Cody waved back at her, elbowing each other a bit as they tried to take the prime spot in the bow. David noticed and raised an eyebrow.

"I'll explain later," Esther said.

The *Santa Julia* pulled up alongside the *Lucinda* again. Handshakes were exchanged all around the deck, and then the team began to cross the rickety gangplank back onto their own ship. This time they brought an additional person with them. Their guide was a slight woman with short dark hair and wide-set eyes named Isadora. She wore a bright-green jacket and baggy trousers that looked almost like a skirt. She scrambled across to the *Lucinda* without a word. Emilio had told them that she spoke no English at all, but she would be able to point out problem areas as they navigated up the river.

Before Esther crossed back over to the gangplank, Emilio stopped her with a hand on the shoulder and handed her a map. It was a rough sketch of the entire river all the way to the lake. The river wound sharply through the land. In places it looked like a long piece of rope had been laid across the map and had its ends scrunched close together, the middle part folding in on itself like an accordion. Emilio's people lived in an elbow of the river. She could see now that water surrounded the hilltop village on three sides, protecting their community while also providing sustenance in the form of fish, water plants, and birds. It wasn't a bad place to live.

"Thank you," Esther said, shaking Emilio's hand and meeting his warm eyes.

"Be careful," he said. "For the sister."

"We will."

"The Big Man is not a friend."

"I understand."

The sun had begun to sink toward the western horizon. Esther climbed onto the plank and clambered across to the *Lucinda*. When everyone had returned to their own ships, they shouted their final good-byes across the water. Emilio raised a hand in farewell, and several of his companions saluted. As soon as the *Santa Julia* pulled away, the *Lucinda* swung around and resumed her journey, leaving the village behind.

They wanted to get as far upriver as possible before the light faded completely, but they were almost out of time. It was surprisingly dark on the river, with almost no distinction between the water and the shore. They had never sailed like this before, in danger of running aground. If something happened to the *Lucinda*, they would have no way of getting home after it was all over. Before long the message went around the ship that they'd have to stop for the night. They couldn't guarantee a safe passage through the river in the dark.

Esther wished they could keep sailing, especially now that they knew Naomi's people were dangerous, possibly even to each other. They had already wasted too much time at the mouth of the river. But David made the final call to wait until morning, and they pulled the *Lucinda* in a bit closer to the shore and dropped anchor. When it hit the bottom of the river, they were able to determine that it was only about forty feet deep, the shallowest water they'd ever experienced.

David ordered a double watch that night, and Esther took first shift. She felt too alert to sleep anyway. She patrolled the deck, staring out at the shore. The river rushed against the banks, sometimes constant, sometimes sputtering and choking like a living thing.

Shadows and strange noises filled the jungle. Breezes rustled intermittently through the trees, carrying earthy, verdant smells. Each time the wind shifted, Esther imagined figures rushing through the darkness toward the *Lucinda*. She had no idea what kind of weapons the people dwelling in the jungle might have. Emilio's compatriots had been helpful, but who knew who else might be living among those trees?

Esther wrapped her jacket close around her and leaned against the outside of the pilothouse. Midnight neared. A strange chirping sounded above the babble of the water. Could it be a bird? She didn't even know if birds sang at night. She watched the shore and the dark depths of the water stretching around them.

Suddenly, there was a crash, followed by the most terrible screeching Esther had ever heard. She bolted upright. The sound pierced through the night like a combination of a seal call and a screaming human child. Esther darted to starboard and stared into the jungle.

She could barely tell any shapes apart through the shifting shadows and the swaying trees. It was so dark. The wailing got louder. The thing was coming closer.

Cody was also on duty, and he ran up to join Esther at the starboard rail.

"What is that?" He clutched a gun in both hands, his round face white in the glow from the deck lights.

"No idea," Esther said. She felt as scared as Cody looked, but he didn't need to know that. She gripped the wrench in her belt.

"It's coming closer!"

"I know."

"Should I shoot?"

"Not yet."

The branches of a nearby tree swayed a little harder than the others. Esther could barely see the outline against the sky, but whatever was making the noise seemed to be in that general area.

"Got a light?"

"Here. It's not very good." Cody handed over a flashlight.

The slim piece of metal felt cool against Esther's palm. She aimed the weak beam at the trees. The noise came again, louder this time, a terrible howling sound. Esther was surprised everyone hadn't already woken up.

"See anything?"

"Nothing." Cody stood a little too close to her, as if hoping she would protect him. She had no idea if she could or not.

More howling. The trees shook. Could it be the wind? More. Esther gestured for Cody to hand her his gun. His hands were shaking badly, and they couldn't afford any accidents. Cody obliged, wide eyes still peering at the jungle.

Esther lifted the gun and looked through the scope, but it was useless in the darkness. Then the branches of another tree moved.

"There!" Cody hissed. "What is it?"

The flashlight beam swept the tree branches. Suddenly a pair of big yellow eyes popped out of the darkness, followed by bared teeth.

"Holy shit!" Esther nearly dropped the light. Cody stumbled backwards and tripped over his own boots. He landed hard on the deck.

"What was that?"

Esther searched for the yellow eyes again. There was a flick of something brown. The trees rustled. Then the movement and the howling were gone.

"I . . . I think it was a monkey," Esther said weakly.

"That hell scream came from a monkey?"

"I saw a tail."

"Great white whale!" Cody said, picking himself up off the deck. "I hope we go back to sea soon."

The crew laughed over the monkey story the next morning. Cody told anyone who would listen about the huge teeth and the body the size of a walrus. It was easier to joke about it in the daylight, but

Esther was surprised at how terrified she had been. She had never felt more out of her depth than she did staring at the shore in the night. She knew precious little about land.

The jungle didn't seem as ominous in the morning, but it still felt like they were journeying through alien territory. With the exception of Cally, they had all seen trees before, but it had been so long that it was like trees only existed in storybooks. Esther had definitely never seen so many different shades of green. Each layer was different, and as the sun traveled across the sky the leaves changed color, shuffling through verdant shades from sea-green to teal to emerald to jade.

It grew warmer as they sailed inland, getting further from the sea by the minute. The trees and plants were dense on the rolling shores of the river, but the fields beyond flattened out quickly. The further they got from the coast, the more the land stretched out. Soon it became a flat expanse like the rolling of the sea, making it difficult to establish any sense of depth or distance.

Every once in a while they'd spot a piece of farming equipment, or a line in the land that looked a bit too straight, evidence of the extinct agricultural industry in the region. It didn't look like anyone had been on land in this area in a very long time. They saw tracks in the muddy riverbanks occasionally, but none belonged to two-legged creatures.

After she'd gotten a few hours of sleep, Esther had returned to the rail. She leaned far over the water, searching for any signs of fish or other river creatures. The river itself was brownish, like kelp, the murky waters impenetrable. It smelled of dirt and algae and rot. She missed the crisp waters of the sea, where the waves reflected the colors in the sky, and the salted wind cleansed and renewed.

The still air grew heavy and hot. Esther pulled off her jacket and tied it around her waist, feeling sweaty and uncomfortable, missing the sea breezes. She went to sit in the shade of the pilothouse facing the bow. David found her there.

"What do you think?" he said. He had removed his sweater and wore a thin navy-blue T-shirt underneath it.

"It's hot."

"Relatively speaking, yeah. Temperatures are still below average for this region, according to what Neal can find out."

"You got him on the satellite?"

"Yeah, while you were sleeping. Connection's not great, but it's good enough."

"Has he heard anything about Naomi?"

"Not directly, but he finally got the Aguamilpa communications guy back on the line."

Esther sat upright. "And?"

"He's still playing dumb about the roster," David said. "Neal didn't want to push it, so he tried to find out how they respond to visitors. He asked if they had any neighbors. The guy claimed there are hostile tribes around them. He talked about tension with another settlement. Neal said he was starting to sound suspicious, so he quit asking questions."

"Think the other settlement is Emilio's village, or is there another one?" Esther asked, thinking about her night watching the jungle. What if there had been someone else out there besides the howling monkey? The trees could camouflage hundreds of people at close range. Unlike the sea, the land offered plenty of places to hide. Even the folds of the abandoned farmlands could conceal strangers. On the river they were exposed.

"Not sure," David said. He wiped sweat from his forehead. "I hate going in blind like this."

"At least we have Isadora to help us find our way."

"Let's hope she doesn't turn out to be a liability if we have to play nice with the Aguamilpa leader," David said.

Cally was patrolling the deck this afternoon, and Cody was keeping her company, even though he'd had a long shift the night before. Cally had pulled her thick hair up into a messy bun. Wispy red curls fell on either side of her face. Cody leaned close to her to say something, and Cally laughed, throwing back her head.

"What happens if there's another lake settlement and we find the wrong group?" Esther said.

"The group we're looking for, the ones Neal has been talking to, are mostly English speakers. That should make it pretty clear."

"Hope so. Anything new from Boris?"

David frowned, fiddling with the sleeve of Esther's jacket. "Marianna's keeping her ears open. Boris left the *Galaxy* a week ago, and no other ships have reported seeing him since. Only . . ."

"What?"

"Boris is tricky. The *Amsterdam* folks are firmly on our side at this point, but I wouldn't put it past Boris to have a few allies we don't know about."

"He's kind of unpleasant," Esther said. "If he's as rude to everyone else as he was to me, I can't imagine he's making too many friends. Why were *you* even friends with him?"

David was silent for moment. "It's hard to explain. I was a teenager when I met Boris. He was older than me, and he was already working on a ship's crew. He was just . . . cool. You never seem to care what people think of you, Esther, but I wasn't like that, especially back then. I wanted to be as cool and uncaring as he was."

"But if you didn't even like him that much . . ."

"Oh, I liked him. He had a certain charisma, and he was very ambitious. I spent a long time trying to be more like him. He liked to rib me a bit, but I put up with his digs because it meant he thought I was worth paying attention to."

"But you're not a teenager anymore," Esther said.

"No, I'm not, but it took a long time for those feelings to go away."

David looked up at where Cally and Cody were still laughing together. Cody stood a little straighter around her, looking a little less like the baby-faced sailor Esther had first met amongst the Harvesters. Maybe Dax was right after all. Cally was definitely being friendly toward him, but then she was nice to everyone.

"Boris was my friend." David adjusted his glasses and met Esther's eyes. "We had some good times together, but he also broke a promise he made to me, and in the end I think he enjoyed holding me down. It took me a long time to realize the man I had admired could be so petty. The one thing he hated more than anything else was a threat to his position. Why do you think he hates you so much?"

"What?"

"Your tech," David said. "It's huge. It's changing everything about the way we live at sea. The *Galaxy* captains are keeping it from their people because they're terrified it will break their hold on their little kingdoms when people can move around freely. Boris knows it's all your fault."

"And what do you think?"

David grinned. "I am salting proud of you, Esther."

She scooted a little closer and took David's hand. This, at least, was simple.

"So what was the promise?" she asked. "The one Boris broke."

Sweat trailed down David's face and disappeared at the neck of his T-shirt. He watched the green riverbank sliding past them.

"This," he said. "He promised to take me on his next expedition to land. He used to sail the *Lucinda* to the Hawaiian Islands to gather soil and plants for the gardening ship. It made him a hero at the *Galaxy*. All I ever wanted was to go with him, but he always had an excuse for why I couldn't come."

"Is it what you hoped it would be?" Esther pulled her knees up to her chest and wiped her forehead. Why was it so rusting hot?

David's mouth lifted in a rueful half smile. "No matter how many times I told myself that not many people had survived, I still pictured us sailing into Manhattan with the skyscrapers rising around us and a whole crowd waiting to greet us."

The trees on the riverbank hung branches out over the water. The *Lucinda* passed beneath one of them, and the shadow swept over David's face.

"At least we're on land, sort of," Esther said.

"Yes. I'd like to explore, though, get my feet on solid ground for a bit longer."

"The river hasn't been blocked since that first wreck. *Lucinda* might make it all the way after all."

"Let's hope so." David smiled. Esther remembered when that smile had been a smirk. He looked content now, despite the sweat running down his face and the alien landscape passing them by. Yes, this was simpler. David and Esther stayed where they were, drinking in the sights of the land around them, as they sailed onward.

The river voyage soon became monotonous. The banks curved around, looping back and forth across the landscape, but didn't change much. They crept further inland, stopping each night. The shores pressed in around them, full of strange noises and hints of living things. It grew warmer by day. Esther found herself getting tired more quickly than she used to, as if the land-bound air were heavier than that at sea.

She missed the familiar rhythm of the ship on the ocean. The constant forward motion of the river made her feel queasy. She couldn't wait to reach the lake, where they'd be back on wide-open water. And she wanted to walk on land again, maybe even take off her shoes and feel mud between her toes.

15. Bridge Town

THREE DAYS AFTER THEY left the sea behind, Isadora tapped her finger on a point on the map Emilio had given them. A large circle had been drawn on one shore and a smaller one on the opposite side, with a line directly across the river.

"Ixcuintla," she said.

"I'm sorry?" David said. He had been discussing the instruments on the dash with Luke while Esther and Zoe tried to get a call through to Neal. It had been harder to reach him the further inland they got. The connections were fuzzy and unreliable.

"Ixcuintla," Isadora repeated. "Ciudad de los Muertos."

"I think *muertos* means dead," Esther said, remembering the names scrawled on the wrecked cargo ship. She looked closer at the map.

"What's this line crossing the river?"

Zoe leaned over to look too. "Think it's a dead point? Like you can't pass beyond it?"

"Maybe it's a place where some of their people died," Luke said.

Isadora frowned and pointed at the map and then up at the horizon. The river bent around before them, so they couldn't see too far ahead.

"*Ciudad*," she said, tapping the big circle on the map, then gesturing upriver. "*Puente*." She traced the line again.

The intercom crackled. Anita was on duty up in the lookout tower.

"Crow's nest to bridge," she said. "Guys, I . . . I see a city!"

"*Ciudad!*" David exclaimed. "I knew I'd heard that word before. It means city!"

"Nice one!" Zoe said.

"Emilio didn't say anything about a city," Esther said.

David picked up the intercom. "Can you see any people, Anita?"

"Not yet, Captain. Looks pretty quiet."

"What do you think?" He rubbed his hands together, smiling broadly. "Shall we have a look?"

"Um, Hawthorne," Luke said, "wouldn't Ciudad de los Muertos mean City of the Dead?"

Isadora reached out and gripped Luke's arm. "Ciudad de los Muertos," she whispered, voice hoarse. "Ixcuintla."

"Ah," David said. "Good point. Let's proceed with caution, shall we?"

They sailed further up the river. Isadora didn't try to stop them from approaching the city. They hoped it would be safe to pass, no matter what "City of the Dead" implied.

They rounded another bend, and there it was, growing on the hilltop like a crust of barnacles. It wasn't very big, perhaps more of a town than a city. Buildings peeked out from amongst the trees and scrub. Antennas spiked up at odd angles. The houses were light-pastel colors but obviously hadn't been painted in decades. The whites and pinks and yellows flaked off the walls, exposing the concrete and stucco beneath.

Esther didn't know much about cities, but this one didn't look like it had ever been impressive. Most of the buildings visible from the river were a single story tall. The one exception, located right at the center of town, was a structure with a tall tower made of tiers. The top tier had a pale-blue dome with a jagged stump on top of it like a broken spire. Next to it rose a slightly shorter but much larger domed roof that was the soft yellow of morning sunlight. Esther was pretty sure it was some sort of church.

The church building looked mostly intact, but she couldn't say the same about the ones around it. Burnt shells of houses scattered across the hilltop. A fire had raged on one side, scorching almost all the way down to the river. As they drew closer, they could see a few burned-out cars, some lying partway in the shallows of the river.

There was no movement at all. It *did* look like a city of the dead.

As the *Lucinda* neared, they figured out what *puente* meant too.

"It's a bridge," Esther said. She leaned forward over the helm, feeling the warm breeze hissing through the bullet holes in the windscreen. "Or at least it used to be."

Concrete pillars rose on either side of the river. Between them a broken roadway creaked downward into the water. It looked like someone had held up a flat stretch of graying cloth and brought their hands together until the middle section dipped beneath the surface of the river. The murky brown waters obscured the broken middle of the bridge, making it unclear how deep the river was here.

"I don't know if the *Lucinda* can get over that," Luke said.

"We better send a boat forward to check the depth," David said. "And while we're at it, I want to explore the city."

"Are you sure we should take a detour?" Esther asked. Ever since Emilio had mentioned that the Lake People had been known to kill each other, she had become increasingly worried about wasting any time on their way there. Her sister had been with them for long enough.

"Yeah, City of the Dead isn't exactly a glowing recommendation," Zoe said. She pulled the headset halfway off her ear. She'd been scanning the radio waves for any signs of life as they approached Ixcuintla, but there were none so far.

"Let's not forget that the first objective of this mission is to explore the conditions on land," David said. "I'd say that includes the biggest town we've seen yet. It won't take long. Let's gather a team."

First they sent the little four-person motorboat over to check the depth where the bridge had collapsed into the river. If it was deep enough, they'd take the *Lucinda* over to the other side. Meanwhile, the crew prepared the main raft to send a scouting team into the city.

In addition to himself, David chose Esther, Luke, Ike Newton, Sarita, Wade, Jackson, and Anita for the exploration team. Wade and Sarita distributed guns to everyone. Esther took only a small handgun and tucked it into her belt. She'd feel better about fighting with her wrench if it came down to it.

"Let's avoid firing those if possible," David said to Wade as they finished handing out the ordnance. "We're here to make friends, if there's anyone living here."

"Sure thing."

"Okay. Stay sharp everyone."

They launched the large inflatable raft and glided slowly over to the shore, picking their way through the drowned cars. They eased over a sunken dingy to tie up at a sloping dock made of weathered wood.

They crossed the dock to the shore, careful to avoid the gaps in the wood. Bushes and mangled trees lined the waterfront. The road leading to the sunken bridge was further upriver, but they found a smaller one climbing directly into the city. David left Jackson to guard the raft and led the way toward the buildings.

The road, now overgrown with scrub, didn't look like it had been well paved to begin with. A mix of hard-packed pathways and broader avenues covered in cracked asphalt led off from it occasionally. The streets were very quiet. The persistent smell of dust and old char filled the air. They didn't see so much as a feral cat as they climbed the hillside.

Esther held her wrench tight and scanned the ramshackle buildings and burned-out cars. They passed a low, wide structure that could have been a grocery store or market of some kind. The roof had caved in, swaying low in the middle of the darkened shop.

There was a flicker. Esther froze. Movement. She was sure of it.

She hissed at the team to stop and slowly approached the structure. Broken windows revealed rows of vacant tables and shelves inside. Foil and plastic packets lay scattered across the floor, emptied of their contents. Esther's heart thudded loud and quick. She breathed. All was still.

There it was again! A flash of motion. A scuttling sound. The wrench grew warm in Esther's palm.

Her boot brushed against a small stone on the ground. She picked it up and rubbed the flat edge. It must have been part of a brick or a piece of tile. She chucked the stone into the building.

A burst of movement. Swirls of black and tan. Something hit Esther's face. She stumbled backwards, swiping at the air with her wrench. She wouldn't go down without a fight!

"Easy." David stopped her with a hand on her shoulder. "It was just a bird."

"Are you sure?"

"Well, several birds. I almost had a heart attack. You okay?"

"Yeah, let's keep moving," Esther said, her cheeks warming. "I don't think there are any people here, though."

"You may be right."

They continued their slow exploration of the town. Apart from a bird here and there, nothing moved.

"This is damned spooky," Wade said after a while.

Luke chuckled. "It's just a bunch of abandoned buildings," he said. "Don't be so nervous."

"What's that thing?" Ike asked. He jogged ahead of the group and led them up another slope of the hill. At the top they stepped out onto a wide square. It was paved, though tough grasses grew thick between the stones. At its center was an open-air octagonal structure with an ornate green roof. Several steps led up to its center.

"It's some sort of gazebo," David said.

"Gazebo? What's that?" Ike asked.

"It's like a shelter. I don't really know what they're for. Weddings, picnics, string quartet performances, I guess."

"Whatever," Ike said. "Can I go up there, Cap?"

"Just be careful."

Ike darted toward the steps, crossing the broad square. The others followed more slowly. The church building with the tower and dome they'd seen from the boat loomed at the far end of the square, beyond the gazebo. It looked mostly intact, even from up close. Soft sunlight cast hazy shadows from the tiers of the tower. A huge pair of doors yawned open at its center.

They crossed the pavement toward the church. Esther scanned their surroundings as they walked, nervous about being exposed. The buildings around the square were nicer than the ramshackle homes in most of the town. They were made of stone or plaster rather than wood, and painted tiles appeared on a few of them. Many of these were broken, delicate reminders of a lost world.

They were halfway to the church steps when Ike screamed.

They whirled around, raising their weapons. Wade and Sarita crouched low, preparing to fire. David and Esther stepped closer to each other and turned, putting their backs together without speaking. Esther raised her wrench and put one hand on the gun in her belt.

"Bodies!" Ike nearly fell down the steps of the gazebo. "Bodies!" he screamed again.

His face was flushed when he reached them. He bent down with his hands on his knees and wretched on the cobblestones.

Sarita's mouth twisted. "Were they fresh?"

"No," Ike wheezed. "Skeletons."

"Don't scare us like that, kid." Wade raised his gun up onto his shoulder. "Just a bag of bones. Surprised we haven't seen 'em sooner."

"How many are there?" David asked.

"Lots. I don't know." Ike looked back at the gazebo as if he expected the skeletons to chase him. "They were arranged in a circle, almost like they planned it."

"Or someone else did," Esther said darkly. She scanned the square, but it looked just as deserted as it had from the beginning.

"Can we go back to the ship soon, guys?" Luke said. He hadn't lowered his gun. "I don't think we're going to find anything here."

"We have to see the church," Anita whispered.

David hesitated. Anita looked at him solemnly.

"Okay," he said. "But be careful. We don't want the whole thing to come down on our heads."

"Wait a second," Esther said. Her eyes had just fallen on something waiting for them in the shadow of the church building.

It was a great big truck. She started toward it, drawn like a fish to a lure.

"Think you can get it working?"

"Depends," Esther said.

She kept her wrench out as she approached the vehicle. It was large, with a wide flatbed and a monstrous cabin. A layer of dust muted the chrome surfaces. She reached for the cabin door. It wasn't locked. The hinges creaked as she pulled it open. The cabin was empty. Esther let out a breath. She hadn't particularly wanted to pull a skeleton out of the truck before she got to work.

There was no skeleton, but there was a key sitting right on the disintegrating seat. It must be Esther's lucky day. She hoisted herself into the truck. The others gathered around, still watching the empty square. Ike looked a little green in the face, but he stood straight. The kid wasn't too bad.

Esther had never driven a car before, but her dad had let her start his Mazda when she was a kid. She loved the way the engine sparked to life at the turn of the key. It was a tactile experience, one of the first things that had inspired her love of engines and machines. She had even crawled around on the garage floor, helping her father fix the car whenever it broke down, which had happened frequently, if she remembered correctly. Those had been happy times.

Esther put the key in the ignition of the big truck and turned it. The engine sputtered. Then nothing. She tried again. *Sput sput sput.* Nothing again. She tried a third time. Still the engine failed to ignite. She climbed back out of the cab and went to inspect the fuel tank. It was bone dry, as she'd suspected. The important thing, though, was that it sounded like there was enough battery left in the thing for the spark plugs to work. That meant it had been driven relatively recently too.

She opened the hood and tinkered around in the engine, fiddling with the connections and looking for rust and corrosion. It had been a long time since she had seen a car engine, and of course she hadn't really known what she was doing back then, but she had enough experience with engines in general to be able to assess the condition of this one. As long as they had fuel, there was a decent chance the thing would run. The biodiesel they made out of algae on the *Lucinda* wouldn't be a perfect solution, but it just might work.

Esther wiped her hands on her trousers and re-joined her friends. While she tinkered with the engine, she had been thinking some things over. It was time to do what she should have done the moment

they learned the men at Aguamilpa were dangerous.

"A town this size will have roads heading toward
other cities, right?" she said.

"The one from the bridge looked pretty big,"
Luke said.

"I bet it goes to a highway," Wade added.

"Do you think we could find a way north?" Esther
asked. "If we wanted to drive inland?"

David looked at Esther sharply. The others considered for a moment.

"Yes," Sarita said. "A road north could be exactly
what we're looking for, especially if that truck runs."

"We can finally get this party started," Wade said.

"This truck won't hold everyone," Esther said.
"Let's see if we can find another vehicle or two in
decent shape."

Luke edged over and spoke to Esther in a low
voice. "Don't forget not to steal my girlfriend. I'll
come with you if you like."

Esther nodded. She had been dreading this, but
she knew what she had to do.

"I think you guys should go overland from here
and head toward Kansas City," Esther said. David
opened his mouth, but she barreled on before he
could say anything. "We're bound to find at least
one more working vehicle, and it looks like there's a
road heading toward the States. No guarantee we'll
find one at the lake. I can continue on in the motor-

boat with a small team. When I find my sister, I'll bring her back here. That way you all can get on your way before winter sets in, and you can proceed with the original mission after all."

"Makes sense to me," Sarita said. "No offense, Esther, but I think we're wasting time on the river. I've taken a look at that map of Isadora's, and I don't think there's a northbound highway leading away from that lake."

"Hold on a minute," David said. "We all agreed to go after Esther's sister. We can't abandon her at the first sign of a road."

"It wasn't fair of me to ask you all to do this," Esther said. "You got me pretty close, and you can continue as planned. This is too good an opportunity to pass up."

David folded his arms. "What happens if that truck breaks down twenty miles up the road? We'll end up walking all the way to Kansas after all. We need you, Esther."

"My sister—"

"I know. I say we continue on the river," David said. "Assuming the *Lucinda* makes it past the bridge, we keep moving and get your sister away from that crazy town. Then we sail right back here, leave the *Lucinda*, and head north in the trucks."

"Look, Cap, time's gonna run out," Wade said. "Trekking through snowy mountains won't be much fun."

"I think we should head north," Sarita said. "It *is* the mission."

"No," David said, a tic in his jaw.

"Can't we vote?" Luke said.

"I'm making the decisions here," David said.

Sarita arched an eyebrow and exchanged glances with Wade.

"Give us a second," Esther said. She hooked her arm through David's and pulled him away from the group. Wade and Sarita put their heads together, frowning at David. Ike drifted over to join them. He nodded at whatever was being said.

"Esther, it's too soon," David said, his usual composure slipping. "We can't split up now."

"We agreed on this," Esther said. "It's time."

"No."

"You can't make that call without talking it over with the crew, remember?" Esther said. She knew this would happen eventually. She had no choice but to continue on. He had to let her go. "Don't spoil your relationship with the crew now."

"They'll do what I say," David said.

"Hey." Esther reached up to cup his face in her hands. Concern furrowed his brow. "It'll be okay. I have to do this, but it's not fair to risk everyone."

"I'll come with you," David said.

"You can't do that." Esther knew it was selfish, but she wanted him to stay with her so much.

She stood up on her toes and kissed him softly on the lips. That's when the first skeleton walked out of the church.

16. The Church

IKE SHRIEKED LIKE AN eel. Luke cursed and pointed his gun toward the skinny figures ambling out of the yawning church doors. There were three of them. They stumbled down the steps toward the group gathered around the truck.

"Pilgrims," one moaned. "More pilgrims."

"Who are you?" David asked. He held up a hand and approached the trio. Their malnourished bodies were barely clothed in scraps of fabric. Two of the three were women, but their bones had so little meat you could hardly tell. All three had limp hair hanging down past their exposed rib cages.

"Pilgrims," the man said again, coming closer to them. "Your journey is at an end. You will find your final rest here."

"We're just passing through," David said. "What can you tell us about this town?"

"Ixcuintla is the sacred town," the man intoned. He had a cultured voice, with a slight accent. "You have come. Your journey is at an end."

"We have food," David said. "We can give you food and water and make sure you're—"

"No food!" the man screamed, stumbling back from him. His eyes grew so wide they looked larger than his mouth.

The women wailed.

"No food no food no food!"

"Heretics!"

"Please," David said. "We just want to help."

"No food! Get thee from us, Satan." The man reached out to hold hands with the women on either side of him. "Sisters, the tempter comes with food. I knew he would try to entice us in our final hours."

"Quickly! We must bar the doors and deny the body!" one of the women said.

"Yes, yes," the other intoned. "Deny the body. Deny the devil."

"We don't want to hurt you," Esther said. "He's not the devil."

"Lies!" the man shrieked. "The devil will tempt you with food in your final hour. Long have we struggled, seeking the idols of survival and sustenance. We have been blind for too long, but no more! We have journeyed here to seek our final solace. We will not eat until the Almighty comes to reveal the truth. We are faithful. We have suffered. In the last moments we will Know, like our brothers and sisters have Known!"

Anita had crept around behind the starved trio. Esther spotted her as she disappeared through the doors of the church.

"We won't harm you," David said. He tried to calm the starving man, but he was growing frantic.

"We have journeyed to the sacred city! This is the final test! We are late, but we will not fail now! Almost seventeen years of death and destruction. Of fighting, fighting, fighting. Killing each other over meat and bread! But now we know the truth. We know peace. No more fighting. No more clawing for food. We are triumphant, sisters!"

He turned and began to pull the two women with him toward the church. One hesitated, looking back at Esther and the others. David reached out a hand to her.

"We can help you."

She stared at him for a moment, then shook her head.

"Too late," she whispered.

They climbed back up the steps toward the church doors. Anita appeared then, skirting around them with a fleeting glance before running back down the steps. The three figures disappeared into the darkness.

"They're everywhere," Anita said when she joined them. "Bones, bodies."

"What kind of hell pool is this?" Wade growled.

"Must be some sort of cult," David said. "Did you hear what he said about the idols of survival and sustenance?"

"The bodies were different ages," Anita said. "I mean some of them looked like they died a long time ago and some were newer."

"Guess now we know why they call it the City of the Dead," Luke said. "Can we go now?"

"Wait," Esther said. "Just because a bunch of salt-addled crazies decided to starve themselves to death doesn't mean we can't gather some vehicles."

"Seems kinda sacrilegious," Ike said.

"I guess I follow the idol of survival then," Esther said. "We need those trucks."

"Let's return to the *Lucinda* and talk it over," David said. "It'll be a different conversation if she can't get past the bridge."

No one could argue with that. They made their way back through the city, leaving the spectral church behind them. Ike fell in with Wade and Sarita and leaned close to talk to them. Anita trailed behind them, looking thoughtful.

Esther still had the keys to the big truck in her pocket, just in case. She noted other vehicles that looked mostly whole on their way back down to the river. It might take a bit of scrounging before they found enough to carry the whole team overland. They couldn't delay.

The three figures from the church left Esther with an uneasy feeling in her stomach. What had driven them—and apparently many others—to believe starving themselves to death was the way to get answers about why this had happened to the world? She had seen people pushed to madness and despair on the sea after the disaster, the first captain of the *Catalina* among them. Now they knew for certain that it had been bad enough on land for other survivors to cope in extreme ways. Esther feared for Naomi. Those poor folks in the church had been harmless, but there was no telling what she had been through or who else she had encountered. There was no telling how she herself might have changed.

David walked beside Esther as they tramped back toward the river.

"You can't ask me to let you go," he said before she could speak. "It's too late for that. If you continue upriver in the motorboat, I'm coming with you."

"You can't leave the *Lucinda*," Esther said. "You've worked too hard on her."

"Then I guess the *Lucinda* will be going upriver too." David picked up a small green banana lying beneath a tree growing almost in the road.

"We have to let the crew decide which risks they're willing to take." Esther took the fruit out of David's hand and tossed it back into the scrub. It could be poisonous. "Didn't you teach me that?"

David frowned and picked up another fallen fruit. He turned it over and over in his hands as they approached the dock.

"Maybe you should be leading the mission after all," he said.

Esther nudged his arm. "I'm a mechanic, not a sailor, remember?"

They pushed their way through the last bit of scrub and arrived at the river. The *Lucinda* had reached the opposite side of the bridge.

"Looks like we can continue on after all, if that's what the crew wants," David said.

"We'll see." It was tempting to let David have his way, but she was afraid they wouldn't have another opportunity to actually find a route north before it was too late in the year. Wade was right. They didn't want to get stuck trekking through snow.

The raft was still waiting for them at the weathered dock for the short jaunt back to their ship.

"Find anything in the city?" Jackson asked.

"It's abandoned," Esther said. "Mostly."

"We found a truck, though," Wade said. He looked at Esther significantly. "A real big one."

"We need to talk," David said. "Gather the crew as soon as we're back on board."

Half an hour later the crew stared each other down across the deck. David had presented them with a simple choice: river or road. A majority vote would decide the issue.

Wade and Sarita argued in favor of leaving the river behind and taking the truck up the north road. Jackson and some of the other Galaxians agreed. They knew their chances of being able to head north diminished each day. Winter would set in before they could make it to Kansas if they didn't move soon. Much of the crew, with the exception of Esther's friends, seemed to agree. They shifted their feet, almost unconsciously turning toward the bridge town and the north road as the discussion continued. They were eager to set off on land toward more familiar regions. Everyone wanted to find their way home somehow.

Then Anita spoke, describing what she had seen inside the church in vivid detail. She was quite poetic in her descriptions of the decimated corpses, all skin and rib cages. She made the prospect of returning to Ixcuintla distinctly less appealing. The crew shifted again, now leaning subtly away from the portside rail, edging closer to the center of the ship.

Esther couldn't bring herself to say anything. She wanted the crew to go north. She wanted them to carry on their original mission and not risk coming within reach of the Big Man at Aguamilpa. At the same time she was unable to voice the argument that would send David and her friends away from her.

"Would anyone else like to speak before we vote?" David asked. Then with barely a pause he turned to Esther's father. "Simon? How about you?"

A hush fell over the crowd as they watched Simon limp to the center of the deck. Esther already knew what he would say. Instead of watching him, she studied the faces of the crew. She knew her father wouldn't ask them to continue risking themselves on account of his family when there was an opportunity for them to travel overland safely. There was too strong a chance the people at Aguamilpa would be hostile if what Emilio had told them was true. Simon was a good man. He had always been less selfish than Esther. He had always been willing to make hard choices.

"I can't ask you to help me find my daughter," Simon said. "You've already gotten us so close, and I think if some members of the crew would like to continue on land they should be allowed to. Thank you for your help so far. I . . . I had given up on my daughter and my wife long ago. Now the impossible has happened, and I may be able to help one of them after all. This simple chance is already an incredible gift. I can't ask any more of you."

No one spoke after he finished. Jackson shifted uncomfortably from foot to foot. Sarita looked uncertain, her eyes a bit misty. Others in the crew seemed to want to step closer, to put their hands on

Simon's shoulders and offer him their help and support.

David nodded, a shadow of triumph crossing his face before he controlled his features. Oh, he knew what he was doing.

"I like Simon's suggestion that some people continue on the road while the rest sail onward," he said. Simon raised an eyebrow at this interpretation of his words, but he didn't dispute it. "Shall we vote? Let's say a line stretches from the corner of the pilothouse to the tip of the prow. If you want to continue on land, step to the side nearest Ixcuintla. If you want to help Simon find his daughter, step to the other side. Take as much time as you need."

David stepped directly to starboard, the side furthest from the bridge town, and waited.

A few people moved immediately. Zoe, Luke, Cody, Anita, Cally. Esther's friends knew their mission wasn't over yet. But some moved to the other side too. Jackson and Wade both took up positions on the port side, nearer the bridge town. It occurred to Esther that one of them would probably be able to fix the truck if needed later on down the road.

Sarita took longer to decide, but she joined her fellow Galaxians on the port side. Raymond followed her, along with a handful of others.

Ike Newton glanced fleetingly at Simon and then gritted his teeth and joined the road team. Perhaps Ike saw this as his chance to break away on his own.

He looked at Simon apprehensively, but Simon just nodded and gave him a small smile.

"Would anyone like to change their minds before we count?" David asked.

No one moved.

He opened his mouth to announce the official decision. Then Dax stepped forward and crossed the line, declaring his intention to join the road team. Cally let out a little gasp. That *was* a surprise. Dax looked miserable about it. He shifted uncomfortably, tugging at the spikes in his hair. Raymond patted him on the back.

Eight crew members had voted to turn onto the north road and head inland. The remaining twenty-one—plus Isadora—would continue on to the lake.

"It looks like the majority has spoken," David said. "The *Lucinda* will sail upriver as planned. Those of you who voted for the road, do you plan to split here and continue to Kansas City on your own?"

The group put their heads together for a moment.

"Yes," Jackson said. "No hard feelings, mate, but I think it's time."

"I agree," David said. "We'll outfit you with supplies and fuel to get you started."

"Let's get to it," Wade said.

Esther felt conflicted as they prepared packs for the group that would take the road. She had wanted more of the crew to join them, but David had used

Simon's popularity to keep the majority with the *Lucinda*. She was sure many of them would have voted to go the other way if it weren't for him. Guilt twisted within her. She was letting David abandon his dream of traveling to Kansas City to keep him with her. She was allowing the team to get further off course in service of her own private rescue mission. She couldn't keep doing this, putting others at risk for her own ends. If the Lake People truly were hostile and hurt any of the crew, she could never forgive herself.

Esther enlisted Anita to help prepare the portable water filters they'd send with the land crew. They made sure the charcoal filters still worked and packed them up again in a hard plastic suitcase they had found floating on the sea long ago.

"Can I ask you a question?" Esther asked her friend as they completed the task. Even though she had known Anita for the same length of time as Zoe, she still didn't feel like she really understood her. It was always hard to tell what was going on in her head.

Anita nodded, her brown hair swinging against her delicate chin.

"Why did you decide to come on this mission even though Toni changed her mind?"

Anita looked up and studied the sleek iron shape of the *Lucinda*. She was quiet for so long Esther worried she wouldn't answer. Anita's sister, Eva, had died on this ship, Esther remembered. She, too, must have mixed feelings about the voyage—and about the potential costs.

"Eva and I left the *Galaxy* because what has happening there was wrong," Anita said. "It was always important to her to do the right thing. I think the right thing is to help you find your sister if you can."

She patted Esther's shoulder and walked away without another word. Esther watched her go, still unsure. It might be the right thing for Anita to do, but that didn't mean it was right for Esther to ask it of her. She had been too wrapped up in the emotion of finding her sister's name to realize it back on the *Catalina*. It was too late now.

Dax's decision to leave them had been unexpected, though. Cally was inconsolable. She could barely speak, and she fluttered around Dax as he slowly packed up his things and prepared to disembark. Grim determination darkened his face.

After talking with Wade about the truck and making sure the team had enough biofuel to get them started, Esther sent Cally to the engine room and stole a quick moment to speak to Dax.

"What's going on, Dax?" she said. "You don't really want to leave the ship, do you?"

"Of course not," he said. "But I'm not welcome here. Cally doesn't like me anymore."

"Yes, she does."

"I'm miserable, Esther. I feel like she's just waiting for the right moment to dump me for *him*."

"I wouldn't be so sure about that," Esther said. "And the road is going to be tough."

"I can handle it," Dax said. "I'm as much a man as he is."

Esther sighed. "I don't want you to regret it."

"I won't."

Cally returned, a plaintive look on her tear-streaked face, and Esther left them to talk—or not talk. Why couldn't relationships ever be easy?

All too soon the road crew had moved their supplies to land, preparing to spend the night in the city and begin the drive in the morning. Esther walked back to the stern deck to wave good-bye to them. She found Cally by the rail, tears streaming down her face. Esther put her arm around her young apprentice's shoulders.

The raft dropped off the last of the gear and pulled away from the road crew, Luke at the motor. Eight people stood on the shore now, surrounded by backpacks and barrels of biofuel. Ike's face was pale, but he looked proud. Simon had shaken his hand and told him to look out for himself. Dax stood beside him, his arms folded tightly around his thin frame.

Luke approached the ship in the raft, nearly there. The *Lucinda*'s engines growled to life. As the ship prepared to leave them behind, the road crew started to look a little nervous. It was official. The group was splitting. It actually eased Esther's conscience a bit. The mission would continue, and those eight would not be in danger from the men of the lake. She was sad to see Dax go, though.

Speaking of which . . . Dax suddenly shouted something indistinct across the water. Then he dove into the river. Cally gasped. Dax paddled frantically, swimming after the raft as fast as he could.

"He's coming back!" Cally shrieked, jumping up on her toes.

Luke heard the commotion and turned the motor. He drove the raft back to pick Dax up and hauled him unceremoniously aboard. Dax clambered toward the bow and waved wildly at Cally. Esther shook her head as Cally squealed and ran for the ladder where Luke and Dax would climb back aboard. *Teenagers*.

The remaining land crew waved at them as they sailed away. The *Lucinda*'s wake trail spread behind them, an arrow pointing away from the spectral city. The sun slanted through the buildings, drenching them in golden-red light. The shadows quickly hid the little crew from view. Anita appeared beside Esther and leaned on the railing. They watched in silence until they rounded a bend and Ixcuintla disappeared.

17. The Riverbank

THE LAND GREW INCREASINGLY marshy as they approached the lake. They left the farmlands behind the day after leaving Ixcuintla. The shores became hilly and green and then mountainous. It was still warm, and the air got muggier by the mile.

The final stretch of the river was wide and rough. According to the map, a dam held back the lake, but the banks of the river on their side of the dam had collapsed. The water spread across a wide valley, leaving shallow areas that the *Lucinda* might not be able to handle.

Isadora knew the marsh well, and she took the helm when they drew near to the dam. She'd guide them through the shallows and help them find a safe place to moor the *Lucinda*. Then they'd have to climb up to the lake on foot.

Little islands began to crop up on either side of the ship, no more than piles of mud. Scrubby bits of grass and bird's nests decorated their tops. The islands seemed to move, oozing outward as if trying to block the *Lucinda*'s path.

Sometimes they disturbed flocks of birds. The creatures rose into the air in droves, looking like water crashing off rocks. Their cries were otherworldly. They undulated in ominous masses over the landscape and swooped low over the *Lucinda*, shrieking.

Esther headed to the pilothouse whenever she wasn't on duty as they picked their way through the marsh. It was crowded, with Isadora, David, and Zoe on duty, but she wanted to know the minute they heard something. She couldn't rest in her cabin as they got closer and closer to the lake.

Finally, on the seventh day after they had left the sea behind they reached the dam. The colossal structure was bigger than any ship. It spanned the river like a great frozen wave, nearly swallowing the sky. Vines spread across it, growing so thick in places that it was hard to tell where the shore ended and the dam began. Water spilled over the top, creating rivulets like giant fingers reaching over the edge. At the center a large chunk of concrete was missing. A waterfall poured out of the gap and thundered down into the marsh. The lake on the other side literally strained at its barrier as if desperate to break through and return to the sea.

The group in the pilothouse fell silent as they sailed slowly toward the dam, listening for warnings from the crow's nest, scanning the shores for signs of movement. Nothing yet. They got nearer, squeezing between two tussocks in the marsh. Suddenly Isadora pointed up at the top of the dam. A tiny figure waved at them from the far right side, near where the jungle encroached on the man-made structure.

"You see that?" Zoe said.

It was a man clad in earthy green. He matched the jungle beside the dam almost perfectly. They never would have noticed him if he hadn't been trying to get their attention.

"Try the radio again," David said.

Zoe had been attempting to contact the Lake Aguamilpa community on the radio for the past day. They should be in range by now, but she had complained to Esther of the poor signal.

"You'd think they'd have better reception on land," she'd said. "I was hoping for radio towers and big old satellite dishes. Turns out trees and hills get in the way of the signal."

Now that they were this close, she tried again.

"Hello? Anyone there? We're approaching on the river in a ship. Can anyone hear us?"

The radio crackled. "We see you. State your business."

"We're fellow survivors looking to share information," Zoe said. "We don't mean you any harm."

"How many of you are there?"

"Fifteen," Zoe said immediately.

Esther and David exchanged glances. They still
had twenty-three people on board including Isadora. Zoe winked.

"Are you seeking food and shelter?" asked the
voice on the radio.

"We're well stocked," Zoe said, "but we've come a
long way. We'd appreciate any help or information
you can give us."

"You may send a small party to meet the Dentist."

"Say again?"

"Send no more than four of your crew to greet
the Dentist and bring your supplications to him.
The Lord has shown you great favor by bringing you
to the Dentist's domain."

"Told you they were wack jobs," Zoe whispered.
"How about ten?" she said into the mic.

"You may send four. Unarmed. If the Dentist
permits, you may call for your companions to join
you later."

Zoe looked over at the others. David was frowning, but he nodded.

"Four it is," Zoe said. "Where do we go?"

"Do you see the Elder hailing you from above?"
said the voice on the radio.

"The man on the dam?"

"Find him on the bank. He will lead you in."

"Roger that. Over and out." Zoe put the headset back on the console.

"The Dentist?" David said.

Zoe shrugged.

"Could be the 'big man' Emilio was talking about," Esther said. "I'm going in. The rest of you should wait until I find out if it's safe." They were so close. Soon she'd know whether or not her sister had really been alive all this time. Her heartbeat picked up, pounding like thunder.

"You can't go alone," David said. "They said we can take four."

"I have to be one of them," Esther said.

"Fine. I'll leave Luke in command and come with you," David said. He raised a hand when Esther started to protest. "I'm the better negotiator. I'll do the talking. Zoe, I need you to stay here and keep in touch with Neal. See what you can find out from his communications man about this dentist character. Then it had better be Simon and Cody. Let's stick with the nonthreatening types to help balance you out, Esther."

She bared her teeth at him but agreed with his suggestion. They didn't want to antagonize these people more than necessary.

"Good," she said. "Cody knows his weapons at least. And he'll keep his eyes open."

"Don't tell them how many of us there are, or about our friends," Zoe said, glancing over at Isadora.

"Agreed," David said. "And I don't plan to tell them what we're after either."

"Well, let's get going," Esther said.

The four of them concealed weapons about their persons and gathered on deck. Esther had hidden a knife in her boot, and her trusty wrench hung from her belt. *Lucinda* had almost reached the far right shore, but they could only get so close before the muddy islands grew too numerous. Cody and David prepared to launch the motorboat. Luke came out on deck to see them off.

"With only four of us, we're in no position to storm the place, but we should be able to confirm Naomi's status," David said. "We shouldn't tell them why we're there until we identify her."

"I agree," Simon said. "I don't even know if she'll recognize us."

"She will," Esther said. She had no way of knowing this, but she had to believe it.

Her father squeezed her shoulder briefly. They were so close.

"Okay," David said. "Look after my ship, Luke."

"Sure thing," Luke said. "I promise not to throw any wild parties while you're gone."

"Great." David shook his hand. "Good luck. If we don't come back, return to the bridge town and begin the trek north. You might be able to catch up with the others."

"Understood."

"Don't wait too long," Esther said. "If it sounds like we're in trouble, get yourselves and the crew out of here."

Luke grinned and flipped his curly hair out of his eyes. "We'll do the right thing," he said.

Esther narrowed her eyes at him, then prepared to climb down onto the motorboat.

"Wait! You can't go yet!" Cally climbed out of the hatch and darted across the deck.

"What is it?" Esther asked.

Cally skidded to a stop in front of them, staring at Cody. He blushed a brilliant scarlet.

"Uh, I just wanted to say good-bye," Cally said. She turned and hugged Esther. Then she hugged Simon and even David, who looked mildly surprised. Finally, she wrapped her arms tightly around Cody's neck. "Be safe," she whispered in his ear. "And I'm sorry." He held on to her waist for just long enough to make a few of the others clear their throats.

Cally pulled back, blinking quickly, and stepped aside so they could climb down to the boat.

Once everyone was aboard, Cody took charge of the motor. No one mentioned Cally, but his ears were still bright red. Esther shook her head. Hopefully that was the end of things. They had to focus on Naomi. They could see her that very day. Her father's eyes were clouded, his face pale against his colorful new scarf.

They pulled away from the *Lucinda* and motored in among the little islands. The water was calm, sparkling in the noonday sun as ripples spread out from their hull. Birds cackled on the islands, watching them. As they neared the shore, they entered a floating mass of some sort of putrid algae. Esther held her nose and leaned closer to the look at the spongy green substance. Tiny insects crawled over it. She couldn't tell if they were feeding off the stuff or trying to burrow into its slimy folds.

"Yuck," she said.

The boat bumped into something, making them lurch. They slid forward a few feet, then stopped altogether.

"Too shallow here," Cody said. "We'll have to wade the rest of the way."

David had also been studying the thick goop around them. "You sure?" His mouth twisted around the words.

Cody stuck the emergency oar into the water and tapped it around their prow, trying to find a way forward.

"Yeah, we're not going any further than this. We can walk from here."

"I'll go first," Esther said, already leaning down to take off her boots.

"Be careful of the mud," Simon said. "You don't want to get stuck."

"It's only about twenty feet to shore," Esther said.

She tied the laces of her boots in a knot and slung them over her shoulder. They beat against her back as she moved to the fore and swung her legs over the edge of the boat. She held her breath and pushed off into the water.

A cloud of flies rose up around her as she splashed down. The water reached past her knees, and it felt viscous and oily on her skin. The smell grew worse, as if something was rotting in the stagnant water. The mud beneath her toes was warmer than she expected, and it felt like she was sticking her feet into a giant living tongue.

"Yuck."

She began to walk toward the bank. Her feet squelched with each step, the water sucking and swirling around them. She looked back at the men in the boat. David and her father watched with looks of mingled concern and disgust.

"It's fine!" she called. "Just a little squishy."

She took another step, and her foot hit a softer patch of mud. She sank down into the bank until she was encased in mud all the way up to her knee.

"Esther!" her father shouted.

"Rust," she cursed. "Stepped in a hole or something."

She tried to pull her foot out of the mud, but the riverbank closed in around her leg. Her other foot slid a little, and soon it too was sinking down into the hole.

"I think I'm stuck," she said. "Give me a minute."

She was no more than ten feet from the solid bank, but the water had risen up to her waist.

"Stop, Esther!" her father shouted. "Don't move. It might be some sort of quicksand."

Esther froze. She sank faster each time she moved. The mud was like a vise around her legs.

"Stay in the boat," she said. "Let me work my way out of this." She twisted around as slowly as possible, looking for a rock or branch to grab.

"I've read you're supposed to lie flat and float to the top," Simon said. "I don't know what you're supposed to do if there's a layer of water, though."

Esther tried leaning forward to flatten her legs out a bit. This brought her face closer to the scummy surface of the water, but she felt the mud give a little. She tried to breathe evenly. *Stay calm. You can get out of this. You have to find Naomi.*

"You're doing fine, button," Simon said.

She could sense the strain in his voice.

"You got this, Esther," Cody said. Then he shouted, "Wait! Hawthorne!"

There was a splash behind her. A wave rippled against Esther's back. David was swimming toward her. He stayed flat in the shallow water, keeping his legs as far away from the mud as possible.

"I said to stay in the boat," Esther said.

Green scum clung to David's blond hair. He stayed flat, which meant the water covered him all the way to the neck. He looked like some sort of sea demon, especially with the queasy pallor of his face.

"Grab my arm," he said, paddling quickly to stay above the mud. "Don't argue."

Esther grabbed David's arm as he kicked forward.

"Esther, relax and lean!" Simon called from the boat. "You're almost there."

Esther held on to David's arm and leaned forward in the water. With each quick kick her legs pulled a little further out of the muck. She kept them as still and straight as possible as David slowly dragged her out of the mud.

"Almost there," he panted.

Esther barely dared to breathe. Finally, she felt the sludge around her left foot loosen. She pulled it the rest of the way out of the riverbed. She kicked a few more times and her other leg pulled free. Immediately, she let go of David's arm and copied his flattened-out posture, floating as close to the surface as possible. They swam the rest of the way to shore through the scum on the water's surface.

"Don't stand up!" Simon called from the boat when they reached the shore. "Keep your weight spread out. There's a big rock to your left."

Esther and David stayed flat on their stomachs and crawled through the mud at the waterline until they reached the rock. They pulled themselves up the wide, flat surface, fingernails digging into the thick moss on the rock's face. Panting, they sat up and looked at each other.

Green goo covered David from head to toe. He must have taken off his glasses back on the raft. He wiped slime from his neck and grinned.

"You all right?" he asked.

"You should have stayed on the raft," Esther said. "You could have gotten stuck too, and then where would we be?"

"You were sinking fast," he said. "I couldn't just let you get pulled under."

"Well, we made it." She laughed. "Do I look as bad as you?"

"Worse. You look like you're wearing thigh-high boots."

He was right. Black mud covered her legs and dripped off them onto the rock. Esther tried to scrape some of it off, but it was very sticky. It smelled every bit as bad as the water had.

"Welcome to land," David said.

"Are you guys okay?" Cody called. He and Simon were still where they had left them in the motorboat. A jagged path through the scum on the water between them and the shore marked where Esther and David had been swimming.

"We're fine," Esther shouted. "Um, I don't think you should come over this way."

"Agreed," Simon said. "We'll head back downriver and see if we can find somewhere to disembark. Wait for us."

"Be careful," Esther said.

Her father saluted, and then he took up an oar and helped Cody push away from the riverbank before they started up the motor.

"I'd give up the *Lucinda* for a shower right about now," David said.

"Tell me about it. I miss the ocean."

"Me too, actually. Isn't it weird?"

"That the second we're away from something all we want to do is get back to it?" Esther said. She scraped at the mud on her legs.

"Yes," David said. "I feel a little land sick. Do you think that was a concept before people started living at sea?"

"No idea, but it's probably because of the mud, not the land. What is this stuff?" She lifted a glob of the green scum closer to her face. It seemed to be made of minuscule webs.

"It's disgusting. That's what it is."

Esther and David scraped off as much of the mud and scum as they could. It left a greenish-brown tinge on their skin as it dried. Esther felt like she was wearing a tight layer of plastic.

They had come ashore about a hundred yards from where the ground sloped upward beside the dam. The trees grew thick here. Insects buzzed around them, some settling on their arms. Esther slapped at them and pulled her boots back on over her mud-stained feet. She stood up.

"Let's see if we can find a path up the hillside while we wait for the others."

"Good idea."

They tramped through more mud to get from their rock to the cover of the trees, but it was thickly packed, and they only sank a few inches. Esther's feet felt heavy. It was warm in the trees, and soon sweat ran in brownish-green lines down both of their faces.

The insects weren't quite as bad here, but it was slow going. Tangled roots rose up to trip them, and some places were impassable due to huge thorny bushes.

"Let's not get too far from the shore," David said as they wove through the undergrowth.

"We'll have to head up there anyway to find that Elder guy." Esther pushed through another thicket of bushes, the branches scraping along her arms. She looked back at David and couldn't help laughing. "We're a mess. Great first impression we'll make on these Lake People."

A couple of yards further on, she stumbled through another thicket and found herself on a narrow stone pathway. The trail wound away from them, but it was definitely going uphill. The path was quiet, and the trees hanging low over the flagstones cast long shadows.

David followed her out. He bent to brush the leaves and mud flakes from his trousers.

"Excellent. Shall we take a breather and then head back to meet your dad?"

"You're not going anywhere," said a stranger's voice.

Three men stepped around the bend in the pathway and leveled shotgun barrels straight at them.

18. Lake Aguamilpa

THE MEN WORE MOTTLED-GREEN and brown clothing, making them blend in with the jungle behind them. The one in the middle had a faded baseball cap pulled low over his eyes. A huge brown beard covered much of his chest. He cocked his shotgun with a loud clack.

"You the ones who came in on the boat?" he said.

"Yes, sir," David said, straightening slowly. "My name is David Elliot Hawthorne. I'm the captain of the *Lucinda*. It's a pleasure to—"

"Where are the others?"

"They took our boat downriver to find a better landing point," David said. "As you can see, we had a bit of difficulty with the mud bank." He smiled ingratiatingly, but it had no effect on the man with the shotgun.

"How many?"

"There are four of us including myself. My companion is Miss Esther Harris."

"Hi," Esther said cautiously.

She watched the other two men, who both wore camouflage clothes like their leader and had beards, one brown and one black. The man with the black beard had his hair pulled back in a long ponytail. He looked Esther up and down, and his mouth lifted in a half smile. She couldn't decide if it was friendly or not.

"We told our companions we'd meet them back by the river," David said. "Mr. . . . ?"

"Name's Thompson."

"Mr. Thompson, we'd better fetch them before we head up to the lake," David said.

Thompson shook his head. He kept his shotgun cocked and pointed at them.

"You wait here," he said. "We'll get your friends. Watch them, Bole."

The man with the ponytail nodded. "I got it."

Thompson and his brown-bearded companion walked slowly past Esther and David, keeping their eyes on them at all times, then strode down the pathway and out of sight.

Bole lifted his shotgun onto his shoulder and held out a hand.

"Sorry about that," he said. "Thompson takes his job real serious, and Jones has the personality of a mud hut. Name's Adam Bole. You can call me Bole. Everyone does."

"Hawthorne," David said, shaking his hand.

"Hawthorne and Harris," Bole said. "You guys from downriver?"

"We're from the sea," Esther said.

"What now? You live on a ship?"

"Yeah," Esther said. "This is our first time coming inland."

"No kiddin'. What kind?"

"A cruise ship," Esther said slowly, not sure how much she should reveal. "We came upriver on a smaller vessel."

"So what's the deal here, Bole?" David said. "Why the hostility from Thompson?"

"We gotta be careful. You're not the first strangers we've met."

"There are others living around here?"

"Naw. It's mostly nomads that cause trouble." Bole took some kind of jerky out of his pocket and started chewing on it. "We try and keep them away, but I don't reckon you're a danger to us if you announced yourselves on the way in. Thompson just wants to be thorough."

"Understood," David said. "What can you tell us about the lake?"

"You'll see 'er soon enough." Bole spit on the ground. "The Lake is our Promised Land, we like to say."

"You traveled here after the disaster?"

"Yeah. We came all the way down from the Old States. Me and my kid sister were livin' in the Rockies for a while, but it got too damn cold, and we decided to travel south." Bole scratched a finger through his beard.

Esther guessed that he was about David's age, around thirty. His eyes were dark brown, and he had a pattern of fine freckles on his cheeks. "So, you two married or what?"

"No," Esther said. "Not married."

"But we're together," David said, a note of ferocity in his voice.

"Right." That half smile flitted across Bole's face again.

Footsteps on the path announced the return of the others. Bole lifted the shotgun down from his shoulder and pointed it at Esther and David again just before his companions arrived.

Thompson and Jones had found Cody and Esther's father. Simon handed David's glasses to him. After a terse round of introductions, Thompson gestured up the path.

"You four go first so we can keep an eye on you. We'll take you to the Dentist."

The group from the *Lucinda* walked ahead. Esther was well aware of the shotguns still pointed at their backs. She fell in beside her father.

"How did it go with the boat?"

"We found a spot further downriver where a big rock juts out into the water. We were able to come alongside it so we wouldn't have to slog through the mud. These gentlemen found us as we were getting the boat tied up."

"The rock is right by the path," Cody said. "This is a good trail, by the way," he said, turning to the lake men. "Did you build it?"

"It was here before," Bole said, striding forward to walk on Esther's other side. "We keep it clear enough. You two took the hard way through the mud."

"Your friend Thompson has been less than forthcoming about the Dentist," Simon said. "What can you tell us about him?"

"He's our leader." Bole scratched at his beard. "The story is the Lord came to him in a dream and promised to lead him through the desert and the jungle to a lake of fish and plenty."

"A dream?" Esther said.

"That's the story. I wasn't with him back then," Bole said. "I met the Dentist's people in southern Arizona. My sister and I were holed up in an old prison town, just two lost teenage kids. They took us in. The Dentist's a little eccentric, but he was right about the lake. Plenty of fish."

The path had begun to wind upward. Wide, flat stones set into the hillside made their passage easier. Thompson still scowled at them, and Jones seemed almost as tense, but Bole chatted freely. He sauntered along beside Esther and offered her some of his jerky. She caught David shooting him a dark look and fought a smile.

The air felt clearer the further up they climbed. Some of the paving stones were broken, but this part of the trail was well maintained compared to the shadowy section below. Before long, the trees began to thin and the ground leveled out.

They reached the final turn in the path. Bole strode ahead, jostling David as he passed. He threw his arms wide and said, "Welcome to Lake Aguamilpa!"

They rounded the bend, and the lake stretched before them, a deep crystal blue. The sun flashed off its glassy surface. The lake was large, its tree-covered banks just visible on the distant shore. Hills surrounded the lake like wide, green arms. The top of the dam was on their left now, a razor line com-pared to the fluid contours of the other shores.

Esther was relieved to see water again. A handful of boats buzzed about on the lake, small things busy fishing. The sight gave her a pang of homesickness. She had a strong urge to run down to the lake and submerge her entire body, or simply float on her back and look at the unobstructed sky.

"Hurry up," Thompson barked. "The Dentist is waiting."

The stone path continued along the edge of the lake for about a hundred feet. They reached a fork where the left-hand path led down to a simple wooden dock and the right one twisted back into the trees. They took the right fork.

Bole returned to Esther's side. "When you meet the Dentist," he said quietly, "you got to keep in mind that he's the supreme authority around here. You don't want to be on his bad side."

"Why? What will he do?"

"Just take it as free advice, Harris," Bole said. "You don't want to meet an angry Dentist."

"Sure, thanks."

The path opened up into a road and they entered a large camp—or a small town, if you were being generous. Cabins lined the road on either side. Many had porches hung with nets. A group of women sat on one of the porches, working on something with their hands. They stopped to watch the strangers pass.

They made their way further into the town. A warm breeze blew dust around their ankles. A man, bearded like their three escorts, trudged across their path carrying a bushel of reeds on his back. Children played in the dirt in the shade of one of the cabins. They too stopped to stare as their group walked up the street.

"Glad to see everyone's so friendly," Cody muttered to Esther.

They reached a square, where another dirt road crossed their path. One side led off to the woods and the other wound down toward the lake, which was visible through a line of scrubby trees by the water.

"I'm off," Bole said. "Got things to do before the roast tonight. You'll be invited of course. Maybe I'll catch you for a dance."

Esther looked up, startled, but he had already turned to stride away in the direction of the lake. His shotgun was slung across his back now, his long, sleek ponytail tangled in the strap. Thompson cleared his throat and gestured impatiently for Esther to keep walking.

They crossed the square and passed a dozen more houses, some with gardens visible behind them. Up ahead a larger building loomed beside the street. Like the cabins, it was made of wood and it had a rustic appearance, like a hunting lodge. A wide porch wrapped all the way around it and out of sight. A tall wooden cross rose from the top like a mast.

Thompson nudged them forward with his shotgun. They walked straight to this building and up the five steps to the porch. Thompson removed his cap and rapped on the double doors. On them was carved a huge volcano. Fire and smoke sprayed out of its conical shape, and tiny wooden figures fled before it.

They waited, standing awkwardly in a group with Jones still looming at their backs.

The doors swung open, revealing a wiry woman in the entryway. She had white hair and deep wrinkles in her round face, and she wore a robe as white as sea foam.

"Welcome to the home of the blessed Dentist," she intoned.

"These are the people from the boat," Thompson said.

"I am Alderflower. Come with me to bring your supplications before the Dentist."

Mystified, they followed her deeper into the lodge. The dark, cool entryway smelled of wood and smoke and something sweet that Esther didn't recognize. The floor was highly polished wood. The lodge felt hushed and formal, and Esther was suddenly keenly aware that she was still covered in dried river slime.

Across the entryway was another set of double doors, which had highly stylized carvings of the lake across their width. Alderflower pushed open the doors and led them through. She seemed to drift like a jellyfish as they followed her white-robed silhouette through the darkened doorway.

Inside was some sort of meeting hall. Benches lined either side of a wide aisle. The poorly lit interior left most of the room in shadow. But at the far end of the aisle a patch of light descended from an opening in the ceiling onto a huge, ornately carved chair.

A man stood up from it as they walked down the aisle. He looked about fifty, a few years younger than Esther's father. He was handsome in a mature way, with deeply tanned skin and very broad shoulders. He was also one of the tallest men Esther had ever seen, at at least six and a half feet.

"I present our blessed leader, the Dentist," Alderflower announced. "May the Lord ever speak through him to guide our steps."

They stopped in front of the dais. The Dentist loomed, arms folded over his broad chest, and regarded them. His eyes were a startling golden hazel, like glistening droplets of petroleum.

"So," he said after what felt to Esther like the world's longest pause, his voice resonating in the shadowy space, "you're the boat people."

19. The Dentist

DAVID STRODE FORWARD TO introduce them, straight backed and proud despite the mud and scum on his clothes.

"My name is David Elliot Hawthorne, and these are my companions, Simon, Esther, and Cody," he said, adopting his smooth spokesman persona. "We have traveled from the sea, where we lived adrift for nearly seventeen years. We are visiting land-based settlements in search of a home. We seek a new life."

"What brought you to us?" the Dentist asked in that deep, resonating voice.

He had a natural charisma. His tone was guarded but not unkind. Esther had to remind herself what Emilio had said about the Big Man at the lake. How the Lake People killed each other when the Big Man said.

"We're from the cruise ship *Catalina*," David said. "I believe one of your followers has been in communication with our ship on the satellite network."

The Dentist made a quick cutting gesture toward Alderflower. "Leave us," he said. "You too, Thompson. Jones."

"Sir," Thompson said. "Are you sure you want to be alone with—?"

"I will not repeat myself." The Dentist barely spoke above a whisper, but Thompson and Jones immediately shouldered their weapons and marched back out the double doors. Alderflower had already disappeared into the gloom behind the Dentist's chair.

The doors slammed shut. The Dentist sat, leaning back with his wide hands on the arms of his massive chair. He studied them without blinking.

"I'm the one who spoke to your ship," he said after a moment. "I have to protect my people from outside influences. The Elders manage the short-range radio at the dam, but I'm the only one with access to the satellite network."

Esther frowned. Neal had been talking to the Big Man, the Dentist, all along?

"You'll know about our database of survivors then," David said without missing a beat. "You provided your roster to add to the List?"

Careful, Esther thought. She was suddenly very sure she didn't want the Dentist to know why they were there.

"I'm afraid not. Your man—Neal, is it?—told me about this List. I deemed it too risky to give that sort of information to strangers. Unfortunately, at the time one of my followers also had access to the network. They have been duly punished for exposing our community against my wishes."

Esther and her father exchanged glances. Punished how?

"Well, we hope our communities won't remain strangers for long," David said smoothly. "We compiled the List to help build relationships and connections with other survivors. We mean you no harm."

"Hmm . . ." the Dentist said, drawing out the sound like a slowly dying engine. "So you say. What's your endgame?"

"We seek a permanent home," David said. "Our mission is to experience life on land firsthand and to scout out possible locations for our shipmates to settle. Your town is impressive, based on what we've seen so far." David swept his arms wide, seeming to take in both the lodge and the town beyond its walls. "We may even like to join you, if you'll have us."

The Dentist put the tips of his fingers together and tapped them against his chin. "I don't know about that," he said. "I can't have outsiders traipsing through my town at whim. I think it's best if you move along." He waved a hand to dismiss them.

"Sir," Simon said, stepping forward. "It's only a matter of time before the human race recovers enough that we can't remain in isolated pockets. The outside world will find you eventually. Don't you want to have greater numbers when that happens? Your community is small still. We could add to it, if our people agree. It could be a mutually beneficial arrangement."

"Simon, is it?" The Dentist frowned, looking him up and down. If Esther wasn't imagining things, he spent an extra second on the bright scarf Simon had received from Emilio's people. "What do you propose?"

"Let us stay with you," Simon said. "Not for long, but if you could offer your hospitality to our small crew for a week or two, we'd be most grateful. You could assess whether or not we would be a good fit for your community during that time."

The Dentist considered this. He studied David and Simon in turn, not bothering to look at Esther and Cody standing behind them. Finally, he leaned forward, unblinking.

"Well, which one is it? One week or two?"

"Ten days," David said immediately. "Will you allow us to stay ten days?"

"This isn't a charity, and I didn't invite you here," the Dentist said. "If you stay and use up our resources, I'll expect compensation."

"Of course," David said. "We'll work for our keep."

"I'm afraid that's not enough."

"We also have a smaller team making an overland expedition," Simon said. "They'll report back to us—and to you—on their findings. They could warn you of potential threats beyond your borders."

"Hmm . . . Promises are cheap," the Dentist said, but he had perked up at the offer of information. He looked between the two men. "What else can you give me?"

David glanced over at Esther. "We can offer expert assistance with the biofuel generator tech. You received the plans through the satellite network, correct? The system is truly revolutionary, and it allows unprecedented mobility."

"Mobility." The Dentist frowned, and his golden eyes cut sideways toward the shadows where Alderflower had disappeared.

"Yes, sir," David said. "Esther here is the inventor, and she'd be happy to get your system up and running in exchange for your hospitality. She could even modify your vehicles to make use of the biofuel if needed."

The Dentist pursed his lips and looked at Esther for the first time. She met his gaze. She hoped the Dentist would believe she really could do it. Some mechanics were skeptical of her abilities because of how young she looked. She tried to stand a little taller. The Dentist's eyes cut toward the shadows again.

"I don't trust this supposed miracle generator," he said after a while. "We live simple lives, powered by the Lake. Our divine mandate is to rely on the Lake for everything, including energy. We are God-fearing folk here. We don't need false idols."

Esther blinked. She wasn't sure how her generator constituted an idol. David looked surprised too, but he recovered quickly.

"We'd like to learn more about this divine mandate and your way of life. Will you allow us to work beside you and share our overland team's findings in exchange for a place to stay for a few days?"

"If I allow you to stay, I'm going to establish some rules." The Dentist folded his arms over his broad chest, tapping his foot on the dais. "I won't entertain the idea of you staying if you won't adhere to them. Is that clear?"

"Of course," David said. "We don't want to be disruptive."

The Dentist didn't return David's placating smile.

"First of all," he said, "I am the divinely appointed guardian of this town. I commune directly with the Lord. It's my duty to protect my people, and I will not tolerate troublemakers. If I say it's time for you to go, I will brook no argument."

"Understood," David said.

"Second," the Dentist continued, "we abide by a strict moral code. I expect your people to follow the laws of the town. I will hold you to the same high standard as my own people."

"How will we know what the laws are?" Esther asked.

The Dentist looked down at her and raised an eyebrow. "One rule is that women are not permitted to speak in public meetings unless they are ordained in the faith. You'd do well to remember that."

"Why aren't—?"

"Women are to be protected and sheltered," the Dentist interrupted, "so they can fulfill their divine roles."

Esther coughed so hard her father had to pat her on the back. It had never occurred to her that someone would make rules that differentiated between men and women. It made no sense.

"My daughter raises a good point," Simon said. "Will we have someone to instruct us in the ways of your people?"

"I'll assign you an Elder. He will tell you everything you need to know about our Code. The third and final rule is that I will not have you enticing my people away. If you try to seduce my followers with outsiders' ways and cause them to doubt the Lord's instructions for their lives, I'll expel you from the town faster than you can say Aguamilpa. Is that understood?"

"Yes, sir," David said. "We look forward to learning from the Elder and working alongside your people. May we use your radio or satellite phone to invite our crew up from the river?"

The Dentist shook his head and stood, looming above them once again.

"We have an important feast tonight," he said, "and we're not prepared for a large group of visitors. You four may stay, but your people will have to come over in the morning."

"Fair enough," David said.

"And one more thing. Do not mention the satellite network again."

"Why—?" Esther began.

"My people don't need to speak with the outside world. Let's not tempt them."

"It'll be our little secret," David said.

The Dentist narrowed his golden eyes, as if he wasn't sure whether or not David was mocking him. Then he clapped his hands sharply.

"I must prepare for the feast. Alderflower will show you out."

The ethereal old woman reemerged and glided toward them. The Dentist watched, unmoving, as his acolyte herded them back up the aisle.

Soon they were stepping back out onto the wide porch at the front of the lodge.

"Was he serious about women not being allowed to speak in public?" Esther asked, turning to Alderflower. "And what counts as a public meeting?"

"Please wait here," the old woman said, ignoring Esther's questions. "Your Elder will be with you shortly." She closed the door, leaving them alone on the porch.

Esther stared after her. What was wrong with these people?

"It's interesting that a patriarchal society has developed so quickly here," Simon said.

"'Interesting' isn't the word I'd use," Esther said darkly.

"You'll need to be extra careful, Esther," Simon said.

"You say that like you expect me to be belligerent toward an authority figure," Esther said. "When have I ever done that?"

Her father gave her a wry smile, doubtless thinking of her thorny relationship with Judith. "Just try not to attract too much attention."

"That man has a choke hold on this town," David said quietly. He brought a finger to his lips and nodded toward Thompson and Jones, waiting at the bottom of the porch steps, shotguns in hand. "You can't cross him, Esther."

"Looks like I won't have a chance."

Esther wanted to find her sister and get out of here as soon as possible. There had been something creepy about how the Dentist talked about the Lord and his duty. There was no sign of the honest religious devotion Esther was used to from Penelope Newton. Even the people in Ixcuintla had seemed genuinely fervent. The Dentist was more like David had been when he spoke for the *Galaxy* captains. He used the words, but she wasn't sure he believed what he was saying.

Despite his impressive presence and resonant voice, Esther had decided she didn't like this Dentist one bit.

20. Lake Town

THEIR ELDER GUIDE TURNED out to be Bole. He met them at the porch after about ten minutes—during which Thompson and Jones scowled and refused to answer their questions—and told them he'd be taking them on a tour of the town. Thompson gave them one final stony glance and loped off, Jones following close on his heels.

"The Dentist called me back on the radio," Bole said. "Gave me a stern talking-to about telling you the rules. He must have thought ya'll are troublemakers."

"It sounds like his rules are really strict," Esther said. "Or am I not allowed to talk to you because I'm a woman?"

Bole laughed. "He's particular about public meetings, but the women run things in the church. Any woman who really wants a say becomes a Shepherd.

You can look into it if you decide to stay. I hear I'm giving you the full tour in case you want to join us."

"We're exploring our options," Simon said.

"Let's get to it then!"

Bole led them down the steps and sauntered into the town, his shotgun still slung across his back. They returned to the crossroads they had passed on their way to meet the Dentist and took the fork leading away from the lake. They walked up a street lined with cabins. Some of the porches were bigger than entire staterooms on the *Catalina*. There was a healthy bustle in the street as people of all ages went about their business.

"Everyone'll be hard at work right now," Bole said. "We farm, fish, and hunt for sustenance. It ain't a bad life."

Esther watched for anyone who looked like her sister as they saw more and more townspeople. The sooner they could find her and return to the *Lucinda*, the better. But Esther had begun to doubt whether she would actually recognize Naomi after all. Every once in a while she'd spot a familiar feature—hair color or skin tone—but none of the faces quite matched up to the image in her mind. She started to feel a bit frantic, like she was trying to hold on to handfuls of water in a dream. What if Naomi was passing her right now and neither of them realized it? These people showed signs of hardship: pinched features, premature wrinkles, scars. There was a good chance Naomi now looked nothing like Esther had imagined she would at twenty-five. As more strangers strode past them, more unknown faces, uncertainty spread tendrils through her mind.

The women wore skirts in earthy tones, as if their clothes were woven from plants or roots in addition to wool. Many had long hair twisted into elaborate plaits. They carried woven baskets full of vegetables or held little children, also wearing handmade clothing. Judging from these garments, the townspeople made most things rather than salvaging and refurbishing as they did at sea. That must be easier on land, where you could actually grow plants and raise animals. The men wore a mixture of the same rough materials and camouflage prints, and nearly all had beards. One had a rifle slung over one shoulder and a dead animal over the other. He slowed to stare at the Lucindans but didn't approach them.

A few people greeted Bole with waves and smiles, but no one spoke directly to the newcomers.

"Folks are real friendly when you get to know 'em," Bole said. "I reckon you'll be best friends by supper time."

"Do you get many strangers here?" Esther asked.

"Oh, now and then," Bole said. "The Dentist says we gotta be careful. My thinking is there are enough of us now that no one would bother doing us harm."

"So the community has grown over time?" David asked.

"Yeah, we get joiners. People hear about our Lake of Plenty, you know? If they commit to serving the Dentist and God's Lake, we welcome 'em with open arms."

A woman wearing the same white garb they'd seen on Alderflower glided by without so much as a glance.

"What are the church's core beliefs?" Simon asked as the Shepherd made her way toward the lodge with the cross on top.

"The Dentist teaches that the Lord came to him in a dream and told him about the Promised Lake," Bole said. "The Lord still speaks to him sometimes and gave him the Code a few years back. He says anyone who follows the Code perfectly will be able to hear the Lord's voice too eventually."

"The Code?"

"It's an addition to the Bible, like a Third Testament," Bole said. "You ever read the Bible?"

"I have," Simon said. "But it has been many years. Is there any chance I could read a copy of this Third Testament?"

"Sure thing," Bole said. "We've got printouts. We only made a few before the last ink cartridges ran out, though. The Shepherds are making additional copies by hand, but that takes time. You'll have to go back to the Lodge if you want to read one."

"I'd like that very much."

"Oh, this whole row of cabins is new, by the way." Bole waved at the side of the street, where simple structures smelling of sharp pine dotted the landscape. "The original buildings are closer to the lake."

The road bent around to the left, meandering among the new cabins. A woman carrying a sleeping baby came out onto one of the newer porches to watch them pass. Her hair was far too light for her to be Naomi. At least, Esther thought so. Who knew how much a person could change in seventeen years?

Esther forced herself to stay calm. Despite Emilio's warnings, the Dentist had given no indication that he would hurt them. She had time to search amongst the townspeople. She had to be patient and she'd find her sister eventually. And she definitely had to stay out of trouble.

"So, about these rules," Esther said, striding beside Bole. "Besides no speaking in public for women, what else do we need to know?"

"You said you're not married, so you can't stay in the same room as a man," Bole said. "We'll find you a place in the single-women's dormitory. Beyond that, there's no stealing, lying, saying anything bad about the Dentist and the Shepherds, disobeying an Elder, breaking curfew, dressing immodestly, hoarding resources, or throwing nonorganic trash in the lake. The lake is the only thing more sacred than the Dentist's word."

"Most of that stuff sounds reasonable," Esther said, "but I have to stay with my crew."

"Sorry, Esther, the Dentist won't compromise on that one," Bole said. "Also, if you come in contact with the locals, you shouldn't speak to them. The Dentist doesn't like it."

"The locals?" Simon said.

"Yeah, there were a handful of Mexicans living in these parts when we arrived. This camp was abandoned, so it's not like we kicked them out, mind, but we've had run-ins over the years."

Esther exchanged glances with Cody, thinking of Emilio, Isadora, and the others.

"What happens if we talk to them?" Cody asked.

"Just don't. They don't speak English anyway, and the Dentist says it's not good for us to intermix."

"He really doesn't like outsiders, does he? Unless they want to adopt his ways."

"Nope." Bole pulled his ponytail loose from where it had become entangled in his rifle strap again. "But you really shouldn't say anything against him. It won't go down well."

They reached the end of the road. A huge, mostly flat area had been cleared of trees and planted with various crops. People were at work in the fields, baskets overflowing with leafy stalks on their backs.

"These are the main community gardens," Bole said, "and that's the smokehouse for anything the hunters bring in that we can't use right away." He pointed to a building at one end of the field, just at the tree line. Smoke emanated from beneath the eaves. "They've been working double time for the roast tonight. The pig and goat farms are on the other side of town."

"What's the occasion?" David asked.

"It's Lake Day, our biggest festival. We're celebrating the anniversary of our arrival here. There will be tons of food and a big 'ol bonfire. Always a good time."

"The Dentist didn't want us to bring more people in from our ship," David said. "Do you think he'd reconsider?"

"Not if he said no once," Bole said. "The Dentist doesn't change his mind much. There will be plenty of time to show them around. Hey, do you guys want to hit the baths before the feast? No offense, but you two kinda smell like the compost bin."

Esther looked down at the green film still coating her skin in places. The mud on her trousers had mostly dried, and it was flaking off like fish scales.

"Definitely. Any chance I could borrow a change of clothes too?"

"No problem," Bole said. "You're about the same build as my sister, only shorter. I'll see if she's got something you can borrow. She lives in the single-women's dorm, so you'll meet her eventually anyway. She'll be at work in the hatchery right now. Follow me."

They turned down a pathway heading back through the town toward the lake. Smaller paths meandered off the main road, some leading to more cabins and others to patches of cultivated ground. One patch seemed to have nothing but grass planted on it.

"That's the soccer pitch," Bole said. "You play?" he asked David.

"It's been a while."

"Might have to challenge you to a match." Bole grinned.

"My siblings and I used to play on the cargo ship," Cody said. "Whoever let the ball get away from them was in for a cold swim." He looked wistfully at the soccer pitch.

"I want you on my team then," Bole said.

They continued along the far edge of the sprawling town. Esther was amazed at how much space there was between all the buildings. It was difficult to tell how many people the town actually supported, because they weren't stacked on top of each other.

They reached a long, low structure with a thatched roof and sides mostly open to the air. A porous wire netting enclosed it. At the far end of the structure was a small log house with narrow, high windows. It made Esther think of an upside-down houseboat, with a roof instead of a hull attached to the cabin.

Rustling and squawking sounds came from the structure. As they neared, they could see that the open part under the roof was divided into smaller squares, all enclosed in wire netting. A narrow path cut between them to the small log house. Each square housed several black-and-white birds.

"Chickens!" Simon exclaimed. "You're raising poultry. What a sight for sore eyes that is."

"This is one of the first structures we built here," Bole said proudly. "The camp was basically a rustic resort for dudes on fishing trips. We found some supplies, but we knew we'd need to figure out how to be self-sustaining. We captured some wild chickens, and we've been breeding them ever since."

Esther leaned close to the nearest cage. The creatures inside regarded her with beady black eyes. The eyes were sharper and more intelligent than that of a fish, and they looked mean. The birds weren't much like the cartoonish chickens she had seen in books and pictures on the *Catalina*. She had never seen a real chicken, as far as she could recall, back when they lived on land. These ones were scrawny rather than plump, with ratty feathers and sharp talons. They pecked at the ground and at each other in an aggressive fashion.

"Do they produce eggs regularly?" Simon asked.

"More or less like clockwork," Bole said. "We can ask my sister. Hang tight for a second."

Bole left them by the edge of the chicken habitat and disappeared into the little house.

Simon crouched down. "I've been wondering whether the disaster would have disrupted the re-production cycles of any surviving creatures," he said. "I'm sure there must have been extinctions, but this is wonderful!" He reached out to touch one of the chickens. It snapped its sharp beak at him. Simon just laughed; Esther stepped back until she was out in the sunshine again.

"We've been at sea a long time, Simon," David said. "The land seems to have recovered a lot more than I thought it would."

"Yes." Simon studied the chickens. "It certainly has."

Bole returned from the log house, followed by a young woman with long black hair tied in a braid over her shoulder. She wore a rough-spun skirt decorated at the hem with a multitude of embroidered flowers. The sleeves of her blouse were rolled back, and in her hands she carried a tiny yellow bird.

"This is my sister, Yvonne," Bole said. "Yve, this is Esther. She's the one who needs the clothes. And this is her father, Simon, and Cody and David."

"Nice to meet you," Yvonne said. She had a high, soft voice, and there was something birdlike about her. She held out her cupped hands. "Adam said you were interested in the chicks. I thought you might like to meet one."

The little bird twisted its tiny, fluffy head back and forth to look at the people gathered around it. Simon stepped forward, and Yvonne tipped the little creature into his outstretched hands. It looked up at him and then pecked at his finger with its sharp little beak.

Esther gasped, but Simon didn't flinch. He brought the creature up to his eyes and began to coo nonsensical sounds to it.

"This one hatched last week," Yvonne said. "I think he's kinda sweet." She bent over Simon's hands and stroked the bird's fluffy, delicate head.

"Do you want to hold it, Esther?" Simon asked, turning toward her.

"No!" Esther said, then blushed when everyone looked at her. "I mean, I don't think so."

"It'll be fine. Here."

Before Esther could stop him, her father took her right hand and plopped the little bird into it. The creature was warm and soft, except for the tiny scratching of its feet against her palm. Esther stood frozen with her left hand beneath her right in case it fell. The feathers tickled her hand as the little bird shifted around to look up at her. It didn't look as mean as the others, but those eyes were definitely too sharp for its own good.

"Please take it back," Esther said.

David laughed and held out his hands for the little bird.

"Esther," he said, "I've seen you fight pirates, battle storms, and confront men three times your size armed only with a wrench, but I've never seen you look so scared."

"I didn't want to drop it," Esther mumbled, wiping her fingers on her grimy trousers. That bird definitely looked like it was up to something.

She watched the other chickens pecking around in their cages while Simon asked Yvonne about feed and hatching ratios. She explained the hatchery operations in her trilling voice. She looked impressed at how much Simon seemed to know about chickens. Esther was always surprised at her father's random knowledge. He had been a college professor before the disaster, and he still read every book he could find.

"Why is it yellow?" Cody asked. He stroked the bird's head and smiled shyly at Yvonne.

"They're yellow when they're born, but they lose their soft baby feathers as they mature. This one will be black and white like the others within a few months. He won't be quite so cute then." She smiled at the little bird.

Esther cleared her throat. "So, Bole said you might be able to lend me some clothes."

"Oh yes. Let me put this little guy back, and I'll grab some things for you. I'm nearly done for the day anyway." Yvonne took the chick back from David. "Why don't you all head down to the bathhouses, and I'll meet you there?" She walked back into the hatchery with the chick.

"Great," Esther said, retreating further from the full-grown chickens in their wire enclosures. "Come on, guys, let's get moving." She spun to head down the path and as far away from the creepy rustling of the chicken house as she could get.

Bole cleared his throat loudly. "The bathhouses are the other way, Esther."

21. Bathhouse

THE BATHHOUSES SAT RIGHT on the shore of the lake. The sun sinking lower over the trees left long shadows across the water. A few boats still floated on the indigo surface, fishing poles spiking out of their sides.

The two identical structures were made of wood like the rest of the town, but with raised roofs. Faint wisps of steam drifted through the gap between the tops of the walls and the eaves. A large mill wheel turned in the gentle current of a small tributary running into the lake. Smoke rose from an enclosed structure between the two bathhouses, and a series of pipes wound in and out of each building.

"This is hands down the best part of the town," Bole said. "We still have running water in some of the original cabins, but we have to filter it in case of contamination. It's wasteful to run the showers, so we set up the bathhouses by the lake. Everyone uses them."

"How does it work?" Esther asked, examining the pipes. She carefully brought her hand close to one to test the temperature. It was much hotter than she expected.

"The flow of the stream powers the wheel, which heats the coils inside the pipes. The water coming into the pipes from the stream gets heated up and then distributed into the two bathhouses. There's a constant supply of freshwater coming through, so it's always clean. And, more importantly, it's always warm!"

"This is a neat setup. Nice and simple," Esther said. "Any chance I could see the original building plans?"

"Yeah, maybe," Bole said.

"All I care about right now is a hot bath," David said.

"Well, help yourself," Bole said. "There's a supply of towels on a shelf inside. I'll grab something for you to wear while your scrub is being cleaned."

"May I come with you?" Simon said. "I don't think I need a bath just yet."

"Sure thing. I'll show you where you'll be staying. Esther, Yve will be here soon, so you can go ahead. That one's the women's bathhouse."

Bole, Simon, and Cody headed back toward the village. David grinned at Esther. "See you on the other side?"

"Can't wait," Esther said.

She pulled open the flimsy door of the women's bathhouse. It was warm and muggy inside. A screen made of reeds separated the entrance from the rest of the bathhouse. A wooden bench sat just beside the door, and there was a tall shelving unit stocked with rough-spun towels in the far corner.

"Hello?" Esther said. "Is anyone in here?"

No answer. She peeked around the screen. The inner part of the bathhouse contained a large rock pool with benches along the edge. The water bubbled slightly, and a layer of steam rose from the surface. Sweat immediately sprung out on Esther's forehead. The room was empty, but there was space for quite a few people.

Esther retreated to the outer area again and sat down on the bench to ease off her boots. She hid her knife in the toe and set them beside the door, checking to make sure it was firmly shut, and peeled off the rest of her clothes. Her trousers were molting like a day-old fish carcass. She grabbed a towel from the shelf and found cakes of hard, gray soap and curved wood implements shaped like tail fins. She took one of each and brought them with her to the inner part of the bathhouse.

She set the supplies at the edge of the rock pool, removed her towel, and stepped into the bath. The water was very hot. She sank into it slowly, the steam rising around her face. She lowered herself down to sit on the floor, the rocky surface rough on her bare legs. Sweat soon dripped from her hair and ran down her neck.

A slight current in the water pulled the dirt from her body and washed it away. She crawled through the pool to examine the apparatus and found only a single pipe leading into it and single hole draining out of it. The flow was constant, though, and it felt amazing on her skin. Maybe they should think about staying here after all! She leaned back and floated beneath the surface. The heat worked wonders on her muscles, soaking into them and releasing the tension that was a near-constant presence in her body. She dipped her head back and allowed the water to swallow her ears with a gentle roaring sound.

Esther hadn't taken a real bath in nearly seventeen years. She remembered how she used to fill the tub with bubbles and give herself a beard and a bubbly white hat. She'd spend hours in the bath, soaking until the water grew tepid or the bubbles dissipated. She'd had a little collection of bath toys, she remembered, two boats and a rubber fish with a hole in its belly that she could squeeze water in and out of. She remembered how her sister would stick her head in the bathroom and tell her to hurry up because it was her turn already. Esther would sink down until the bubbles surrounded her face like a lion's mane and pretend she couldn't hear Naomi. She was remembering more of her sister every day, peeling back the layers of memory.

"There you are!" said a voice directly above her.

Esther bolted upright, banging her elbow against the edge of the rock pool. Yvonne had appeared in the bathhouse. She was stark naked, with one hand on her hip and the other around a towel.

"I got you some clothes. I want to bathe for the feast tonight before the crowds arrive."

Esther retreated to the far corner of the pool, right by the hot input pipe. What did Yvonne mean by crowds? She curled into a ball to cover herself a little bit. Yvonne didn't seem to notice. She set her towel down, bending over the bench. Esther averted her eyes.

"So, what do you think?" Yvonne asked.

"About what?"

"The bathhouse, of course. Have you ever seen one like it?"

"No, this is a first," Esther said. "It's shared, I see."

"Of course," Yvonne said. She unwound her braid and shook out her long, dark hair. "The Code is very strict about modesty, but it's not the same in the bathhouses. Relax."

Esther stayed where she was as the other woman joined her in the water. Yvonne sighed and leaned back, her hair spreading out around her body.

"Ahh, that's so nice after a long day of work."

"I guess." Esther studied her own knees, which still bore a stubborn film of green.

"My goodness you're tense," Yvonne said. "You haven't even really started, have you?"

"I'll be quick." Esther spotted her soap, far enough away that she'd have to stand up to get it.

Yvonne noticed her discomfort and giggled.

"Here," she said kindly, retrieving the soap and the curved wooden instrument. "You ever used one of these before? You scrape your skin with it. Gets the dirt off a lot faster, especially once you've worked up a sweat. I can help you."

"That's okay," Esther said quickly. She reached for the soap and the piece of wood. Yvonne had one too and she demonstrated how to scrape it along her arm after lathering up with the grayish soap.

It was a little awkward, but as Esther sloughed away the grime from her trip into the muddy bank of the river, she felt much better. Soon her skin had returned to its normal color. The swift current through the bath drew most of the soap and dirt away immediately, leaving the water clear.

Yvonne chatted about the town as they bathed, telling Esther what seemed like a year's worth of gossip about people she had never met. Esther listened carefully for any mention of her sister.

"So, who was the tall blond with you?" Yvonne asked after a long story about some girl making eyes at some guy at the last soccer game. "He's kind of dreamy."

"That's David. He's . . . my boyfriend I guess you'd say."

"Really? Are you going to get married?" Yvonne perked up, leaning forward through the layer of bubbles swirling around the surface of the bath.

"I don't know," Esther said.

"Have you ever—you know?"

"What?"

"You know . . . kissed?" Yvonne dropped her gaze and blushed, which was surprising coming from a woman who had no problem standing naked in front of a stranger.

"Well, yeah, of course. We've been together for a few months."

"Together . . . as in *sleeping* together?" Yvonne's eyes were suddenly as round as a fish's.

Esther nodded, starting to wish she hadn't said anything.

Yvonne gasped. "Don't let anyone hear about that, Esther. You're not married!"

"What's the big deal? We're adults."

"But that's one of the worst things you can do under the Code," Yvonne whispered. "We have to save ourselves for our husbands. It's God's will for our protection. You'd better marry him soon."

"But I'm not from here," Esther said. "I don't live by your Code."

Yvonne sucked air between her teeth and looked furtively around the bathhouse. She leaned closer, her breasts dangling in the water.

"You need to be careful if you decide to stay here, Esther. I mean, I won't judge you, but don't let people hear you talking about your fornications."

"But—"

"I'm serious. People found out about my friend meeting a man in secret and now she's locked up."

"What?"

"If you break the Code, you could be—"

Suddenly voices exploded in the entryway. It sounded like an entire engine crew had decided to come in for a bath all at once. Their laughter echoed around the bathhouse.

"Yvonne, what's the punishment for breaking the Code?" Esther asked, her stomach lurching.

Yvonne shook her head. "I shouldn't have said anything."

The babble of voices grew louder, and a few women came around the corner of the partition, towels in hand.

"What's your friend's name, Yvonne?" Esther said quickly. The chances were vanishingly slim, but she had to be sure.

Yvonne shook her head and whispered, "Just be careful."

Then more women were flouncing around the edge of the partition and hopping into the pool, all their nakedness on display. Esther scanned their faces as quickly as possible. Why had she been so certain she would recognize her sister when she left the *Catalina*? It had been so long. Were any of these women even the right age to be Naomi? At least one among them could be around twenty-five, but her hair was golden and straight. She stopped dead when she noticed Esther.

"I told you there were strangers here!" She grabbed the arm of the older woman next to her. "Didn't I tell you, Sue Ellen?"

"This is Esther," Yvonne said. She shot Esther a warning look, as if she expected her to start shouting about her immoral behavior. "She came up the river on a ship."

"Didn't I tell you there was a ship?" The golden-haired woman shook her friend's arm hard. "My Johnny went out to meet it."

"Okay, okay. Hold your goats, Jemima," the older woman said.

Then all the women started talking over each other, their rapid-fire voices drowning out the sound of running water. Esther scrutinized their faces, tried to catch familiar tones of voice, but the chatter threatened to overwhelm her.

"Where did they come from?"

"Is there really a ship?"

"It's been a while since there were strangers in town."

"It's only been two years."

"No way!"

"Three at least."

Esther should have realized there would be multiple people in the town who could easily be her sister. She picked apart their appearances, eliminating possibilities one by one. That woman was too old. That one too young. Two were black. She didn't *think* any of the others were Naomi, but how would she know her for sure?

The golden-haired woman jutted out her lip. "Two, because Johnny and I have been here for three, but Thompson and them—"

"You've been here for three years, Jemima, or I'll eat my gardening gloves."

"Two. I think I'd know."

"How many people are with you?" demanded a woman with smooth, dark skin and tight braids cascading around her face.

"I heard four," said Jemima.

"No, definitely five."

"Four!"

"There are four of them," Yvonne said. "The others are men."

"You're just in time for Lake Day!" Jemima said. "The whole town will be there!"

Sue Ellen waved a piece of soap at her with a tanned hand. "Are you thinking about joining us?"

All the women stopped talking at once, staring at Esther like she was a fish in a bowl. Caught off guard, she answered quickly, explaining that they were traveling in search of a new home on land, and then she dipped beneath the surface of the pool to rinse the soap out of her hair. The water in her ears blurred their voices for a moment. She'd have to be careful. People lived differently on land, and she needed to show them she was thinking about adhering to their way of life.

Esther climbed out of the rock pool, grabbed the rough towel, and made an excuse about having to meet her friends. She retreated to the entryway and sat on the outer bench, shivering in the sudden cool of the air. She would find her sister at the feast that night. The whole town would be there. She would know her when she saw her. She'd have to.

Yvonne soon joined her and gave her a dark-blue blouse and a heavy brown skirt embroidered with pale-blue flowers, like the one she had been wearing earlier. She also handed her a pair of soft shoes made of some sort of animal skin. She refused to answer any more of Esther's questions, nodding significantly at the partition and the group of women behind it.

"We'll talk later," she said.

The men were nowhere to be seen outside, but the village bustled with people getting ready for the feast. Yvonne showed Esther where to leave her dirty clothes in a large woven basket near the lake. Washboards sat beside it, drying in the late-afternoon sun.

"No one could think those belong to anyone in the town. You'll get them back," Yvonne assured Esther as she dumped her mud-stained clothes. She kept her boots and tool belt.

Yvonne brought Esther to the single-women's dormitory, pointing out a spreading tree beside it so she'd be able to find it again. Names and hearts were carved all over the tree trunk. Esther spotted the initial N inside one of the hearts, but that could be anyone, of course.

Inside the dormitory a dozen women were busy getting ready for the festival. Yvonne fired off names too quickly for Esther to catch. Most seemed to be in their early- to midtwenties. Esther searched their faces and watched for signs of recognition, feeling overwhelmed. None of them looked close enough to the image she had in her head, but wouldn't Naomi live here if she was in the town? Unless she was married already. That was a strange thought.

Some of the women wore trousers when they came in, but all changed into full skirts covered in embroidery as they prepared for the evening. They combed and braided each other's hair and coated their eyes and lips in homemade kohl and rouge.

"Let me do you," Yvonne said.

While she worked at Esther's face with a thick charcoal pencil, another young woman attacked her hair with a comb and twisted it into a short, painful braid across the top of her head. Her bangs fell out of it immediately, so the woman brushed them to the side and stuck a pin into the braid to hold it, making her wince. Yvonne tried to apply some sort of paste made out of berries to Esther's lips, but she pushed her hand away. No need to go overboard.

While Esther put up with these ministrations, she studied the dormitory. It had bunk beds and space for twenty, though only twelve of the bunks looked occupied. These were decorated with drawings and covered with handmade quilts and embroidered pillows. Evidence of "land life" popped up here and there: potted flowers, bundles of sweet-smelling herbs, things carved out of wood. Esther had never seen so much wood in her entire life.

"Hey, ship girl!"

"Huh?"

The girl who had fixed Esther's hair, whose name was Betsy, tapped her on the shoulder.

"You live on a cruise ship, right?"

"Yeah, I've been there ever since the eruption."

"What's it like being on a ship all the time?" Betsy asked. She had a round, ruddy face, and she'd applied a liberal layer of rouge to her cheeks. She was twisting her own hair, long and thick like seaweed, into an elaborate plait. "Isn't it cramped?"

"Well, it's all self-contained, so you can't really get very far away from anyone," Esther said. "You guys are so spread out here. You must always be walking.

But the sea is wide open, at least. And it's what has kept us alive all this time, just like your lake."

"Did you only eat fish?" Betsy looped the finished braid on top of her head and began sticking more pins into it. One snapped, and she tossed it aside. Esther picked it up and saw that it was brittle and covered in rust. "We eat fish from the lake too, but at least we have some variety. What about vegetables? What do you do for vitamins?"

"We eat a lot of seaweed," Esther said. "It's quite nutritious."

"You're pretty short, though." Betsy turned toward her and put her hands on her hips. "Is that because you only eat seaweed and fish?"

"I don't know."

"You're even shorter than Na— "

"Betsy!" Yvonne said shrilly. Her hand slipped, and the red paste she'd been applying to her lips smeared like blood on her chin.

"Oh right. Gotta go. Talk to you later, ship girl." Betsy flounced off to the other side of the dormitory, but Esther had heard enough. She grabbed Yvonne by the arm and led her firmly to the cabin door. A few of the women looked up as they passed, but Yvonne didn't protest.

Outside on the porch, Esther turned to face Yvonne. "Naomi Harris," she said.

Yvonne's face twitched. It was enough.

"You have a friend named Naomi, right?" Esther said. Her skin buzzed like she'd been shocked with electricity. Dread and hope mingled in her chest. "She's not the one who got locked up, is she?"

"I can't talk about—"

"Answer me."

Yvonne looked around fearfully, but no one passing by the dormitory on the path paid them any attention. She bit her lip. "Yes, okay. We're forbidden to talk about Codebreakers. Please don't tell anyone."

"Naomi is a Codebreaker?"

Yvonne nodded, looking like she might cry. "How do you know about her?"

"What does she look like? Tell me that first."

Yvonne twisted her hands deep in the folds of her skirt.

"She's short, and she has dark, curly hair. Her nose has a bit of a hook and, well, Esther, she looks a little like you and your father."

Esther squeezed her eyes shut. It *was* her. She knew it had to be her.

"Is that why you're here?" Yvonne asked.

"She's my sister. We're here to get her. How long before she's let out of lockup or whatever?"

"She's not . . . she's going to be . . ." Yvonne gave a little sob and she clutched Esther's arm. "You have to take me with you."

"What? No, we can't—"

"If they find out I told you anything, I'll be in serious trouble."

"You don't want to live at sea, Yvonne."

"No, but I don't want to . . . If you get her out, you have to take me away with you before the Dentist finds out." Yvonne's grip tightened like a sailor's knot.

"Wait, calm down." Esther tried to pry Yvonne's fingers open. "What will the Dentist do?"

Yvonne bit her lip, eyes wide. "I can't talk about this."

"Look, we'll work something out," Esther said. A horrible possibility was beginning to dawn on her. She couldn't bring herself to voice it. "Are you saying Naomi won't be let out? Where is she being kept?"

"You can't, Esther," Yvonne whispered. "There will be guards. Someone will get hurt."

"Rust. Just tell me—"

The dormitory doors burst open. Then the women were spilling out of the doors, chattering, laughing, surrounding them like a flood. Betsy looped her arm in Esther's and dragged her down off the porch. Yvonne joined the crowd, eyes wide, but she made no effort to get any closer to Esther.

Betsy prattled about the feast as she pulled Esther along with the other women. Esther tried to stay calm, but the top of her head felt like it was floating up toward the trees. She didn't think

Yvonne would say anything about what they were up to. She'd gather the others and make a plan. They had to find out where the Codebreakers were kept and exactly what sort of sentence the Dentist had in mind for Naomi's indiscretion. There was work to do.

Even so, Esther had to fight to stay anchored to the ground. It had been confirmed: her sister was alive.

22. Lake Day

THE GROUP OF WOMEN traipsed down to the waterfront, not too far from the dam. The shore had been entirely cleared of trees here, and long tables covered a sparse grass lawn. A huge pile of wood stood at the water's edge, casting shadows in the fading light. A large platform had been set up nearby with a wooden podium on top.

Esther stopped at the end of an aisle between the picnic tables and scanned the crowd for Naomi in case she was already out of lockup. People streamed from the town, laughing and greeting each other as they found seats at the long tables. Esther estimated nearly four hundred townspeople had gathered by the lake already, with more coming. She watched hopefully for anyone who looked like her sister. Yvonne couldn't have meant Naomi would never be released. Or worse . . .

"Esther, over here!"

David rose from a table near the aisle and waved her over. He wore rough handmade clothes like the townspeople. He still stood out, though. His straight posture and the way he carried himself distinguished him from the men of the town, who were all a little bent from hard labor.

"Who is *that*?" Betsy asked, staring at David appreciatively.

"They're together," Yvonne said, reappearing on Betsy's other side. She peered at Esther like a frightened goby fish.

Betsy's mouth twisted in a frown. "The good ones are always taken."

"His name's David," Esther said. "Thanks for the clothes, Yvonne. I'd better join my friends."

"We'll see you tonight," Yvonne said. Then she added shrilly, "Don't forget you're staying with us!"

"Got it. See ya."

Esther finally extracted her arm from Betsy's grasp and left the other women behind. She sat on the bench between David and her father. Cody leaned over the table to listen in.

"Good news," Esther said in a low voice. "It's definitely our Naomi. I hear she looks just like us."

Simon reached forward to grip her hand. He started to say something but stopped and squeezed her hand harder instead.

Cody pumped his fist, keeping it low so as not to draw attention to them. "Right on, Esther!"

"I'm impressed as always," David said. "We haven't been able to get Bole to tell us anything useful."

"I got the truth out of Yvonne. But there's a problem. Naomi's locked up somewhere for breaking the Code."

"What?"

"I don't know where she's being kept or what they're planning to do with her, but we have to be extra careful not to let anyone else know why we're here."

All the color drained out of Cody's face suddenly. He stared over Esther's shoulder.

"Evening, folks." It was the Dentist.

He stood close behind them and put a hand on David's shoulder, so he couldn't turn around. He was so tall he seemed to block all the light from their little group. Esther silently willed Cody to wipe the guilty expression off his face.

"How are you enjoying your stay in our town so far?" the Dentist said.

"It's very nice," Esther said, carefully polite. She couldn't tell whether or not he'd overheard what she had said a minute ago. "The bathhouses are impressive."

The Dentist didn't even acknowledge her.

"We were particularly impressed with the poultry breeding program," Simon said.

"Ah, glad you could look around those," the Dentist said. "And you?" He patted David on the shoulder familiarly.

"Your facilities are admirable," David said. "Especially the bathhouses." He winked at Esther.

"They are popular," the Dentist said. "Enjoy the feast and let our Elders know if you have any questions about our culture." He nodded at Cody and Simon and took his hand off David's shoulder. He hadn't made eye contact with Esther. She frowned as he moved along the table to greet another group.

"Bole's sister, Yvonne, asked to come with us when we leave with Naomi," Esther said when the Dentist was out of earshot. "She's afraid of what will happen to her if the Dentist finds out she shared information."

"We can't make any promises," David said.

"I agree," Esther said. "But she might help us, so I think we need to keep the option open."

"Fair enough."

"Hey folks." Bole jogged over to their table and leaned in between Esther and David. "What'd I miss?"

"We just had a visit from the Dentist," Simon said.

"Aw, scrub. Hope he doesn't mind me leaving you alone for a second. I'm gonna lose my Elder privileges."

Bole squeezed onto the bench, forcing David to shift down to make room for him.

"How was the bathhouse, Esther?" Bole asked.

"Um, great. Very relaxing."

"You look real pretty. Yve lend you that skirt?"

"Yeah," she said.

"Nice," Bole said, looking her up and down.

"When will the feast get started?" David said stiffly.

"Hold your goats, man," Bole said. "There's plenty of food for everyone. We got the ceremony first."

There was a bang from over near the lake. A dozen men had gathered along the edge of the podium. Thompson and Jones were among them. They fired shotguns over the water—probably blanks—one right after another. Everyone turned in their seats to face them as the echoes reverberated across the lake.

After all the shotguns had been fired, a dozen women wearing matching white robes climbed up to the podium. Alderflower was the oldest of the bunch, and the others ranged from middle age all the way down to a girl who couldn't have been more than sixteen. These must be the Shepherds. They carried huge bunches of flowers in their arms. One by one they tossed their flowers onto the wood pyre beside the podium, then retreated to the back of the stage.

Alderflower stepped forward. "He has promised," she intoned.

The women behind her repeated the words. *"He has promised."*

"He has led."

"He has led."

"He has called us. He has delivered us to the lake. We are saved because of the lake."

The women repeated the words. Another round of shotgun fire roared across the water.

"In the days of darkness," Alderflower continued, "the Dentist heard a voice in a dream. The Lord called the Dentist to lead us to our salvation, to lead us to a lake of plenty, a lake of fish and flower, a lake of sustenance and blessing. And we followed!" Another shotgun blast. "Today we gather to remember the day of our salvation. Ten years ago the Dentist brought us out of our tribulations!"

The crowd stood to cheer. Some drummed on the tables and hollered. As the people applauded, the Dentist walked toward the stage. He had donned a coat embroidered with bold patterns of black and midnight blue. A flash of fire red embellished each shoulder. He looked larger than life, like a king from a storybook.

The cheers grew louder as the Dentist reached the podium. He smiled, pressing his large hands together and bowing toward the crowd. The Shepherds gazed at him with what could only be described as adoration. Esther felt an uncomfortable

sensation in her stomach at the sight like nausea—
or fear.

Finally, the assembly quieted.

"My friends," the Dentist boomed, "thank you for
your support. Thank you for your continuing devotion to the Code. When the Lord spoke to me, he
told me I would find a people more devout than I
could hope. You are that people."

Thunderous applause rose from the townspeople, sending shivers down Esther's spine. This was
just weird.

The Dentist held up his hands, waiting for quiet.

"Today," he said, "we mark the tenth anniversary
of our deliverance. We renew our commitment to
the Code by giving back to the lake. Today we offer
these flowers as a fragrant sacrifice, a representation
of our promise to uphold the Code."

Alderflower waved for the youngest of her aco-
lytes to hand a burning torch to the Dentist. He
held it high over his head, his eyes glimmering in
the light like twin flames. Alderflower said a short
prayer, and then the Dentist tossed the torch onto
the waiting pyre. The wood and sacrificial flowers
went up in a blaze of smoke and applause.

Another woman in white stepped forward and
led the Shepherds in a hymn. Soon the others
joined in, voices rising from the crowd as one.

The Lord has brought us to the lake,

The lake of fish and sun.
The sun will shine upon the lake
And each and everyone.

The Lord has saved us from the ash,
The ash of death and dust.
The dust did fall upon the land
Until the Lord saved us.

The Lord has called a holy man,
A man of strength we trust.
We give our trust to Chosen Man,
Our friend the good Dentist.

Esther coughed into her fist. Bole glanced at her sideways, then went back to singing.

The Dentist gave the holy Code,
A Code to show the path.
The path leads to a righteous life
For each and every one.

The Dentist nodded in thanks as more cheers spread through the crowd. Esther leaned toward Bole.

"What happens to people who break the Code?"

"Small-time reprobates get put in lockup," he said, his breath warm on her face.

"What if they do something really bad?" Esther wasn't sure how bad being caught with a man was for unmarried women here. She was still trying to get a handle on the Lake People's customs.

Bole hesitated. Then he whispered, "We offer grave offenders back to the lake."

"What do you mean?"

"Breaking the Code is real serious, Esther."

"You drown them?"

"It's better than a firing squad. But today it'll just be the ash from the flowers and some of the roast. It's symbolic."

Esther's heart beat like thunder in her chest. She chose her words carefully. "Does everyone agree with executing people like that?"

"Look, the world has changed," Bole said. "What else are we going to do with serious Codebreakers? Allow them to continue eating up all of our resources without contributing anything?"

Simon had been listening in. "Who decides whether the Codebreaking is bad enough for a death sentence?" he asked. He met Esther's eyes, and she could tell he was struggling to keep his voice casual. He, too, must want to grab Bole's collar and wring the information out of him.

"It's up to the Dentist," Bole said. "Last I heard, there were two or three people in for the chop. I'm kinda surprised they didn't have one lined up for tonight. Maybe they didn't think it would make a good impression on ya'll."

The Dentist had moved closer to the bonfire. He was still talking about offerings and the blessings of the lake, but Esther found it hard to focus on his words. He loomed like a big, dark shadow before the fire.

"Doesn't this bother you?" she asked.

"It's a little messed up, I'll grant you that," Bole said, "but what do you expect us to do? Codebreakers put the rest of us in danger. I reckon the Dentist has got it right. And if the Lord wants us to give them to the lake, it don't bother me one bit."

Esther could *almost* see the logic in eliminating people who were a danger to the community rather than allowing them to continue using up resources. But her sister was under the Dentist's thrall. Of course, Naomi couldn't actually be in line for execution, not for so small a crime.

Esther resisted the urge to ask more questions. They couldn't have Bole wondering why she and her father were so interested in Codebreakers.

The Shepherds sang another hymn, and when the last notes faded away, one of the women scooped a container of hot ashes out of the bonfire with a shovel. Remnants of burnt flowers floated away on the breeze.

The Shepherd handed the container to the Dentist. He lifted it over his head for a long moment. The townspeople held their breaths or whispered quiet prayers. Then the Dentist drew back his arm and hurled the ashes into the lake. There was a hiss and a splash. The cheers of the crowd rose over the lake once more.

"May the Lord grant it so," the Dentist said. "Now bring forth the feast!"

23. Feasting and Dancing

MEN WEARING BANDANAS OVER their faces stoked the fire, and others brought out huge slabs of meat, including a whole pig, already partially cooked, which they hung over the bonfire on spits to char the skin. Wood smoke filled the air, drifting over the gathered townspeople and obscuring the stars. The aroma of roasting meat permeated the crowd.

Now that the ceremony was over, the townspeople stood and moved about, talking to friends at other tables while they waited for the food to be ready. The Dentist and his band of Shepherds vacated the stage, finding seats at random among the people.

Cody asked Bole about the meat, and Bole promised to take him on a hunting expedition, saying something about wild pigs and spears. Esther only half listened. She couldn't help searching the crowd for Naomi, just in case. The news of the executions was worrying, but she couldn't imagine Naomi's offense warranted the ultimate punishment. That had to be reserved for murders and the like. But there was no telling what sort of punishment she would receive. If the Dentist learned what they were after, it could jeopardize Naomi's position further. They had to find out where she was being kept—and soon.

The other townspeople began to notice the newcomers, and a few came over, seeking introductions. Bole conducted his role as their keeper or whatever he was with glee, clearly enjoying the attention he got as the Elder in charge of the visitors.

"What did you have to do to become an Elder, Bole?" Simon asked during a lull in the greetings.

"Oh, I'm one of the originals," Bole said. "I traveled to the lake with the Dentist, so I'm automatic. All the men from the first group—thirty-six of us—are Elders. I'm the youngest of the bunch. Any other guy who wants the job has to work up to it. That's why Thompson's got such a chip on his shoulder. He hasn't had a chance to really prove himself since he came to the lake."

"So he didn't arrive with the Dentist?"

"Nope. Thompson's crew were nomads. They figured they'd be better off settling at the lake than scrounging in the wilderness forever. I wonder sometimes if the Dentist doesn't raise him to Elder because he was their leader before. What's to keep his stalk from growing too high, you know?"

"What does the Elder role entail?" Simon asked.

"We're sorta the Lord's honor guard. We protect the community, guard prisoners, keep an eye on visitors like yourselves."

Esther leaned forward. "So these pris— "

"Look! The food's ready," Bole said. "We're real informal here. You can help yourselves." He offered Esther a hand as she climbed over the bench. "Say what you want about the Dentist, but he was right about the lake of plenty. We've been eating like kings ever since we got here."

They followed Bole toward the bonfire, where the food was set up buffet-style along the edge of the stage on wide wooden trays. Esther had never seen so much land food in her life. There was grilled fish from the lake, of course, but also vegetables, chicken, and glorious golden ears of corn. A burly man in a sleeveless shirt sliced huge slabs off the roast pig, steam rising around him. Luke would be upset he had missed the barbecue. They piled their plates high, and Esther realized she hadn't eaten since they left the *Lucinda* that morning, except for the single piece of jerky Bole had offered her hours ago.

Bole accompanied them back to their table to join them for the meal, though David took the seat next to Esther before he could. As they dug into their food, Simon and David asked Bole polite, careful questions about the town. If he was in the Dentist's inner circle of Elders, they couldn't trust him no matter how friendly he seemed.

Esther concentrated on her food. The succulent meat dripped with hot, fatty juices. It was stringy, and the tendons caught in Esther's teeth as she gnawed at the bones. It tasted delicious, but Esther had begun to feel a bit queasy. Her head felt hot and heavy. She tried to shake it off. It was probably just because she wasn't used to this kind of food. She was worried, out of her depth. She needed to work her way through this situation, figure out how to fix it. Naomi needed her.

She looked over at a group of white-robed Shepherds filling plates with food at the buffet. They carried the plates over to the Dentist, who was deep in discussion with a group of older men. The men barely glanced up as the women laid down their offerings. Then the Shepherds stepped back to watch the Dentist eat.

Esther frowned. She wasn't sure what she had expected of the lake town. She was surprised that the community was so fully established, with its own customs, traditions, and even its own brand of religion. She remembered how Penelope Newton had taken charge of the religious life on the *Catalina* and it had morphed into something that may not have resembled her old faith. The End Times had consumed every discussion, and Penelope had tried for years to connect the events of their world with the prophecies she studied in the scriptures. Some people on the *Catalina* had found solace in what she was trying to do. Others had stuck to their own faiths in their own ways.

But here the Dentist had created his own religious framework, expanding on an existing religion and twisting it for his own ends rather than trying to fit the new world into the old way. He had positioned himself as both prophet and admiral. If the people's fervency was any indication, his bid for power had worked.

"Wanna dance with me, Esther?" Bole said suddenly, snapping Esther's attention back to the table. "The band's setting up now. Gotta claim the first one."

"Um, okay, sure."

David shifted beside her.

"Great! I'll go dump our plates. Meet you at the end of the table." Bole stood and jogged toward the bonfire.

"I'll see what I can get out of him," Esther said in response to the flat look David gave her. "You should go dance with Yvonne. She thinks you're dreamy."

Esther walked between the tables, dodging the townspeople milling amongst them. The people chattered and laughed, many offering each other bites of their food. The town was a little like the *Catalina* in that everyone seemed to know each other well. It would be idyllic if Esther hadn't just found out that they killed anyone who didn't conform to their rules.

Now that all the meat had been cooked, the townspeople added more logs to the bonfire, causing sparks and flames to leap into the sky. The fire roared like storm winds. Esther spotted the Dentist at the end of the table nearest to it, still surrounded by the group of men—Elders, perhaps? The fire threw harsh shadows across his face. He raised a wooden stein to his lips. Was he watching her?

Esther turned her back on the Dentist and found Bole waiting for her.

"Can you dance the reel?"

"Huh?"

"It's a line dance. You just have to do what everyone else does."

"Okay." Esther reached for Bole's shoulder, but he pushed her hand down.

"No, you stand here." He positioned her on one side of a wide patch of dirt, stepped four paces away, then faced her.

Other couples joined them, the women on one side and the men on the other. David and Yvonne stepped into line four couples away from Esther and Bole.

"What do we do now?" Esther called across to Bole.

"Wait for it . . ."

A fiddler moved to the front of the stage, where a four-piece band had finished setting up, and the music began. It was an energetic song with a fast tempo. The women on either side of Esther stepped toward the men, looped their arms through their partners', and spun them around. Esther stood frozen, unsure what to do. Before she could move, the women had returned to their places. Then the line of men danced forward. Bole looped his arm in Esther's and spun her in a wide circle.

"You're going again next," he said. "Get ready."

This time Esther advanced when the other women moved and tried to mimic the way they grabbed their partners' arms. She accidentally punched Bole in the stomach when she came forward. He just laughed and guided her around in a circle again.

Then the dancers were moving far too fast. Stamping. Twirling. Stepping this way and that. Esther tried to fumble through the movements, concentrating hard on the feet of the woman next to her. Her skirt swirled around her legs. She wouldn't have a chance to get information from Bole with this kind of dancing. There was no time to actually talk!

The lines separated, and then the couple at one end met in the middle and danced and twirled between the two lines while everyone clapped in time to the fiddle. Another couple followed, doing different steps. How was she supposed to know what to do?

David and Yvonne were next, and he twirled her down the line, spinning her in perfect, tight circles all the way to the end. How did *he* know how to do that?

When it was Esther and Bole's turn, she leapt forward and closed her eyes, allowing him to guide her through the movements. The world spun around her as Bole dragged her inelegantly down the line. She heard laughter, but she kept her eyes closed until they reached the end and he released her.

When she opened her eyes, the last couple was spiraling its way down the line, and then all the couples were off again, stamping and twirling and clapping in an ever-faster rhythm. Esther barely made it through the remainder of the dance. Her head was pounding when the music finally stopped.

Everyone cheered, and Bole patted her on the shoulder.

"You did great!" he said. "Wanna go for another?"

"No! I mean, thank you, but I need a break. Shall we sit down for a minute?"

"I've promised a dance or two to another girl. I'll catch you later." Bole deposited her on a bench and trotted off to find his next partner.

Winded, Esther watched him go. There went her chance to get information. It had all happened so fast! Maybe she didn't like dancing after all.

She shifted on the bench and glanced across the table where Bole had left her—directly into the petroleum-gold eyes of the Dentist.

"Oh, um, hello," she said.

"Evening," the Dentist said. He studied Esther silently, expressionless. His companions were nowhere to be seen.

Esther wasn't sure what to say, so she simply held his gaze and waited for him to speak again.

"I heard a rumor," the Dentist said. He turned his stein slowly between his wide hands, the contents swirling around and around. "Someone asked you whether they could leave the town with you. And you said yes."

"Who told you that?"

"I gave clear guidelines," the Dentist said, "about spreading dangerous ideas among my people. Don't test me."

"Or what?" Esther said.

The Dentist smiled. "You remind me of someone."

"Really."

"Oh yes. Enjoy the rest of the dance, Miss Harris."

Before she could respond, the Dentist stood and left the table. He disappeared into a group of townspeople.

By the time Esther got back to her table, she was shaking.

"Are you okay, button?" her father said. "You look flushed."

"The Dentist knows we're up to something," she said. "Just had a weird conversation with him. And he used our surname. We never said it in the lodge. Thompson, Jones, and Bole heard it, though. And Yvonne knows. At least one of them is reporting back to the Dentist on us."

"We must be extra cautious then," Simon said. "Are you sure you're all right?"

"Fine. Just out of breath from the dancing," Esther said. Why wouldn't her hands stop shaking?

David returned from the dance with Yvonne in tow. She was flush with laughter, and she collapsed onto the bench beside Esther.

"He's quite a dancer," she said.

David smiled politely and sat down next to Simon.

Cody hurried up to rejoin them too. He had apparently been taking a closer look at the bonfire, because there was a smudge of charcoal on his face. But he wasn't smiling, and he looked like he had something to say. He stopped short at the sight of Yvonne sitting with them.

David noticed Cody and jerked his head slightly at Esther. She turned to distract Yvonne while Cody leaned in to whisper something to David and Simon.

"Can you teach me how to do that dance?" Esther said. "It was fun, but I was a mess."

"Of course!" Yvonne giggled. "You just need to learn the count, and then it's easy. Let me show you."

She tugged Esther from her seat and steered her to the middle of the aisle. As they moved, Esther's head spun like an out-of-control turbine.

"Okay, the reel is on an eight count. Do you know what that means?"

"Uhh . . . not really."

"It's the rhythm. First let's clap. One, two, three, four." Yvonne beat her palms together. The noise was sharp, cutting into Esther's skull. "Five, six, seven, eight." The people around them were talking too loud, their laughter shrill. "One, two, three, four . . ."

Esther's balance wavered. She looked back at the men. Cody seemed to have finished telling them what he had found out. David did not look happy about whatever it was.

"You know, on second thought," Esther said, "I'm not feeling too well. I think I'll call it a night."

"Are you sure?" Yvonne said.

"Yeah. You should go dance with Cody. I'm sure he'd enjoy it." She returned to the table, her steps sluggish. "David, would you walk me back to the dorm?"

"Gladly."

"I'll teach you tomorrow then," Yvonne said. She grabbed Esther's hand and whispered in her ear. "Don't let him go inside the dorm. Remember what I told you." Then she pulled Cody away and skipped back toward the dancers.

"I'll fill her in," David said to Simon as he offered Esther his arm. Both their faces were grave.

"Get some rest, Esther," Simon said. "And be careful." He turned to watch Cody and Yvonne walking away, concern furrowing his brow.

Esther and David made their way through the crowd toward the town. A handful of older people shuffled away from the tables, leaving the dancing and noise behind. Esther and David walked in silence, waiting for the others to disperse toward their cabins and leave them alone. Esther still couldn't shake the pounding in her head.

"Esther, you're really warm," David said. "Are you feeling okay?"

"It's been a long day," Esther said. "What did Cody find out?"

"The *Lucinda* has been sent away."

"What?"

"Thompson told Cody that the Dentist contacted Zoe on the radio and told her I ordered her to retreat several miles downriver. They're not going to allow the rest of the crew to come into town. The Dentist thinks we're up to something, but he doesn't know what."

"Salt. So we're on our own?"

"For now."

"I talked to the Dentist," Esther said. "He definitely suspects something."

"We need to move fast. I don't like being isolated from our crew. Let's meet tomorrow morning to make a plan. I'll see if I can learn anything else tonight. They put the three of us in an empty cabin, though, and I understand the curfew is strictly enforced. You might have better luck with your roommates."

"Okay. I'll work on Yvonne. Be careful, David. We can't afford any mistakes here."

"Don't worry about me. Get some rest." David squeezed her hand but didn't lean in to kiss her. Instead he bowed over her hand, brushing her palm with his fingers, and turned to go.

Esther climbed the stairs to the dormitory next to the spreading tree. It was deserted. All the women would be at the festival for a while yet. Esther made a slow circle around the large room, looking for any hints that could help them. Several of the women had carved their names on their bunks or embroidered them on their pillows. Esther couldn't find any evidence of Naomi here at all. Why did her head hurt so much?

She kicked the soft moccasins off her feet and sat on her own bunk. Her lids felt heavy, her eyes scratchy and hot. She lay down on top of the quilt Yvonne had found for her. She should get undressed, but she wanted to rest for a minute first. Shadows closed in around her.

24. Fever

WHEN ESTHER AWOKE, SHE had a vague awareness of people moving around her, but all she felt was heat. Or was it cold? She was shivering. Her head pounded and spun. Was there a storm? Something wrong with the engines?

She descended into blackness.

The next time she clawed toward consciousness, she heard voices.

"Can't believe she's so hot . . ."

"She needs more blankets."

". . . didn't realize anything was wrong. I just went to work, and when I came back . . ."

The sea swirled around her. She was in a volcano. Where were her storm goggles?

"Should we get her friends?"

"They went out with the hunting party."

"Can't break the fever . . ."

". . . need to . . . soon if she's going to have a chance . . ."

The waves pounded down on her skull. No, she was trapped beneath the engine block. That's why she couldn't move. She should call for Cally, but she had no voice.

She wanted her mother. She saw her rising out of the sea, foam and starfish in her hair. Naomi, still a little girl, held her hand. She pointed at Esther, and Nina smiled. Then a wave swallowed them both.

The next thing Esther knew she was being lifted. Arms strong around her. They smelled like dirt.

Light in the trees. Still moving. An engine sputtering to life.

She felt something soft. It was dark. Blurring in her ears. She was in the bath with that almost-too-hot water. No, she could breathe this time.

Sensation faded again.

25. Inside

ESTHER AWOKE WITH HER face covered in sweat. She wiped her forehead, her fingers shaking. She felt like she'd spent the entire day carrying heavy parts from the engine room to the top deck.

She blinked rapidly, and the room around her came into focus. She was no longer in the single-women's dormitory. Her surroundings were sterile. White plaster walls. A narrow, high window with no curtains. She lay on a hard bed, which was the only thing in the room except for an empty chair.

The door was made of heavy steel, and it was closed. Esther remembered her captivity on Calderon Island a few months ago and felt a tug of panic.

She sat up shakily and examined her arms. A tube sticking from one of them snaked toward a stand with a glass bottle full of liquid. Esther had heard of IVs before, but she'd never had one. This one looked like it was made out of an old soda bottle. She eased the tube out of her skin and pinched her arm to stop the trickle of blood.

That heavy steel door made her nervous. Was she a prisoner? Had the Dentist already figured out why they were really here?

Then it hit her like a swinging boom. Naomi! Her sister was here at the lake somewhere. Alive. Maybe in danger.

Esther slid off the bed. She was a bit unsteady on her feet, but she could at least hold herself upright. If she *was* imprisoned and not just in an infirmary, this might be her chance to get answers.

From the weak light slanting in through the window, Esther guessed it was either approaching evening or she was in a deeply shaded area. That didn't help her much. Had she been in here for almost a full day? The window was too high to see out, and she didn't trust herself to climb on top of the chair at the moment. She crept to the door and listened.

There was no sound outside her room. She counted ten heartbeats, then tested the doorknob. She gasped in relief when it turned. She wasn't locked in. The Lake People couldn't have figured out what she was up to yet. She pulled the door toward her, finding it surprisingly heavy. She was weak. Her arms were noticeably thinner than they should be. Had she had been sick for longer than a day? She remembered then that the *Lucinda* had been sent away. What of her father, David, and Cody?

She peeked out at a corridor lined with identical doors. It was fairly long. She didn't think she'd seen a building this big in the town, apart from the Dentist's Lodge. This didn't feel like that polished wooden interior. She crept out of her room, but there was no one around to stop her. The hall was deathly quiet. There was a set of double doors at one end of the corridor. At the other end a heavier-looking door had a panel with two buttons next to it. There was something familiar about that.

Esther walked toward it unsteadily, and she was within ten feet before she realized it was the door to an elevator. Of course! Her brain must be a little scrambled by her illness.

Esther stood before the elevator for a split second before making her decision. She might never have another chance. She had to learn as much about this town as possible if she was going to find Naomi. She hit the button.

Esther held her breath as the elevator car arrived, preparing an excuse for being out of bed, but when the doors opened the little box was empty. She stepped inside and examined the panel of buttons beside the door. The building had only four levels. The first three were neatly labeled: G—Infirmary; B1—Storage; B2—Detention. B3 had a button but no label. She wondered briefly what was down there, then pushed the button for the Detention Level.

The elevator descended. This was too easy. Esther clenched her fists, wishing she had her tool belt with her. Almost there.

When the doors opened, the Dentist stood before her.

Esther stared at him, her heart sputtering and racing. Her reflexes were slow. She felt foggy.

"Hello, Miss Harris," the Dentist said. He didn't seem surprised to see her.

"I'm lost," Esther said.

"Indeed you are. You're heading in the wrong direction, I'm afraid. You've been ill."

"I—"

"You'd best return to your room. Luckily, I'm heading that way myself. I'll escort you."

"Okay," Esther said. She tried to sound groggy, and it didn't take much acting.

The Dentist stepped into the elevator with her. She shifted so she could look down the corridor behind him. The Detention Level was one long room separated into compartments with rusty metal bars, making Esther think of the chicken hatchery.

In the cage closest to the elevator doors, just to the left, sat a young woman.

Esther froze, hope stopping her breath. The young woman had curly dark hair lying lankly on her forehead. She was short.

And she had Esther's mother's nose.

It was Naomi. Esther was sure of it. They locked eyes for perhaps two seconds. Then the elevator doors closed.

When Esther looked up, the Dentist was watching her.

"See anything interesting?" he said softly.

"What's in there?"

"That is our detention facility, as I'm sure you know, seeing as you hit that button."

"I feel kind of out of it," Esther said. "I think I've been sick."

"Yes," the Dentist said. "But you're feeling better now I trust."

"Not really."

"Then you must get more rest."

The elevator doors opened, and the Dentist steered her out. He guided her down the hall, his grip firm. Esther was reminded how very tall he was. Her head didn't even come up to his shoulder.

She waited for him to confront her, to accuse her of trying to steal one of his prisoners. He obviously knew she was sneaking around on purpose. She didn't want to play games. Did he know specifically about her connection to Naomi, though? There was a good chance Yvonne had told him everything, but she couldn't give anything away just in case.

"What is this place?" she asked.

"The Bunker. Don't worry. We have very good nurses."

"What's in the lowest level?"

The Dentist didn't answer. He guided her firmly back into her room. Before closing the door, he gave her a final long look, his golden eyes glistening.

"Get well soon, Miss Harris."

The lock clicked behind her.

Esther collapsed onto the bed, her heart racing. Naomi was here, two levels beneath her feet. She was in a cage, but she was still alive—at least for now. It was really her. Esther could barely process it. Alive. Alive. Alive. She felt feverish, triumphant. But the short walk up and down the corridor had taken a toll on Esther's weakened body. She slept again.

When she woke, a sleeping David Hawthorne occupied the chair by her bed. He still wore the clothes he'd borrowed from Bole, the shirt open at the neck.

Esther rolled onto her side to face him. "Psst, David," she hissed. "David Elliot Hawthorne!"

He jerked upright, disoriented. His eyes were red, and his hair wasn't quite as perfectly combed as usual. When he saw she was awake, he leapt off the chair and knelt by her side.

"How are you feeling?" he said quietly.

"A little shaky. Are we prisoners?"

"No, this is the infirmary. The hospital."

"I know. But there's a prison here too. Have you seen—?"

"Shh. Not now, Esther." David glanced significantly at the door. "You had a fever. The Shepherds think you caught something from the muddy river. It's a wonder I didn't get it too."

"How long have I been here?" Esther asked.

"Three days."

"What? Salt! What's been happening out there? We need to—"

"They've been taking good care of us," David said, jerking his head toward the door again. "I was worried. I wasn't sure you'd make it."

"I'm a little the worse for wear, but I should be fine. Have you heard anything from the *Lucinda*?"

"They're still on the river about a day's journey out. I talked to Zoe and reassured her that we're fine here." David raised his voice a little. "I told her how warmly we've been welcomed and that the lake might be a great place for us to settle. The others are impatient to see it, of course."

David looked at Esther warningly, and she cast about for a safe question to ask.

"How is my dad?"

"Simon's fine. He was here until about an hour ago, when I made him go get some fresh air. You scared us both. It's good to see you awake." David leaned in as if to kiss her cheek, but instead he put his face close to her ear and whispered, "They're listening to everything. We'll talk when you get out."

Esther grabbed David's shirt and kept his face close to hers.

"I saw her," she hissed. "Naomi is in a cell two levels below us. But the Dentist saw me sneaking down there."

"He hasn't confronted us." David frowned. "What's he waiting for?"

"I don't know, but we need to move fast. Can we get the others up here to help?"

David pretended to adjust Esther's pillows and whispered, "The Dentist claimed it was a misunderstanding that they got a message telling them to leave, but he's dragging his feet on giving us permission to bring them in. He keeps saying they need to prepare to give the visitors a proper welcome."

"We should have a plan in place for when they arrive," Esther said, possibilities whizzing through her mind like a spooling engine. "We can't afford to waste time."

"You need to focus on getting better," David said. "I'll work on a plan with Simon and Cody."

"I can't just sit here."

"I understand. But don't get caught sneaking around again." David stood. "I'll go get your dad. Don't want him finding out you've been awake for a whole thirty seconds and I haven't told him yet." He looked over at the door and raised his voice. "And I'll bring you some berries, Esther. They're swell here."

"Can't wait."

26. Sisters

WOMEN WEARING THE WHITE-ROBED Shepherd's attire tended to Esther in the infirmary. Her primary caregiver, a woman in her sixties with lank, gray hair, went by the name Whitefern. Esther wanted to leave the infirmary as soon as she was able to stay conscious for more than an hour, but Whitefern kept her on a very strict schedule. She bustled around, fussing and clucking like one of Yvonne's chickens. She fed Esther soup four times a day and wouldn't allow her to hold the spoon herself. She even accompanied her to the bathroom. She alternated between chattering about the blessings of the lake and lamenting her many ailments: aching back, failing eyesight, bum knee, various rashes and boils. The only body parts that didn't seem to bother her one bit were her teeth.

Being confined to bed at Whitefern's mercy was incredibly frustrating for Esther, but she did her best to smile at Whitefern often and thank her for her care. She had to keep up the story that she and her companions might settle at the lake. She tried to appear moved and impressed by the work of the Shepherds.

As long as the Dentist continued to pretend he didn't know they were lying about their real reason for being there, they had time to work out a plan. And Esther had time to do some reconnaissance.

Unfortunately, Whitefern sat up with Esther for the entire first night after she regained consciousness. Esther had planned to sneak back into the basement at the first opportunity, but she didn't count on the woman's diligence. Whitefern knitted with a pair of wooden needles all night long, at it every time Esther woke and tried to slip away.

On the second day Esther was conscious—her fifth day in the Bunker—Cody came, along with David and her father, to visit. The men tried to keep their conversation to neutral topics. They told her the townspeople had warmed to them in Esther's absence and had taken them on scouting, hunting, and berry-picking expeditions. Cody regaled her with the tale of David's quest to pick berries for her and his subsequent fall into a bramble patch, resulting in small scratches all over his arms.

The men were trying to deflect suspicion and put the townspeople at ease by throwing themselves into the life of the lake. Cody took to it natu-

rally, and he even accompanied some of the townsmen on their nightly curfew patrols. As the youngest among them, he found everything fresh and
exciting, and the townspeople seemed to enjoy introducing him to new experiences. Simon had managed to get his hands on a copy of the Code to
study, and David was getting to know the Elders to
find out who was most influential.

They were all doing their part, but Esther knew
there was something only she could do. Her father
must know it too, because before they left he leaned
close to hug her and said, "Please keep safe, button.
I don't want you taking unnecessary risks. I almost
lost you."

"I'll only take necessary risks."

"Esther . . ."

"I'll be fine, Dad."

Esther knew what she had to do. There was only
so much the men could accomplish out there. They
had to find out how many guards the Detention
Level had, how they'd be armed, and how difficult it
would be to get Naomi's cage open. They needed
answers about the Bunker itself before they could
make a move. That was up to Esther.

But on the second night, Whitefern was just as
assiduous in keeping an eye on her. Esther began to
wonder whether the woman slept at all. She fought
drowsiness, hoping to catch the woman drifting.
Sleep pulled at Esther like an undertow. She finally

gave up and fell asleep to the sound of clacking knitting needles.

She dreamt of her mother tapping her fingernails along the countertop in their sunlit kitchen in San Diego. Naomi darted through the room toward the open front door, a stack of books clutched to her chest. She disappeared into the blazing outdoors before Esther could call out to her.

David and her father visited again on the third day and reported that the Dentist had finally given them permission to bring more of their crew up to the village from the *Lucinda*. Through a frantic, whispered discussion—interspersed with loud statements about the weather for the benefit of whoever was listening outside the door—they agreed they would try to get Naomi out of her cage while the townspeople were preoccupied with welcome activities for the crew. It might be the distraction they needed. They didn't know yet which day the crew would arrive, but Esther needed to get the information about the Detention Level soon.

Fortunately, that night—the third after Esther woke up from her fever—Whitefern fell asleep at her bedside. Esther had seen her take something from her pocket and pop it surreptitiously into her mouth. A short time later she had stopped complaining about her back pain. She settled into her chair, and soon her head began to nod, her knitting needles slipping down her lap.

Esther watched Whitefern's head nod for half an hour, fighting to stay awake herself. She felt much better than before, but she still grew tired easily. She had to be back to her full strength when they made their move.

When Whitefern's head finally drooped to her chest, Esther waited for a count of one hundred to make sure she wouldn't jerk awake. Whitefern's breathing grew deeper. She seemed to be settling in for a nice long nap.

Esther climbed carefully out of her bed, begging it not to creak. Whitefern didn't stir. Esther had put her socks on earlier in preparation, and now she crept across the room without a sound. She held her breath at the door and eased it open to escape for the second time. Or at least that's what she tried to do. She met resistance at the door handle. Whitefern had locked them in.

The woman began snoring like a walrus. Esther crept back and eased her hand into the pocket of Whitefern's robes. Her fingers rattled a bottle of pills. She held her breath, but Whitefern didn't move. She slid the pills out of the pocket and set them on the floor so they wouldn't make more noise. Then she reached back into the woman's robes and found a bundle of keys. She pulled them out and tiptoed to the door.

The third key she tried fit the lock. With a final glance back at Whitefern's sleeping figure, Esther crept out of the room.

The pitch-dark corridor greeted her. There were often people walking the halls during the day, but it was quiet now. As far as Esther knew, there were only one or two other patients in the infirmary right now. She'd seen a young man hobbling to the bathroom, his ankle in a cast, and she'd heard Whitefern talking in gruesome detail about another patient's severe hives with a Shepherd called Thistlebloom.

Esther tiptoed down the hallway to the elevator. As long as she didn't run into the Dentist again, she would use the "lost and disoriented" excuse with any guards she encountered. If she met the Dentist, it was probably a sign that her luck had finally run out.

The elevator car was waiting for her when she hit the button. Esther clenched her fists as the doors closed behind her. She descended to the Detention Level.

The doors slid open. She couldn't see anyone in the beam of light from the elevator. The Detention Level was quiet and dark, like the upper corridor. Esther stepped into the square of light spilling out of the elevator, barely breathing.

It was silent. Still. Her heartbeat thudded in her ears.

Then the elevator doors closed, making Esther jump. The darkness was complete.

Esther stayed where she was, clenching and unclenching her fists. She listened for any hint of movement.

"Who's there?" said a voice in the darkness. A woman's voice.

"Don't be afraid," Esther said, taking a few tentative steps toward the speaker. "What's your name?"

"Naomi. Who are you?"

"Are you Naomi Harris? Originally from San Diego?" Esther walked closer. She reached out blindly and felt the cold bars of the cage. "Your birthday is July 27."

"How do you know that?"

"I know you," Esther said, her words catching in her throat. "My name is Esther Harris. I . . . I'm pretty sure you're my sister."

There was a long silence. A deep breath.

"I don't have a sister."

"I know it sounds crazy," Esther said, her throat constricting, "but we escaped, Naomi. Dad too. We were on the boardwalk in San Diego, and we got away on a ship. We've been living at sea ever since the disaster. We thought you were dead until a few weeks ago. We came to get you."

"You don't understand. I really don't have a sister. Never have. And I've never met my father. He left my mom before I was born. I'm sorry to disappoint you."

Esther felt like the earth had suddenly stopped spinning. It couldn't be. The coincidences were too unlikely.

"But . . . you were born on July 27. And you escaped from San Diego! And your name . . ."

"I think Harris is a pretty common name," Naomi said. Then she was speaking quickly, the words tripping over each other like ripples. "I didn't escape from San Diego. I lived there, but my mom and I were visiting my grandmother in Texas when the volcano blew. We fled south when all hell broke loose and lived on our own until we met the Dentist on his way down here to the Lake. I don't know you."

Esther felt like she'd been struck dumb. She had been so sure that this was the same Naomi Harris. It had to be her. She had seen her with her own eyes.

The darkness was oppressive, like a thunderhead. The bars of the cage warmed in Esther's grip.

"Look—Esther, right?—I've never heard of anyone who escaped from San Diego. The ash fall was too thick there."

Something touched Esther's hand. Naomi had reached out to her through the shadows, taking her hand.

"I'm really sorry, Esther, but you'd better go. You don't want to get caught."

Esther felt a cyclone spinning in her head. She had *seen* her. Yes, she had been feverish, but she had recognized her!

"I don't believe you," Esther said. "You are my sister. I don't know if someone's making you lie or if you're messed up because of everything you've been through . . ." Esther's voice faltered. She remembered the skeletons stumbling out of the church, moaning about how starvation would reveal the truth. She tightened her grip on the hand in the darkness. "I'm getting you out."

"Esther," Naomi whispered, "you have to go."

"No. Dad and I will take you away from here. It'll be okay."

"I won't go with you," Naomi said firmly. "Don't try, Esther. This is my home, and I'll accept the punishment for my actions. I follow the Dentist. I don't have a sister."

"We're working on a plan. Just hang tight for a little while longer," Esther said. Doubt crept in, insidious like a hidden leak in a ship's hull. Had she been so wrong? She had turned everyone away from the original mission. The team had split, maybe forever. Her father was here, in danger, when he should be safe on the *Catalina*. And for what?

No, Naomi was traumatized. She needed help.

"Be ready when we come for you." Esther squeezed Naomi's hand one more time and headed back to the elevator. Before she hit the button, she stopped. "Will they execute you?"

Naomi made a sound, something between a sigh and a sob. "I betrayed the Dentist. The Code is clear. I have to die."

"No, you don't," Esther said. "We're getting you out."

"Don't worry about me," Naomi whispered. "Please, Esther. Don't put yourself in danger. You have to go."

Esther peered through the bars of the cage. Her eyes had adjusted to the darkness enough that she could see the faint outline of the woman's head. She turned sideways, and Esther was sure she saw her mother's nose.

"Just hold on for a few more days," she said.

Esther snuck back to her room without encountering anyone. She returned Whitefern's keys and then lay back on the lumpy pillow, feeling empty. It was stupid to think Naomi could have survived San Diego. She had endangered the entire crew, chasing after an impossible dream. She had risked everything. She had let hope blind her to reality.

And yet she couldn't believe Naomi was telling the truth. No matter what she said it *had* to be her. And she was going to be killed unless Esther did something about it. She may have said she wouldn't come with them, but Esther couldn't accept that. She would drag Naomi out of this prison kicking and screaming if that's what it took.

27. Weeds

IN THE MORNING WHITEFERN told Esther she would be released from the Bunker after lunch. She could return to the dormitory, but only under strict instructions not to exert herself. Whitefern gave Esther back her own clothes, which had been freshly laundered, her tool belt, and her boots. Esther felt around inside the right boot. The knife she had hidden there was gone. Whitefern met her eyes sedately, as if daring her to ask about it.

Whitefern bustled her out of the Bunker after a hearty lunch of chicken soup. Esther got her first look at the building's exterior. It was a long bungalow made of concrete, with most of the levels underground. High, narrow windows were spaced at regular intervals around the structure. A name had been painted on the wall long ago, many of the letters now faded beyond recognition. Esther could make out only one word: "hydroelectric." The building must have belonged to whoever once operated the dam, but whether it had been living quarters or some sort of facility she couldn't say.

The building was located in an isolated clearing surrounded by a dense thicket of trees and scrubs. A single dirt road led away from it. A vehicle waited for her at the head of the road. Bole was the driver, and in the front seat Esther saw—

"Cally! When did you get here?"

"This morning!" Cally leapt out of the front seat to give her a big hug. She had flowers twisted into her hair. "It was a serious hike up from the river. My first hike ever! They told us you were being released today, and Bole said it would be okay for me to come along in the jeep. My first jeep ride ever!"

"Just don't mention it around the Dentist and you're good to go," Bole said, grinning at Esther.

"So this is the jeep?" Esther asked. The car—painted in camouflage colors matching Bole's clothes—was open to the air, with a cracked windshield and a roll bar over the top of the seats.

"Yeah, she's held up well all things considered," Bole said. "We try not to drive too much to conserve fuel. That stuff's hard to find. Hop in."

Esther climbed into the backseat, and Cally returned to her place in the front. There was no seat belt, so Esther gripped Cally's seat as Bole fired up the engine. She must have been brought to the Bunker in a car in the midst of her fever, but otherwise this was the first time she had ridden in one in sixteen years.

The jeep bounced away from the Bunker along the dirt road. It felt strange to ride in a car again, almost surreal. It was another thing reminding Esther that she was out of her depth. She'd had a hard time untangling everything she'd been feeling since she walked into the Detention Level and Naomi denied knowing her. She had to focus on what she could control: her plans for what to do next.

"How are things on the *Lucinda*?" Esther asked as the jeep bumped against every rock and dip.

"They're fine," Cally said. "We left a few people behind to keep watch. There are ten of us in the town now, counting you. Zoe was super upset that she couldn't come over, but she has to stay on the comms."

The jungle flew past them, and Esther watched for milestones so she'd be able to find her way back to the Bunker. They passed two other paths disappearing off into the trees, but as far as she could tell, the Bunker was the end of the line. It shouldn't be too hard to get back.

"Where are we headed?" she asked.

"We're helping with the farm this afternoon," Cally said.

"The Dentist says you've gotta earn your keep now that you're feeling better," Bole said.

They broke through the trees and reentered the town. They passed the chicken coop, where Yvonne waved enthusiastically at them. It was a bright day, and lots of people were out and about.

"Everything is so amazing here," Cally said. "Isn't walking on dirt and rocks strange, Esther?"

"I guess . . ."

"I keep feeling like I'll trip. I saw some of the women wearing these soft-looking shoes. Don't you think they hurt?"

"They must be used to it."

"And the dust! I knew *about* dust, but it's so strange to have it floating around in the air. It's like sea spray, except it makes my throat scratchy."

As they bumped along through the town, Esther spotted Cody stripping bark from a pile of logs with some other young men. He straightened from his work at the sound of their approach, accidentally knocking over a few tools that had been leaning against the logs. He raised a hand in greeting, and a whirl of dust from their tires surrounded him.

Esther leaned forward to get a look at Cally's face when they saw Cody, but the jeep jolted her roughly, and the moment passed. Cally was far too occupied with her observations from her very first morning on land to pay attention to her admirer. She and the others had doubtless been warned to act like they wanted to join the Lake People, but Cally's enthusiasm was genuine. Esther liked seeing the town through Cally's eyes. She had been so focused on Naomi and the Dentist—and being knocked flat by fever—that she hadn't had much chance to appreciate the wonder of it. They were on *land*.

They drove toward the community gardens near the smokehouse. The field stretched toward the tree line like a frozen green wave, the plants bristling in neat rows. Half a dozen others from the *Lucinda* were already at work.

"We got you guys pulling weeds today," Bole said.

"What are weeds?" Cally asked.

"Fast-growing plants that pop up where you don't want 'em."

"Why wouldn't you want them?"

"They choke out the good plants. These babies need room to grow."

The jeep lurched to a stop beside the smokehouse. Esther and Cally followed Bole out into the field.

A group of women were showing the Lucindans, including Dax and Anita, which plants to pull. Esther recognized Betsy from the dormitory and Sue Ellen from the bathhouse among them. Thompson and Jones stood watch nearby with a handful of other men. Thompson's eyes cut toward Esther and the others when they arrived. Then he went back to scanning the trees for signs of trouble.

Cally went over to join Dax and kissed him on the cheek, earning a disapproving stare from Sue Ellen nearby. Apparently, Cally and Dax were back on good terms. Sue Ellen made her way over to the young couple, obviously preparing a lecture on appropriate behavior for the newcomers.

Esther spotted her father further out in the field. Simon was on his knees with his hands in the dirt. Long rows of leafy green plants spread around him, bearing some sort of bulbous, greenish fruit. When Esther walked up to him, he sat back on his heels and smiled.

"How are you feeling, button?"

"Much better." She squatted beside him in the dirt.

"Have you learned anything new?" he asked after glancing over at the nearest townswoman. Betsy knelt about ten feet away, but she was busy showing Anita the proper way to break up the dirt around the weeds with a little shovel.

Esther hesitated, remembering Naomi saying she didn't have a sister or a father. Remembering her insistence that she wouldn't leave the town if they tried to break her out.

"I talked to her," she whispered. "It's definitely our Naomi."

Simon smiled, blinking rapidly. "Any news on her sentence?"

Esther lowered her voice further, wishing there was a better way to break this news to her father. "She's going to be executed."

Simon looked up sharply. A grim shadow crossed his face, like a storm cloud over the sun. Tension stiffened his shoulders, and he dug his fingers into the dirt. He took a second to compose himself. Then he reached for another weed and said, "When?"

"I don't know. She said she betrayed the Dentist."

"Betrayed?"

"That's the word she used," Esther said.

Simon worked at the weed for a moment, easing it out of the earth with practiced hands. "That doesn't sound like a transgression of chastity, does it? I wonder if there's more to her crime than Yvonne told you."

"I've been thinking the same thing," Esther said. "It doesn't matter as long as we can break her out. I want to try tonight."

Simon looked at her then, and she couldn't read his expression. Concern and determination, yes, but there was more to it. Pain? Guilt? He looked down and yanked another weed from the earth with none of his earlier gentleness. A fine spray of dust coated his trousers.

"I'm not sure that's a good idea, Esther," he said. "Our friends have been closely guarded since they arrived." He nodded toward Thompson and the others. "We may want to give it a few days before moving, in case their attentions relax."

"Okay . . ." Esther said slowly. They had talked about using their friends' arrival and subsequent welcome as a cover for their big move. She didn't like the idea of waiting any longer than necessary. "I thought we would do it when they got here. David was saying—"

"I've already spoken to David about it," Simon said.

There was a strange note to his voice. Was he hiding something from her?

"Oh. So I guess we'll give it a day or two then . . ."

Esther's father clearly had something on his mind that he didn't want to share with her. But then she was hiding something from him too: the very real possibility that she had been wrong and it wasn't their Naomi after all. Maybe a day or two would give Naomi time to come to her senses. She had to leave with them. She had to know them.

Betsy moved a bit closer to Esther and Simon and kneeled down to work a single row away. She hummed the tune to the reel they had danced at the bonfire night.

"So, let me show you what we're doing here," Simon said brusquely, handing Esther a threadbare pair of gloves. While Betsy pulled weeds nearby, Simon explained how to tell the difference between the weeds and the scrappy tomato plants. "Tomatoes! Aren't they beautiful?"

"They're green."

"They have a ways to go yet before they're ripe," Simon said. He looked up at the men lounging by the smokehouse. "I don't know if we'll get to enjoy these ones ourselves."

They worked down the lines side by side. Esther could see why her father enjoyed gardening. It was amazing to dig her fingers into the crumbling soil. She took off the gloves and let the earth fall over her skin. She almost felt bad pulling out the weeds. They were living, growing things that had found a place to set their roots. They had worked hard to be here. They deserved it.

By the time they reached the end of their respective rows, the sun had strengthened, warming the earth and sending sweat down their faces. They flopped down in the dirt to take a break. Betsy brought a wooden bucket and a big spoon over to them. She offered it to Simon first.

"Would you like some water, sir?"

"Thank you. It's Bethany, right?" Simon said.

Esther looked up. Her father never got people's names wrong.

"Betsy."

"So sorry, Betsy. Thank you." Simon had to use both hands to steady the spoon while he drank deeply from the water, seemingly to keep from shaking. He handed the spoon back to Betsy and went over to talk to the others from the *Lucinda*. There was definitely something strange about him today. He made Esther think of a coiled spring, ready to leap into motion at the slightest nudge. And he was usually so calm!

"It's good to see you up and moving around," Betsy said, coming over to sit beside Esther.

Betsy wore a skirt even though she had been working in the field, and it billowed out around her in a near-perfect circle as she sat.

"Thanks," Esther said. "I'm still a little shaky on my feet."

"You gave us quite a scare," Betsy said. "I was afraid you were going to die, but the Lord brought you through. It must have been a Lake Day blessing."

"The Shepherds took good care of me."

"It's fun having visitors." Betsy smiled and combed her fingers through the ends of her long hair so she could retie her braid. "Are ya'll really thinking about staying here and joining the community?"

"Maybe . . ."

"Johnny and Jemima Jones did it. They were wandering around in the wilderness before. It's much better here by the lake."

"I'll give it some thought."

"Good. Well, we better get back to work. We've got a whole field to finish."

"Sure." Esther followed Betsy back into the field and settled in to pull weeds beside her. "Hey, Betsy?"

"Yeah?"

"Why are there only women from the town working in the field?" She nodded toward Thompson and Jones and the other men watching from the shade of the smokehouse.

"Those men are here to protect us, of course." Betsy chuckled like Esther was a child. "Besides keeping us safe, the men do all the hunting and fishing, and we women cultivate the land and care for the livestock. How do you do it at sea?"

"Uh . . . we don't really have different roles for men and women on our ship. There are women on the fishing crew, and one of our main leaders is a woman."

"Like a Shepherd?"

"She's more like an Elder, I think, or even the Dentist. She doesn't have anything to do with religion at all." Esther wondered how Judith was holding up. She hoped the *Catalina* was still staying aloof from other ships until they were sure where Boris was headed. She had nearly forgotten about him with everything that had happened since they left the *Catalina* behind.

"Fascinating," Betsy said.

"I guess."

"But who keeps you safe?" Betsy asked.

"We keep each other safe," Esther said. She remembered fighting side by side with Zoe and Dirk to defend the *Catalina* when it was attacked at the *Amsterdam Coalition* that summer. It hadn't occurred to her to stay back while the men protected them.

"Who are you afraid of anyway?" she asked. "The lake doesn't seem like it's in danger of being attacked."

"You don't know what it has been like, Esther." Betsy sat back on her heels for a moment, clutching a weed in her palm. "I was on my own for a while. When men find women alone on the road . . . Well, I think it's better this way. I thank God every day that the Dentist found me. He knows what's best for us."

"I'm sure he does," Esther said. She studied Betsy out of the corner of her eye. She seemed content with town life, like Yvonne, but she had obviously been through some hard times. There was a reason this place was a sanctuary for so many. Most of the women here appeared happy. They weren't afraid, despite living under a strict code that demanded their silence and controlled their behavior—right down to who could share their beds— under the threat of death.

She wished she knew what Naomi's betrayal had been. Something still didn't add up about her punishment.

Esther had a feeling they would need all the allies they could get, though. Betsy seemed devoted to the Dentist, but she had likely also been friends with Naomi. She had almost mentioned her name the day Esther arrived. Would she be willing to help? Esther needed some way to find out how Betsy felt about the rules—and rule breakers.

"Have you seen David?" she asked. He was as good a topic as any if she was going to hint at Code-breaking.

"The blond? He and a few of your people went fishing."

"Really? I wish I could have gone with him."

"Esther, women don't fish here."

"I've done it before," Esther said. She grabbed hold of a particularly tough weed and tried to yank it out of the earth.

"We each have our roles. It's God's will."

"If you say so. Anyway, I miss being with David." She did her best to sound lovesick. It helped to think about how Neal used to talk about Marianna. "He's really wonderful. And the way he makes me feel . . ." She gave a huge sigh. "Do you have anyone like that, Betsy?"

Betsy looked up, a pink cast to her face. "Actually, there is someone I've had my eye on. He's an Elder. I'd love to marry an Elder."

"Oh yeah?" Esther leaned closer. "Have you ever gotten him alone and—?"

A long shadow was suddenly cast over their work. Thompson loomed above them, his shotgun barrel sticking out behind his shoulder. He wore the same cap pulled low over his eyes.

"You can go fishing tomorrow if you want," he growled.

Esther blinked. Exactly how long had he been listening in?

"Are you sure?"

"You're a guest, aren't you?" Thompson said, adjusting his cap. His bushy beard hid his expression. "I say if a girl wants to fish, she can fish."

"Thank you," Esther said.

"Meet me at the dock after lunch."

"Okay."

Betsy gaped at Thompson as he stalked back over the field, not bothering to weave among the tomato plants. She looked a little panicked.

"I don't think you should be friends with Thompson, Esther," she said.

"I'm not sure I'd call that being friends," Esther said. "What's wrong with Thompson?"

He was now hovering over Cally and Dax, watching them work. Dax glanced up and gave a little jump.

"He's . . ." Betsy looked around again. "He's trouble. He speaks against the Dentist sometimes. That's wrong, Esther. I've seen him breaking curfew when he wasn't on duty too."

"Yeah?"

"I told the Dentist about it, obviously." She lowered her voice. "And I hear he even talks to the Mexicans when he comes across them on patrol."

"And that's bad?"

"Of course. It's only a rumor, though. Maybe I should tell the Dentist Thompson's taking you fishing."

Betsy started to stand, but Esther shot out a hand and gripped her wrist. She smiled through gritted teeth.

"Don't do that, Betsy. I'm sure he doesn't mean anything against the Dentist. He's just being nice."

"Under the Code we're supposed to tell the Dentist if anyone is doing something he wouldn't like, even if what they're doing isn't specifically forbidden. You'll need to learn that if you stay here."

"It's just a fishing trip," Esther said. "I miss being out on a boat. It can't hurt."

"Okay . . . Just watch out for Thompson, Esther. He's not a very good Code follower."

"I will. And thank you for the warning."

Esther sent up a silent prayer of thanks to Thompson. She had been a little too close to asking Betsy about Codebreaking. The woman couldn't be trusted. Not even a little bit. Thompson on the other hand . . . He was a puzzle.

28. The Lodge

WHEN THE WORKDAY WAS done, the crew made their way to the bathhouses to clean up for dinner. The hot water felt great after the hard day's work. Cally and Anita were more comfortable with the whole communal bathing situation than Esther had been. Cally couldn't stop giggling from the moment her toes hit the water to when she climbed back out again and wrapped herself in a towel, her hair dripping like red kelp.

Yvonne met them outside. "We're having a dinner for your crew in the Lodge," she said. "It won't be as fancy as Lake Day, but we want to give the newcomers a proper lake welcome. It'll be a double celebration because you're better!"

She hugged Esther suddenly and released her almost as quickly, as if she was afraid it wouldn't be okay with her.

Esther patted her lightly on the back. "Sounds good," she said. "And thanks."

Esther introduced Yvonne to the others, and they walked toward the Lodge together.

"Will the whole town be at the feast again?" Esther asked.

"Goodness, no!" Yvonne said. "Everyone prepares their own food at home and eats with their families. This will just be a few Elders and their wives, the Shepherds, and a couple of us single folk. We often eat together anyway."

"What about the Dentist?"

"He'll be there. I'm sure he wants to meet all of you"—she glanced back at Cally and Anita, who had fallen behind to pet a domesticated dog that had trotted across their path—"in case you decide to stay at the Lake."

Lights glowed from the cabins like the warm lights of a faraway ship. There was something safe and homey about it. Esther imagined living in a town like this, where the people of the *Catalina* could spread out over the land but still be close enough to occasionally eat together. They could help each other grow things. They could fish. They could have pets. Parts of the life here didn't seem so bad.

They reunited with the rest of the crew on the large porch overlooking the crossroads. The group from the *Lucinda* had cleaned up, and they looked awed and serene after their day on land. Everyone was in good spirits as they made their way through the two sets of double doors and into the Lodge. In the same big meeting hall where they had first met the Dentist, the chairs and benches had been pushed back to make room for a single long table with places set for about fifty. The Dentist's massive chair sat at the head, but the Dentist himself hadn't arrived yet.

Bole waved at Esther when she came through the doors with the other women. He had applied some sort of grease to his black beard so it looked extra shiny. He stood by a smaller table, where a pale-yellow liquid, possibly lemonade, was being served in jars.

"My brother has been talking about you," Yvonne said. "He's super excited you're well again." She looped an arm through Esther's and walked with her toward the long table to find seats.

"But I'm with David."

"Oh, he knows. He doesn't mean anything by it," Yvonne said. "He flirts with all the single women. He's done it too much now, though, so I don't know if anyone will actually say yes to him when he's finally ready to court properly."

"He must be happy about all the newcomers then," Esther said.

Bole had sauntered over to introduce himself to Anita. She smiled shyly at him, twisting her pale fingers together.

"How about you?" Esther asked Yvonne. "Do you have someone to . . . court?"

"I wish." Yvonne glanced around and lowered her voice. "I had a crush on Louis when I was younger too, but he only ever had eyes for Na . . . for *you know who*."

Esther looked around the hall quickly. She didn't want to miss a chance to get information if Yvonne was in the mood to talk. Babble filled the room, but no one was too near to them. The Lucindans were finding places at the table amidst the townspeople trickling in to join the feast. Among them Esther recognized some of the women she'd met the day of the feast and a handful of Shepherds and Elders. There was no sign of either Thompson or Jones.

Esther pulled Yvonne into a chair beside her and leaned closer, a neutral expression plastered on her face.

"Louis is the one she was caught with?"

Yvonne nodded, tears welling up in her eyes.

"They've always been crazy about each other," Yvonne whispered. "But the Dentist didn't approve. He kept demanding that Louis work harder before he'd give them his blessing to marry, but they couldn't stay away from each other."

"You need the Dentist's permission to get married?"

"He's our *leader*, Esther. God gives us leaders to guide us." A woman Esther didn't know sat down a few seats away on Yvonne's other side, but she immediately turned to talk to the man on her left. Yvonne leaned even closer, and Esther could feel the breath of her whisper on her cheek. "Louis is a hard worker, though—truly he is. He's good and kind. I know it's not a good enough excuse to break the Code, but they really and truly love each other."

David came into the Lodge then, entering like he was about to give a speech. He was with a few men—Elders, Esther assumed. He stood out—tall, handsome. His white-blond hair was lighter than anyone else's, but it was his presence, his posture that made him stick out from the crowd. Esther couldn't imagine how anyone could look at anyone else when he was in the room.

"I think it's a great excuse," Esther said.

"I thought the Dentist would make an exception for her," Yvonne whispered. "He's looked the other way before, and she's . . . Something changed, that's all."

Yvonne looked around again to make sure no one was listening. A pair of Shepherds glanced over at them from the other side of the table, then resumed their conversation.

Yvonne bit her lip and whispered fiercely, "You have to help me when you get her out, Esther. I'm not brave like Naomi. I can't stay here as a Code-breaker."

"It'll be okay," Esther said. "What happened to Louis?"

"He'll be offered to the lake for sure," Yvonne said, voice quivering.

The Dentist strode into the room. All chatter ceased, and the townspeople stood. Yvonne tugged Esther out of her seat too. The Dentist strolled to the head of the table, taking time to greet people on his way, pressing hands and patting shoulders. He wore his heavily embroidered jacket again, and it made him look even taller and broader than he already was. Esther felt her stomach clench like a fist.

"My friends," the Dentist said when he reached his chair, "welcome to Lake Aguamilpa. I hope you'll enjoy your stay. Our people will guide you in our ways as they introduce the bounty of the lake to you. It is our hope that you will want to live a life of goodness and truth. When the Lord first called me in a dream, he told me some would doubt us. But he also told me that others would see the blessing and the joy to be found here. I urge you to learn our ways so that you too may find salvation."

"May the Lord grant it so," murmured the townspeople.

"Now"—the Dentist clapped his hands together—"let us eat."

Everyone sat. Esther's father had taken one seat beside the Dentist, and David took the other. Anita had ended up on Esther's other side, and Bole sat beside her. He leaned forward to grin at Esther, stroking his sleek beard.

A flurry of women brought out the food on large platters like buffet trays. The people passed them around the table and then placed them in the middle after everyone had taken their portion. There wasn't quite as much food as they'd had on Lake Day, but it was still an impressive spread: creamy corn, sweet roasted peppers, and fish coated in a rough batter and fried to a golden crisp.

Bole chattered about this and that during the meal, while Anita nodded politely. Esther asked him a few questions, but she kept her attention on the head of the table. David spoke to the Dentist, obviously turning on the charm. He had always been good at getting people in power to listen to him.

Esther ate steadily, hoping David would learn something useful tonight. She wished they'd taken this opportunity to go get Naomi, but he must have a good reason for delaying. He'd be making good use of his diplomacy skills right about now.

Suddenly, however, the Dentist sat back in his chair and narrowed his eyes at David. Esther wished she could hear what they were saying. David offered him a platter of roasted peppers, speaking rapidly, possibly backtracking. The Dentist looked down at the platter suspended in David's hands but didn't take it. His golden eyes took on a dangerous glint.

Esther felt for the wrench in her tool belt, wishing Whitefern hadn't taken her knife. Something was wrong. David had made some sort of misstep, and he knew it.

Then her father put his hand on the Dentist's shoulder and stood.

"May I have everyone's attention, please?" Simon said.

Faces turned toward him around the table. Esther held her breath. The Dentist didn't smile.

"I'd like to propose a toast," Simon said, "to the Dentist and to this fine community. We've been around the world since the disaster, but I've never encountered so much warmth. It reminds me of being at my grandfather's farm in Pennsylvania. I want to thank the Dentist and all of you for bringing us back to a simpler time. We can all learn a lot from you. To the Dentist!"

"The Dentist!"

Glasses clinked. After a long moment the Dentist nodded.

David still held the platter, but he recovered his composure and scooped some peppers onto his own plate. Esther released her grip on the wrench. Her father could handle this.

Simon drew the Dentist's attention for the rest of the meal. The Dentist watched him even when they weren't speaking. Esther desperately wished she could hear what they were saying. She'd have to steal a minute with her father after the meal.

The Dentist didn't stay long after everyone had finished eating. The townspeople stood when he left, watching him go with reverence in their eyes. The people really believed he was some sort of prophet. Their devotion, though clearly well meaning, made the situation all the more delicate. Esther remembered how quickly Betsy had been willing to turn Thompson in for suggesting something the Dentist wouldn't like.

As soon as the Dentist left, the atmosphere became more relaxed and casual.

"Shall we help clear the table for dessert?" Yvonne said.

She, Esther, and Anita gathered up an armload of plates and carried them to a large kitchen located through a side door in the main meeting area. Esther noticed that only the women had helped to clear the table. This must be another one of their divinely assigned roles. The Elders kicked back in their chairs, some taking out pipes. When Dax turned up in the doorway of the kitchen with a fistful of forks and spoons, Betsy chased him out again and told him to relax while she washed up.

The women talked and laughed as they worked. When the dishes were done, they helped carry a platter of sweet fruits and berries drenched in cream back out to the main hall. Everyone helped themselves to the dessert. They ate standing and mingled with the people they hadn't sat next to.

"This is more like our usual routine," Yvonne explained. "You missed out while you were sick, Esther. The single folk cook here most nights there isn't a picnic or barbecue, and then we hang out until curfew."

"Why do you even have a curfew?"

"It's for our protection. Nothing good can happen after midnight."

Betsy directed a few of the women to draw up chairs in a circle for a game. Cally and Anita joined them, and within a few minutes Cally stood in the middle of the circle, acting out whatever had been written on a scrap of papery bark in her hand. Bole gathered another group on the dais, where he set up a target made of a board padded in cloth and began to throw little metal darts at it. That sort of game would be much more difficult at sea, where the floor had a tendency to move. Esther's father surveyed the target, his hand in his chin, while some of the Lucindans went up to give the darts a try.

David caught Esther's eye and jerked his head toward the exit. She met him on the porch outside the second set of carved wooden doors, which stood open to let in the breeze. The moon hung heavy over the town. Part of the lake was visible through the scrubby trees on the shore, shimmering like steel.

"I learned something about the last group to join the Lake People," David said. "Thompson's crew."

"Yeah?" Esther glanced back into the Lodge, but the others were still occupied with their games. Laughter spilled through the doors.

"He's afraid of them," David said. "The Dentist. I asked him what would happen if we decided to stay but set up our own camp nearby to allow our people to get used to their ways, and he responded very aggressively. He said we'd have to follow the Code wholesale or it wasn't worth the risk of letting a bunch of strangers near the town. Then he said last time they'd added strangers they were more trouble than they were worth. I thought he was going to send us away then and there. I tried offering him your tech again, but that just made him angry. Your dad pulled a nice save there."

"I noticed."

"Yeah, it was the right move to focus on how this town is like 'the good old days.' I don't think the Dentist believes most of the stuff he spouts, but that's one thing he means. My theory is he didn't like the way things were going in the world before the disaster. He reset everything to his liking, and he's invented a world that is a throwback in many ways. He only wants people in his town who buy into his ideas, though."

"Do you think he really believes the Lord gave him instructions in a dream?"

David considered for a moment. "Doubtful. He's capitalized on the myth, though."

"I guess." Esther folded her arms. The town was quiet around them, the lights from the cabins glowing brighter. "So he's threatened by Thompson and his crew?"

"By Thompson. By any technology that would let his people move around or reconnect with the outside world. He's terrified of losing his position. He's like the *Galaxy* captains in that way. Another leader could supplant him pretty easily if he got enough of the men to agree. Thompson, the leader of the newest group, which hasn't had as much time to buy into the cult of the Dentist, is the likeliest candidate."

Esther frowned, running her fingers over the cool metal of her wrench. "Thompson offered to let me go fishing out of the blue. Then Betsy warned me that he wasn't a good Code follower."

"Interesting," David said. "What's his angle?"

"Not sure. He hasn't been all that friendly so far."

"Yes. What about Bole? Your fan?"

Esther rolled her eyes. "He's an Elder. He *seems* like a nice guy, but he's been with the Dentist for a long time. He has every reason to be loyal." She remembered what Naomi had said. *I follow the Dentist. I don't have a sister.* "The Dentist does have a hold over people. Otherwise, why would they put up with all the rules and ceremonies?"

"People want someone to follow." David leaned on the porch railing. A light breeze ruffled his hair. "When the *Galaxy* captains decided to stay at sea, we were happy someone seemed to know what they were doing. In the chaos after the disaster we needed order. We needed a strong hand. Must be the same here."

Esther nodded, thinking about her father. He had led the *Catalina* in the days after the disaster. He had provided structure and routines for the people. Even though he wasn't particularly authoritarian, like Judith had been for the past six years or so, he still provided necessary order. But it became a problem when the one giving orders got a little too used to the power.

"Hey, let's forget about all that for a minute." David put his arms around Esther and drew her close. "I'm so glad you're well again. I don't know what I'd do without you."

Esther leaned her head on his shoulder. His heart beat in her ear. They were alone on the porch, and the town was quiet. No one would see. She wrapped her arms around his waist, putting her hands under his shirt so she could feel his skin against hers. They swayed in the moonlight, dancing without music.

"It's a good thing I got a fever," she said. "Otherwise, it might have taken a lot longer to find Naomi."

"Are you absolutely sure it's her?" David asked.

Esther hesitated. She had promised to always talk things over with David. They were a team. It was only fair for him to know that Naomi herself had denied the connection. She had claimed she wouldn't go with Esther. That might be reason enough for them to give up and leave the lake before they got any of their people in trouble. But Esther was sure she could convince Naomi to go. Whether she was lying for some reason or just confused, Esther couldn't give up on her.

"It's her," she said.

"Good."

David leaned down then and kissed her face, her neck, brushed his fingers through her hair. Shivers ran over her skin like electricity. Esther wanted so badly to find a quiet spot where she and David could just be near to each other. But they couldn't give the Dentist any reason to watch them more closely than he already was. Naomi was too important.

After too short a moment David sighed and released her. Esther felt colder the minute his hands left her waist.

"We can do this, Esther," he said.

"I know."

They went back inside the Lodge to join the others. It was Betsy's turn to play the acting game, and she was flapping her elbows like fins and squawking while the women in the chairs shouted guesses.

Esther was fairly certain she was supposed to be a chicken. Esther scanned the group on the dais. Cody was trying out the other game. His dart hit the inner part of the target, and all the men cheered.

"Do you see my dad?" Esther said. "He was over there earlier."

"He probably went to bed early," David said lightly. "You should head back to bed soon too, Esther. You still need rest."

Esther narrowed her eyes. She thought they had been standing by the Lodge's only exit. She started to say as much, but when she turned, David was already striding away from her to rejoin the men.

29. After Midnight

SOMETHING TAPPED THE WINDOW by Esther's bunk. She sat up. There it was again. *Tap.* A pause. *Tap.* She wondered how someone could swim up and reach her porthole before she remembered she was on land, in the women's dormitory. The window wasn't that far off the ground.

There was another tap.

Esther crept from her bunk and peered outside. An object struck the smoky glass as she reached it. Someone was throwing stones at the window. She couldn't tell who in the darkness. She sensed movement at the edge of her vision. Shadowy figures gathered beneath the spreading tree near the cabin, the one with a trunk carved full of names.

Esther looked around the dorm. The other women all appeared to be sound asleep. She was probably the only one of them worried enough to sleep lightly. She tiptoed to the door and snuck out with barely a creak.

The town was hushed. Peaceful. Long moon shadows stretched across the ground, making the buildings look like they were deep under the ocean.

A dark shape beckoned to Esther from the shadows. Heart thudding, she followed him toward the tree. As her eyes adjusted, she recognized Cody's round shoulders. She started to relax—until she realized that Thompson was waiting for them, leaning against the tree trunk.

Esther opened her mouth to ask what the hell was going on when she realized a third figure was sitting at Thompson's feet. He was clutching his leg, which twisted at an odd angle.

It was her father.

"Don't make any noise, Esther," Cody began.

"What the hell is going on!" she whispered hoarsely, dropping to her knees beside her father.

Simon's face was tight with pain, but he managed a small smile. "I'm fine, button."

Simon's leg wasn't just twisted. It was mangled. Long rows of scratches ran down its length. His blood glistened black in the darkness.

"I found him caught in the barbed wire fence," Thompson growled.

"Couldn't see it in the dark," Simon said. "By the time I realized what had happened, I was too tangled up to escape. I fell trying to extract myself and wrenched my old injury."

"What were you doing?"

"He was on his way to the Bunker," Thompson said. "Tried to go through the jungle, but we have it fenced out there."

"The Bunker?" Realization hit Esther like a swinging boom. He had been trying to rescue Naomi on his own!

"I don't want to know what he was trying to do," Thompson said. Esther could sense tension coming off him in waves, even though his posture was casual as he leaned against the carved tree trunk. "It would be worse for him if one of the Elders found him, so I cut him loose."

"He was helping me back to my cabin when Cody found us while out with the curfew patrol," Simon said. He sounded remarkably calm considering the amount of blood coating his legs. His hands were torn up badly too, leaving dark smudges as he tried to shift his injured leg. "He insisted on coming to find you."

"Damn right!" Esther said. "What were you thinking?"

Thompson cleared his throat warningly. "I told you I don't want to know what he was doing."

"Why are you helping?" Esther asked. "You're not going to report him to the Dentist?"

"I still might if I decide you're a danger to me and mine," Thompson said. "You seem like good people, though." He stood and picked up the shotgun that had been resting against the tree. It glinted in the weak moonlight. "I'll trust you to patch him up. This never happened."

"Okay," Esther said, wanting desperately to ask more. She knew he wouldn't answer, though. "And thank you."

Thompson grunted. "Don't be late for fishing tomorrow."

Then he disappeared into the night.

Esther turned her attention back to her father. They had to stop the bleeding and wrap him up as best they could. She'd need to grab blankets or something from the dormitory. She had no idea how they were going to hide this injury in the morning.

"You could have been killed," she said, fighting the urge to cry in frustration. "Why didn't you let me help?"

"I'm sorry, Esther, but I can't lose one daughter trying to save the other," Simon said.

She was startled by the raw tone in his voice. She would die to help her sister, but she hadn't considered the situation from her father's perspective before.

"We're in this together, Dad," she said slowly.

"It's my fault, Esther." Simon grimaced as he shifted his leg again. "I should never have assumed they didn't survive. I should never have decided to stay at sea when there was the slimmest of chances."

"You had no way of knowing—"

"It doesn't matter. I left them. It has been almost seventeen years! I should have come back to look for them sooner." He took a shuddering breath and fell silent.

Esther didn't know what to say. Why hadn't she anticipated this? Her father had spent so long keeping his pain and guilt from her. Of course he would want to try to make it right without hurting anyone else. She understood that feeling all too well.

Something rustled in the darkness. There was a noise, perhaps a bird.

"We should get you back to your cabin," Esther said. "And I'll wake up Anita. She's better with injuries."

"David stayed out late with some of the Elders to keep them occupied," Cody said. "I'll run ahead and make sure none of them are around before we move him."

"Wait. David knew?" Esther hissed, remembering their stolen moment on the porch. She hadn't seen her father after that.

"I asked him to keep your attention elsewhere," Simon said. "And that boy will do anything for you."

Esther swallowed her retort. It was odd to hear David being called a boy. She knew her father had as much a right to put himself in danger to help Naomi as she did. She was annoyed that they went behind her back, though. They may have been trying to keep her safe, but none of them were safe anyway. David knew that as well as she did. The nerve of that boy!

She'd deal with him later, though. Esther left her father beneath the tree and crept back into the cabin to wake Anita. She didn't wait for an explanation, quickly gathering up blankets and clothing and following Esther out into the night. Esther prayed their luck would hold and none of the women would realize two of the strangers were out of bed.

Esther and Anita helped Simon back to the little cabin the men had been sharing. David was still out. Apparently, the curfew didn't apply to Elders and their friends. Anita and Esther got her father patched up and put to bed. They concocted a story to tell the townspeople about how he had decided to go for an early-morning jog and he had tripped and fallen into a bramble patch. It was a bit thin given the extent of his injuries, but it was the best they could do.

"We could say he was attacked by a wild boar!" Cody suggested.

"That would have made a bit more noise than a trip," Simon said. "I'd have been screaming bloody murder for one."

"I guess. Bole told me they can be as big as dolphins."

"And a lot less friendly."

"So what do we think about Thompson?" Esther said. She was wiping the last of her father's blood off her hands and knotting up the sheet they had used to clean his wounds.

"He's been nice enough to me," Cody said, "except for that first day."

"Nice might be a stretch," Esther said. Thompson was still a mystery. She'd see what she could get out of him on their little fishing expedition tomorrow.

"Well, not nice," Cody said. "But he doesn't seem all evil and controlling like the Dentist."

"I agree," Anita said. She checked Simon's bandages once more and stood. "Don't move around too much. Your knee will take longer to heal than the scratches, but you don't want to open up your scabs."

"And don't try anything stupid again," Esther muttered.

Simon frowned. "I'm afraid I won't be trying anything for a while." He met Esther's eyes steadily. "I failed."

"I'm sorry, Dad." Esther got down on her knees beside his bed.

The others stepped away to give them a moment. A single lamp burned beside Simon, casting shadows across his tired face.

"You can't feel guilty about this forever," she said. "You've been there for me all along. That's why you didn't look for them. You kept me safe, and you did a great job of it." Esther fiddled with the edge of the quilt on her father's bed. She should have said something sooner. She should have thought about what he must be going through. "It can't have been easy, being alone like that. You have to forgive yourself."

Simon sighed, a sea-deep sound. He cupped Esther's cheek for a moment, his thumb resting on her two thin scars.

"You'd better get back before you're caught."

Esther hugged him tight, and then she and Anita hurried through the town to their own cabin. They made it back into their beds well before first light.

30. Fishing

WHEN ESTHER ARRIVED AT the dock the following afternoon, Thompson and Bole were waiting for her. She had decided to bring Cally along. If the townspeople didn't want women going fishing, that was too salting bad.

"Thanks for offering to take us out on the lake," Esther said to Thompson.

He nodded stiffly. She couldn't tell if he was hiding a smile or a scowl behind his beard. She was keenly aware of how vulnerable they were now that Thompson knew they had been sneaking around. Just because he didn't like the Dentist's Code didn't mean he was their friend.

"That's the whole point of this place!" Bole said.

Despite his joviality, Esther wondered whether he had been sent along to keep an eye on them—and on Thompson. She couldn't forget he was still a member of the Dentist's favored circle. But he *was*

Yvonne's brother. Esther wished she knew who to trust.

"I can't wait to see what it feels like to sail on still water," Cally said. "It'll be great. My first time on a lake!"

Bole chuckled. "Wouldn't want you to miss it."

They headed down to the dock. Thompson fell in behind them, his heavy feet pounding loudly on the wooden boards. A fishing boat waited for them at the end of the dock. It was about twenty feet long, with a simple open cockpit and a collection of fishing poles sprouting from its stern like spines.

A few men had already gathered, including Cody, who had acquired a wide-brimmed straw hat from somewhere. Bole ushered them onto the boat. When everyone was on board, Thompson fired up the motor, and they pulled away from the dock. Esther breathed a little easier with the motion of the boat.

"I figure all you sea people can fish real well," Bole said as he sat beside Esther and began untangling a fishing line.

"The Dentist won't mind?" Esther asked, reaching out to help him.

Bole shrugged. "He said to keep you folks busy. Gotta earn your keep and all. Too bad your dad couldn't come."

Esther didn't answer. The story of her father's injury had gone over well enough at breakfast that morning, but she was feeling more anxious than ever about making a move soon.

The water rippled around them as they sped across the lake. It was so calm compared to the sea, with barely any wind. It was good to have water beneath her again. Esther felt healthier than she had in days. On land she constantly had the sense that she was being held down, pulled toward earth, caught in quicksand. But on the water they swept forward, skipping free across the surface.

The lake was quite big, and it was an odd shape, like a cross or a starfish. It settled in the cracks between several hills, so the water spread outward, long fingers reaching into the contours and crevasses of the hills around it. The hills cast strange reflections across the surface of the water.

Sunlight danced over the ripples around them. Esther leaned over the side of the boat, allowing the spray to coat her face. She opened her mouth, and water landed on her tongue, clear and unsalted.

Near the center of the lake they slowed. Thompson cut the power to the motor and allowed the boat to drift, rocking a bit from the movement of the fishermen.

Everyone chose a fishing pole, and someone handed around a tin can full of dirt-covered, wriggling worms. Esther pinched one between her fingers and studied it closely.

"What are those?" Cally squealed. "I've never seen anything so gross in my entire life."

"It's an earthworm. People use them for bait on land," Esther said.

"Ew. Do I have to touch it?"

"It's not nearly as slimy as an eel."

Cally took the tin can and peered at the worms. "Fish eat these?"

"Fish eat anything," Esther said.

She poked her hook through the worm's body. It continued to writhe. She quickly dropped it into the water and allowed the line to unravel.

"Here. Use this one instead, Cally." Cody had come over to their side of the boat. He held his fishing rod high above his head to avoid poking anyone in the eye with it. "It has a lure. The captain says to be careful not to lose it. I'll use the one with the worm."

"Thank you," Cally said as she exchanged fishing poles with Cody and examined the lure made of bright yellow and white feathers. "This is pretty. They should do this for all of them."

"You have to keep it moving," Cody said. "That way the fish will think it's a bug."

Cody put his arm around Cally to demonstrate how to reel in the lure so it looked like it was skipping on the lake. As he did, he lost track of his own line, and soon it was tangled up with Esther's.

"Watch it, Cody!" she said.

"Gee, sorry. Let me fix it."

"I got it. I'm going to the stern." Esther disentangled her line and moved back beside the outboard motor, where it was less crowded.

She dropped her hook again. Her line sliced the water. Gentle ripples coursed away from the fiberglass hull of the boat. Being on the water reminded Esther of that weightless floating feeling the sea provided. She felt homesick.

Her line twanged, and something tugged on the end. She jerked the tip upward and began reeling in her catch. Several people shouted around her.

"I got one!"

"Me too!"

"Looks like we found the school, kids," Bole shouted.

The fish on Esther's line had plenty of fight in it, and soon she was sweating. She was still a little weak from her illness, but within a few minutes she had reeled in the fish and pulled it up to the boat.

Esther had seen a lot of fish in her life, but this was the ugliest she had ever encountered. It had very thick gray lips and a mottled brown and green body. She brought it over to the bucket, where it joined two others swimming in tight circles in a bit of water.

"That's a nice bass," said Thompson. He stood at the helm, one hand on the wheel. He carried his shotgun slung across his back even here.

"Do they taste any good?" Esther asked.

"The uglier they are, the better they go down," he said.

"If you say so. Can I get another one of those worms?"

"Here." Thompson handed them over.

"Thank you." Esther hesitated. It was now or never. "Thompson?"

"Yeah?"

"Why did you help us last night?"

"Told you it never happened."

"But do you and the Dentist—?"

"I know what you're getting at," Thompson said. "You're barking up the wrong tree. My beef with the Dentist is my own business."

Esther didn't know what "barking up the wrong tree" meant, but she got the gist. She doubted Thompson would join them in acting directly against the Dentist. But would he give them away? They were running out of options, and Naomi was running out of time.

They had filled three buckets with bass by the time the sun began to sink.

"The lake must want to welcome you to our town," Bole said. "Just like it welcomed us. We got a ceremony tonight to thank it."

"Is that some kind of religious thing?" Cally asked.

"Yup. We're making an offering to the lake."

Esther froze. "What offering?"

"I don't want to freak you out," Bole said. "Remember the sacrifices we talked about a while back?"

"You mean executions," Esther said.

"They're killing someone?" Cally looked horrified.

"Don't worry, they only execute criminals," Bole said quickly. "When people break the Code real bad, we offer them back to the lake. It's better than doing it to an innocent person. We're advanced like that."

"But why?" Cally said.

Panic swirled in Esther's stomach. She wanted to throw up. Naomi was going to be killed. They had to do something. She judged the distance between their boat and the shore. Too far to swim. They had to go back. Now.

"How else would we deal with criminals?" Bole was saying. "Keep feeding them in lockup when they're not contributing anything to the town? It would be too dangerous to keep them around."

Cally was growing distraught. Cody put a hand on her arm to try to calm her, and she clutched his hand.

"Can't you just send them off somewhere? You know, maroon them?"

"This way's guaranteed to keep everyone safe," Bole said. "And the lake still gets its sacrifice."

"That's crazy."

"Hey, the lake saved all our lives," Bole said. "It gives us sustenance. I know it sounds lame, but it really is our promised land. We need to show our gratitude."

Esther felt dread spinning and spooling within her. How could he be so nonchalant? They had to get back to town. She hurried toward the cockpit.

"Thompson? We need to go back."

Thompson didn't answer, but he was already firing up the motor for the journey to shore.

They crept toward the dock at a deathly slow pace. Esther wished she could commandeer the helm.

"Can you show us how fast this thing goes?" she said.

Thompson grimaced, but he throttled the engine, and they shot across the lake. The sunset had turned the sky a dark-golden yellow like burnt corn. The trees stood sharp against it, reminding Esther of how far from the sea they were. The sun would sink below the tree line long before it met the actual horizon as she was used to thinking of it. She forced down the panic, contained it like a fire in a fuel cell. She had to stay focused.

When they finally reached the dock, the townspeople were already streaming toward the shores of the lake.

"Where's everyone going?" Esther asked.

"We're back a little late," Bole said. "It's almost time for the ceremony."

"The execution?"

"The offering, yes," he said, giving her a cautious look. "Don't you want to thank the lake for the bounty it has provided today?"

"Of course," Esther said. "I need to go find—"

"Hold on," Thompson said. "This isn't a vacation. You need to clean the fish like everyone else."

"But the ceremony—"

"Won't start without us. Those people are going to get good seats. You'll be able to see well enough. Come on now. We've got fish to gut."

Bole had already started off toward the town, mumbling something about Elder duties. But the rest of the men remained, standing around the Lucindans in a loose, too-casual circle. Esther bounced on the balls of her feet, preparing to make a move.

Then Thompson took a few steps closer to Esther and said under his breath, "Pick your battles. Trust me."

Esther nearly hit him. This *was* her battle! But there were too many men around. Even with Cody's and Cally's help, there was no way they could get through these guys without sending up a warning. They'd never even get close to the execution site.

Jaw clenched, she set to cleaning the fish. It was torturous to sit there bent over the dock with a fish knife in her hand while the moment of the execution ticked closer. Each time Esther drove the knife into the belly of a bass to remove its entrails, she imagined a knife going deep into her sister. She stripped the fillets off the brittle, translucent bones, seeing the tender flesh of her sister's arms, still the size of an eight-year-old girl's. Esther cut her own thumb twice as she rushed through the cleaning. She ignored the pain and the blood.

After she was done, Esther rinsed her hands and the fish knife in the lake. When no one was looking, she tucked the knife into her pocket. She would be ready when they brought out her sister. She would not allow Naomi to die.

31. Sacrifice

THE WHOLE TOWN HAD already gathered by the time Thompson let Esther, Cody, and Cally go. They ran toward the cleared part of the shore where the Lake Day feast had been held the week before. The picnic tables were full. The Dentist stood at the podium with his band of Shepherds. The Elders and other guards surrounded them. Esther's heart pounded, rapid like a machine gun. The ceremony had already started.

"The crime is confirmed. The Code is clear," the Dentist said. "Let us purify our community through this act."

No, no, no! We're too late! Esther scanned the crowd, desperation making her vision blur.

All heads turned toward the town. Some of the townspeople's faces seemed lit with an inner glow, near rapture. Other people in the crowd, however, maintained carefully neutral expressions as they went through the motions of the ceremony. Not everyone was fully committed to this, but they didn't try to stop it either. The lake had given them enough that they were willing to put up with human sacrifices in order to stay.

Someone was going to be killed tonight, dumped into the lake like bycatch. Fear wrapped itself around Esther's heart. Her hands found the fish knife she had stolen. *Please don't let it be Naomi.* She stood at the edge of the crowd. She only had Cally and Cody with her. The others from the *Lucinda* were on the opposite side of a long aisle leading straight to the Dentist's podium. They were too far away. She needed their help.

Four men marched through the town, approaching the assembly by the lake. They formed a box around a fifth figure. A large canvas bag covered the prisoner's head. The group wasn't close enough for Esther to tell whether it was Naomi, but the prisoner was definitely the shortest in the group.

The four guards were big and beefy, their muscles straining under their camouflage shirts. Could she take them? Even if they were unarmed, she wasn't sure she'd be able to get through all four in time. And then there'd be the rest of the town to face. She needed backup.

The five people started down the aisle between the tables. Esther gripped the knife so hard her hand ached. As soon as they were past, she darted across the aisle to join the Lucindans at their table right in the middle of the crowd. There was no sign of David, but her father was there, his legs swathed in makeshift bandages. He too had his eyes fixed on the figure being led down the aisle.

Esther perched on the edge of the outer bench beside him, her feet facing the podium so she could launch herself forward when the time was right. There was no time to plan, no time to coordinate their attack. But if she rushed forward the Lucindans would follow. They would keep the Elders off her back for long enough.

The townspeople began to drum rhythmically on the picnic tables. *Ba-bum. Ba-bum.* Esther held her breath. *Ba-bum.* She was ready. She'd kill the Dentist and anyone who got in her way before she let them hurt her sister. She had to pick the right moment. There could be no mistakes.

Ba-bum. Ba-bum. Ba-bum. She drew the fish knife and held it against her leg, where no one could see it. The wooden handle warmed in her palm. Almost time.

Then one of the guards shifted out of the way as he adjusted the sack over the prisoner's head. The prisoner had very broad shoulders and a strong, narrow waist. That was definitely a man. It wasn't Naomi.

Esther's father put a bandaged hand on her shoulder.

"Not her," he whispered. "Don't."

Esther sucked in a breath. She forced herself to relax, shuddering as the aftereffects of dread hit her. She had been seconds away from launching herself at the Dentist.

The pace of the drumming picked up as the group moved slowly up the long aisle. The prisoner shuffled along with his covered head down, but he didn't try to run away. If Esther was being led to her own execution like that, nothing would stop her from going down fighting. But the man seemed almost calm in the face of this madness.

The group reached the front of the crowd, right beside the lake. A tall pyre of fresh wood had been set up where they'd had the bonfire on Lake Day. *Please don't tell me they're going to burn him to death*, Esther thought wildly. She imagined the biting terror the man must be feeling right now.

The Dentist raised a hand and the drumming ceased. Silence spread through the crowd.

"This man," the Dentist said, "has disobeyed our most solemn laws. He has caused the fall of an innocent. He has forever ruined one of our sisters. Tonight he will pay the price."

The men moved the prisoner closer to the cold pyre. Esther felt Simon's hand tighten on her arm and realized she had begun to stand without thinking. She glanced at him and he winced, no doubt from the pressure on his injuries. She sat back, shaking. The only thing that kept her from running to save the man was the knowledge that it would doom Naomi for good. And probably the rest of them too.

A rowboat appeared on the darkening waters of the lake. It was a simple vessel manned by two figures. It pulled as close to the shore as it could get. The four guards pushed the prisoner out into the lake. At least they weren't going to throw him onto the pyre. They splashed forward until they reached the boat, where they lifted the man into it and then removed the canvas bag covering his head.

Esther wasn't close enough to see the details of his features, but she guessed that he was young, perhaps in his late twenties. His head had been shaved close. His beard—if he had had one like the rest of the townsmen—was gone. The men in the boat lifted something up and placed it around the prisoner's neck. It was heavy, judging by the way they strained to lift it. The prisoner hunched over as the object pulled him closer to the bottom of the boat.

"It is better," the Dentist intoned, "to have a millstone tied around the neck and to be drowned than to cause one of my children to sin."

The rowers pulled further away from the shore. Then they reached into the bottom of the boat and pulled up a large stone with a rope looped through a hole in its center. This was what had been tied to the prisoner's neck. They pushed him close to the edge of the boat.

"Whatever you do, don't react," said David's voice from Esther's other side, calm and firm. She hadn't even noticed when he had arrived and sat down beside her. "This isn't our fight."

She couldn't tell if he was speaking to her or to himself. His words echoed Thompson's earlier: *Pick your battles.*

The Dentist looked out over the crowd, an almost feral expression in his eyes. There was something here. A personal grudge against the prisoner perhaps?

The Dentist raised both hands and said, "We offer this man to the lake in penance for his sins and for ours. May we always uphold the Code."

"*May we always uphold the Code,*" the people repeated.

"May the Lord grant it so."

"*May the Lord grant it so.*"

Then the rowers pushed the stone and the man into the lake. He sank without a sound.

There were no cheers. Esther was grateful for that at least. A few bubbles rose where the man had disappeared. Ripples spread out across the water.

Esther knew the fear of drowning well. It was synonymous with the fear of death for anyone who lived at sea. They had all pictured it: the sudden silence, the panic as whatever had pulled you beneath the water held you down. She had imagined those moments of struggle a thousand times. And then silence.

The bubbles stopped rising. The ripples dissipated. Triumph bathed the Dentist's face for an instant. The sacrifice was complete.

Afterwards the Lucindans gathered in a tight knot as the bonfire was lit for another barbecue. Esther breathed quickly and shallowly. It took all her willpower not to launch herself at the Dentist, who was now chatting with a few Elders by the fire.

David tried to distract her by asking about the fishing, but that only made it worse. Bole and Thompson had kept them out on the water so they wouldn't hear about the preparations for the sacrifice. David had been out with a hunting party, and the leader had taken him on a long detour, so he arrived back even later than Esther. She scowled at the people around her, these seemingly open-faced and innocent townsfolk who danced and farmed and played soccer. They had allowed this to happen.

"Would it help if you knew his crime?" David asked. "It's possible he deserved it."

"They made a spectacle of it," Esther said. "Why would they do something like that in front of everyone and then immediately begin a meal? Even if he deserved to die, it's sick."

"I agree," Simon said, his face very pale. "It was unheard of in the modern world—before the disaster—for human sacrifice to be part of a religious celebration. The Dentist has an unprecedented level of influence to get away with something like this. His people must be very afraid of him."

"He didn't do it in front of us by accident," David said. "This was a warning."

"We have to get Naomi out," Esther said. "Now."

"We can't get caught," David said. "If the towns-people put up with this for one of their own, we can't expect any mercy for outsiders like us."

"I can find my way back to the Bunker," Esther said. "I think I know how to get inside the building, but it was too dark to get a good look at the lock on her cage. We'll have to improvise."

"I'll ask the Elders to find out for sure, but I'm guessing they won't have sacrifices two days in a row," David said. "Tonight bought us time, if nothing else."

"The real question is, how do we get Naomi out without putting everyone else in further danger?" Simon said.

Esther studied the Lucindans. David and her father. Anita, her face a little green. Dax with his arm around Cally, who was wide-eyed and solemn. Cody, his round baby face looking a decade older beneath his silly straw hat. Then Esther caught sight of Yvonne sitting by herself at the edge of the crowd. Her face was streaked with tears, confirming Esther's suspicion about the identity of the prisoner. *Louis*. The man her sister loved.

She knew what she had to do.

"We don't," Esther said, her path suddenly as clear as seawater. "You guys have to take the whole crew out of the village. Otherwise, we'll just end up with more people in jeopardy."

"You'll need help," David said.

"I don't think numbers will make much difference. Everyone has to get away from here, and then I'll sneak her out." Esther put her hand in her pocket to make sure the fish knife was still there. She felt the smooth edge of something else in her pocket too, and it gave her an idea. She smiled.

"What do you have in mind, Esther?" Simon asked.

"You have to leave too, Dad," Esther said. She lowered her voice, looking between David and her father, the two men she trusted more than anyone else in the world. "If too many people stay behind, they'll get suspicious. Take the others to the *Lucinda* and wait for me out of sight of the dam. Or return to Emilio's people if you have to."

"You can't do this alone," Simon said.

"I have to," Esther said. She gripped his hand, clutching his fingers to avoid hurting his cuts. She remembered grabbing his hand as a child, holding on as he protected her from a world gone haywire. "I have a plan to get Naomi out of the Bunker, but we can't start a fight. Most of the people here are decent." Esther glanced at Yvonne again. Betsy had gone to sit beside her, putting an arm around her shoulders. "Get everyone out of here, and I'll join you."

"Are you sure?" David asked.

Esther was glad he didn't say she couldn't do it.

"She's my sister."

"She's also my daughter," Simon said. "And so are you."

"Dad, for my plan to work I need to be fast and completely silent. Your injuries would only slow me down. We can't keep arguing about it. It's time to move."

Her father was quiet for a long moment. He rubbed at his knee and frowned at the bandages wrapped around his badly mangled legs. "Okay," he said with a sigh. "I trust you, Esther."

"So do I," David said brusquely. "We'll return to the *Lucinda* first thing tomorrow. All we need is an excuse to leave you behind."

Esther smiled. "I've got a plan for that too."

Esther was not at all sure she could get Naomi out, especially if she really didn't want to leave, but she had to make David and her father believe she had a plan. She would not allow anyone else from the *Lucinda* to be harmed. She had been selfish for too long. If she was killed, then so be it. She couldn't abandon the young woman in that cage whether or not it was really her sister. She would make sure no one else suffered for her mistakes.

32. Departure

THE LUCINDANS ATE BREAKFAST in the Lodge the following morning. The Dentist took his place at the head of the long table. As before, a few single people and prominent Elder families had been invited to share the meal of scrambled eggs and fried green peppers. The Lucindans sat together at one end of the table. They had already been warned of the plan. Esther hoped they could all act.

Immediately after the meal David raised his voice a bit. He didn't stand, so it would look like he only meant to address his own crew. It was showtime.

"Everyone," he said, "I've been doing some thinking. We've enjoyed the hospitality of the good people of the Lake, but I think we're not as good a fit here as we had hoped. I believe it's time we continued our journey in search of a new home. The snows could already be starting in the high mountains. We should be on our way before our path becomes too dangerous."

"Do we have to go so soon?" Cody asked. "I like it here. And I still haven't gone on a wild boar hunt!"

"There are things I'd still like to do too," David said, "but after last night I'm not sure it's the right fit for the whole *Catalina* community."

A few of the townspeople had leaned in and were listening to their conversation.

"I'm not sure everyone would be able to follow the Code anyway," Dax said. "And that's important here."

"Perhaps we've imposed on our friends here for too long," Simon said. "It may be time."

"I agree," Anita said.

"It's settled then," David said.

"Should we continue on foot from here?" Simon asked.

"No, let's return to Ixcuintla to get vehicles," David said. "We can try to catch up to Jackson's team on the road."

"If we move soon, they won't be too far ahead," Simon said.

"Let's pack up after breakfast then," David said.

"Wait!" Esther shouted. She blushed when the whole table turned to look at her, including the Dentist. *Good.*

"What is it?" David asked.

"I don't want to go yet."

David gave her a withering look. "It's not up to you."

"But we've only just started learning about the farming life here. I haven't done so many things. And the Shepherds were so kind to me when I was sick. I want to stay longer."

"I've made my decision," David said.

"No!" Esther stood up from her table, accidentally knocking over a jug of goat's milk. "I want to stay a few more days. This is a good place. It's safe and there's plenty of food."

"I'm the leader of this expedition," David said. "We leave today."

"I don't want to—"

"You know what, Esther?" David said. "I've about had it with your insubordination. You want to stay? Fine. The mission will be better off without you."

"Fine! I'll stay then." She jutted her lip out in a pout, then pulled it back again. Too much. She didn't dare look at Cally or she might laugh. "The lake is better than the sea anyway," she said.

"Oh *sure*. That's why. Tell the truth, Esther." David stood, his face a thunderhead. "This is about *him*, isn't it?"

Esther blinked. "I don't know what you're talking about." And she really didn't. This wasn't part of the plan.

"You think I don't see the way he looks at you?"

"Who?"

"You know who. I shouldn't have believed you'd be faithful. You're a fickle woman, Esther. You do what you want without regard for anyone else's feelings."

"Is that what you think?" Esther sputtered.

"Yes," David snarled. "You're too immature for me anyway. And selfish. You'd never make a good wife."

Betsy's mouth hung open. The other townspeople shifted in their seats, looking discreetly down at their scrambled eggs.

"Excuse me." That seemed far enough to Esther. "You think you're so smart, but you're not the world's greatest captain. Not even close." She needed to get back on script. What was she supposed to say again? Right. "I know now there are better people to follow. Better leaders."

"I suppose you think *you* should lead," David said. "You always think you know better than everyone else, that it's up to you to do the right thing."

The other Lucindans began to appear uncomfortable too. Dax's jaw looked like it might fall off. Esther's face grew hot.

"We've decided to move on," David continued. "So pack your bags."

"You can't tell me what to do, Hawthorne," Esther snapped.

"That's enough." David lowered his voice danger-ously. "You're out of the crew. Everyone else, get your gear. We leave at 1100 hours."

The Lucindans mumbled their assent. Cally no longer looked in danger of giggling. Esther couldn't look at any of the crew. She focused on her plate, fuming. Some of what David had said hit a little too close to home. She looked up at him, and he glared at her. She jerked her gaze away and found herself locking eyes with the Dentist.

He wore a slight smile. She couldn't tell if he knew what they were up to or not, but she was al-most too angry to care now. How dare David say those things in front of everyone! And to call her fickle after everything they'd been through!

She stood, shaking with anger, and stalked over to the Dentist's chair.

"Sir," she said, "I'd like to ask your permission to stay at the lake. When I was ill, the Shepherds took such good care of me . . . I like what I've seen of your life here and . . ." She had practiced this speech, but she was forgetting some lines. Salting David Elliot Hawthorne. He threw her off. The fight was never supposed to get that personal. "And I've made friends here. Please, can I stay?"

The Dentist studied her, pressing his fingers to-gether beneath his chin.

"I'll work," Esther said. "I'll earn my keep, and I swear I'll follow all the rules of the Code." Some-thing Betsy had said floated back to her. "The road isn't safe for women, and I want to stay somewhere I'll be protected. The others can go on without me."

"We *will* hold you to the Code," the Dentist said. "And you'll have to swear to serve the Lake, as we all have."

"Of course."

"And I will not stand for insubordination. Understand this well."

"Sir, I have no problem following the orders of a *worthy* leader." Esther shot a glare at David. He had begun to usher the Lucindans toward the doors. Cody hadn't even finished his breakfast, and he forked a few more bites into his mouth as he stood.

"Very well," the Dentist said. "You could do with a steady hand. I'd urge you to find a husband sooner rather than later."

Esther nearly swallowed her tongue, but she forced a smile. "I look forward to my new life here."

A slow smile spread across the Dentist's face. There was no way he believed her. He was playing along for his people's benefit. How much did he know? She didn't break eye contact with him until the door closed behind the Lucindans.

The crew gathered their belongings quickly. They hadn't unpacked most of their stuff, so they could move at a moment's notice. Cally and Anita had already collected their knapsacks from the single-women's dormitory when Esther returned there after breakfast. She changed back into the skirt and blouse Yvonne had given her. She had to show her commitment to becoming a woman of the town.

She went out to see her friends off, though. They would hike back down to the river and be on their way within a few hours. She might never see them again. There was only a slim chance this would work.

A few townspeople gathered to say good-bye to their visitors. Esther stood beside Yvonne as her friends prepared to head into the jungle. Thompson and one of the Elders emerged from the village to accompany them down to the river, shotguns resting in their hands once again. Thompson met Esther's eyes for a minute, his expression cloaked. He was still a loose wire, one she hadn't been able to tie down. She hoped she wouldn't regret it.

Esther's father hugged her fiercely before turning and limping down the path, assisted by a walking stick one of the townspeople had fashioned for him. As he disappeared into the trees, she could still feel the warmth of his arms.

She still hadn't told him the whole truth. If she failed in this attempt, at least her father would know she had been doing it out of love for her family. And he would never find out that Naomi claimed not to know them. That was all she could give him.

There were tears in Cally's eyes when she said good-bye.

"Be careful, Esther," she whispered. "I need you."

"You'll be okay," Esther said. "Don't break too many hearts."

Cally sobbed and hugged her again. Then she marched down the path, leaving Dax and Cody to follow in her wake.

David didn't look at her at all. He shook hands with the Dentist, who had come to see them off. She wanted him to glance at her, to give her some sort of sign that they were okay. But he avoided her gaze entirely, standing straight and elegant as ever. Then he walked away from her without saying good-bye.

Esther was still scowling at the bend in the path where David had disappeared when the Dentist turned to her.

"I believe it's time to get to work, don't you think?"

"Yes, sir," Esther said. She wiped angrily at the tears welling up in her eyes. "And thank you."

The Dentist smiled, and Esther felt a viscous hatred, like oil sliding through her stomach. It was his fault she had to say good-bye.

Esther followed Yvonne back to the hatchery and spent the day helping her feed the chickens. The evil birds made her cringe, but it kept her busy. She would make her move at nightfall. By that time the *Lucinda* should be under way. Her friends would be safe, even if she never saw them again. She had a pretty good idea of what to do. She just had to pull it off. A few chickens were nothing. Esther would not let herself be afraid.

After work Yvonne dragged her off to watch a game of soccer. She seemed to think Esther was nursing a broken heart and wanted to distract her. Yvonne assured her there would be plenty of nice-looking men at the game.

They sat in the grass with a few other women and watched. The teams were Elders against ordinary townsmen. They wore armbands in two different colors to help tell the teams apart. The goals were wooden posts with fishing nets spread between them to catch the ball. The ball itself had been repaired many times, and the canvas patches were almost as numerous as the white and faded black ones.

"I wonder where Thompson is," Betsy said, flopping onto the grass next to Esther and Yvonne.

"He usually plays?" Esther asked.

"He's team captain," Yvonne explained.

"He should have been back from walking your people to the river by now," Betsy said. She studied Esther carefully as if waiting for a reaction.

"Maybe he had work to do," Esther said.

"He never misses a game."

As far as Esther knew, there had been no plans to mess with the guards. The Lucindans were supposed to make sure the Lake People knew they were truly leaving. She hoped David hadn't done anything rash. They couldn't afford mistakes at this stage. Her bigger fear, though, was that Thompson had acted against them after all.

The game was fast, and the men shouted and laughed at each other as they played. A handful of children kicked a makeshift ball around on the sidelines. Esther wondered whether her sister used to sit with Yvonne and Betsy to watch the games. Had Louis played too? Had his former teammates been among the men who pushed him into the lake to drown?

Loathing for the Dentist filled her. She was sure he was the one responsible for all this. Life in this town could be so good. In other circumstances it was exactly the sort of place she would have liked to create for her friends from the *Catalina*. But this town only accepted those willing to follow exactly the same set of moral guidelines and pay lip service to the Dentist's version of God. For everyone else this place was not the folksy paradise it seemed.

At halftime Bole jogged over to sit beside them. Yvonne pulled Betsy away, winking at Esther.

"Hey there." Bole sat in the grass beside her.

"Hi. You were great," Esther said.

"Thank you. I heard about what happened between you and Hawthorne. Sorry about that."

"It's okay," Esther said. "I'm looking forward to a fresh start here."

"I get it," Bole said. He smoothed down his beard and tightened his long ponytail. Then he whipped a dandelion from the grass and tucked it behind Esther's ear. "I'm sure you'll need time and all, but I wanted to tell you I plan to officially court you just as soon as I can."

Esther blinked. "Uh, I'd like that."

"Thought you would." Bole grinned.

"I might need a little time, though. I hope you understand."

"Sure thing. You're probably kinda sad right now. Courting's no fun when you're sad."

"Thank you for understanding," Esther said. "I need someone who really understands me." As if on impulse she leaned in and hugged Bole, wrapping her arms around his sweaty waist.

"Aw, you'll be all right." Bole patted her on the back. "Hey, don't forget about propriety."

"I'm still getting used to how you do things here," Esther said, smiling tremulously.

"Don't worry. I'll help you." Bole adjusted the dandelion in her hair and grinned. Then he leapt up and returned to the field.

Betsy and Yvonne had much to say about Esther and Bole as they watched the rest of the game. For a community with strict rules about what couples could and couldn't do, they seemed to love any hint of romance. Esther let their conversation wash over her, wrapping her hands in her skirt. She thought she knew now what David had been doing. The Dentist and the townspeople might not have believed she really wanted to live like the Lake People, but a lovers' quarrel was another matter. Bole was only helping the illusion. She should have realized what David was doing at breakfast, but she had been too angry. Her reactions had been totally genuine. That must have been what David had planned. Damn it, the man knew her too well.

She felt a bit bad about misleading Bole, but none of that mattered. She only had to keep up the charade for the rest of the day. She was done wasting time.

Late that night when the other women were asleep, Esther climbed out of her bunk. She changed back into her own clothes and carried her boots to the door. It creaked a bit when she opened it, but none of the women stirred.

Clouds obscured the moon and stars. Deep, dark shadows filled the village. Esther caught a glimpse of the evening curfew patrol heading away from the women's dormitory, going the opposite direction as the Bunker. Good. Right on schedule. Cody had managed to find out the patrol timetable during his time helping out with virtually every task in the town. He had made genuine friends, and Esther suspected he would have liked to stay here in other circumstances. He had learned there was usually only one pair of men doing rounds at any given time. But it just took one to raise the alarm.

Esther sat on the stoop and pulled on her boots. She was tying her second lace when the dormitory door squeaked. It was Yvonne, wearing a thick woolen nightdress.

"Where are you going?" she whispered. "We're not allowed out after curfew."

"I wanted some fresh air. Go back to sleep, Yve."

"I'm not stupid, you know," Yvonne whispered. She closed the dormitory door behind her, careful not to let it slam. "Tell me what you're up to."

Rust. "Will you promise not to raise the alarm until morning? No one's going to get hurt."

"I swear."

"I'm getting Naomi out of the Bunker."

"I knew it!" Yvonne squealed. "Let me help you."

"I don't want you to get in trouble." The path in front of the dormitory was still empty, but that could change any minute.

"She's my best friend, Esther," Yvonne said. "I would free her myself if I could, but I have nowhere else to go. Will you take me with you?"

"I don't want to give the Dentist any more reasons to come after us. I'm trying to do this without getting anyone killed."

Yvonne folded her arms. "Then I'll raise the alarm right now."

"Yve . . ."

"You can't leave me behind, not if you're really breaking Naomi out. I can help!"

Esther couldn't have Yvonne warning anyone, and she didn't want her to take the fall either. Enough people knew Yve had been friends with both Naomi and Esther. They could put the pieces together all too easily.

"Actually, there is a way you can help me," Esther said, realizing that one part of her plan could go a lot smoother than she'd anticipated with a little help.

"Yeah?"

Esther stood and put her hand in her pocket. "Yeah. I don't know how to drive." She withdrew the key she had taken from Bole's belt when she hugged him at the soccer game. "Want to help me steal your brother's jeep?"

33. The Bunker

THE JEEP BUMPED ALONG the darkened road. They kept the headlights off until they were several hundred yards outside of town. Getting the vehicle had been fairly uneventful. Yvonne knew Bole usually parked it in front of his cabin at the far edge of town—and he was a sound sleeper. They had simply taken it and driven off down the road. Until he woke up in the morning, Bole would be none the wiser. They should be long gone by then. Yvonne claimed her brother would never give them away, but they couldn't afford the risk.

The jeep's engine rumbled far too loudly. Every time they bumped over a root or the engine coughed, Esther was sure they were going to be discovered. Yvonne wasn't a particularly good driver. It felt like she was swerving to hit every dip and pothole on purpose.

Yvonne bounced up and down on the seat, both hands clutching the wheel. "This is so exciting!" she said. "I can't believe we're going to bust her out. Do you think we'll go to hell?"

"I don't believe in hell," Esther said.

"What will we do when we get into the Bunker?" Yvonne asked.

"Don't worry about it," Esther said. "You'll be waiting outside."

"But—"

"If we get caught, you can say I threatened you and made you drive me out here. If you come in with me, it'll be harder to pull off that excuse."

"So what's the plan?"

Esther released her grip on the jeep door to put her hand on the stolen fish knife. Something made a rattling noise beside it in her pocket. Most of the plan revolved around those two objects.

"Don't get caught," she said.

They passed the second of the two side roads Esther remembered from her drive with Bole and Cally.

"Turn off the lights. And slow down."

Yvonne obliged. She clicked off the headlights, immediately plunging them into blackness. The jeep slowed to a crawl, allowing time for their eyes to adjust to the dark.

An animal made a cawing sound in the scrub. The trees took on scraggily, alien shapes, like malevolent creatures. Esther's heart leapt into her throat. She breathed slowly. She needed to stay focused. She would be spending a lot more time amongst those trees soon. She couldn't get freaked out now.

They reached the end of the road. The jeep bounced down the rough gravel path to the Bunker. Yvonne cut the engine and allowed the vehicle to roll to a stop.

"Okay, wait here," Esther said. "If anyone finds you, tell them I said I'd hurt you and your family if you didn't drive me out here."

"Got it." Yvonne squeezed her hand. "Be careful, Esther."

Esther got out and approached the front door of the Bunker. It was locked, of course, so she pulled out the fish knife and went to work on the screws holding the hinges to the wall. She had checked to make sure this was possible back when Whitefern had released her from the infirmary. When the hinges were removed, Esther used her wrench to pry the door open. There was no alarm. That was a relief. She'd had no way of knowing for sure whether or not the Bunker had an automatic alarm system.

The disconnected door was very heavy, but this was the easy part. Esther leaned it against the wall and looked down the gloomy corridor. Yvonne was still waiting, peering wide-eyed over the side of the jeep. Esther took a deep breath and entered the Bunker.

Inside, the infirmary level looked just as it had before. It was quiet, with no guards in sight. The place was designed to keep people in, not out. She had to assume there would be guards in the lower levels, though.

Her boots squeaked on the floor as she walked to the elevator at the end of the corridor, passing the room where she had stayed during her illness. When she pushed the button, the elevator took a minute to arrive. That made Esther nervous. Someone had taken it down to the lower levels, and they hadn't come back up.

She waited next to the door so she'd be out of sight from the elevator car, preparing to leap forward with her knife raised. The doors opened. The elevator was empty. Esther slammed a hand against the door to hold it open and stepped inside. She pushed the button for the Detention Level. The easy part was almost over. Had it been too simple?

The elevator descended into the earth. Passed the Storage Level. Esther breathed slowly. *Almost there.* Descended further. The light for the Detention Level lit up as the elevator slowed. The doors began to open. Light poured through the crack. Someone was in there. Esther threw herself back out of sight. She wanted to see how many there were before she attacked.

Esther pressed herself against the wall, praying the guards would think some fluke had caused the elevator doors to open, praying they wouldn't start shooting straight off. They shouldn't be able to see her in this position.

But from this angle she could see into Naomi's cage.

It was empty. A periwinkle blanket sat abandoned on the bench, but Naomi was gone.

"Rust," Esther hissed.

Instead of jumping out, knife raised, she let the elevator door begin to close. Was she too late?

A hand banged against the edge of the door, stopping it just before it shut.

"You made it."

It was David.

34. Detention Level

SALTY HELL," ESTHER SAID. "I almost cut your hand off. Where's Naomi?"

"The cages were empty when I got here," David said. He gestured down the length of the Detention Level. The lights blazed, but there were no prisoners or guards to be seen. The door to Naomi's cage stood open.

"When was that?"

"Hours ago. I followed a Shepherd in and hid in an empty hospital room. But now the whole place is deserted. I don't like it."

"Why aren't you back on the *Lucinda*?" Esther asked.

"Thought you might need backup. Your father took everyone to the ship, and I circled through the jungle. I found the hole Thompson cut in the barbed wire fence when he got Simon out. Ripped my sweater, though." He held up his arm. A raw red scratch peeked through the tear in the fabric.

"What was with everything you said at breakfast?" Esther asked. She scanned the Detention Level again as she spoke. Yes, it was definitely empty. "You laid it on a little thick."

"I trust you with my life," David said, "but you're not a very good actress. I had to surprise you and make you really mad if the Dentist was going to believe you wanted to stay."

"That's what I thought," Esther said. "Afterwards, I mean. I *was* angry. It may have worked on the townspeople, but I'm not sure the Dentist bought it."

"You might be right. My guess is he got wind of what you were up to and moved Naomi," David said.

"But then there'd be guards here waiting for me."

"There were. I took care of them already. They're over behind the desk."

"Really?"

"I'm not completely incapable," David said. "It was one of the Elders I've met before and some young kid. They were surprised to see me instead of you, and that gave me the second I needed to incapacitate them."

"Are they dead?"

David missed a beat. "No." He looked toward the far side of the room. "At least, I don't think so."

"Nicely done," Esther said. "But we'd better move."

"Any idea where they would take your sister?"

"My guess is the bottom level here. The one without a label," Esther said.

"I agree. You armed?"

"Sort of. I have a fish knife and my wrench."

"The two goons behind the desk were kind enough to supply us with guns," David said. He slung a hunting rifle forward from his back to his front and went over to the desk to pick up another one. He put it in Esther's hands.

"Okay, let's go."

They stepped back into the elevator. David was about to press the button when Esther put her hand on his arm to stop him.

"I need to tell you something," she said.

"That you love me?" David said.

"No, don't change the subject."

"You don't love me?"

"Of course I do," Esther said. A grin flashed across David's face. "No, you need to know something about Naomi." She met his clear green eyes. "When I talked to her a few days ago, she told me she never had a sister. She said she is from San Diego, but she was in Texas when the volcano blew."

"I thought you recognized her."

"I did! I mean, I think it *is* her. She might be brainwashed or traumatized or lying to keep me out of danger or something." Esther swallowed. "Also, she kind of said she wouldn't come with me if I tried to rescue her."

David's face emptied of expression. He stared at her as if waiting for more information.

"I'm still going down there," she said. "And I brought some pills that I nicked from Whitefern in case we need to make her come quietly. Do you want to wait upstairs?"

David sighed. "You're killing me, Esther. Let's get this over with. We've come this far, and I don't like the idea of letting anyone else get sacrificed to the lake if we can prevent it."

He pressed the button for the lowest level. The elevator descended. They checked to make sure the safeties were off on their guns. Esther pressed her arm against David's for a moment. She was glad she wasn't alone.

The light for the bottom level glowed yellow. The elevator car slowed. Esther held her breath.

The doors opened. They burst into the room together.

"That's far enough." The Dentist stood up from a chair in front of the elevator doors and calmly pointed a revolver at them. He had been waiting.

The Dentist wore blue-and-white-striped pajamas, which were too short for his tall frame. He was alone, except for a figure huddled in an armchair in the corner. Naomi.

The bottom level of the bunker was outfitted like a first-class stateroom. There was a small kitchen with a table, a couch, two bunk beds, and a large woven rug on the concrete floor. One entire wall was made of open shelves stocked with row after row of canned food, paper goods, and tanks of propane. A computer on the table was plugged into a brick of batteries, and a massive water tank filled most of the space at the back of the room. At a glance it was obvious a handful of people could live here for a long time.

Esther took it all in in a flash.

"Are you all right, Naomi?" she called.

Naomi lifted her hands to show that they were tied with a thick cord.

"He found out you were coming."

"Yeah, I guessed that by now."

Esther hadn't lowered her gun. Neither had David.

The Dentist cleared his throat. "I warned you about filling the heads of my children with ideas about the outside world." His golden eyes seemed to glow in the darkened space. "I told you not to seduce my people away."

"You can't kill her," Esther said. She scanned the room for signs of other men. Her eyes landed on a jumble of miscellaneous parts set up in a way that looked familiar, a bucket overflowing with goopy green algae beside it. Esther realized it was a highly amateur attempt at assembling her generator.

"I can do what I please," the Dentist said, his deep voice dangerously calm. "This is my town. Now, I have a message for you. I've recently acquired some new allies, and they asked me to convey their greetings before I execute you."

"Boris," David said immediately. "He's your ally, I assume."

The edges of the Dentist's lips drooped a little, as if some of his surprise had been ruined. "Yes," he said.

"He wanted to gloat when you told him we'd be walking into a trap," David said.

"It's two against one," Esther said, still trying to sort out the connection between the Dentist and Boris. How long had they been in touch? "If you shoot either one of us, the other will take you out."

She kept her attention on the Dentist's trigger finger. She wouldn't hesitate.

"Actually," the Dentist smiled, "he wanted me to tell you that he sank your ship. The *Catalina*, is it? He thought you'd like to know."

Esther gasped, and the muzzle of her gun drifted off the Dentist for an instant. He fired.

The pain that exploded in Esther's arm was nothing compared to the way her heart imploded in her chest. David shouted her name, looked toward her. Other shots were fired. Naomi pitched out of her chair and lay flat on the floor. Esther tried to lift her gun, but she couldn't move her arm.

Not the *Catalina*. It couldn't be true. She couldn't believe it. She thought of Bernadette and Reggie, of Byron and his family. The Cordovas and the Newtons. Neal. Judith. The people that had been her family. The ship that had been her home.

Her blood dripped onto the concrete floor. Her knees were cold. She realized she was crouched on the ground. When she looked up, the Dentist was still standing. David was on his knees, the sleek barrel of the Dentist's revolver pressed to his forehead. *No.*

Time slowed.

Everything was falling apart.

"Now then," the Dentist said. "I thought that might get your attention, Miss Harris. Here's how this is going to work. I will shoot Mr. Hawthorne here and then throw you in the lake in front of my people to remind them what happens to anyone who crosses me."

David's gun was behind the Dentist, where he had kicked it. Too far away. Naomi lay prone on the floor, but she wasn't bleeding. She twisted her head a fraction and met Esther's eyes. She had to know her. Would she help them?

"You're afraid," Esther said. The Dentist's eyes flickered back toward her, but his hands remained steady, gun pressed against David's skull. "You're afraid of your people. You're terrified they'll turn against you."

Naomi eased her tied hands forward in front of her body, staying face-first on the floor. She was out of the Dentist's line of sight. Their only hope.

"All men in power fear their people," David said. Despite the gun barrel pushing into his forehead, he sounded calm, collected, sophisticated even. He sounded like himself. "I've seen it before. Your new friend Boris is the worst of the cowards."

"I'm already tired of listening to you," the Dentist said, sighing. "I'm not interested in your dramatics."

Naomi inched forward, any sound she made muffled by the woven carpet.

"That's why you met us here alone," Esther said. She had begun to feel light-headed. She was losing blood. She couldn't let the Dentist pull that trigger. "If you knew we were coming after Naomi, you should have had guards with you, not just waiting for us up on the Detention Level. But you didn't. You're here alone."

"I thought *you* would be alone, as it happens," the Dentist said. "I can handle one woman."

"That, and you didn't want any of your men to come down here," Esther said. *Hurry up, Naomi.* "You've got this place well stocked—your own private survival bunker—and you don't want anyone else to know about it. It's supposed to be your fail-safe if your people ever decide they've had enough of you."

"You think you're rather clever, don't you?" the Dentist said, lip curling.

"No, not really," Esther said. "Naomi is the clever one."

The Dentist spun to look at Naomi, and she shot him at point-blank range with David's gun.

35. The Radio

H E WAS LYING," DAVID said.

They were still in the Bunker. He was wrapping a tourniquet tight around Esther's arm with the cord the Dentist had used to tie up Naomi. The bullet had hit just above Esther's elbow. It felt like every bone in her arm had shattered. She pressed her wadded-up jacket against the wound while David worked. She could barely move the fingers of her left hand, and she was shivering.

"Esther, listen to me!" David said. He put his hand under her chin and lifted her face up so she'd meet his eyes. "He was trying to distract you. He was lying about the *Catalina*."

"He sounded serious to me," Naomi said.

She sat in the armchair again, staring at the man she had just killed.

"You're not helping," David said dryly.

"Um, I just saved your life," Naomi said.

Her face was ashen, and she looked like she might throw up.

"We have to find out for sure," Esther said. She felt like she was speaking through a fog bank, but her senses were sharpening. The pain helped. "We need to get back to the *Lucinda* and call them on the satellite phone."

"You can call from here," Naomi said. "That computer is linked up to a satellite dish on the roof. He doesn't let anyone else use it."

"Do you know how to work it?" Esther asked.

"I've never used the phone part before," Naomi said.

"I'll do it," David said. "I've probably had a bit more experience with computers than you two."

"Let me finish that then," Naomi said. "There's a first aid kit."

She stood on wobbly legs and retrieved the kit from the shelf closest to the door. Esther watched her. There was something strange about what Naomi was doing, something that didn't add up, but she was too shaken to identify what.

"Hold still," Naomi said, kneeling in front of Esther while David went to the computer. She opened a packet and pulled out a chemical-soaked cloth. "This'll sting."

Naomi used the cloth to clean the wound in Esther's arm. There were spatters of the Dentist's blood on her face and in her curly, matted hair. She definitely had Esther's mother's nose.

"You *are* my sister, aren't you?" Esther said. "Why did you pretend you didn't know me?"

Naomi bent lower over Esther's arm, avoiding her eyes. She finished cleaning the wound and reached into the first aid kit for a bandage. The first aid kit she had known exactly how to find.

"Wait, you've been down here before, haven't you?" Esther said. "More than once. You know about the computer and where to find things. I thought the Dentist didn't let anyone down here."

Esther pulled her arm out of Naomi's hands, trying to ignore the raging, burning pain.

Naomi's brown eyes swam with tears. Two of them rolled down the hook of Esther's mother's nose.

"He . . . he was like a father to me," she said. "He saved me from the ash. And I just . . . I just . . ." Naomi trailed off, staring at the Dentist's body.

"What do you mean he saved you?" Esther said.

David looked up from the computer, where he had been tapping at the keyboard.

"The Dentist," Naomi said. She sniffled, wiping at the blood on her face. "Dr. Robert Dagan. He was treating me when the volcano blew. He saw the ash coming through the window and carried me down to the basement of the clinic without a word. Mom was in the waiting room, but he wouldn't let me go to her." Naomi's voice faltered. She swallowed back a sob. "We took refuge in the basement storage room and survived on the oxygen stocked there for surgeries. We were underground for weeks, but he shared his air with me." Naomi looked up at Esther. "I wanted Mom and Dad to come for me, but they never did."

Esther let out a breath, pain throbbing in her arm. So Naomi hadn't been with her mother when the ash fell after all.

"We waited until we were almost out of oxygen," Naomi said, "and then the Dentist rigged up suits for us out of the medical gear in the basement, and we dug our way out. It had rained, and buildings were flattened all across the city. It was horrible."

Naomi tentatively reached out to Esther and held up the bandage for her arm. "Let me finish that."

Esther let her resume bandaging the wound, gritting her teeth against the pain.

Naomi focused on her hands and continued. "We dragged all the oxygen tanks and protective masks we could find in a shopping cart and used them until they ran out. Even then the air smelled like poison. I thought we would die after all, but we just kept going. We walked until we found a car that wasn't completely clogged with ash, and then we drove from town to town, looking for somewhere to stay. We scavenged for canned food for years. We moved on whenever nomads or gangs of desperate people turned up. The Dentist promised we would find a safe place one day. He said God would look out for us. I felt safe with him. We eventually decided to band together with other survivors, and the Dentist made them feel safe too. He told us about a place where there was a lake full of fish. I think he'd been here before on a fishing trip. He might have even had a dream about it, but I don't know for sure. We traveled across the border and through the desert to get here. We were attacked along the way. More than once. We lost people. But the Dentist kept us together."

"Was he really going to execute you, though?" Esther asked. This image of the Dentist as a savior didn't match up with the fact that Esther had discovered her sister in a cage. "Or was this an elaborate ploy with Boris to get us away from the *Catalina*?" Her voice caught on the name. It couldn't be true. She couldn't have lost her home, the people who had survived with her for years. Not on the same day she got her sister back.

"I really am—was—condemned." Naomi sat back on her heels, looking around at the food and survival gear stacked all around them. "But it wasn't because of Louis. Robert—the Dentist—changed over the years. I don't know if he planned for the religion to take off like it did, but he embraced the prophet role. He got more authoritarian, and the rules got stricter. He became more and more afraid of the outside world. He went from helping every stranger we came across to fighting them off unless they'd swear to live exactly the way he wanted. He talked about remaking the world in his own image. I think he went a little crazy. Really, everyone in the world has gone a little crazy."

Esther swallowed hard, remembering the skeletons in Ixcuintla, the ruthless leaders of the Calderon Group and the Harvesters, even the *Galaxy* captains, who refused to let their ships install her technology to keep the people under their rule.

"So what *did* you do?" she asked.

"The List, Esther. I sent our roster to your friend on the *Catalina*."

"That was you?"

"I was the only one who was allowed into the Bunker. He planned to keep me with him if the worst happened—again—and he had to take refuge down here. I knew about the satellite network and that Robert was keeping news of the rest of the world away from the community. I tried to talk him into letting us contribute to the List. Your friend wouldn't give us access to the other names without a roster, and I wanted to see if anyone I knew had survived."

Naomi took Esther's hand then, squeezing their bloody palms together.

"And he said no."

"Yes." Naomi looked down at the Dentist's body, then turned away again quickly, her eyes welling up. "I snuck down here one night and transmitted our roster. But Robert found out before I could even get a look at the List."

"And Louis?"

"We had been caught together once before," Naomi said. "Robert had turned a blind eye for me then. But giving out our roster was a betrayal he couldn't look past. Of course he couldn't tell the community about the List because they'd all want to see it too. Instead he had Louis arrested that very day. We'd been really good about following the rules. Louis was doing what Robert wanted in the hopes of winning his approval." Naomi gave a little sob, her shoulders quaking. "It wasn't his fault."

"How does Captain Boris fit into all this?" David asked. He had been listening intently from across the bunker.

"Captain Boris and the Dentist first made contact on the satellite network months ago," Naomi said. "I don't know what their arrangement was exactly, but I believe Boris asked the Dentist to keep you occupied when he found out you were here. He must have promised some sort of protection at the mouth of the river. The Dentist has considered that a vulnerable position ever since his attempt to get rid of the locals living near there failed."

Esther closed her eyes, listening to the clack of keys as David resumed work on the computer. She should have known Boris would have allies. No wonder the Dentist had been so quick to let them stay. It had given Boris plenty of time to act against the *Catalina*. She should never have let so much time pass.

"As far as I know," Naomi said, "Boris was never aware of our connection, but Robert put it together pretty quickly after you arrived. You and I both look like Mom, and I have Dad's curly hair."

Esther nodded. She stared at the woman her sister had become. Naomi looked older than her twenty-five years, her face lined and solemn. She had been through hell here on land. But there was still one more question.

"Why did you tell me you weren't my sister?"

Naomi looked down at her hands. "The Dentist figured out what you were after. He knew your last name from the Elders, and he must have seen the resemblance between us. All he had to do was check the List. I was already in here by then, and he came to see me the day you and Dad arrived. I could hardly believe it was true. But I didn't get a chance to hope I could be with you. The Dentist . . . he told me he would release Louis if I claimed I didn't know you and told you to leave me alone." Naomi looked up and met Esther's eyes fiercely. "When you turned up outside my cell, I panicked. I've spent a long time telling myself I don't have any other family but the Dentist. There was a chance to save Louis, and I didn't want you to get hurt trying to help me. I lied."

Esther remembered how the words had poured out of Naomi when she told Esther the fake story about being in Texas when the disaster happened. She had been trying desperately to protect the people she loved.

"But you shot the Dentist," David said. "Dagan."

"He broke his promise," Naomi said, pain and fire in her expression. "I did what he asked, but he killed Louis, drowned him in the lake even though he didn't do anything. And he was going to kill you too. I had to stop him."

Tears coursed down Naomi's cheeks. She looked down at the Dentist again, seemingly unable to pull her gaze away. Her shoulders quaked. Esther wondered if she should hug her. The woman was practically a stranger. She was almost glad her busted arm gave her an excuse not to. It was a lot to process, and the shock of being shot in the arm was making her brain foggy. She wished she could have saved Louis yesterday. But if she had tried, she'd never have made it here.

"Figured it out," David said suddenly. He hit a button on the computer, and a beeping sound filled the room. "I'm calling the *Catalina*."

Esther held her breath as they waited for someone to answer. Her wound throbbed. She prayed that David was right and the Dentist had been lying. The computer continued to beep—indicating the satellite phone ringing in Neal's Tower, she hoped.

Then the beeping stopped.

"No," Esther said.

"I'm sorry, Es— "

"Call them again."

David tapped the keyboard, and soon the beeping noise filled the room again. The signal traveled across the land, over the sea, bouncing up to the heavens and back. Time stretched like a tug line pulling toward the breaking point.

The beeping stopped. Esther's heart skipped a beat. There was a crackle. Then—

"This is the *Catalina*."

Esther gasped as Neal's voice filled the Bunker.

"*Catalina*, this is Hawthorne. What's your status?"

"A little busy here," Neal said. "We're on the run. I got a tip from the *Amsterdam* rig boss. Boris knows where we are, and the destroyer is after us. Your plan didn't work, unfortunately."

"Sweet salt and rust," Esther said. She leapt up and darted over to the computer. The sudden movement nearly made her pass out, and she collapsed onto David's lap in front of the computer. "Neal! It's Esther! Is everyone still alive?!"

"Yeah, we're fine, except for the whole part about Captain Boris chasing us. Without the *Lucinda* we're sitting ducks."

"What's your present course?" David asked.

"We're sailing for the coast as fast as we can," Neal said. "But the destroyer is faster. They'll be on us in a few days."

"You've gotta head straight for the Santiago River," Esther said. She felt rattled, ripped about like a flag in a storm. But it didn't matter. The *Catalina* lived. "We'll come for you."

"Are you on the *Lucinda* now?" Neal said. "I haven't been able to get ahold of Zoe today. The connections on the river have been hit and miss."

"No, but we're less than a day's journey from where they're supposed to be," Esther said.

"Did you get Naomi?"

"Yes! She's here with us now."

"Awesome! Hey, Naomi! I'm Neal!"

Naomi looked up, surprised.

"We don't have time to talk right now," Esther said. "Can you get in touch with Marianna and see if there's any way she can buy us time?"

"She's trying," Neal said. "She's in danger herself."

"If we sail through the night, we might be able to make the coast in three or four days. We'll be with the current this time. Meet us at the mouth of the Santiago as fast as you can."

"You got it."

"Okay, we've gotta go now, Neal. I don't know what's wrong with Zoe's link, but if the *Lucinda* is still afloat we'll be there to meet you."

"Sure thing. Come as fast as you can. Bye, Naomi!"

The line cut out.

"Well, what are you waiting for?" Esther said to the others. "Let's get going!"

36. The Drive

ESTHER, DAVID, AND NAOMI found Yvonne still waiting for them in the jeep. She had curled up on the seat and fallen asleep.

"Wake up, Yve," Naomi said, shaking her shoulder gently.

"Naomi, is that you? Are you alive?" Yvonne rubbed her eyes blearily.

"Yeah, I'm okay," Naomi said.

She still seemed shaky. She must be exhausted after what she had been through tonight. Esther would need to rest soon too. She was a little worried about the giant hole in her arm.

"Can you drive us down to the river?" Naomi asked.

"The river?" Yvonne rubbed her eyes.

"You know the way, don't you?"

"Yeah, but it's a rough road," Yvonne said. "If we dent the jeep, my brother—"

"It's an emergency."

"I know, I know. But only because you're still alive."

Yvonne climbed out to hug Naomi and usher her into the back of the jeep. David lifted Esther over the side to put her on the backseat and then climbed into the front. He handed her one of the rifles they had taken from the Bunker, helping her balance it on the edge of the jeep so she could fire it with one hand if she had to. She grabbed him by the front of his shirt before he turned back around, planting a panicked, joyful kiss on his mouth. They had done it. David brushed her cheek with his fingers and turned back to the face the road.

They set off through the jungle. When they reached the first turnoff, Yvonne spun the wheel hard. They rumbled deeper into the trees, bouncing over a rougher, newer road. Pain chopped through Esther's arm. She glimpsed a barbed wire fence through the thicket.

Naomi explained what had happened to the Dentist in clipped words. Yvonne kept turning to stare at her, and each time Esther was sure they were going to pitch off the road and into the scrub.

"So . . . so the Dentist is *dead?*" Yvonne said for the fourth time.

"Yes," Naomi said miserably. She looked over at Esther, eyes wide and tearful. Esther wasn't sure what to make of her yet. She had been through a lot, but at least she was no longer pretending not to know them. But the lake had been her home for a long time, and it must be hard on her to leave it. Speaking of the lake . . .

"Yvonne," Esther said, "you probably don't have to come to sea with us now that the Dentist is dead. I'm sure your brother would protect you if you want to go back after dropping us off."

Yvonne burst into tears. David grabbed the wheel to keep the jeep from veering off the road.

"Thank you!" Yvonne squeaked. "I don't think I'm cut out for this. I want to go home so bad!"

"A lot will change in town now," Naomi said. "Maybe you can help them make it better than it was, for everyone."

"Oh good. I was going to miss my little birds so much," Yvonne said.

She took hold of the wheel again as they continued to bounce through the trees. David turned back to wink at Esther.

Esther looked over at her sister again. In the darkness she could have been sitting next to the spectral shape of her mother. This was so strange.

"Naomi," she said, "after this is all over, do you want to find out if they'd let you stay too? You said before that you didn't want to leave."

"I know," Naomi said after a moment's hesitation. "I think I want a fresh start. And there are too many memories at the lake. I'd like to stay with you and Dad, at least for a little while."

Esther smiled. "Sounds good. We just have to save the *Catalina* first."

The sun was beginning to peek over the treetops by the time they rolled down to the riverside. The *Lucinda* waited for them far enough downriver that she couldn't be seen from the dam. They had to abandon the rough dirt road for the final yards and drive through the underbrush, bouncing and rattling along. Yvonne got the jeep as close to the water as possible and began honking the horn. Esther and the others leapt out and shouted for the crew.

A few people were standing watch on deck, and more tumbled out, rubbing their eyes and staring at the ruckus on the riverbank. In short order the crew launched the raft and sent it over to pick them up. Zoe was driving. She stood up next to the motor as she approached the shore.

"Geeze, I'm glad you got her," Zoe said, "but couldn't you have announced your presence a little more quietly? It's still early."

"The *Catalina* is about to be attacked!" Esther shouted. "We need to get under way now. They're almost defenseless. Why isn't anyone fixing the comms?"

"Didn't know there was a problem. Cally and Dax had the night shift," Zoe said. "I'm going to murder those two."

"Doesn't matter now. Boris is heading for the *Catalina* in the destroyer. We need to meet them at the mouth of the river."

"All aboard then," Zoe said. "You look terrible by the way, Esther."

"Good to see you too."

David and Zoe helped Esther into the raft, while Naomi hugged Yvonne good-bye by the jeep. Esther sank down onto the bench and looked back at her sister.

"You'll be okay," Naomi was saying to Yvonne. "Take care of the girls."

"I will," Yvonne said. "I'm going to miss you."

"You too." Naomi hugged her again and turned toward the raft.

Suddenly Thompson stepped out of the trees, his camouflage clothing making it look like part of the jungle had come to life. He had his shotgun in his hand, and with a few quick steps he moved between Naomi and the raft.

"Hold on a minute," he growled.

Naomi and Yvonne gasped. David stepped back out of the raft onto the shore. Esther teetered on the bench, her head swimming. Zoe put one hand on her shoulder to steady her, the other reaching for her pocketknife.

"It's all right," Thompson growled. "I don't want trouble."

"Where did you come from?" Yvonne asked.

"I've been watching the *Lucinda* all night," Thompson said. "I had to make sure they weren't going to come back and attack the lake. Thought it would be my chance to prove I'm a better leader than Dagan."

"The Dentist is dead," Naomi said.

Thompson adjusted his cap. "I see," he said. "Are you folks really just going to leave?"

"We don't want any trouble either," David said carefully.

"Naomi? You sure you want to go with these people? I'll stop them if they're taking you against your will."

"No, it's okay," Naomi said. "This is my family. Yvonne can explain everything."

Yvonne squeaked, but she nodded when Thompson looked over at her. "She has to go with them," she said.

"There will be a power vacuum up at the lake," David said. "If you let us go in peace, we won't come back."

He hesitated for a second and then lowered his rifle so it hung from his shoulder on the strap. He raised his hands in a calming gesture.

After a full minute Thompson did the same.

"Unlike the Dentist, I don't mind contact with the outside world," Thompson said. "Within reason. Things are going to change real quick around here, but let's keep lines of communication open. I've heard a rumor that we might even be able to get our hands on a satellite phone."

"It's in the Bunker," Naomi said. "Bottom level."

"Thought it might be," Thompson said.

David stepped forward and shook Thompson's hand. "Let's keep in touch."

"Sure. Why not?" Thompson turned to Yvonne. "Can you give me a ride back up the hill? After that I'd be honored if you'd let me cook you breakfast."

Blushing and sputtering, Yvonne made room for Thompson in the jeep. She waved to Naomi and Esther and drove the jeep through the brush toward the road. The growl of the engine faded as they headed back toward the lake.

David offered a hand to Naomi and helped her climb into the raft. Zoe fired up the motor and drove toward the *Lucinda*, waiting for them on the river. Faces lined her railing as the crew watched them approach.

"Sounds like you've got a story," Zoe said. "I've been sitting here staring at the shore for a week. That's the last time you get to go on an adventure and leave me behind."

"Agreed," Esther said. "But it's not over yet."

They reached the *Lucinda* and climbed aboard. Esther wanted to kiss the deck she was so happy to be back on a ship. Naomi looked around shyly at the crew, who had gathered to stare at her. Esther nudged her reassuringly with her uninjured arm.

She noticed that they were almost exactly the same height.

Then their father limped out of the pilothouse, leaning on his walking stick. Simon stopped when he saw Naomi and Esther. He stared at them for a few moments, and then he dropped the walking stick and covered his face with his hands. Esther gave Naomi another nudge, and she walked forward to hug their father for the first time in nearly seventeen years.

The crew cheered. Esther reached for David's hand.

"Thank you," she whispered.

He didn't answer. He didn't need to.

Simon held Naomi's face in his bandaged hands and whispered something Esther couldn't hear. Then he was waving her forward, holding both of them tight. Their family was together again. The bullet hole in Esther's arm burned like a lightning strike, but she let her father hold them close.

Then she pulled back, wiping away the tears with her good hand. They had one more family left to save.

"Let's go help the *Catalina*."

"You guys go below and get some rest," David said. "I'm taking my baby back from Luke. We're on our way."

37. Seabound

THE CREW WORKED QUICKLY. David and Luke got the *Lucinda* under way. Anita extracted bullet fragments from Esther's arm with a pair of pliers and then sewed her up as best as she could. While she worked, Esther sat with Naomi and her father, side by side on a single bunk, and filled him in on everything that had happened. It helped to distract her from the pierce and pull of the needle and thread. Then Naomi told her story.

She cried a bit while she talked. There had been dark roads as she found her way through the ash-drenched wreckage of the world. While Esther and Simon had spent a storm-swept, uncertain life at sea, Naomi's life had been one of dust and thirst and blood. And along the way the Dentist had been her only anchor.

"So . . . your mom wasn't with you the whole time?" Simon asked.

"No. She waited in the reception area while I was in the dentist's chair," Naomi said. "I don't even know if she made it out of the waiting room when everything happened. We couldn't get to it when we dug out. I've always assumed I was the only survivor from our family."

"We thought so too," Simon said. He touched Naomi's hair, as if to confirm she was really sitting next to him. "I wanted to go back for you, but I thought there was no way you could have survived. I'm so sorry."

"You had Esther to look after," Naomi said.

"Yes." Simon smiled. "And now Esther's looking after us."

Esther grimaced. Anita had just tied off the last of the stitches. "I'm doing a bang-up job," she grumbled. "This hurts like hell."

"So we're going to help the *Catalina*, which is your main ship, right?" Naomi asked. "And Captain Boris is after it?"

"Yeah. He's mad because we stole this ship, the *Lucinda*, a couple of months ago," Esther said. It had begun to dawn on her that they were heading toward a battle they might not be able to win. The *Lucinda* was armed and faster than the destroyer HMS *Hampton*, but Esther didn't think they could defeat the *Hampton* in a head-to-head conflict. This could all end here anyway. She looked around at her reunited family, wondering if she should leave

them at Emilio's village. This was her fight—hers
and David's. At least her father would still have a
daughter now. She owed it to all the people on the
Catalina to help them if she could.

"He's able to chase us now because he's using an
energy technology Esther invented and shared with
the world," Simon said. "She's turned out to be
quite handy."

"The Dentist knew about that," Naomi said. "He
tried building one for his secret bunker, but he
didn't want to let anyone else hear about it."

"He said he didn't trust it," Esther said.

"He didn't trust it in the hands of his people,"
Naomi said, "but he definitely wasn't stupid. He
knew how useful it was. He didn't want his people
to be able to drive away whenever they wanted because of an abundance of fuel. I can't believe that
was yours, Esther. And you gave it away?"

"Yeah, that's a long story. It helped our enemy,
but it won us some . . . friends." Esther stared at
Naomi without really seeing her. *Of course.* If she
didn't feel like her arm was about to fall off and her
brain dissolve into a shell-shocked mush, she would
have thought of it sooner. "I have to go up to the pilothouse. Time to call in the cavalry."

Anita helped her up the ladder while Naomi
went to rest. Their father hobbled to his own bunk
to lie down as well. There would be more time for
them to catch up later. Esther would make sure of
it. Meanwhile, she had to make a few phone calls.

The satellite connection was spotty as they sailed further away from the lake, running back toward the sea. But whenever they had a clear signal, Esther called everyone she could think of. Everyone who had asked for her advice on how to install their systems. Everyone who had mentioned how useful it was. Everyone she had met on her journeys of the past year. She called the Calderon Group and the Harvesters. The aircraft carrier. The *Sebastian*. The *Scurvy Sea Dog* and the *Santa Anna*. Every ship that had ever stopped at the *Amsterdam Coalition*. She knew they wouldn't all come, but she had to try.

As they sailed back toward the sea, she begged every ship she reached to set their course for the mouth of the Santiago River. The *Catalina* was on her way there. And so was Boris. She called in every favor she could think of, banking on the goodwill she had begun building up the moment she transmitted her invention across the airwaves.

And the other ships answered. They sailed across the sea, fleeing the life of isolation and distrust and conflict they had lived since the disaster. They owed Esther for their mobility. And now they were coming to help.

For three days and three nights the *Lucinda* sailed and the *Catalina* fled. Other ships reported in whenever they caught sight of HMS *Hampton*. And other ships headed toward them. Neal blasted the coordinates for a rendezvous point across the airwaves. The ships converged on the river mouth on a point almost within sight of the shore. They drew together, ready to help the *Catalina* through her darkest hour.

Esther's arm was in agony, but she barely slept, barely looked away from the river as they sailed onward. Isadora, their river guide, took the helm at night, trusting her instincts and experience to get them through the dark. The haunted bridge town slid past them in the blackness. By day the jungle on the riverbank gave way to rolling fields and scrub. Abandoned farms sprang up and faded away around them. They were almost there. It was going to be very close.

On the afternoon of the fourth day, the *Lucinda* approached the cargo ship blocking the mouth of the river. The *Santa Julia* was waiting for them. Emilio had been keeping watch, ready to let them know at the first sign of the *Catalina* or the *Hampton*.

The tide was approaching its highest point. They would be able to slide right past the cargo ship. They helped Isadora totter over a wooden plank to the *Santa Julia* to return to her people. Esther had tried to get Naomi and Simon to go with her and wait safely in the village on the hill, but they refused.

"Not after I just got my daughters back," Simon had said. "We're with you."

Emilio waved at them from the deck of his ship. Simon pointed at Naomi, smiling broadly. Emilio clapped his hands and smiled back. They lost sight of him as the *Lucinda* pulled forward. They sailed slowly past the swirling waters around the drowned cargo ship and the names of the dead.

The *Catalina* was supposed to be waiting for them at the rendezvous point just a mile away, beyond the reach of the breakers. They were almost there.

But as they pulled past the cargo ship and headed for the invisible line where the river met the sea, they heard the first shell.

"It's time," Esther said.

She returned to the pilothouse and stood beside David. Her arm was in a sling, and she wouldn't be much use on deck.

The rumble of explosions floated across the water, faint still, like distant thunder. Somewhere the battle had begun.

They sailed across the wide river delta toward the sea. Fog hung low over the horizon, glowing as the afternoon sun struggled behind its veil. David leaned into the wind whistling through the bullet holes in the screen. His glasses were still cracked. They'd have to do something about that someday.

Zoe was on standby at the radio. Luke had gone to help with the weapons. Cody and Anita and Dax and Cally and the others would be out there too, preparing to make a final stand to protect their home. Esther had wanted to make Cally and Dax, the youngest among them, wait below, but they deserved to be on deck. The *Catalina* was their home too.

Esther squinted into the haze. The fog bank drifted lower over the water like a cloud of ash. They couldn't see any other ships yet. There was another boom, another shell. They had to be almost there.

They sailed straight. The *Lucinda* tossed in the choppy water as they crossed the border between river and sea. Waves burst beneath their hull. They were almost to the coordinates Neal had sent out. The *Catalina* had to be there somewhere. Where were the other ships? Booms shuddered somewhere on the cloaked sea. Were they already too late? Esther willed the view to clear.

"We can do this, Esther," David said, keeping his eyes fixed on the fog-laden horizon.

"I love you," she said.

Then a shell exploded directly in front of their hull.

"It's the destroyer!"

"Damn Boris," David said. "His timing is horrible."

He spun the wheel, swerving the *Lucinda* hard to avoid more shells. The destroyer loomed suddenly before them off their starboard side, large and gray and dangerous. It was a hulking, luminous mass. The big gun on the prow pointed directly at them. David turned the *Lucinda* into the mists and fled before it.

"I still can't see the *Catalina* through all this soup," Esther said.

"Where are the others?" David asked. "We could use them right about now."

"Maybe no one came," Zoe said.

"They'll be here," Esther said.

She kept her eyes peeled. Boris knew they were there now, but the *Lucinda* was agile. She darted back and forth in the coastal waters, skirting around the larger warship, enticing it to follow them like a sailfish teasing a shark. The *Lucinda*'s draft was shallower than the *Hampton*'s. She could get closer to the shore, maneuvering around the heavier, slower destroyer. Further in the waves crashed roughly against the land. They were perilously close. It was dangerous for them, but it was worse for Boris.

Another shell landed in the sea, not as close to them now.

"I've got an answer for him," David said. He grabbed the intercom. "Fire at will."

Gunfire ripped the fabric of the mist.

"Hold!" David said.

Then he turned the wheel hard again. By the time the *Hampton* answered his fire, the *Lucinda* had moved away again, further out to sea. David turned the *Lucinda* and raced parallel to the shore. They sailed into the fog, searching the ghostly soup for other ships.

"Wait. I see something!" Esther peered through the fog, gripping the dash with her good hand. The wound in her other arm ached as her muscles tensed.

Slowly a white-gray shape emerged from the mist. It was the *Catalina*. She tossed in the waves, dangerously close to running aground. Her decks looked top heavy above the churning surf. Esther had forgotten how big she was. How battered and beautiful.

"She's listing badly," David said. "She's been hit."

"Are we too late?"

"Can't tell."

"We aren't too far from shore," Esther said. "She just needs to hold on a little longer. Ready, Zoe?"

"Ready!"

Zoe put a hand on her headset and hit a button on the control panel, engaging the satellite network. She switched on the mic. All their friends should be able to hear them.

"This is the *Lucinda*. We're at the rendezvous point. We have a visual on the *Catalina*. Approach the *Hampton*."

They waited for a crackle through the speakers, but there was nothing.

"Where are they?"

The *Catalina* lurched in the waves before them. The fog lifted a little. The *Hampton* closed in again, speeding out of the haze, its massive shape looming above the *Lucinda*.

David spun the wheel and managed to get be-tween the *Catalina* and the *Hampton*, their small, sleek ship the last bastion of defense between the *Catalina* and a final killing blow. The destroyer swung around, no doubt readying another shell, all its guns trained on them.

This was it. They were going to be blown from the water, destroyed within sight of land. Esther gritted her teeth for the first impact.

Then another shape emerged behind the de-stroyer.

"It's the *Charley!*" David shouted, pumping his fist in the air. "The Calderon Group is here."

The newcomer swept toward them, the big har-poon missile on her deck swinging around to point at the destroyer. Esther imagined the Calderon pi-rates preparing their weapons, shouting sharp or-ders across the decks.

Another vessel burst from the mist, large and rust-bitten. Guns cocked. Sailors ready. Then an-other, small and deadly. Another.

"There's the *Sebastian!*" Zoe shouted. "And that's a Harvester ship, I'm sure of it."

"Look, there's another!"

"And there's Adele's ship!"

One by one ships sailed out of the haze. Souped-up, rusty, weather-beaten, enduring. They didn't engage the *Hampton* and didn't draw too close to the shore, instead sailing through the clouds, forming an honor guard around the *Catalina*, defenses ready. Esther's call had been answered. Their friends were here to help.

"Okay," Esther said. "Call the *Hampton*."

"You got it, boss," Zoe said. She hit a few buttons and then turned up the speakers.

A voice filled the pilothouse. "HMS *Hampton*."

"This is Esther Harris on the *Lucinda*. Is Captain Boris there?"

Silence. A muffled sound. Then: "Speaking."

"Hello, Boris, this is Esther."

"You're too late," Boris said. "I already put a hole in the hull of your precious *Catalina*. I decided to let her sink slowly. But you? You I'll destroy."

"Sorry, Boris. You're the one who's too late. You might want to take a look at your radar. Or better yet, look out the window."

The other ships sailed closer. They surrounded the *Catalina*, some moving in front of her, forming their own flotilla. The *Lucinda* was still the closest ship to the destroyer, but the others were gathering, threatening like storm clouds.

"See all those ships?" Esther said. "Those are people who have been able to use my energy technology to travel all over the sea. They can sail all the way to the shore—this shore, in fact. All these people came when I asked them for help because I helped them. Do you remember when I asked you to help me save the *Catalina* all those months ago? You said no. Well, these people said yes, now when

I need it the most. And they are going to blow you out of the water if you come any closer to my ship."

"You think your words scare me?" Boris said.

She could almost hear him spitting into the radio.

"No," Esther said. "But the simple facts should scare you. You're outnumbered. It's over. You can go back to nursing your grudge at the *Galaxy*. If they'll have you back that is. I hear Marianna let a rumor or two get out among your own people. They've heard some folks are moving back to land. They might want to do that too. They'll definitely want to choose for themselves. You'd better hurry back if you want to salvage anything of your hold over them. And you can leave me and my family alone."

Boris was quiet for so long Esther thought he had hung up on her. The *Hampton* still floated before them, its giant steely form tossing in the waves.

"Is my friend David Hawthorne there?" Boris said.

"I'm not your friend," David said. "I should have realized that a hell of a lot sooner. Go home, Boris."

"I always knew you'd move against me," Boris hissed.

"I tried to move away from you, actually," David said. "I found myself a real friend." He grinned at Esther.

"Enough talking," she said. "Boris, you and the *Hampton* have thirty seconds to hightail it out of here, or I'll send my people after you. And don't even think about causing problems for us again."

"Fine," Boris spat. "Keep your sinking ship. My work is done."

The connection cut off.

Zoe switched the satellite phone back to her headset and asked a few of the gathered ships to follow the *Hampton* back out to sea. The *Charley* volunteered a bit too enthusiastically. Esther wouldn't be surprised if the Calderon Group decided to relieve the *Hampton* of some of its choicest weapons along the way. Other ships that hadn't made it to the coast in time offered to keep an eye out and make sure Boris went all the way back to the *Galaxy Flotilla*. It was over. Almost.

The *Catalina* listed badly. She really was sinking. Esther felt her heart constricting as they turned in a wide circle and sailed closer. They could see now that there was a nasty gash low in her portside hull. It was near the bowling alley, Esther realized. At least it was far from the cabins. But the sea would already be flooding into her, filling the engine room and all the lowest spaces in her belly with water faster than the pumps could get rid of it.

Esther remembered hiding in those spaces, taking refuge, growing up. That vessel had carried her home.

Some of the lifeboats were already moving away from her, every seat filled. The people escaped from her sinking decks with nothing but the clothes on their backs, leaving behind everything that had made up their world over the past sixteen and half years. They were oddly calm, embracing the solemnity of this moment. Their life at sea was over.

There were over a thousand people on board, and they no longer had enough lifeboats for everyone. But the other ships that had gathered to help them sent their own lifeboats to pluck the survivors from the *Catalina*'s decks as she went down. They carried the Catalinans to shore or back to their own ships for the time being. David sent the *Lucinda*'s raft and motorboat over too. Every little bit helped.

The *Catalina* sank slowly, and with the help of so many boats they were able to get everyone off her in short order. They worked together to whisk the people away to safety boat by boat as the old ship went down. The mists lifted a little, framing the *Catalina* like curtains on a stage.

Esther joined her father on the deck of the *Lucinda* as the boats retrieved the last few survivors from the *Catalina*. They'd had to pull further away to avoid the drag of the sinking vessel. They watched her languish, the sea swallowing her in a slow, sad embrace. They were within sight of the shore. The *Catalina* had finally made it back to land.

Esther looped her uninjured arm through her father's and rested her head on his shoulder. They stood watch together, not speaking, bearing witness, quietly saying good-bye.

The last boat to leave the *Catalina*'s decks was a navy speedboat they'd had since their first weeks at sea. It headed straight toward the *Lucinda*. As it got closer, they could pick out the faces of the last of their friends abandoning their home.

Reggie drove the speedboat. A battered guitar leaned beside him. He looked ten years younger as he sailed away from the *Catalina* for good. Neal sat on one of the benches, his headset around his neck, the wire dangling free. The wind blew his mousy hair back from his forehead.

Judith stood on the other side of the motor in the stern, arms folded. She stared back at the *Catalina*. The speedboat carried her further and further away from it, but the whole time Esther watched her, Judith didn't look away. She watched the *Catalina* until the speedboat stopped in the shadow of the *Lucinda*.

When Judith finally turned, her face was wet with tears. She didn't wipe them away, didn't try to hide them. But she looked lighter, looser. They had made it. They had survived. Judith had seen them through until the very final moment, and she had been the last one to leave the *Catalina*'s decks.

Simon reached down to help Judith onto the *Lucinda*. Once on deck, she hugged him and Esther tight, failing to notice Esther's arm in a sling. Even though the pain made Esther want to scream, she hugged Judith right back.

Then the three of them looked toward the *Catalina*. The sea had reached her uppermost decks now. The foredeck was covered. Neal's Tower sprouted up like a lone periscope. Water sloshed over the windows, already working at some of the patches they had installed over the years. Foam and sea spray hugged her angles, her battered white-gray surfaces.

Then with a final gurgle the *Catalina* slipped beneath the surface of the sea.

38. Land

ONE YEAR LATER

ESTHER DUG HER TOES into the sand as she walked along the beach. The grit was wet and cool. Her boots hung around her neck, tied at the laces. She dodged a bit of debris—a mangled plastic chair—leaving footprints in her wake.

The tide was all the way out. It was the best time to gather salvage and collect sea creatures. Eating land food had been a nice change over the past year, but she still preferred seafood. A crab scuttled along the beach, its legs leaving miniature tracks in the sand. Esther darted forward to pick it up, her boots banging against her chest.

She pinched the crab around the middle and examined its soft underbelly while its legs waved wildly. There was a wide pattern on the pale shell. This one was a girl. She placed it back on the beach and let it scuttle toward the sea. It would return to the seafloor and help repopulate the blasted planet with new life.

The next wave swept the crab up and surged around Esther's bare ankles. She turned her face into the wind and looked out at the sea. The upper decks of the *Catalina* were visible a few hundred feet out. It was always like this at low tide. Twice a day the waters receded and her crown emerged from the surf, a memorial to their life at sea.

Esther often timed her visits to the beach for low tide. She'd put on her goggles and swim out to the wreck to walk atop the *Catalina*'s decks. Barnacles grew thick on her now. Sea grasses and coral had begun to spring up in places. Fish darted in and out of her corridors in flashing, brilliant schools. The last of her paint had been worn away. Every time Esther visited, another section had corroded or a wall had opened. Every time the *Catalina* had sunk a little further into the sand. The sea would overtake her one day, and she would truly become a part of it.

Esther breathed in the ocean air. It was a warm day, sunny like many of their days had been that summer. The farms along the riverbank were doing well. They were planning a real harvest festival for the next month. They'd invite everyone: the Lake People, the folks from Emilio's village, the former Catalinans, and all the crews that were in port then.

They had removed the cargo vessel blocking the entrance to the river and begun building a port town on the Santiago River. The town itself was located atop one of the hills about two hours upriver. They knew better than to build anywhere too near the sea. But they *were* building. They were making a new life. Their town would become a city, a hub bridging the gap between land and sea. Already ships came from all over to trade, to exchange information, and even to settle on land once again.

David emerged from the sea then, wearing striped swimming trunks that Cally's mother had made for him. He waved one hand at Esther and lifted a bulging plastic bag high in the other. Water glistened on his white-blond hair and made tracks down his tanned chest as he trudged through the shallows toward her.

Further up the beach, Esther's father and sister walked side by side along the waterline. They found joy and solace in long, slow talks, still getting acquainted after all this time apart. Simon was writing about the aftermath of the disaster, and Naomi was proving to be a willing research assistant as well as one of his best sources. They spent hours every day interviewing travelers and studying any eyewitness accounts they could get their hands on. Neal helped them by connecting them with new sources whenever he came in contact with someone with an especially interesting story.

Esther had had her father to herself for all these years, so she didn't mind. She didn't have much in common with Naomi, so getting to know her again had been a slower process than she had expected. Their lives had been so different, and for the first few months they had orbited each other, slowly figuring out how to talk like sisters again. But Esther had David and Zoe and Neal and Cally and even Judith. She could let her sister spend a little extra time with their dad.

"Great haul today," David said as he joined her. He opened the bag to show her the scraggly, waving legs of a couple of giant lobsters.

"They're bigger than the last batch," Esther said.

"And tastier I hope." David fell in beside her. "What's on your mind?"

"How do you know something's on my mind?"

"I know you, Esther," David said. He stopped her with a hand on her arm and tilted her face up to his. "I know you, and I love you. That'll never change, even though everything else has."

"It's good to be back," Esther said. "I'm glad we took a day off today."

"I miss the sea too," David said. "I know you like fixing the combines and working your magic on the cars, but I can tell you miss it."

Esther nodded. It was a different life on land. There was still a lot of building to do as their town slowly took shape. The farming was difficult. They had to coax the land to support them, but the former Catalinans were working hard. Their numbers had nearly doubled over the past year as people heard about the new settlement and decided to join them.

Esther had more than enough to do with her own projects, but she sometimes missed the wind in her face and the whir of a marine diesel engine under her hands.

"Maybe it's time we took the *Lucinda* on another trip," she said.

"Sweeter words were never spoken," David said. "I was thinking we could check out the Panama Canal. Assuming we make it through another winter, I say we sail south next spring. Luke, Zoe, and Cody should be back from Kansas City by then."

"I like the way you talk," Esther said.

A horn honked much further up the beach. Cally stood up from the front seat of the jeep and waved her arms over her head.

"Hurry up, you guys! I'm hungry," she called, leaning on the horn.

"I'm beginning to think Reggie shouldn't have taught her how to drive," David said.

Esther laughed. "She'd have figured it out on her own. You got enough of that lobster for everyone? Dax should have the pot going by now."

Cally had broken up with Dax again last week, but he had shown up, bright-eyed with his hair on end, when they packed up the jeep for their trip to the beach that morning. Everything was back to normal.

"Yes, ma'am," David said. He leaned in and kissed her softly, a hint of salt and sand on his lips. Then he smiled and jogged up the beach toward the jeep.

Esther fell in beside her father and Naomi as they followed him up the beach.

"It's too bad Judith couldn't come today," she said.

"Penny and I had breakfast with her this morning," Simon said. He had married Penelope Newton in a simple ceremony last winter. Esther had been *extra* nice to Penelope that day. Naomi really liked her, and at least she made their father happy. "Judith's keeping herself more than busy. She's drafting a trade agreement for all the ships that want to use our port. I haven't seen her so happy in a long time."

"That's good," Esther said.

"I hear Dirk is going to run against her in the next election," Naomi said.

"Just a rumor," Simon said. "As a matter of fact she's asked him to be her running mate. It's a smart move. She may have actually managed to neutralize him."

"I don't envy him one bit," Esther said.

She noticed something metallic sticking out of the sand. She stopped to extract it and brush off the grit. It was some sort of motor. Wires trailed out of it, but the components didn't look too rusted. Excellent. She knew just how to use this in her next project.

"Can't you guys walk any faster!" Cally called.

She and David sat in the front seat of the jeep. The Harris family climbed into the back. Cally fired up the engine and drove them back toward their campsite further up the beach, where Dax awaited the lobsters. Sand spun out from beneath their wheels like sea spray.

They settled in around the fire and boiled the lobsters, talking as the sun set over the rolling sea. The waves crashed beneath them, hiding the *Catalina* from view again. But they were okay. Life on land was good. And they still had the sea.

Acknowledgments

THIS SERIES HAS BEEN three years in the making. I can't even begin to express my gratitude to everyone who helped me along the way.

The following people read *Seafled* at various stages: Rachel Marsh, Geoffrey and Allison Ng, Trine Bradshaw, Laura Cook, Willow Hewitt, and Julie Young. Thank you for your vital feedback. I'm especially grateful to Willow for spending hours sorting through the problems in the third draft with me and—more importantly—for helping me fix them.

My two critique groups have been essential throughout my *Seabound* journey. Thank you to Sarah Merrill Mowat, Brooke Richter, and Rachel Andrews, and to Laura, Willow, Rachel, Betsy Cheung, Jennifer Brown, and MaryAnna Donaldson.

Ayden Young gave me technical advice throughout the series. Thanks for being as excited about following rankings and sales graphs as I am.

I'm grateful to the Author's Corner for talking strategy and whimsy in equal measures, and to Amanda Tong and the Nanowrimo crew for all the company.

Marcus Trower, my editor, and James from GoOnWrite, my cover designer, helped me make these books polished and professional. Thank you for everything you taught me in the process.

And thank you to the readers who have encouraged me along the way, including Joyce, Janie, Julie, Galina, Angela, Linda, Sara, Yvonne, Stephanie Z, Stephanie B, Moses, Wayne, Whitney, Leslie, Miriam, Kelly, Asa, and all the rest! Thanks, especially, to Stephanie Z for naming the Dentist.

This book is dedicated to my husband, Seb, without whom none of this would have been possible.

Thank you so much for reading.

Jordan Rivet
Hong Kong, 2015

ABOUT THE AUTHOR

Jordan Rivet is an American author from Arizona. She lives in Hong Kong with her husband. Prone to seasickness, she likes to watch the ships in Victoria Harbour while standing on solid ground.

Also by Jordan Rivet:
Seabound
Seaswept
Burnt Sea

61080420R00290

Made in the USA
Lexington, KY
28 February 2017